W9-BJN-302

THE SPIRIT OF '76

DEDICATION

Dear Hunter:

Although all the characters in my novel are invented, it would have been impossible for me to create Marshal Markov without the advice that you gave me from your admirable knowledge of Russian life and letters. Therefore, I dedicate this book to you.

Your aging and affectionate father,

Holmes Alexander.

THE SPIRIT OF '76

A Political Novel of the Near Future

Holmes Alexander

ARLINGTON HOUSE·PUBLISHERS
81 CENTRE AVENUE • NEW ROCHELLE, N. Y. 10801

The excerpt from *John Brown's Body*, from the *Selected Works of Stephen Vincent Benét*, Holt, Rinehart and Winston, Inc., copyright, 1937 by Stephen Vincent Benét, copyright renewed ©, 1964 by Thomas C. Benét, Stephanie B. Mahin and Rachel Benét Lewis, is reprinted by permission of Brandt & Brandt.

The excerpt from *A Study of History* by Arnold J. Toynbee, abridgment of Volumes I-VI by D. C. Somervell, 1947, is reprinted by permission of Oxford University Press, Inc.

Library of Congress Catalog Card Number 66-25069

MANUFACTURED IN THE UNITED STATES OF AMERICA

THE SPIRIT OF '76

A PRELUDE

The Muse of History, a stubborn wench, is never going to rescind the verdict on what happened to Federal Aviation Agency One that Thanksgiving Day, 1975. Besides, her veracity is forever affixed by the instantaneous, electronic recordings of the fatal flight.

"Hello, Skyfloat. This is Executive Extra. Sixty miles south of Boston now. Leveling at cruising altitude, forty-two thousand feet. Our bearing is two-four-zero degrees. Over."

"Okay, Executive Extra. Cleared for Forrestal Airport, Washington. If you see three F-200-B's at your topside, they'll be the security Air Force aircraft."

"Roger—out."

Two minutes later at 15.34:

"Come in, Skyfloat. Executive Extra here. Reporting moderate clear air turbulence."

"Take it up to forty-five thousand, Double X. Security aircraft reporting perfect weather at that level."

"Moderate to severe turbulence now. Do you have us in the scope, Skyfloat? We are losing altitude."

"Read back, Double X."

"Excessive vibration of cabin controls. Severe turbulence

mounting. Altitude thirty-eight thousand . . . thirty-five . . . and now thirty-two."

"We have you in the scope. Are you level?"

"This is Executive Extra. We are still losing altitude at thirty thousand feet. We are in six-tenth cloud with radar indicating one fighter-type aircraft on our tail."

"Executive Extra, there is no security aircraft near you. Climb to original altitude on bearing one-five-oh. Aircraft at your level is unidentified private jet or National Guard ship. Repeat instructions."

By now it is 15.45. The Skyfloat, a four-motor Douglas-15, carrying advanced equipment and a ten-man crew, is over New Haven. It is keeping, by routine procedure, about a half hour's flying time ahead of FAA One. Skyfloat has lost voice contact with its precious transport. The principal scope shows a blotch of milky white. The sensitizers have reported to the aghast Skyfloat skipper that a mid-air explosion has occurred at the pinpoint position of FAA One.

Chapter One

Samuel Tilden Lepol, 37th President of the United States, had celebrated the 355th Thanksgiving Day by delivering an appropriate message to nearly one hundred thousand persons in and around the Boston Common. He spoke at high noon on a plain pine-board platform. He stood on a slab of redwood from his native California. Into the slab had been driven fifty silver nails, representing each of the states, and the President himself had driven the golden spike that emblematized the United Nations. On that day he wore one of the dark blue pin-striped suits that had become his formal garb. Gibing Democrats liked to point out that the vertical stripes were calculated to make his not-very-spare and not-very-tall figure seem more impressive. The fact that the President chose to stand on the block of lumber aroused a would-be humorist in the press party to pass a remark recalling the old rumor that Tom Dewey used to wear built-up shoes. This was the last untoward comment that anybody would remember hearing about the doughty and appealing statesman who was so soon to die.

He couldn't know that this would be his last utterance. Yet he was one of the fortunate few who speak so portentously that were they cut off in the midst of any address it would stand the test of time. President Lepol likened this occasion at Boston to that memorable day in 1620 when the Pilgrims stood upon the New World's shore.

"We, too," he said, "have made landfall at the New Atlantis. For we in this country are the Pilgrims of Peace who have left oppression and prejudice far behind. The starry banner has grown from the unlucky number of thirteen stars to a spangled field of fifty. Today that flag no longer seeks to wave in the lone splendor of narrow nationalism. The golden spike of brotherhood is a nobler metal than superficial silver can ever be. As I have often said, the title of 'Mr. President' is to me less exalted than the one which spontaneously grew up and became attached to my efforts in the last campaign. I will always answer proudly to the cognomen given me at that baptism of public service—'Lepol for the People'! Not merely for the 200 millions who call themselves Americans, but for the 4 billions who are citizens of the world.

"That is what this Thanksgiving Day means. It means that this country, having joined the family of nations, may now rejoice to have left the stormy seas of international strife behind us—and rejoice that no nation, large or small, no people of whatever color or origin, is now outside the fold of universal fraternalism.

"The journey has been arduous, and our safe arrival cannot mean, any more than it did for the Pilgrim Fathers, a surcease from responsibility. Ours is now, in Lincolnian language, to bind up the wounds, to care for those who have suffered, and with malice toward none and Federal aid for all, to go forward and to make our New Atlantis a homeplace where all may breathe the air of freedom. I say to all who hear my voice or read this humble statement: ask and you shall receive—seek what is desired, and you shall find."

The words, as Lepol knew, were wafted by satellite transmitters to the cities and hamlets far away, whipped into fast translation, and offered as hope to billions of hearts. He had undertaken, more than any man who had ever held the office, to lift it above the last clinging mud-driplets of isolation. Indeed, this man had sensed that "Mr. President" was a shopworn handle to the fast-growing minority of American Negroes who had yet to see one of their own race in that post which was supposedly open to every American boy. What was "Mr. President" to the huddled masses of New Zealand, a country into which had swept a few years ago the vast yellow tide of immigration from the Indochina peninsula and Malaya? What could the provincial title stand for to the restless, suspicious, energetic citizenry of the new giant of the East, the striving regime of continental China? But when he dared call himself "Lepol for the People," he was speaking, as no man ever had before, to the boundless constituency of all humanity. The autumn air seemed fraught with poignancy, as if a new age were closer than the orator was aware.

The multitude in the Common which had stood silent, as if fearful of missing some nuance of meaning by interruption, broke into roaring applause as he finished. Lepol threw out his arms, with the palms extended toward them in that characteristic gesture. Wave after wave of cheers rose and climaxed, only to rise and crest again, as he turned right and left, then completely around and back again to the rostrum, his arms and hands still open, offering at once manly affection and the promise of an abundance at his command.

That last message, world-wide and heart-deep, still emanated from his glowing presence as he took the arm of the venerable Massachusetts' Governor Brooke, and fell in behind the flying wedge of Secret Service men that would take him to the Thanksgiving dinner at the State House there in Boston.

Three members of the press party, chosen from the general pool, had ridden from Forrestal Airport, Washington, to the Honey Fitz Airport, Boston, on the Presidential plane. These same three accompanied the President to the State House. The others, fourteen in number, went by bus to a less sumptuous feast of turkey and cranberries at a dining room set aside and equipped as a makeshift news room in the air terminal. The meal would not be served for another hour, giving time for highballs and the filing of stories. Two of the newsmen, columnists by trade, had more time for analysis than the others did, and this pair, amber tumblers in hand, chose to sit outside in the patio where a bronze statuette of Mayor Fitzgerald, grandfather of politicians, presided.

"No doubt," said the older of the two, a compact man of sixty who wore a fierce white mustache and chose to speak with a faint though not native British accent, "you will attack that speech from your congenital right-wing bias, Philip. I found it quite magnificent."

The other man tilted his whiskey at a speculative angle, seemed to study its composition for omens and did not at once answer. He was just past thirty, light brown of hair, grey of eyes, lithe-figured but showing the strain in his serious, aesthetic young face of hard work not unmixed with a share of disappointment as to its results. Any observer would have noted the contrast between the men, as well as the residual antagonism that lurked in their professional relationship. Philip Obermeister's brown tweed suit had evidently served him for more than a few autumns, for it had the gloss of long usage although its cloth was immaculate and the creases had been newly ironed. The other man, Calvin Borton, was in tan flannels, which did him and his tailor top credit. Both the point of his breast-pocketed handkerchief and his gold cuff links sported Borton's monogram.

"My bias isn't apt to shape many opinions," Obermeister answered the older man's sally. "That's the consolation of being an unpopular writer instead of being both popular and profound as you are, Calvin. But one thing did strike me as a noteworthy omission in this year's Thanksgiving message. Somehow I didn't hear any gratitude expressed to the Heavenly Father. Lepol took all the credit for peace and prosperity, present and future, to himself and his Administration. I didn't like his downgrading of the national office either. What the hell is he running for in '76—the chief magistracy of these United States or regency of the known universe?"

Borton chuckled, but managed to give his amusement a customary touch of condescension.

"You see, my dear Philip, the man thinks big—and you can't get used to that, not in a Republican anyhow. But you're right about one thing. It was the kickoff speech of next year's campaign. That's how I'm going to write it, anyhow. Lepol for the People is playing one-upmanship on the Finnigan Clan, who are sure to control the Democratic nomination now that the Johnson-Kennedy feud has killed off competition in the party. Lepol is a cinch to be the first two-term Republican since Eisenhower, and he may be the first to put his own son in direct succession. Keep your eye on Dwight D. Lepol for the GOP race in California. He's already got campaign posters that call him Young Ike, and I guess you know who's making a Thanksgiving appearance in Berkeley a few hours from now. No less than the First Lady herself."

"Juno, goddess of know-it-all," nodded Phil gloomily. "A few years ago the idea of a political dynasty was downright distasteful to the American people. Nowadays, it's taken for granted. No, Calvin, I admit there's a lot I don't like about all this. When people cease to be jealous of their liberties, that's when they lose 'em. Thanksgiving is supposed to be a national religious festival—the only one we have in this country. But there's the President literally making a stump speech on the East coast, while he's got his imposing wife making something of the sort on the West coast."

"Politics is growing up, that's all," yawned Borton. "The presidency is a bigger prize than ever. You can't blame ambitious men and families for doing what's been done over the centuries in Europe and Asia."

"But we're not Eurasians," answered Phil hotly. "We're Americans with our own traditions and I hate to see them smashed to smithereens in these dammed power grabs."

"You're behind the times, my boy. Speaking of power plays, I suppose it didn't go unnoticed by you that Lepol gently eased the skids under his Vice President by sending him to Buenos Aires for that Conference on Aid and Security. I'll bet you a new suit the Republican ticket next year won't include Jeremiah Chase of Old Virginny. No indeed, the new man for the tail of the ticket will be a horse of another color."

Phil blushed at the reference to a new suit, but let the insinuation pass. "A Negro running mate, you think? That'll mean the Attorney General."

"The Honorable Erasmus Hannibal can't miss this time," nodded Borton like an oracle. "Barely missed last time. In '72 Lepol pulled the slickest combination since the Kennedy-Johnson ticket of 1960. Sam knew he had to have Jerry Chase if the party was going to get the last vestige of the right wing vote. But that vestige has at last faded away. The GOP slate will be Lepol-Hannibal—but don't write it. That'll be my Sunday piece and everybody will know you stole it from me."

On this disagreeable and snobbish thrust, too pointed to be unintentional, Borton arose and, opening the glass door, went into the dining room. Phil watched him summon another drink with an imperious gesture to a passing waiter, and saw him take a solitary seat in a corner, producing a small, leather-bound, elegant notebook from an inside pocket.

"Poor fellow," thought Phil.

Borton, that vain and inconsiderate man, had no friends among the press corps. He did not seek intimacies at the working level. In fact, Borton conveyed the impression that he was slumming just by consenting to travel with a group, and he did so rarely. Phil knew the man's habits and idiosyncrasies; he'd begun his Washington apprenticeship as a legman for Borton. "Remarkable person, though," Phil murmured as he took out his own notebook which was the utilitarian kind used by stenographers for dictation. "When I used to work for him, he never let me forget that his sources of news were of the highest and most confidential. I'm sure he's been to a White House dinner lately, and probably heard directly from the President what the next year's ticket is going to be. Cal seldom writes by surmise. He's never without the inside line. He's proud of it. Only I wish for his own sake he weren't so arrogant. A fellow needs friends even at Cal's high level and . . ."

An unexpected voice obtruded upon the young man's reverie. "You shouldn't sit around and think so hard, Mr. Obermeister," this voice said, not unpleasantly. "I could almost read your mind."

The speaker presented a remarkable appearance. She was a well-formed, honey-haired woman of about Phil's own age, dressed in becoming powder-blue slacks and blouse, and she was equipped with a number of mechanical reporting devices that were attached to her person by small leather thongs and straps. As Phil looked up, she swiftly aimed a micro-camera, dangling from a neckpiece, and clicked its lever.

"Do you object?"

"So ordered," he laughed. He liked Eula Breck very much. People called her the Mechanical Maiden in some derision, but he admired her astonishing virtuosity as a reporter and writer of contemporary history. She worked for a slick-magazine chain, she had a television program of her own, and she'd written the best book he'd read on the presidential contest of three years ago: *People's Choice* '72. It was an open secret that Miss Breck would be writing another history on the coming contest—*People's Choice* '76, no doubt. Her ability to do so much work, and do it so well, was partly explained by her reliance on mobile automation. Along with the camera she carried three voice-recorders, one for taking interviews, one for dictating her own observations and the other—as was suspected among her colleagues—for reportorial eavesdropping.

"Sit down, Eula. Can I get you a drink?"

"No thanks. It dulls the edge of snoopery. I might as well confess I was sitting on the other side of Mayor Fitzgerald's likeness and catching your conversation with Cal Borton. Bit of a prig, isn't he?"

"He's just a poor, mixed-up pundit," said Phil, "but he . . ."

"Writes like a million dollars."

"So do you, Eula."

She liked a compliment as much as most women, and repaid it by sitting beside Phil and giving him a fleeting kiss on the cheek.

"Excuse my eavesdrop, Phil. Other people's actions and opinions are my business, same as yours, only I'm a natural gatherer of data. Sometimes the tone of a conversation is more important than the content. I couldn't resist taping you and Cal. Liberal intellectual vs. conservative ditto. The arrived pundit hard at work patronizing the upward struggler. Fascinating to record what each of you perceived in a presidential address which may become historical. I'll get many more reactions before the day's done. My instruments are scrupulously objective, even if I'm not."

"You're a Lepol admirer."

"Practically his high priestess," Eula assented. "Any man who could rescue the Republican party from near-oblivion and post-

Goldwaterism has got to be a colossus. I like everything the President stands for—egalitarianism, globalism and electoral majorities."

"All right. You like his aims. How about his methods?"

"The end justifies the means, I say."

Phil smiled. "It's funny to hear that from a liberal. I wasn't around in the days of McCarthyism. I'm told that persons who said they approved his aims, and didn't care how he achieved them, were considered beyond the pale. The very essence of high morality is to care about methods. We all would like to get rich—but not by stealing. We like to overcome our competitors—but not by murder."

"My, but you're a fundamentalist," exclaimed the young woman. "I'm afraid history has passed you by, Phil. But let's have a fair exchange. I've told you how I feel about Lepol. Is there anybody left in public life now that Goldwater's retired whom you admire?"

"Yes. . . . I'd give very high marks to the Vice President."

"Jerry Chase?" she mocked him good-humoredly. " 'Just for a handful of silver he left us / Just for a riband to stick in his coat.' "

"I admit I didn't like that phase of his career. I sometimes wish Mr. Chase had turned down Lepol's offer of the vice presidency spot. But I don't quite believe he deserted his conservative principles just for a place on the national ticket. I like to think he was promised a voice in White House policies, and that he hoped to keep a lid on Lepol's far-out liberalism."

"Hasn't succeeded, thank heaven," said Eula. "Phil, I had a reason for asking you the question. Now I'm going to give you the house prize for a nice interview. We've still got time before Thanksgiving dinner to hear another Thanksgiving message."

She unhitched a transistor radio from her belt and set it on the table before them, bending her richly shimmering head of hair as she examined and twiddled the dials. Phil regarded with some interest her slender back, the dainty lines of a shoulder strap and bra-buckle outlined through the stretched blue blouse. The ideological antagonism between himself and Borton did not exist in the case of this comely girl of the Left. Green eyes darted him a thoroughly unprofessional and almost coquettish glance. She wasn't so absorbed with business as not to have felt his appreciative gaze. He said quickly:

"You won't be able to get Juno Lepol's broadcast. It's not yet noon in California."

"I'm tuning in for Buenos Aires. Voice of America will carry Jerry Chase. He speaks from the Embassy there. Hah—Eureka!"

The tiny instrument caught up a deep, well modulated Southern voice in midsentence . . .

" . . . because faith in the Lord is more important to America than any other defense, military or material, against real and imagined peril.

"The Puritans said, 'Put your trust in God, my boys, and keep your powder dry.' They were putting first things first. Early Americans believed—and we must revive this credo—that all our man-made protections won't save us if ever our reliance on the Almighty is lost. Indeed, such loss of faith in Heaven would make national self-defense useless and an enemy attack unnecessary for our destruction. Losing that faith, we would be goners as a nation and a people.

"Documents like the Declaration of Independence—like the Federalist Papers—like the Gettysburg Address—are, of course, secular in nature. Yet there is the suggestion of a religious sermon in each of them. It just isn't possible for anybody to understand America, or to speak about her or to love her, without acknowledging that she was in the beginning, and in all her finest hours, as Lincoln phrased it, a nation 'under God.'

"That doesn't mean, and never did, that we claim to be God's chosen people. It means that we have chosen God. It means and will mean, so long as we remain a nation, that we Americans have taken God as the foundation rock for our political philosophy and for our nationalism. Nobody ever claimed that the Declaration and Constitution were handed down from Sinai like the Decalogue. But it's incontestable that our sacred documents were written in the light of Judeo-Christian belief to almost the same extent that the so-called classics of the Communists were written in the brimstone glow of the Marxian dialectic."

"Wow!" said Phil.

"Why, that trigger-happy s.o.b.," exclaimed Eula.

The distant voice resumed:

"American religio-political traditions can be traced through ancient and massive records. They go back to the first Thanksgiving Day in 1621. They extend through hundreds of proclamations—messages, addresses, resolutions—by the Continental Congress, by General George Washington, by the Congress of the Confederation, the national Congress, by governors and legislatures of the states, by Federal and Confederate armies in the field and by the navy at sea. As a nation we are accustomed to seeing 'In God We Trust' upon our coins, to asking grace at our family dinner tables, to saying prayers before court and legislative sessions and—until a decade ago—before the opening of school sessions. The President of the United States is sworn to his office, and I to mine, by a solemn oath in the name of God. None of this seems unusual or unnatural to us. But when the United Nations was founded in 1945 and set up soon afterwards with international headquarters in New York City, a startling fact came home to us—hard! Not every nation by any means relates its political life to its religious life. The United States is different in this way, and in many other ways, and we should be proud of that—we should try to remain different in many regards. Let us always conduct our affairs as Lincoln described us—'this nation under God.' And let us commence every enterprise, of war and peace, with these words of the Puritan motto: 'Trust God.' I thank you."

Eula silenced the transistor. She gave a low whistle.

"Extremist!" she said with scorn.

Chapter Two

Meanwhile the Finnigan clan—those three stalwart brothers and their mother—were meeting in Manhattan. The penthouse suite of the Hotel Hilton Uptown was one of three places reserved, under pseudonyms, in the attempt to get a place that wouldn't be bugged. That practice of surveillance had become more prevalent than ever since ratification of the 29th Amendment which forbade wire tapping and other forms of snooping, as well as private possession of firearms. Nobody except a few law-abiding citizens paid faithful attention to the law of the land, with the result that every government bureau and most large industries relied heavily upon their snooper staffs, and criminals and spies went about secretly armed.

But the Finnigans had felt reasonably secure as they gathered to watch President Lepol's telecast from Boston and to hold their first formal council for the campaign of '76. Ma Finnigan sat enthroned in an armchair before the set, and the three brothers were lined up on a sofa where she could watch them.

A household name: Ma Finnigan. Born Nellie Clarkhunter, she was a daughter of the Philadelphia dynasty of demagogues which had pushed out the last of the old patronage-fed bosses—that great race of swagmasters—for political control of that city. Nellie had been a taut, wholesome, energetic, athletic girl. At sixteen she had broken the women's high jump record in the Atlantic Coast Amateur Games. At eighteen she won the Woman's Marathon from Harrisburg to Independence Hall. There was a one-sided romance with a golf pro around her twentieth birthday, and shortly afterwards her engagement was announced to a suitable young legislator from Maryland, himself twice divorced. The society page of the *Baltimore Banner* described Miss Nellie Clarkhunter as follows:

> She reminds one of suspended motion in white tights hovering over the highjump bar, or of a pair of stout, tireless legs on a sylvan tow path. When you see her, you think of time-out on the hockey-field, rather than of happy hours at the honky-tonk. If she someday becomes first lady of Maryland, a thought that friends say is not absent from her fiancé's mind, she will reign with a grace that is to the manor born.

Nellie didn't care for the compliments. First of all, the passage was a near-plagiarism on a panegyric once addressed to the second Mrs. Nelson Rockefeller by historian Theodore White, and Nellie was not one for second-place honors. Besides, she'd always wished she were pretty and winsome instead of being so sturdily built. Finally, it wasn't difficult to see that her arranged marriage, hailed by the controlled Eastern press, was little better than a process of wheel-and-deal between two factions of the political managers. If there was going to be any finagling, she'd do it herself.

"Dammit," Nellie told a country club chum, "I want to make it on my own. Nobody's ever going to fall in love with me—I'm too sweat shirt for that. But I'm going to be heard from, and don't you forget it. I read where a rich man once said he was going to make his son President. Well, any parent who just repeats that statement is a cheap piker. I'm going to have three sons, and *each* will become President, one after the other, naturally. You laugh now. But you just wait and see."

Nellie was often to denounce this boast as apocryphal, but her subsequent career fixed it forever in the national folklore. The man she finally married, Little Joe Finnigan, a Vermont wheelwright, survived her driving energies only long enough to become progenitor of the sons. She named them by the ABC's, a handy identification method—Andrew, Barney and Chester. Her widowhood was a dynamic matriarchy during which she liquidated the St. Albans Wheel Company, and used the proceeds as a building block to establish the Green Mountain Space Facility, Inc. A typical entrepreneur of her own generation, which produced millionaires exclusively by government contracts, Ma Finnigan was seldom at home except for weekends. But she supervised her brood by remote control. She could say of her sons, as the Roman matron had: "*These* are my jewels."

In an age that could produce synthetic diamonds, the Finnigan brothers were indeed shaped to gem-like perfection. A cleverly concealed laser-wave device (a direct line to the Republican National Committee at 1625 Eye Street, N.W., Washington, D.C., Zip Code 20140) showed them there on the sofa at the Hilton Uptown and preserved the picture as well as the ensuing conversation for this book of history which you are now reading.

Andrew, Barney and Chester Finnigan were crew-cropped men, for the luxuriant hair-growth that symbolized political power in the Kennedy era was long out of vogue. They were meaty specimens, somewhat reminiscent of Tammany Hall types in the Boss Tweed period, since all fashion seems to run in cycles. But in more important ways the Finnigans represented the mores of the middle decades of the 20th Century in which they had grown to manhood. So faithful to their dentists had they been that their cavity-free teeth shone like constellations when they so much as opened their mouths to speak, and looked like marble hedgerows when they grinned. No candidates were ever better equipped for television performances, or for flashing "hiya-fellow" friendship on the exhausting hand-shaking tours that had become the *sine qua non* of contemporary statesmanship.

For the rest, the Finnigans were finished intellectual products of an age. Each had graduated high in his class from an Ivy League college. Each had pressed on to take his doctorate in advanced studies: Andrew in political science, Barney in business administration, Chester in physics. The matriarch had clearly foreseen that "education"—that is, the accumulation of academic credits—was the way to the top in the Kennedy-Johnson Age.

In the breakup of that epoch, when furious Democrats were butting heads like mountain goats, and often dying like embattled elk with their antlers locked, the Finnigans played it cool. They had done just enough military service to put it in their records, and sufficient welfare work to affix their names to the right committees. All three married wives who were joiners, organizers, social workers and accomplished speakers. Andrew was now Governor of New York. Barney was a senator from Pennsylvania. Chester had followed the distinguished example of Elliot Roosevelt and become Mayor of Miami Beach.

Today they, with Ma Finnigan, studiously watched the presidential telecast from Boston. When it was over, the three filial glances did a sharp eyes-right to the matriarch, now a thin, steely figure who always dressed in dove-wing gray and wore a fresh rose at the shoulder.

"Bad luck," said Ma after a thoughtful pause. "I was hoping Sam would put his foot in it."

"Me too," exclaimed Governor Finnigan gloomily.

"Andy!" snapped the old lady. "How many times must I tell you never to use that expression? If there's any one thing that finally overthrew the two-party system it was Republican me-tooism carried by Sam Lepol to the nth degree."

"Well, it couldn't have happened without the Kennedy-Johnson fracas," grumbled the Governor in self-defense.

"That's right," Ma agreed. "The Republicans had to get lucky with a me-too all-outer at the time of a Democratic split. Just the same, me-too is an expression that gives me the all-overs. But never mind," she added soothingly, "it's time you fellows started thinking for yourselves. I'm an old woman. I can't keep on being your think-tank forever. Who's got a bright idea on how to whip Lepol next November?"

"Lepol didn't say anything about giving up the only two overseas Navy bases we have left," observed Senator Barney Finnigan, a member of the Armed Services Committee in Washington. "Why doesn't Andy here come out for turning Guantanamo Bay back to the Cubans, and giving the Saigon Navy Base back to North Vietnam?"

"Yes, that's not a bad thought," Ma Finnigan agreed. "It always pays to put a priority on peace and disarmament. But Lepol knows that as well as we do. It's such an obvious move that we can't be sure he won't do it himself at the psychological moment. But let's keep it in mind. What else?"

The Mayor of Miami Beach had quietly left his seat and gone to a portable book shelf which was transported with the Finnigans wherever they held these family gatherings. Chester Finnigan consulted the index of a volume and brought the book back with him to the sofa.

"My idea," he said, "is that Andy here hasn't got much chance in a confrontation campaign against Lepol. But let's not forget that the Democratic registration in the nation is still three-to-one over Republican registration. Back in 1960 when Jack Kennedy was being called the inexperienced candidate, he reached into political history for a red herring. Just listen to this."

The others became attentive as Chester read:

> Ann Arbor, Michigan, October 28, 1960, John F. Kennedy speaking: "Your choice is very simple. Do you want Mr. Nixon and the party of McKinley and Harding, Coolidge and Hoover? Or do you want Kennedy-Johnson and the party of Jefferson and Jackson, Cleveland and Wilson, and Franklin Delano Roosevelt?"

Ma Finnigan nodded vigorously. "Good boy, Chet. When in doubt, turn to the example of JFK. Of course, the party appeal will work better this time than it did last time. Andy is going to unify the Democrats on a Convention platform statement that goes all the way back to the days of Old Hickory—'To the victors belong the spoils.' Right, Andy?"

"Yes, Ma'am," the Governor said emphatically.

Senator Finnigan cleared his throat and said: "There's another thing to keep in mind when we look at Sam Lepol and become discouraged with the prospect of beating him. It's true that he's so far been able to out-demagogue us Democrats. But let's never forget—the man's a Republican, isn't he? And Republicans are just naturally dumb about politics. Lepol was running scared last time. But this time he's an odds-on favorite, and that's just when the Republican stupidity streak comes out."

"That's true as a generality," their mother agreed. "But we can't count on it in Lepol. He's smart."

"Tom Dewey was supposed to be smart," the Senator pressed on. "But in 1944 he let General Marshall talk him out of making an issue of Roosevelt's conduct of World War II. And in 1948 Dewey was so far ahead of Harry Truman that he took his hands off the handle bars and fell on his face."

"Maybe," grinned the Governor, showing his telegenic teeth, "I could get Lepol to meet me in a television debate. That was Nixon's big mistake against Kennedy."

"Too pat," said Ma Finnigan. "I'm not against trying it, but Lepol won't bite. None of you fellows has yet suggested the basic strategy."

"Divide 'em and conquer," the brothers said in something close to unison.

"Right. If Lepol runs with Jeremiah Chase on the ticket, we'll get the big metropolitan press to rip 'em apart on the liberal-conservative axis. If Lepol dumps Chase and puts a Negro on the ticket we'll have to nominate a Negro who can call theirs an Uncle Tom."

"Ma, you're a genius," cried her youngest son generously.

"Let me remind you what somebody once said. 'Genius is the infinite capacity for taking pains.' That's all there is to it. Think and plan, boys. Think and plan."

The brothers fell into a brown study, from which the Mayor was first to emerge.

"Ma, what about the so-called Lindsay syndrome? Would it work on a national scale?"

"Go ahead, son."

"Well, in 1965 Congressman John Lindsay, a Republican, put together a fusion ticket in his election for Mayor of New York. He got the Liberal party endorsement for himself. He chose another Liberal to run as Comptroller. He chose a Democrat to run for President of the City Council. Lindsay asked all of his followers to vote for these two. And each of these two asked their followers to vote for Lindsay."

"I get it," said the Governor. "I should choose a Socialist to run as Vice President with me. And maybe promise to appoint a liberal Republican as Secretary of State."

"It might work," Ma Finnigan ruled after they had awaited her decision. "We'll keep all these ideas on ice till we meet again. But I don't want you boys to let any optimism go to your heads."

"We won't, Ma," said the Governor speaking for the others. "We all agree that Sam Lepol will be a tough man to shave."

Chapter Three

Another woman of politics, Juno Lepol, had listened with considerable interest to the presidential Thanksgiving message. Juno had hoped to have her son with her for the occasion, but it was breakfast time at Berkeley, California, and Dwight D. ("Little Ike") Lepol was not an early riser. So Juno, alone and apprehensive, sat with coffee and honeydew before her in the bright bubble that was her quarters at the Sheraton Sunset Motel, and watched Sam's performance. She followed the speech from a typescript on the table before her and occasionally jotted down a critique. The President seemed to be speaking without notes, and had no lectern before him, but in fact he was merely reciting the words from a small memo-prompter concealed in the knot of his necktie. The speech was the joint product of his ghost writers and of a computer in the White House basement where popularly accepted ideas were scientifically collected and stored for use.

No major candidate for years had dared rely upon his own convictions, much less his language and intellect. The mass movement toward raw democracy put an inexorable demand upon telling the people what they wanted to hear. The highest forensic skill had become the ability to talk down to the people's level, and at the same time to combine this form of condescension with the subtle deceit of making the people think that they were thinking for themselves.

President Lepol did all this exceptionally well, and yet his wife was not wholly pleased. Sam lacked something. Sincerity, of course, though that hardly mattered any longer. No, she thought, aiding her cerebrations by jotting notes on the typescript, the missing ingredient was something else. He had hit the lowest common denominator so far as the substance of his remarks was concerned. The computerized surveys were infallible in their findings that people enjoyed the endless emphasis upon security—peace abroad, prosperity at home. People reacted favorably to the theme of giantism—the bigger the better! Visions of political uniformity, of globalism, made them think they were thinking big thoughts of their own. Everybody belonged to the Master Race! It was Hitlerism without hate, without the perils or the sacrifices of conquest. Everybody was part of the Reich which was going to dominate the world for thousands of years to come!

"However," Juno's fine, precise penmanship was recording, "Sam has become such a trained seal in delivering this message that there's a risk of losing rapport with the voters in a hard campaign such as the one that lies ahead. It's almost as if he could turn up the audio volume of that memo-prompter and let the audience listen to it instead of to him. I keep feeling a premonition that something could go wrong for us in the election. The people are ripe for some candidate who offers them a change of tune. I don't believe Governor Andy Finnigan would supply it. He's a synthetic man the same as Sam is, and the Democratic party will write a platform with different words to the same tune that the Republicans are playing. I suppose there's nothing to worry about so long as we've got nobody except the Finnigans to lick. But we're vulnerable just the same. If a candidate came along with real audacity—with personality—with a strong set of convictions—well, it would be Katy-bar-the-door for Lepol and the Finnigans too. Of course, there's no such person in sight unless it's . . ."

She paused in her writing here, the small pen suspended. She read back over her stream-of-consciousness jottings. Audacity! Personality! Convictions! While her mind was still on this searching track, she allowed the pen to descend and describe what was in the deepest, fear-ridden reaches of her mind. She closed her eyes while the instrument wrote. She opened them and read the name —Jeremiah Fielding Chase.

An absurd fear, of course. Jerry Chase was embalmed in the vice presidency. Sam had taken care of that, though not without some cost in the coin of political promises. Very few people knew the terms of the bargain that had brought Chase to the Lepol-Chase ticket, but that deal wouldn't matter much longer. At the propitious moment Chase would be liquidated and the promises would have no force or effect. A "Dump Jerry" movement was already in progress among the party leaders. Researchers were at work trying to dig up some scandal in Chase's private life or family—to concoct one, if necessary, though it probably wouldn't be. The precedent of the "Dump Lyndon" movement in the early months of 1963 came to mind. Then, as now, the facilities of quiet, efficient federal investigation could be counted upon to produce results. Lyndon had had his Bobby Baker, and had managed to build a well-concealed fortune greater than the one inherited by John F. Kennedy. If it hadn't been for the Dallas tragedy, Vice President Johnson would have been off the 1964 ticket and the menace of his ambitions wholly expunged.

Even before those days, Juno remembered, there had been the two abortive schemes to detach Richard Nixon from Eisenhower's coattails. In 1952, the schemers had caught Nixon with a slush fund and he'd barely saved himself by that maudlin telecast which featured the dog, Checkers, and his wife's cloth coat. Then, in 1956, with the beloved Ike a cardiac case, and Nixon seemingly more likely to succeed than any man in history, the conspirators had tried again to bounce him off the ticket. They'd failed, it's true, but that was because Nixon was immensely clever and because Ike lacked the ruthlessness to destroy a man who had been so loyal. Well, those circumstances didn't exist in the present setup. Jerry Chase wasn't clever—not even very ambitious—and if Sam Lepol wasn't pitiless when it came to axing a colleague's career, his wife—thought Juno with a tight smile—could play Lady Macbeth in real life as well as on the stage.

She folded the typescript and inserted it between the leaves of her diary, into which she would later transcribe some of her thoughts. A glance at her wristwatch showed her it was nearly nine o'clock. At noon today she was scheduled to take the leading part in a Thanksgiving pageant, "Liberty Unlimited," at the University of California football stadium. Dwight D. would play the role of interlocutor. She hoped he hadn't stayed out too late with that flighty ingénue, Cassie Croker. It was important to Dwight's political future that he make a good appearance before all the young and future voters who would be present. He was already a state senator of California—a good beginning. With another glance at her watch, Juno decided to give him a quarter-hour more of sleep.

Young Ike at 29 was too old for bed checks, and she had no idea what time he'd come in—but undoubtedly not early. The lack she had noted in her husband—no personality, no boldness—was superabundantly supplied in Young Ike. A smile of confidence and satisfaction lighted the mother's beautiful face as she thought of those over-trained automatons that Ma Finnigan was pointing for the White House.

Fifteen minutes passed. Juno rose in her flowing white negligee, went through the connecting bathroom door and peered into the adjoining bedroom. She froze in her tracks with shock. His bed was made and unoccupied, giving the room the emptiness of a tomb.

She did not cry out, but the hot bolt of fright caused her to sway and to clutch at the doorknob for support. Something had happened to Young Ike! Dreadful visions of a smashup on those murderous freeways assailed her lively imagination. Juno could all but hear the crash of rending steel and see the limp, lifeless bodies spread upon the gory concrete. Or—her frantic mind raced on—what if Young Ike had eloped with the feather-brained Cassie? Juno could envision, too, the black splash in the tabloid press: President's Son Goes to Gretna. Oh, dead or alive, Dwight seemed born to rend her heart. What hopes and dreams she had for this wild, brilliant, attractive son. How he represented for her the ultima Thule of life's desire. She was already First Lady of the Land—but ambition attained would always be for her ambition stimulated. To be a President's wife—why that was nothing compared with being a President's mother. She had merely married Sam, but Dwight D. Lepol she had borne in labor and raised in anxiety.

There was no one else in all the world she loved except Dwight. Sam—he was a clod, a boor, a political synthetic whom she had instrumentalized into the presidency. If she had the choice of Sam dead or Dwight living—why, it would be no choice at all. If it were a matter of the President getting involved with a fluffy little adventuress and bringing the ugliest kind of notoriety upon the White House, Juno would have preferred it a thousand times over to some folly on Dwight's part that would threaten her plans for him.

Heavens, she didn't care how many affairs he conducted outside the glare of publicity. She expected him to horse around awhile and then to marry—in fact, marriage was very much in the scheme of things for a man who was destined for national scrutiny and leadership. But the wife had to be most judiciously selected, indoctrinated and pledged to the fulfillment of the husband's career. A girl like Cassie, gay and pretty as a field flower, thoughtless and sportive as a lark, would never do.

Juno staggered back to her own room and there, on the verge of collapse, beheld a talisman which caused an instantaneous lifting of the heart. On a tripod by the desk stood a mighty symbol without which she never travelled—the Great Seal of the President of the United States. Technically, it did not belong to her presence. Only the chief executive himself was entitled to have it around as the emblem of his rank. But Juno had overruled authority long ago on this matter as well as others. The Constitution had never contemplated any recognition of a royal consort, but national usage in the instances of Eleanor Roosevelt and Jacqueline Kennedy had gone a long way toward doing so, and Juno had claimed the distinction of being a presidential co-equal by common law.

The sight of that glorious certificate braced the woman. It lifted her spirits. She stood before it with a feeling that the ordinary torments of uncertainty and suspense of life were not for her. Had Dwight been in an accident, the Secret Service would long ago

Arena girls, commenting on the dates that the tall, stately Juno kept with the rather short representative loudly remarked in the dressing room: "Eckstrom, you could eat your dinner off the top of his head."

"I intend to," was Juno's rejoinder.

Often, as she looked back over the years, Juno would bless her adolescent adversities. If she hadn't been ashamed of her parents, she wouldn't have striven to rise above them. If she had been petite and cute, she might have been less aggressive. If she had been truly talented for the stage, she might not have looked for another outlet to find it in politics. Though not more than a half-inch taller than her husband, she seemed to tower over him, not only because she walked in high heels but also because she had the dominant vision in many ways. When they campaigned together for re-election in Sam's district, she was already measuring the competition for the Senate. When he made the Senate and seemed content to settle comfortably for a long stay in that most exclusive of clubs, she worked for his appointment as Secretary of Housing and Urban Development. As soon as Sam had command of that enormous, open-end budget for building the homes and paying the rent of half the population, Juno hired the aging ghost-writers who had worked for John F. Kennedy and other notables and caused them to produce the mammothly merchandised volumes by Samuel T. Lepol.

Poor Sam! In those days of struggle he revealed to her many weaknesses that had to be overcome. For one thing, he was a patrician by birth and breeding. He liked cultivated, well-washed company at private country clubs and in sumptuous living rooms and libraries. She discovered that his favorite authors were the Victorians, Thackeray and Samuel Butler, both of whom were frank about their distaste for poverty in all its revolting forms, whether the shabby-genteel or the starved and ragged. Another of Lepol's favorites was the whimsical Charles Lamb, whose candid essay on the insufferable nature of poor relatives was the most-thumbed item in all of the Lepol books.

Worse still, Lepol had a chuckling fondness for Joel Chandler Harris' *Uncle Remus*. He could imitate the plantation dialogue at length. When she caught him in abandoned laughter, reading the Tar Baby story to Dwight D., Juno snatched the book from him and flung it into the fire.

"Sam, will you never learn? I've told you a hundred times that the whole literature of the comic Negro is completely out of the mainstream of American thought."

"But Juno, that tale is a masterpiece of folklore. Nothing is more true to life than that old darkie sitting there and making up animal stories for the little white boy. Those were days when the white and black races really did get along. Why can't they get along now? Sometimes I wish . . ."

"All of this class propaganda must be taken from my house and destroyed. Thackeray, Butler, Lamb, Edith Wharton, Henry James and all the rest that deal with privilege and closed society. Books like that couldn't even find a publisher in this day and age."

"That's because the literary liberalissimos have gone in for book burning worse than Hitler. The egghead critics have a censorship of their own, either ignoring or panning any book that offends the pure faith. I don't mind running for office as a lunatic leftist if that's what the times demand. But dammit, Juno, even rabbis tell Yiddish jokes and Irish priests still get a laugh out of Pat and Mike jokes. I think it's just as prudish not to mention race as it was when our Victorian ancestors weren't allowed to admit a woman had legs."

"You think—! You wish—! Sam Lepol, if we'd done things your way, you'd still be building up seniority on the Committee on Internal and Insular Affairs."

"I sort of liked it there."

"I know you did. You'd be perfectly satisfied to go on writing rivers and harbors authorization bills and sitting around the pork barrel with your cronies. What an example you'd have set for Young Ike here. You promised me when he was born back in 1946 that you'd get out and try to make yourself President if I let you name him after your bridge-playing friend at the NATO Supreme Headquarters."

"All right. I promised. I'll do it, too."

"Not if you don't give yourself a strong brainwash. I'm not going to mention those prejudiced, upper-class books again. They must go! I want you to fill the shelves with volumes like Lillian Smith's *Strange Fruit* and James Baldwin's *The Fire Next Time*. If you must delve into the distant past, you can pick books about suffering people—the American Indians and those Okies of John Steinbeck and the victims of the pogroms in Russia and any good historical novel about the tortures of the Spanish Inquisition or the Roman galley slaves."

"But, Juno, why must I read about human suffering? I like people."

"Sam, you are studying for high political office. You must major in the hardships of the lower classes. I realize that there's very little privation and no tyranny whatever in America any longer. People never had it so good. But you can't go around telling people how lucky they are. You must develop an outgoing wave of sympathy."

"Juno?"

"What?"

"It puzzles me. I'm really very fond of people. Some, more so than others, I admit that. But you and all the ultra-libs go in for loving whole populations in the mass, and wallowing in accounts of their agonies. Yet you don't really like people, do you?"

"What a ridiculous question, Sam."

But she never answered it. Except to herself in that tell-tale diary. Paging back to her stage days, Juno found a number of entries concerning contacts she had made with the great and near-great of the theater. Most of these successful entertainers, as she vividly recalled, were sympathetic persons who knew that they could give pleasure to audiences. They enjoyed the knowledge. They liked people, all right, individually and in numbers. But the diary recalled to her mind that there had been exceptions. A few wealthy and celebrated stage persons were downright misanthropes. They were loners. They were grouches. They actively despised the howling crowds, the shy autograph seekers and the young aspirants like herself who came for help and advice.

Item in the diary:

> With even a modicum of thespian ability, I can rise above Lincoln's dictum. I can fool all the people all of the time into believing that I care for their sniveling desires and their fawning attentions. I can campaign from Long Island to Waikiki Beach, shaking slimy hands, kissing misbegotten babies, making drooling addresses—and nobody will know how I loathe it. What's more, I can transmit some of my pretense to Sam. He's a difficult case. So sentimental. So transparent. He'll sit all night with a sick friend, but cringe at the sight of some boisterous constituent who yells in his face and calls him "Ole Buddy." Still, to know Sam's weakness is to be warned. I must break up his close masculine friendships that get in my way. I must coach him in the emotional mooching of the multitude.

In the interregnum between Sam's election and presidential inauguration, Juno had a very bad moment. She appeared on the Eula Breck program called "Between Us Girls." On this particular evening it was a panel show with two newspaper columnists, Borton and Obermeister, as well as Miss Breck, questioning the incoming First Lady.

Breck: Mrs. Lepol, why did you give up the stage?

Juno: My dear, it gave me up.

Breck: Aren't you being too modest?

Juno: To be frank, I discovered something larger than the stage of the theater. I learned that all the world's a stage.

Breck: And all the politicians actors?

Juno: You are putting words in my mouth, Miss Breck. I don't like that.

Breck: I'm sorry. Mr. Obermeister, your turn to question.

Obermeister: Mrs. Lepol, you may know that you are sometimes referred to as Juno who, among other things, was the goddess of wisdom. Would you tell our audience—what is the deepest wisdom that woman can learn from life? Is it love?

Juno: A woman doesn't learn that, Mr. Obermeister. Love comes naturally if it comes at all.

Obermeister: If—?

Breck: Next question. Mr. Borton?

But for Juno, the occasion was spoiled by her fluff. "If it comes at all," she had answered. That ingenuous young man had seemed actually hurt by her equivocating response. His serious gray eyes expressed a sorrow for her—for her who in a few days would become the mistress of the White House. It was as if he had blundered into her secret. He was embarrassed for himself and her. That night she sought the diary:

Item:

> But I do love. I love Dwight. He is the very extension of myself.

At eleven o'clock Juno buzzed her son. He answered over the hotel phone with a semi-conscious grumble. But an instant later she heard his electric razor humming from the bathroom along with the spurt of an additional shower. She was already clad in a grey gown, those inevitable and glinty serpents of blonde hair (her trademark, by now) coiled about her brow under the prim pilgrim bonnet. Dwight joined her soon, wearing a dark blue wash-wear which would purposely be the only modern garb of the pageant. He carried a sheaf of sides—his cues and dialogue.

"Ike, you haven't learned your lines, have you?"

"It wouldn't have helped. My head is seething like a reactor. My tongue feels thick as a carpet. Let's go, Mom."

The open car journey, heavily guarded, was a matter of minutes to the stadium. They entered by the players' tunnel into the home team locker room where Juno assured herself that a pale but eager Cassie, wearing her Scarlet Letter, was among the waiting cast. Juno let a Secret Service functionary accompany her further into the stadium for a trouper's take of the house. The stands themselves were not filled, but hundreds of students and guests sat on the gridiron grass that surrounded the stage-in-the-round. Juno returned in satisfaction to the locker room and addressed her supporters:

"We have a fine crowd. We must give them our best."

For her it was more than just another show. The allegorical script belabored a familiar theme, global togetherness, but the appearance of a President's wife was a bold innovation. She had applied her forward strategy of campaigning both for the present and the future office at the same stroke. Dwight would have the best scenes and as much as twenty minutes of national television coverage. Just so he was sharp. But he would be, she knew. He was adept at rising above his hangovers. Why had she fretted about that empty bed this morning? Nothing would happen to Young Ike. He was too important in her plans for the national election which followed the one in which Sam could hardly lose. Besides, no untoward event could take place without her knowing right away. There was Secret Service with its radiophones and open circuits. She would always have the cold comfort of being the first to hear bad news.

"On stage," called the director. "Places, please."

Juno led the procession of actors through the cheering throngs to the stage. At 12.10 Pacific Coast Time, the show was on. That would be 15.10 on the Atlantic coast. The first scene showed the arriving Pilgrims and the kneeling Indians. Just before the first intermission, at 12.40, the interlocutor gave a decision that the Pilgrims were trespassers in the New World. They would have to weigh anchor and begone to their previous inhospitalities unless the Indians should pass an immigration bill to make them welcome. Back through the cheering audience Juno led her troupe. A pale Secret Service agent, radiophone in hand, met her in the locker room.

"Mrs. Lepol?"

"Yes?"

"I must give this message just as I received it. The plane has been rammed. The President is dead."

Chapter Four

Calvin Borton, Philip Obermeister and Miss Eula Breck, with the eleven other reporters, had departed Boston on the press plane about a half hour ahead of FAA One. It is a customary procedure which allows coverage of the President when he lands from any journey. Phil and Eula took seats together in the aft lounge where they were joined by Calvin Borton. There was only some broken conversation at first because the two assistant press secretaries for the White House, Vic Silver and Paul Stewart, took a while to pass out authorized texts of the Thanksgiving Address. The three scribes in the lounge seats, like good professionals, fell to work searching the written text for any hidden significance or inconsistencies with the spoken version.

"Here's a gimmick," said Phil, turning to Eula after a close perusal. "In the passage on page six where the President was promising everlasting prosperity, he predicts that the third-quarter deficit in the federal budget will be three-quarters-of-a-billion dollars less than was anticipated in June. But he doesn't say that the Bureau of the Budget overestimated on purpose so as to make red ink look like black ink. And he doesn't say that the national debt has just passed through the $900 billion ceiling. By next Thanksgiving we'll be talking in trillions of debt instead of billions."

Borton removed his heavy hornrimmed reading glasses to give Phil a withering stare.

"You have the best nineteenth century mind since Robert Taft, Obermeister. What difference does it make how high the national debt goes? We owe it to ourselves, I daresay."

"But we keep running deficits in good times as well as bad, Calvin. I don't claim to be the economist that you are, so you tell me—is the Government so different from other corporations? Isn't there bound to be a day when the rent comes due, so to speak?"

"Preposterous. The circulation of money is like the circulation of the body's blood."

"Yes, I've heard that one before, Cal. It sounds to me like economic doublethink. When there isn't any logical answer to a very obvious predicament, the only way out is to talk gibberish."

"You dolt! No doubt, if I were to recite an ode by Pindar, you'd call it gibberish just because you don't speak the language."

"But I don't see any reason why the language of national finance in a democratic country should be conducted in Greek or in an unintelligible jargon. I have great respect for your intellect, Cal. Why don't you tell me, in plain words, please, what's good about a deficit?"

"There are deficits *and* deficits," said Borton pityingly. "Some are good. Some are bad. A planned deficit, such as this country has run since the Kennedy Administration, is good."

Eula giggled. "Scotty Reston wrote a column about that. He said that you don't plan a deficit any more than you plan an illegitimate baby. The Kennedy Administration got caught, that's all—and tried to make a virtue of necessity. I'm on your side, Mr. Borton, but let's not kid ourselves."

Borton glared at the girl. He wrathfully donned the hornrimmed glasses to return to his reading and to end the conversation. Eula Breck's new giggle burst its bounds in a real peal of laughter.

"Sorry. But for a moment you looked just like a cartoon of Barry Goldwater in those goggles. It struck me so funny I . . ."

Her remark had been overheard. Her amusement was so infectious that others in the cabin had to stifle their snickers. To laugh aloud at the world-famous columnist, Borton, would have been scandalous. Yet the thunderhead scowl behind the spectacles did make him look all the more like those 1964 Ed Harpoon cartoons of Goldwater. When Borton snatched off the spectacles and rose indignantly from his seat, a definite crisis was building up in this small but news-spreading group.

"I am going up front," Borton announced. "I may say that I'm unaccustomed to traveling in the steerage, and I won't make the mistake again."

But as he began his withdrawal, its dramatic effect was smothered by a hoarse voice over the public address system.

"Seat belts, everybody. This is an emergency."

Borton sank back. In the hush of the cabin, there was only the concerted click of metal seat-belt fasteners. Silver and Stewart, the press secretaries, emerged from the flight deck. The former carried a hand mike, the latter was wearing earphones.

"First announcement," said Silver into the mike in the same hoarse voice. "This plane will land at Forrestal on schedule. We will not divert. Repeat. Diversion is not authorized. I now have very bad news."

Accustomed to flying, the listeners did not hear the humming of the motors. Nothing mattered but the awaited statement. Hands reached automatically for pads and pencils. The two secretaries wouldn't be standing in mid-aisle if this plane were in danger. It had to be—everybody seemed to know it—bad news about that other plane.

Vic Silver, a veteran of the wire services before he took the White House job, looked exactly as if he were dictating a momentous story over the phone. He seemed entirely unaware that he had a visible audience. His concentration, showing in the intense gray face that now glistened with sweat, was wholly on the content and presentation of his material. He began to speak, slowly and distinctly, at a measured rate of delivery.

"President Lepol died this afternoon just twenty minutes ago in a mid-air collision over Connecticut. All crew members and passengers on Federal Aviation Agency One were lost.

"Wreckage of the presidential plane struck the ground fifteen miles northeast of Greenwich and four minutes after being hit at 15.34 hours, Eastern Standard Time, by an unidentified single-motor jet. Damage from fire and impact is total. Bodies are being identified by medical components of state and local police. A detachment of Connecticut National Guard which happened to be marching nearby has secured the area pending arrival of federal troops and officials.

"With the Vice President out of the country, and not yet contacted in Buenos Aires, Attorney General Hannibal has proclaimed an unlimited national emergency until the new President can be reached."

Silver lowered the microphone. He took a handkerchief and swabbed his face. For a moment the silence that followed his voice was as absolute as death itself. Eula Breck's gasping sob broke the spell. Reporters stared into one another's faces as if looking for confirmation of the unbelievable. Oaths were ejaculated. Tears were seen on cynical, masculine cheeks. Phil put his arm around Eula's quaking shoulders and drew her to him for comfort. But the pause was brief. Professionalism was the take-charge factor.

"Vic? Anything whatever on that unidentified jet?"

"Yes, but I'll have to go off-record. Paul here—" Silver gestured to Stewart who was pressing the headset against his ears—"is monitoring everything that comes into our flight deck. We've never worked under an unlimited emergency situation. We don't know the ground rules. But here goes off-record. You'll have to verify when we get on the ground."

"Go ahead, Vic!"

"The jet remains unidentified so far as we've been told. Security aircraft that escorted FAA One saw it strike the tail assembly of the larger craft and fall to pieces."

"Is there a search?"

"A search is being conducted for some markings of the collison vehicle."

"Doesn't anybody know where the unidentified jet took off from?"

"There are conflicting reports thus far. One report says that the jet was a private aircraft, probably owned by a business concern in the Boston area."

"What does the other report say, Vic?"

"It says the jet originated out of Otis Air Force Base, and that it has a National Guard registry."

"Vic, was the crash an accident?"

"No comment whatever on that, fellows. I'm sorry."

"Anything else?"

Silver turned to Stewart. They conversed in whispers. Silver resumed the hand mike communication.

"The Vice President, that is, the new President, Jeremiah Chase, has now been officially notified through the American Embassy at B.A. He is expected to take the oath of office immediately, probably over live television, and to return to the United States without delay."

"What else, Vic?"

"I guess it's all right to give you this. It's very public in California. The former President's widow, Mrs. Juno Lepol, was between scenes at the Berkeley stadium when informed of the tragedy. She insisted upon going to the stage in her costume, accompanied by her son, and making the announcement of the tragedy in person."

The reporters took a moment to envision that macabre and melodramatic scene. They all knew Juno. They had seen her in action. But before anybody could put a follow-up query, Silver announced that the plane was making its descent on Washington and that he would see them next at the White House press room.

When the plane landed, eleven of the reporters hurried to the White House, which would now be the news center of the world. But the two columnists, and Eula, were more interested in background and off-beat reactions. Each rushed to the parking lot, jumped into his car and headed in his chosen direction.

Chapter Five

Still smarting from the brief clash with the unspeakable Obermeister and the Mechanical Maiden, Cal Borton gunned his Chevrolet Slipstream out of the parking lot and up the ramp to the John Philip Sousa Freeway. Forrestal Airport lay in the flatlands that used to accommodate the Anacostia Navy Base. Ringed with highrise apartments, the area was jocularly known in journalese as Laker's Acres—named for the jaunty millionaire investor who had begun in Washington as a Senate page boy and found ways to build his fortune by doing private favors for senators who afterwards preferred not to have the connections known.

Very few of the flats were let to families, for the management catered to Government girls by a side investment in beauty parlors and dress shops, as well as by a kennel and veterinarian establishment which took care of the police dogs. The orgy of gang-type rapes in the late 1960's had set the fashion for women to adopt the use of these fierce animals. Laker's Acres was known as the safest place for unmarried girls to live.

All but a few of the tenants had evidently left Washington for the holidays, but two open vehicles, with mistress and protector in the front seat, rushed up the ramp and into the Freeway at the same time Borton was making his entrance. He swerved to avoid one, nearly sideswiped the other and, almost in the teeth of the snarling Alsatians, lost control of his car which performed a vicious ground-loop across the concrete. On an ordinary day, he would have been hopelessly in the path of thundering traffic, but the road was nearly untraveled today. So he straightened his course and drove on.

The incident warned him that his nerves were out of hand. That seemed understandable, considering that he had received shocking news only a short while before, but Borton knew that the thing which really jarred him was what had happened before the announcement of the President's death. That ridiculous boy had not only disputed him in public, but had come off with no worse than an even break in the ensuing argument, and then that impudent girl had laughed at Borton, and set the whole lounge to snickering.

Mortifying! He couldn't remember such a thing ever happening before. He was used to rapt attentiveness when he gave his opinions, and the company in which he usually gave them was far more erudite and select than the one of the afternoon. For years he had lunched regularly, when in town, at the refectory table in the Professional Club, and it was a bold person among the senators, lawyers, authors, clergymen and retired ambassadors who dared to cross conversational swords.

When he dined out, at the White House, the embassies and the mansions of the rich and mighty, he was always the focus of a respect that bordered upon deference. In the capitals of the world, Borton was the sought-after guest and the honored consultant. More than thirty years of opinion-giving and opinion-making through the top journals of the English-speaking world had fixed his position, rarely challenged and never before derided.

As he crossed the Sousa bridge into downtown Washington, he reached into his breast pocket for the small, square, silver box in which he carried the tranquilizer pills prescribed by his doctor for periods of stress. The medication hadn't been intended for such unexpected use as this: being teased by other reporters. It was intended to calm him when the overload of profound research and of protracted periods of difficult writing became oppressive. A bachelor, there was nothing much for him to do in his tall, elegant Georgetown home except to study the intricate dynamics of the world's civilization, modern and ancient, and to worry about what drastic calamity would bring about the fall of Western culture, a debacle he had many times predicted.

Calamity Cal! He could remember now, with an effort, when people had called him that, although more in awe than disrespect. Time after time, his warning had helped, in ways that not many persons knew, to avert the catastrophes that he foresaw.

As a very young man he had been invited to the Oval Room to drink those tart martinis that Roosevelt enjoyed mixing. Once Cal had been there just at the time the fall of France had opened world conquest to the Nazis. He couldn't be certain, but he was nearly so, that a chance remark of his own had been the basis of FDR's denunciation of Fascist Italy, given at the University of Virginia. "The hand that held the dagger has plunged it into the back of her neighbor."

Cal had been a privileged early morning walker with Harry Truman not long before that telegraphic bombshell had exploded under General Douglas MacArthur and blown him out of the Far East Command in time, Cal felt, to save the U.S.A. from the dangerous folly of bombing the Red Chinese ports and bringing on war with Russia.

Eisenhower, Cal reflected, he hadn't known well, but he'd been in on those consultations with White House advisors that brought about the decision to destroy Joe McCarthy. Kennedy—? Well, Jack liked to slip away to Cal's home in Georgetown, and it was there the President had rehearsed the American University speech that signaled the decision to make the first Nuclear Test Ban Treaty.

Borton recalled how he had fallen out with Johnson, a cornball autocrat, and had gone over to help Sam Lepol make a living organism out of the GOP, which had nearly expired when Goldwater took it out of the pure air of the twentieth century.

Yes, many a time he, Calamity Cal, had sensed an imminent smashup of the Western World: Nazism, adventurism under MacArthur, bestialism in McCarthy and the apocalypse of nuclear rivalry. Humanity was always just escaping annihilation by the skin of its teeth, as Thornton Wilder had written, and was always lucky enough to have men of foresight around at just the right time.

Borton, taking his pillbox in his palm, rattled it and let it slide back into his pocket. He wouldn't seek artificial relief. He needed all his faculties today. He would operate on raw nerves, if he must. For the meaning of that little hassle on the press plane was coming through to him now. Despite all the progress the country had made under President Lepol, there remained a residue of reactionism in the nation, else a whippersnapper like Obermeister wouldn't have any readers at all, and nobody would think it at all funny for a silly girl to make that uncalled for reference to Goldwater. The fact that this untoward incident had taken place at very close to the time of Sam Lepol's death was what had so depressed and agitated him, thought Borton. For he had felt, from the very instant of the fateful announcement, that this violent ending of the President's scrupulously protected life was no accident!

Intuition! He had nothing else to go on at this moment. But a newspaperman without intuition would be a sterile creature. True, the only sound basis of reporting had to be facts—facts—nothing but facts; and yet this intuition, born in seekers of truth and developed by years of experience, performed as a spark that often lighted the search. An adult lifetime of keeping watch over the mortality of the human race had convinced Borton that accidents just don't happen in matters of high importance. No, for behind every seemingly fortuitous happening of gravity, there was a discoverable causation, and Borton could feel it in his bones.

What he felt now was the positive belief of foul play. An action by somebody, perhaps a conspiracy by many persons, had brought about the downing of FAA One. Sam Lepol was his friend, and later he would mourn for him, but right now the mission was one of detection and exposure, so that the nation and the world would understand and avenge this crime.

Borton, once more in control of his nerves, confident that his instincts would lead him to discovery, wheeled into Independence Avenue and parked boldly on the all-but-empty street in front of the marble palace that housed the Federal Aviation Agency. Among the hundreds of functionaries he knew in this town was one Frank Foley, a lame duck Senator from Idaho. The President had saved Foley from the horrid fate of going back to Pocatello by appointing him chairman of the security division of this agency. There was just a fair chance, Borton believed, that Foley would be in his office on a holiday. Foley lived in a small apartment with a harridan of a wife and used his work as an excuse to get away from her. Besides, the tragic news had been out for almost an hour, and it would be natural for Frank to rush to the office where he might be of some help in this emergency.

"If he isn't here, I'll telephone him to come down," thought Borton as he flashed his White House press pass at a bewildered watchman and punched the button of the automatic elevator for the fifth floor. The sight of artificial light behind a frosted pane of glass caused him to exclaim, half-aloud, "By heaven, he is here."

The heavy-set Frank Foley, ashen-faced and coatless, sat crouched on a straight-backed chair. He had been watching the agency departmental teletype printer that was clacking out the latest reports. He swung his ponderous body with an effort.

"Cal! I thought you'd be on the scene of the crash or near it. My god, can you believe it?"

"I considered getting a charter flight to Greenwich, but I couldn't think of a better person than you to fill me in on what really happened, Frank."

"Happened?" Foley waved him vaguely to a leather visitor's chair. "I'm getting the developments as fast as they come into the agency, but I'm sure you know as much as anybody does, or more—you generally do."

Cooped-up bureaucrats often exaggerated the inside knowledge of the free-moving press. Borton had played upon this illusion before, but he had to be very careful now or Foley would sense that he was here on the sort of fishing trip that desperate reporters engage in.

"My god, Frank, I came here to get away from the rumors. I knew you'd be on the job. Not only were you a close friend of Sam's, but your agency is going to wear the horns in this affair—maybe just the goat horns, but maybe the horns of the villain as well. It's the FAA's responsibility to clear a traffic lane for the

President's plane. From the little I've already heard, the press is going to hang the blame right here."

"What—on me?" cried Foley, going from ashen to linen.

"Not on you personally, I hope. On the FAA, for certain. But you know how the American people like to believe there is a plot somewhere. You personally have charge of internal security in the agency. I don't think for a moment there was any dirty work. Yet we both know that mid-air collisions are practically unheard of."

"Cal! Look at this." Foley ripped off a yellow tearsheet and thrust it at Borton. "Clear air turbulence! That plane dropped 10,000 feet in two minutes time. If there's one meteorological phenomenon that nobody can predict or control it's CAT—clear air turbulence. We have volumes of study on it, and no conclusions worth a hoot."

"Wasn't there a law suit not long ago?"

"Yes, siree, there surely was. Standard Airlines Flight 1030 hit CAT at 40,000 feet and a couple of drunken passengers in the aisle fell down and got their teeth knocked out. They sued because the seat belt sign wasn't on."

"I read about it, Frank, but it's out of my mind."

"Case went to the U.S. Court of Appeals. It was thrown out. A three-to-nothing opinion called the accident an act of God. Standard Airlines held blameless. They couldn't prevent it—neither could we. There's my official verdict—act of God."

"Frank, FAA could have prevented that National Guard jet out of Otis from being where it was."

"The hell you say," cried Foley hotly. "If the President's plane had been at the prescribed altitude that little jet wouldn't have been within miles of it. I'm not even going to admit it was a National Guard plane until we pick up the pieces and read the markings. After all, what other evidence do you have that it wasn't a civie jet except that one of the Air Force planes reported seeing a parachute?"

Borton was scanning the tearsheets as fast as he could. Contraband material, so far as the press was concerned. CAT—no announcement of it had been made on the press plane, but there it was. Yes—another surprise. One of the Air Force pilots had reported seeing a parachute blossom out of the air-strewn wreckage.

Borton said, "It would take awfully quick reaction on the part of the collision pilot to eject himself and hit the silk."

Foley reached for the tearsheets. He set them aside from Borton's unfinished perusal.

"Yes, that's true. And I don't believe it took place. We have no aerial pictures to prove it, either."

"Is there a search laid on to find the 'chutist?"

"There is, Cal. An all-service alert has gone out. But take it from me, the 'chutist won't be found. Why not? Because he doesn't exist. In all that aerial debris from two colliding planes, it would be easy for an Air Force pilot to believe that he sighted a parachute. So far, no verification."

Borton's mind raced. Ordinarily, only military pilots, including National Guardsmen, wore parachutes. If an innocent Guardsman out of Otis had escaped the crash and floated to the ground, he would in all probability have made the fact known by now. But an aerial assassin, taking to the silk, would behave like a guilty person. He would stay in hiding as long as possible. Experienced Air Force pilots, such as those who flew security for the presidential plane, weren't given to hallucinations. If a chute had been reported in the air, there was an informed presumption that there must have been one—soon lost sight of, very likely, in the excitement of seeing the presidential plane in distress.

"Frank, why do you doubt that the collision jet originated out of Otis?"

"Several reasons. An authorized military plane would have been ordered away from the area of a presidential flight. Second, it took amateur flying to cause this sort of crash. There aren't any amateurs in jet planes."

"There's a long-shot guess—the crash may have been deliberate."

"Cal, it couldn't have been deliberate. Nobody, in the air or on the ground, could have predicted that FAA One would hit CAT and lose 10,000 feet of altitude at just that combination of coordinates in the sky. No, siree—I'll make my report. The President's death was an act of God."

"Frank, I've got to be skeptical. Every reporter must be. I'll agree on the high improbability that a National Guard pilot climbed up, saw FAA One in a break in the cloud ceiling, rammed and bailed out. But there's another suspect in the picture. What about that private or corporate jet which has been reported in the area?"

Foley took another scan of the incoming sheets, got up, massaged his fat face with his hands and looked at Borton in gray fatigue.

"Yes, we reported a civie aircraft in the vicinity. Everything else being equal, we'd know exactly what it was, where it was, who it was. But, Cal, we don't get a flap like this every day. When FAA One got hit—things went blooey! We've tried to keep up with the sudden dispatch of search and rescue planes, the sealing off of the crash area, the bringing in there of extra forces and dozens of V.I.P.'s who demanded clearance. Our circuits are jammed with messages."

Borton nodded sympathetically. "I'm trying to help you. The press is going to climb all over your agency for letting this tragedy happen. If there was a breach of security, you're in deep trouble. Now, then—let's assume it wasn't a National Guard plane that did the damage. What about the other one known to be within interception distance?"

Foley rustled through the accumulated tearsheets. He found what he was looking for, took a pair of shears and clipped the item. Borton reached eagerly for the clue, but Foley held it against his stomach. The two men stared until Foley relaxed.

"You're my friend. As much as any newsman could ever be. If you ever tell where you got this tip, I'll swear you're a liar."

"I won't tell, Frank."

"This civie jet plane took off from a small field near Brookline, Massachusetts."

"Brookline?" Borton gasped.

"That's what I said."

Borton repeated the word, this time in a cry of sheer exultation.

"Brookline!" That intuition of his! That extrasensory beam of guidance! Brookline, Mass.—the home of the infamous Nathan Hale Society. Now he understood why he had flared up in anger when Obermeister began blabbing that reactionary line against deficit budgets. Right-wing kookism! A mortal danger to the country! And by heaven, the most vociferous kooks of all were those wretched Nathanites with their inflammatory slogans. "Get us out"—meaning out of the UN. "This country is a Republic—keep it that way!" "Impeach Chief Justice Thurgood Rustin!" And all the rest.

"Nathanites!" Borton fairly croaked the word, but his tone contained satisfaction as well as loathing. He'd known it all the time—deep in his subconscious he'd felt that awesome conviction. Sam Lepol's death—no accident! It was cold, cruel, calculated murder. Some dastardly Nathanite had gone up in a plane and rammed FAA One.

"Frank! What else do you have? A name? A registration number? Anything at all?"

"Yes, but I don't want my fingerprints on any speculative story—understand that. Bear in mind the CAT. Our inspectors will take several days to reconstruct what happened—if they ever do. The plane that took off from Brookline is registered to the Nathan Hale Society, all right. It was cleared to fly to New Haven, but it never reached there. The pilot's name was Miles Standish Smith—I think he's a fairly well-known speaker on the ultra-conservative circuit."

"Lord—yes," breathed Borton. "Smith is president of the Nathan Hale Society. A wild-eyed, far-out radical-rightist. Just give me that registration number—that's all I ask."

A few minutes later, the name and number committed to paper as well as to memory, Borton bolted down the five flights of stairs. He wouldn't risk one of those freak incidents of getting trapped in a stalled elevator. Besides—who could tell? If this were a widespread conspiracy, a noted liberal spokesman like himself might be a marked man. He must get to a typewriter and bang out a special column. There was still time to make the early edition of the *Washington Standard*, a morning paper that went on the street about seven o'clock of the evening before its dated release. Borton leaped into his car, turned on the radio as well as the ignition, and took a moment to calm himself. This was no time for getting flagged down by the police who were now in evidence along the street, augmented by small squads of soldiers. The tense voice of an announcer came from the dashboard radio.

"We continue our coverage of this tragic day. President Lepol's body has now been definitely identified at the crash site in Connecticut. We repeat for late listeners. With the country without a President in residence, Attorney General Erasmus Hannibal has declared a state of unlimited national emergency. . . . He has requested the President pro tem of the Senate and the Speaker of the House to recall all members of Congress from the holiday recess. He has requested all governors to call out the National Guard on a standby basis. This emergency will automatically lapse as soon as the new President, Jeremiah Chase, takes the oath of office. There is an unconfirmed report that Mr. Chase will speak to the nation by television from Buenos Aires very soon. Stay tuned for further announcements."

An M.P. at the corner of 14th street and Independence Avenue flagged Borton to a stop, examined his press pass and waved him on. Borton kept the pass in his hand, holding it out the window to other policemen. They allowed him to make two right turns that brought him into Pennsylvania Avenue, and he proceeded slowly amid gathering crowds to the flashy glass-and-granite Standard Building.

Most reporters would have gone straight to the city room, but Borton took a small elevator marked "Private" and shot himself to the seventh floor. The door opened on the beige-carpeted suite of the publisher, Dennison Lancaster. The svelte secretary, Sara Lewis, red-eyed from weeping, did nothing to halt Borton's direct steps to the inner office where a tall, over-tailored man stood yelling into a telephone.

"Keep on trying! No, I won't speak to the Ambassador. Make him understand that I've got to get Jeremiah Chase—nobody else will do. Who the hell does he think he is? Have you told him who's calling?"

Lancaster banged down the phone and collapsed into the chair behind an immense executive desk.

"Hello, Cal. Terrible, isn't it? We've got our presses rolling for a special edition, but I'd like to lead the top news story with a personal interview. Hell, by the time the television gets another hour's air-time, there's not much use telling readers that the President has died in a plane accident. I want to get Jerry's pledge in print that he'll continue Sam's policies—at least that'll be a fresh story."

"Story?" shouted Borton, crashing both fists to the publisher's shiny desk. "I've brought you an exclusive that will sizzle your front page. Stop the presses and tell that sniveling woman to wheel me in a typewriter."

"Now, look here, Cal. You're a big shot and all that, but you don't tell me how to run the *Standard.*"

"This is one time when I do. Just listen. It wasn't an accident, Denny. It was an aerial assassination. I've got the proof. I've got the name of the killer, and the serial number of the plane."

Lancaster's jaw opened. For a moment he was dumbfounded. Then he got up from the desk and put his good-looking, nervous face close to Borton's.

"Are you sure—absolutely sure?"

"I got it from an FAA official, but off the record. The President was killed by a Nathanite, Dennison."

"My god," breathed Lancaster. "Of course, he was. I believe it—I believe it. That missing plane out of Boston."

"It was actually out of Brookline, Denny. While I'm working you can double check the registration somewhere. Now will you get me a typewriter?"

Lancaster picked up the phone. "Hold everything downstairs, Miss Lewis. And wheel your machine into this room."

Chapter Six

When Phil Obermeister left the Forrestal Airport parking lot and reached the top of the ramp, he saw what happened to Borton's car. It performed a screeching description of the letter S, narrowly avoiding two other automobiles before coming to a dead halt athwart the Freeway. Phil stayed where he was until he was sure Borton was out of danger. Preparing to drive on (he was going to the Pentagon for a fishing expedition), Phil saw in the rearview mirror that Eula's car stood on the ramp behind him. He got out and walked back with the enjoyable notion of seeing her once more.

"I'm sure our friend Calvin has some deep-inside sources. How about you?"

"I'm strictly an extrovert, Phil. I go where the action is. I'll pack a luncheon, take my K-9 and head for Greenwich."

"The best I can do is prowl around and try to get lucky. There's something very unlikely about what we know so far."

"Don't wear yourself out," said Eula. "Come over to Laker's Acres and use the telephone while I'm getting ready."

He nodded, returned to his car, and followed her to the next turnoff. She led him through a bright-tinted lobby where a sparkling fountain threw up its graceful breaking lines. The elevator brought them to a wide, cheerful hall and she unlocked a door that opened into a bright, balconied living room that was hung with water colors.

"My spare-time labor," she said. "If you've never visited Laker's Acres, you'll see that the landlord knows single girls. We like dainty, pleasant quarters which are hard to find in other parts of town. Those buttons—" she indicated white discs set on each of the four walls—"are the hanky-panky alarms. If I push one, the janitor is up here pronto with his dog."

She unharnessed herself of equipment while he tried to follow these remarks.

"Girls don't like hanky-panky?"

She was in the kitchenette building two sandwiches.

"It's the time, the place and the man, my friend. Sure, we like it. But the emancipation of women has reached a level that isn't well understood. We insist upon options. There are fifty members of the V.C. in this complex alone, and the campuses are increasing our membership in quantum degrees."

"V.C.? That meant Viet Cong not so long ago, Eula."

"Now it means Virgin's Club. There's the phone. I'm going to shower and change."

She disappeared through the bedroom door, giving him a glimpse of a frilled dressing table and a lace-canopied tester bed before she closed him off. Phil gave a shrug and sat down in a spindle chair before the phone. He remembered now hearing something about those clubs at the women's and coed colleges, but he'd put it down for a fad or a hoax. He had been in love only once that mattered, and since then his acquaintance was largely among divorcees who, naturally, couldn't qualify for the V.C.

But the idea of the lovely Eula, sexy-looking and in her middle twenties, but virginal by choice, was intriguing. A man could wolf it around Washington, writing politics and high-powered personalities, without really knowing what went on in the America that lay around him. Phil shook himself out of these reflections, brought his mind back to work, taking the Bell credit card from his pocket while he tried to think of some profitable call. On a shelf within reach of his hand was the blue-bound Congressional Directory. He opened to the state maps and soon found that Otis

Air Force Base lay in the Ninth District of Massachusetts. He turned to the state lists and found the Congressman to be Timothy Calkins who, it appeared from the biographical section of the Directory, was also a colonel in the Air National Guard.

"How're you doing?" came Eula's voice through the door.

"I think I've got my man. At least it's worth a try."

While he was placing the call, he heard the spurt of the shower, resolutely pushed aside the delightful vision of Eula under its rain (doubtless with a hanky-panky button near at hand) and listened to the hard ringing of Congressman Calkins' home phone. He instantly recognized the lawmaker's twangy Northern voice.

"Tim? This is Phil Obermeister in Washington. It's pretty dreadful, isn't it?"

"I tell you, Phil, I still can't believe it. I was driving home from the State House where I'd just had one of those good Democrat-to-Republican talks with the Governor when I heard about it."

"Tim, I don't know how much has gone out over the air, but we were told on the press plane that a small jet out of Otis . . ."

"Yes, I'm in uniform and I'm going over there to stand by on alert."

"I was wondering if you had a name—who was piloting the jet in question?"

"Come off it, Phil. You couldn't expect me to tell you that."

"I don't see why not, sir. You're a member of the House Armed Services Committee as well as a ranking military officer. You have a right to know, and you could easily find out."

"I do know. I've already found out. But that doesn't mean I'm going to issue a press release."

"This isn't a general release. When a reporter asks a direct question—I've never heard you duck one before. There isn't any security on the man's name that I know of. In fact, if he's alive it's in the public interest to make his name known. He might be recognized by someone who reads the name in print."

"What do you mean alive? How much do you know down there?"

Phil gulped. He wasn't much at lying. But he could tell when a self-important politician was itching to give. Sometimes it paid to act wiser than you were. He made a wild stab.

"We think he might have got out by chute, Tim."

He heard Calkins clear his throat to think that one over, so he pushed a little harder.

"You certainly have some responsibility to your own District, Tim. A lot of your constituents will remember this day. And there's your military unit. If a man's missing, I can't see how it's wrong to give his name. You'll soon be running for the Senate and—well, the American people still have a right to know."

"Can you keep it off the record?"

"Any way you like it, Congressman. Tell me his name—I'll tell nobody where I got it until you give me permission."

A tone of secrecy entered the distant voice. Phil reached for his notebook and laid it on the table.

"This man is not a constituent of mine. He came to Otis from the Puerto Rico Guard to engage in two weeks of routine training. Carlos Martinez—captain and pilot. He took off in the only plane that left the field this morning, and that's everything I know."

"Thank you, Tim."

"Protect me. I trust you."

"Good-by."

Phil looked up to see a barefooted, well-kimono-ed Eula reading the name he had written.

"Mean anything?" Eula asked.

"No, but I have a friend who is up here from San Juan to study medicine at Georgetown. The only trouble is . . ."

"What?"

"Joe Freedman, my friend, has more prejudices than a cat has fur. His father was Cuban—killed trying to invade Castroland at the Bay of Pigs."

"What about it?"

"As for that Freedman—in an old time saying, he sees a Communist under every bed. To hear him talk, half the population of Puerto Rico wants annexation with Red Cuba under Sanchez Barbaquito. There's at least a fifty-fifty chance that Joe will tell me this Carlos Martinez is a Communist—and then where shall I be?"

Eula looked at the young man's serious face, gone almost somber now with troubled thoughts. He had a strong aquiline nose, high curving forehead, and she judged he had been much blonder in his youth, for the thick hair was just a shade off being golden brown. His cheekbones were high and prominent, and the rest of the face sloped down beautifully—complete with a definite dimple in the cleft chin. But the distinguishing characteristic in the open, handsome face was its sensitive quality. Her heart went out to him in this seemingly small, momentary quandary, and she felt the yearning to bend down and fold his head against her heart. But he might not understand. He could easily take an expression of sympathy for something she didn't intend. Men didn't need much to set them off when they were in a woman's flat where she had already disrobed.

"What do you mean, Phil—where would you be? If you had information that the man who possibly killed the President, accidentally or not, was a Communist, I should think you'd have a red-hot piece of news."

He shook his head. "For a rabid Red-baiter like Joe Freedman to finger Martinez as a Commie, you see, wouldn't make it true. It would be a lead, but it might be exaggeration. It might mean that Martinez was no more than a Socialist, a believer in government ownership of the means of production and exchange, but not with any connections to Moscow or Peking. Not that my friend Joe would be lying—he'd believe exactly what he said, but that wouldn't make it true."

"But aren't you—a—?"

"Do you find it so hard to say?" he smiled up at her a little sadly. "Yes, I'm one of those reactionaries you keep hearing about. Not a member of any group. I wouldn't join any organization—not even a trade union. I'm an anti-Communist too, which is something else than just being a non-Communist. And finally, I'm an opinionated journalist. These are all reasons why I try to stay out of the way of temptation."

"Tempted?—to do what, Phil?"

"If I thought I'd found a Communist name to use in a story, I'd be tempted to sensationalize it. Especially under the circumstances of covering the death of a President. I just don't know anybody else in town except Joe Freedman who might possibly identify Martinez, and I don't think Joe is an unprejudiced source."

"But, if Joe tells you Martinez is not a Communist, you'd believe that, wouldn't you?"

"Yes, I would."

"Call him," said Eula. "See what you get. I'll be right back."

She closed the bedroom door behind her with a reluctance she felt abashed to admit. What a sweet fellow. Such a wonderful guy. Most of the newsmen whom she knew were idealistic despite their cynical talk, but she'd never met one so—well, so damned sincere about his professional virtue that he would walk wide of temptation. There was a chastity about Phil—almost like her own, she started to say to herself as she got into her underwear, but that wouldn't be true. His was instinctive, whereas she had arrived at her own convictions by the process of hard reasoning. If she was going to have sexual intercourse with a man, she wanted it to be a complete experience. She wanted marriage. She wanted children.

A whole lot of young women had lately reached the same conviction, but hers was an intimate, introspective decision, and had nothing to do with what others decided. Eula selected a pair of dark slacks and a heavy woolen blouse. She chose a pair of stout walking shoes, judging that she might be on her feet for a good many hours. She paused before the mirror to give her blonde hair a sweep or two with the twin silver brushes. As an afterthought, smiling back at herself and her purpose, she made a tight O of her lips and colored them generously with lipstick. She left the mirror, turned back, took a dabbler from a fragrant bottle and touched her ear lobes with perfume.

When she reached the living room, Phil sat where she had left him, but he was grinning sheepishly.

"I phoned Joe. He wasn't home."

"You could have spared yourself all that anguish."

"Yes. But I also phoned the WAC officer on duty at the National Guard division at the Pentagon. She divorced a good friend of mine, but I like her. Without any explanation I asked her to look in the current orders for exchange training to see if there was a Captain Carlos Martinez listed there. She did. He was."

"Did you get a scoop?"

"No. I got his age—twenty-four. His home address—301 Esperanto Drive, Santa Cruz, Puerto Rico. And one thing more. It's rather strange. On the card where officers on training missions put down who's to be notified in case of accident, he listed the Honorable Erasmus Hannibal, Department of Justice."

Eula pocketed the sandwiches and began hanging the equipment of her trade on herself. Phil came over to lend a hand.

"What do you make of that last?" she asked. "Why the Attorney General?"

"I haven't a clue. As soon as I see you off, I'm going over to the *Washington Express*. I'll give the city editor the top copy and put the black sheet on the wire to McKay Syndicate in New York. By that time I'll have thought of something else to do."

He followed Eula to the cellar and emerged with her into the compound where the dogs were kenneled. She told him to wait, went among the cages, and returned with a toothy monster on a leash.

"Sorry I didn't kiss you good-by before," she said. "It just wouldn't be safe now. Bosco would tear you to ribbons."

He could think of no answer to that. They parted in the driveway.

Chapter Seven

Otto Ozenski, a grim, bushy-haired Pole, ten years an American citizen, wearing a livid scar on his forehead as a memento of leading a costly escape across the Berlin Wall, was reading the Obermeister copy in the city room of the *Express*.

A tabloid, the *Express* didn't go in for depth stories like the *Standard* and the *Dispatch*, its two Washington rivals. Ozenski believed in splash—lots of it. He ran Obermeister and two other right-wingers on the editorial page, but he doubted that they sold any papers for him. Splash—one- and two-word headlines when he could get them. RAPE—KILL was a favorite. RED PLOT was another. He resented violence and loathed Communism. He had reason. He'd lived under both and he lived by exposing both. He liked being a journalist of sensationalism. He was dissatisfied with the sheet of typing that columnist Obermeister had left behind. The lead paragraph read:

> Carlos Martinez, 24, captain in the Puerto Rico National Guard, is the missing man in a wide search for the pilot who smashed into the late President's plane.
>
> Captain Martinez left instructions, in event of accident, that U.S. Attorney General Hannibal be notified.

Ozenski stopped reading there. He knew Obermeister had tried without success to reach Hannibal for comment. All right! Man unreachable . . . town under martial law. But the story was too thin. Top news, sure, but thin. No other medium even had the name of Martinez. But name, rank, age—not enough. An American President lay killed, and there was a pattern. Booth, Lincoln's killer, a secessionist. Those three who tried to slay Truman, revolutionaries. Zangara, the man who fired at Roosevelt, an anarchist. Oswald, Kennedy's assassin, a Marxist. So what about Martinez? Otto Ozenski, Red-hater, knew every other Red-hater in Washington.

"Tommy," he shouted across the desk to his assistant editor, "get me Joe Freedman on the horn. If he doesn't answer, send a reporter to his house and wait till he comes. But get him—get him."

Two minutes later Tommy shouted back: "Freedman on the horn, Otto."

Ozenski grabbed the phone. "Hey, Joey. Can you jump a cab and come on down? I don't trust the wires under martial law. Yeh—I've got a fella's name I want to ask you about."

Slowly the city filled with khaki, blue and green. A lumbering convoy from Fort Meade disgorged its soldiers in the knolled playground that surrounded the Washington Monument. The men clumped off in columns at shoulder arms, or double timed with their carbines swinging at their sides in clenched fists. As darkness fell no onlooker could tell what the troops were up to, though they seemed everywhere on the move. Bluejackets from the Norfolk Navy Base arrived incongruously in railroad cars, Marines in green battle dress were landed in cargo planes and swept in from three different airports by buses commandeered from the Capital Transit Service.

Gradually, in the dead still coldness of this November evening, the shape of the maneuver became discernible. The military was isolating Pennsylvania Avenue. Shoulder to shoulder, the men at arms took ranks on both sidewalks of the Avenue. Two ranks faced the historic thoroughfare, two others faced heaving crowds in the parks and side streets. The fifth rank stood against the White House picket fence in reserve. The Avenue became bare of all traffic save the roaring military cars and motorcycles, interspersed by a few waddling tanks. The blockade's east flank rested at Union Station and its west flank at Washington Circle where the Father of the Country sat stalwart and heroic on his huge bronze charger. NBC and CBS, making a hasty treaty of necessity, had set up cooperative camera towers opposite the two centers of interest—the White House and the Justice Department, about a mile apart. Now it was NBC's turn. Hundreds of thousands of persons in the city and hundreds of millions in the nation stared at their television screens. Many must have wondered what had happened to the central event of the day: the President's death. It seemed faded into insignificance.

"Charles Cotton for NBC: You see the White House bathed in yellow lights as our cameras focus from a perch in Lafayette Square. The Mansion tonight has its usual complement of liveried servants, harried staff members and waiting newspapermen, but in the only sense that matters it is empty and forlorn. This morning the country had a President—he lies dead in a mortuary in Greenwich, Connecticut. Tonight we have another President—or do we? One thing is certain—nobody at this hour is under oath to fill the office. Several times during the day we have been told to stand by for the appearance of the President-designate, the Honorable Jeremiah Chase, who so far as we know is in Buenos Aires. We are now told that Mr. Chase will address the nation at 9:00 p.m. Eastern Standard Time, exactly forty-five minutes from now, but this has not been confirmed as yet by the Justice Department, which at this moment appears to be the seat of government.

"Here is a sensational piece of news just published by the *Washington Standard* under the front page byline of columnist Calvin Borton. It reads:

> Positive identification has been made of the man responsible for the death of President Lepol. A prominent member of the Nathan Hale Society, Miles Standish Smith, was piloting the small jet plane that rammed the presidential airliner in mid-air. Smith and the violent vigilante group in which he served have long vilified the late Samuel Tilden Lepol and have called for his overthrow. Evidence strongly suggests that Smith, who may be dead or alive at this writing, became the first aerial assassin of an American President. Search parties in New England are combing three states for the killer's person or body.

"Please stand by for further announcements."

Screens flickered and a new face and voice took up the running story:

"This is Ned Amberson of CBS. We are shooting from the roof of a building opposite the Justice Department which you see on your screen. In his office on the fourth floor, Attorney General Hannibal is now the most powerful man in America—I should say he is the only figure of power and has been an invisible one all day. Our reporters in the press room just across the hall from his office have not seen him for hours. But dispatches are regularly released in his name. The latest of these is a reiteration of the national emergency which, the Attorney General insists, will be lifted as soon as the country has a sworn President.

"The Attorney General has repeatedly pointed out that under the 25th Amendment to the Constitution, the President must nominate a Vice President who in turn must be confirmed by both Houses of Congress. Thus far, the President-designate has not taken office, has not nominated a Vice President and the entire Congress is scattered for the holiday weekend. Under these circumstances, the Attorney General declares that a vacuum of power would exist if he had not taken measures to fill it.

"Here is a sensational piece of news. The *Washington Express* has just published a six-inch headline reading, 'RED KILLS SAM.' It is based in part on a byline story by columnist Philip Obermeister and in part on additional information supplied by Editor Otto Ozenski. Here is the lead paragraph:

> Positive identification has been made of the man responsible for the death of President Lepol. A prominent member of the Communist Pan-Caribbean Party, Carlos Martinez of Puerto Rico, was pilot of the National Guard jet that downed the President's plane. Martinez and the Pan-Caribbean Party have long called for the overthrow of President Lepol. Search parties in New England are combing the countryside for Martinez, who is reported to have escaped the crash by parachute.

"Please stand by for the President-designate's address now rescheduled for 9:30 p.m., Eastern Standard Time."

A jut-jawed Nicholas Katzenbach . . . a tousled Robert Kennedy . . . then all the way back through the red-headed Frank Murphy of the Roosevelt regime to the handsome Edmund Randolph of George Washington's cabinet.

Thus the Rogue's Gallery, as the press called the portraits of former Attorneys General that enhanced the curving corridor walls of the upper stories of the outwardly stalwart and inwardly decorative Department of Justice.

"A black skin among the palefaces. Yes, I'm proud to think that my picture will make for high visibility when the time comes. You can quote me straight. Please do."

Thus had spoken Erasmus Hannibal at a press conference in January, 1973, just after his confirmation by the Senate. He had gone from the conference with his friend Cal Borton to lunch at the famous refectory table at the Professional Club. It was another "first". No other Negro had ever put his feet under that privileged board. Indeed, no Club member other than Borton, it was said, would have had the temerity or the status to bring it off.

Their friendship had begun at the Democratic National Convention of 1948 in Philadelphia. A famous political wag had written a piece that was the chuckling talk of the town.

"The best oration of this boozy clam bake was thundered last night by one Erasmus Hannibal, a round-chested, bullet-skulled delegate of Michigan, on the subject of equal rights. The Hon. Mr. Hannibal bellows like William Jennings Bryan, but he is the color of a good ten-cent cigar."

One not amused at this raillery was Hannibal himself. Borton found him on the Convention floor that morning fuming and sputtering, beating his curvacious chest and butting his bullet-shaped head at thin air.

"Who does that anthropoid ink-slinger think he is? I've got a good mind to climb into those press seats and punch him on his pudgy nose."

"Calm down, Mr. Hannibal. He paid you a compliment."

"Compliments like that I can do without. He gets personal

about my complexion, does he? I will express an opinion on his ancestry—the dirty German swine."

"Come on. I'll buy you a beer," said Borton. "You're supposed to be a political comer in Michigan and I want to know you better."

The friendship deepened down the years. Hannibal became Attorney General of his state, then its governor. Kennedy made him a U.S. Circuit Judge, and Johnson raised him to the Circuit Court of Appeals. Hannibal quit the bench in a dudgeon when the Supreme Court, in effect, fixed the traffic ticket given to a Russian diplomat by a Negro cop. Hannibal publicly resigned from the Democratic party and registered as a Republican. Borton wrote it up:

> Judge Hannibal would be a great American—if he could only forget he is an American Negro. He asks us to forget his color—but he never forgets it. He is one of the most race-conscious men in the country—and he should be the least. He is so brainy, so personable, so widely esteemed that the GOP would like to nominate him for Vice President on the Lepol ticket of 1972. The one thing that might prevent it is that he carries his racial chip on his shoulder, and might turn the campaign into a freedom march.

Hannibal resented the column at the time, but it sobered him. After Jerry Chase beat him out for the vice presidential nomination, Hannibal got to thinking that maybe Borton was right. The way to help the Negro race was not by putting on scenes and tantrums. He had taken the sophistic line that there was no difference between black and white. Well—there was. Not only in visible color—in lots of other ways, too. Most everywhere, he had to admit, Negroes were the hoodlums of the street, the breeders of vast numbers of illegitimate babies, the soakers-up of relief and special-favor money which came largely from white pockets. The American majority was willing to forget all this group delinquency whenever a Negro individual made good on his own and proved himself a useful citizen. That was true in his own case. It could be true for all Negroes—it really could. But they too often behaved like Africans. He had to confess it. Small wonder if they weren't widely accepted, regardless of all the laws about equality.

When Hannibal accepted the appointment as Attorney General, he vowed to set an example for his race. He could never be a white man, but he could be a man—just a man—whom people would call a good American, not a good Negro American. It was easier to make the resolution than to keep it. Hannibal regretted the provocative remarks about his portrait. He set out, once more, to become an Attorney General who would be remembered for his works and not his skin. He undertook to make speeches before Negro and mixed groups, telling them that the individual was what counted in America, urging his fellow Negroes to remember they had duties as well as rights, urging sympathetic whites to stop preaching self-pity to Negroes.

"For my race," he said at a Howard University commencement, "I say it is time that we took an accounting. Yes, we were enslaved by the white man, but we were emancipated by him also. In no other country throughout history, have a dominant people fought a war of brothers' blood to free a docile and supine minority. In our lifetime we have seen this same dominant majority pass law after law for our benefit. . . .

"This country has gone so far in its liberalism—so far in its welfare to the Negro as to threaten the national solvency with inflation and bankruptcy. We should pause to remember that an economic depression will hurt poor people before it hurts rich people, and that when it hurts the big money-earning corporations and individuals who pay the big taxes, it will take the bread and the jobs of those who live from hand to mouth rather than on their dividends and savings.

"Furthermore, we should pause and remember that a century and more of freedom is not too brief a time for a race of people to prove its worth. If we Negroes remain the inferior race, it must be because we have not stirred our stumps to become otherwise. Yes, it is late—but not too late to mend. Go to your jobs. Look to your families. Return to your churches. Behave like responsible Americans.

"I do not give advice that I shun to take myself. As Attorney

General, I am going to try to make the great American experiment work, not by flaunting my color, but by showing that we all live under the same colors—the red, white and blue of the flag and the American Constitution."

With that bold and bruising speech, Hannibal felt he had found the meaning of his private and public life. He had come to maturity as a man and statesman. Yes, the President had been chilly to him in public about those remarks against liberalism, but in a quiet talk in the Oval Office, Lepol had urged the Attorney General to experiment with a few more such lectures on the Negro problem which years of soft treatment had failed to solve. And the Negro leaders had been huffy for a while. In fact, his own wife and his three children thought he had over-played the paternal sternness, as they thought he did in the home as well.

But despite such disapproval, Hannibal felt he had been in the right. He had demonstrated the prime quality which his reading of history had taught him to admire in other statesmen. He had showed himself willing to be unpopular in a large cause. Churchill had done this when he seemed to come out against "peace" at the time of Munich. Lincoln had done it when he took the stringent war measures of drafting able-bodied men and suspending the writ of habeas corpus. Cleveland had done it is as a matter of course. Many of these statesmen had been criticized at the time of controversy, only to be exonerated by history.

This was the state of the Attorney General's mind as the fateful Thanksgiving day began. He took his family to the Episcopal Church in Spring Valley and thanked God for all their blessings. He ate his turkey and cranberries, took a brisk walk in Rock Creek Park and drove to his office to catch up on some work. One of the watchmen on duty in the corridor came banging at the Attorney General's door.

"My god, General, the President is dead."

The circumstances were such that he had little time to think and no opportunity to seek advice. Not another cabinet officer, not a ranking member of Congress was in town. Hannibal turned on the office television to keep in touch as best he could. He sent the watchman to tell the switchboard operator to summon the entire

Justice Department staff—did his authority extend any further than that? He called a man he knew who worked for American Telephone and Telegraph Company and asked him to get an emergency call through to the Embassy at Buenos Aires.

From then on, hour after hour, there were things that had to be done—and nobody except himself on hand to do them. Troops and medical teams must be sent to the crash site, and a security system thrown around the tragedy until clarifying details could be ascertained. The confused reports of a parachute falling out of the wreckage suggested something that he dreaded to take under consideration—yet it had to be considered. The crucial matter of getting a new President into office, and back into the country, seemed to him the over-riding responsibility. But what could he do to expedite it? He had notified Jeremiah Chase through the embassy. He had been assured that the President-designate had received the announcement and would make a television appearance in due time.

But two hours went by and the Attorney General began to think terrible thoughts. What had happened in Buenos Aires? What might happen here? What would be the wages of inaction if some adventurer—some enemy—physically moved into the empty White House?

Four hours went by. By now the troops he had ordered up were moving into place. He was surprised at the cooperation of the military commanders to whom he snapped out these emergency requirements. Nobody questioned civilian control of the military. None disputed that the man nearest the top, himself in this instance, deserved instant obedience. It would have been self-deceit, as the Attorney General admitted later, to say that he didn't tingle with a sense of unexpected power as those crowded hours rolled by. But he could say with equal honesty that all he had worked for was to hold that power in safety until he could gladly relinquish it to its proper custodian.

Six hours were coming to an end, and so, he thought, was the crisis. The President-designate had now set 9:30, forty-five minutes away, as the definite time for the telecast. Mr. Chase had sent word that he would fully explain the delay, and would carry out all the necessary official functions.

For the first time since early afternoon, Erasmus Hannibal switched off the television. He dropped down on the office couch, drew some coffee from the percolator there and lighted his pipe. He was alone in the ornate, high-ceilinged, chandeliered inner office, but by now he had two other cabinet members standing by to help out with any last minute decisions. They had driven to town from nearby vacation spots, and come directly here. In a room across the hall, Seth Phillipson of State had set up a temporary headquarters to handle any matters dealing with foreign affairs. And just beyond a connecting door sat Secretary Silas Knockery of Commerce who had been Lepol's campaign manager. Phillipson—man of peace. Knockery—man of politics. They had arrived too late to be helpful thus far, but Hannibal was glad to have them aboard. He looked at his wristwatch. Thirty-six minutes to airtime. In little more than a half hour the United States would once more have a President.

Hannibal's comforting pipe was just beginning to draw. A breathless aide ran in with a copy of the *Washington Standard*—its ink hardly dry from the press.

"Sir," cried the aide, "the Borton column has just named the assassin—and it's a Nathanite!"

"Good Lord," groaned Hannibal. "That's all we need. Son, take this paper to Secretary Knockery next door. And ask him to step in here, please. I'm going to need him on this."

Silas Knockery, tall, pink-faced and portly—a political crossbreed, in appearance at least, between Leonard Hall and Jim Farley, didn't "step"—he lunged into the Attorney General's office. He was waving the paper and shouting.

"I knew it! I never had the least doubt of it. The moment I heard of Sam's death, I knew some damned crazy reactionary had killed him. Act of God, the FAA says about the crash. God—nothing. Hate! Naked, loathsome hate! Sam Lepol was a beloved man. Every red-blooded American should get out his gun and shoot the first Nathanite he sees."

"Please, sit down," said Hannibal. "We've got to think fast. This news will hit the country like a ton of bricks. I wonder if the President will hear about it before he speaks. I could phone him—"

"Don't do it," said Knockery. "You're still in charge here, Erasmus. Make a statement right away. Order a roundup of all known Hale Society members. Listen, man—I'm thinking of the future of the Republican party. Yes, of your political future, too. Nothing you could do would be more popular. You'll be nominated on the first ballot in '76 if you jail the Nathanites. It's high time somebody did."

"Thirty minutes till Jerry's airtime," said Hannibal, glancing at his watch.

"Don't leave anything like this to Jerry Chase," rasped Knockery. "You know as well as I do what he is. Calls himself a conservative. But if you ask me, he's further right than that. I wouldn't be surprised if he's a Nathanite himself. It's a secret society, don't forget."

"He'll soon be President of the United States, Silas. It'll be his decision. The buck stops with him. No, even if a Klansman had killed Sam, I wouldn't order mass arrests. That's not the way we do things under the Constitution."

"What the hell do you know about the Constitution," yelled Knockery. "Your ancestors were running around in loincloths when the ideas for that great document were taking shape in the great civilizations of Western Europe. Did anything of the sort ever come out of the African jungles?"

"My ancestors came to America about the same time yours did, Mr. Secretary—in the middle of the seventeenth century. I'm sorry I asked your advice. Get out my office."

Knockery stormed out of sight. Hannibal leaned back wearily on the couch. His pipe had gone out. The coffee had turned cold. He bent and held his head in his brown hands. Time seemed to stand still. These last, dragging minutes of his power were the most excruciating of all. Even after Jerry Chase took the oath, he would still be five thousand miles away—as much as six hours flying time from Washington. Besides, the President-designate couldn't have the full facts before him. He couldn't know the temper of the country, and how it might react in blind fury over the report that Borton had published. Oh, it would be easy, thought Hannibal, to do nothing—nothing at all. He'd already done much—some people would say too much—in marshaling the troops, alerting the governors, declaring the national emergency so as to be ready for any explosion of the crisis. Well, it had happened—this news was explosive.

The aide was in the doorway again. He was bringing another newspaper.

"Son, before you give me any worse news, get to the phone there and call Governor Brooke of Massachusetts. Tell him I expect him to use his National Guard to protect the Hale Society headquarters in Brookline, and to provide sanctuary for all its members against mob violence. Tell him that's an order. I'll verify if necessary."

"Yes, sir. But you'd better read this."

While the aide went to the desk phone, Hannibal shook the *Washington Express* to full length. RED KILLS SAM. Hannibal opened to the story on the inside page. But he read it on the jog. He was trotting across the corridor and into the room occupied by Secretary Phillipson. That tall, gray, willowy, sweet-faced man already had a copy of the *Express* on the desk before him. The long, delicate, pale fingers trembled as he held the sheets, but that was from age and not from panic.

"Fifteen minutes, Mr. Secretary," said Hannibal elliptically.

Full explanations were not necessary to Seth Phillipson. That good, gray shepherd of international peace had a mind that made a computer look like a snail in reaching well-weighed conclusions. Already, as Hannibal knew, Phillipson had savored, tasted, chewed, swallowed and digested every bit of information in the *Express* story, and had applied it, collated it, adjudged it in relation to the myriad facts and probable reactions that made up the gaseous, insubstantial planet of the world's state of mind called the Situation.

"Sit down, my friend," said Phillipson gently. "Briefly, we have the allegation here that a Communist, not a Nathanite, has slain Sam Lepol. We do not know which, if either, allegation is true. But the truth does not matter so much at the moment. What matters is what Jerry Chase's reactions will be. Frankly, we know him to be a leaner toward conservatism. In the imprecise jargon of our unfortunate times, that means he is anti-Communist. More frankly still, I have always regarded Jerry as quick tempered. He is an impulsive Virginian—inclined to act now, think later. Did you know that the head of the Russian State is coming to Lepol's funeral?"

"Thirteen minutes," said Hannibal.

"That's time enough," said Phillipson. "You must use the powers you have assumed in this crisis. You must turn off the switch."

"Do what?"

"You must act through the Federal Communications Commission to blank out the President-designate's speech from Buenos Aires. In the name of peace."

"Are you serious? You know I can't do that."

"Technologically, it's possible. For years the Russians used to jam the Voice of America."

"But—"

"A hot-blooded statement by Jerry Chase against the Communists would be disasterous, General Hannibal. Worse—he might take some hot-blooded action. The accusation here is that a Cuba-connected Puerto Rican has murdered our Chief Executive. For all we know Jerry Chase will give some Nathanite order such as, 'Lob one into the men's room at Havana.' "

"I don't believe it, Mr. Secretary."

"We can't take the chance, General Hannibal. Pick up the phone and call the FCC—in the name of peace."

"Sir, you said it was technologically possible. What if it is? Constitutionally, it would be indefensible to cut the President off the air."

"Erasmus, you force me to be brutally candid. You're a good fellow. But let's never forget you're a Negro. The philosophical roots of the Constitution go back to Plato and the Schoolmen. The roots were cultivated in centuries of Greek thought, Roman law, the Renaissance, the Enlightenment, and English jurisprudence. I am sympathetic. But these matters are beyond your comprehension. As the senior member of the presidential cabinet, I order you to cut Chase off the air."

"Until the dust has settled?"

"Yes."

"In the name of peace?"

"Yes."

"Mr. Secretary, time runs short. I must speak succinctly. You can go to hell."

Hannibal wheeled and hurried back to his own office. The aide stood at the desk with a quacking phone in hand. Hannibal took the instrument from him.

"Governor, this is the Attorney General. You've heard my orders. I hold you responsible for protecting the Nathanites in your state. While you're about it, I want you to protect all persons accused of being Reds. The Constitution, sir—it must be preserved."

Five minutes. Hannibal waved the aide from the room. He went to the couch, knocked the cold ashes from the pipe, refilled and lighted it. He drew hot coffee. He reached for the television and switched it on, then settled back to hear the new President take over the powers of office.

Chapter Eight

The face that soon would fill the telescreens of the nation and the world was a handsome one. It was ruddy with outdoor living. It was crowned with soft but lively iron-grey hair. The blue eyes were surprisingly round and full of sparkle. The nose was prominent and strong. The mouth was wide and firm when in repose, but the mobility of humor appeared as soon as the owner spoke or smiled.

In the final five minutes before airtime, Jeremiah Chase stood calmly before the cluster of mikes and cameras which had been set up in the second-floor hallway of the palatial marble American Embassy at Buenos Aires. He gave the men with the hand cameras their innings before the speaking started.

Chase wore an immaculate, white summer suit. He was six feet three, weighed 180 pounds, was 45 years old. He had extraordinarily broad shoulders, long arms, a splendid chest, a hard, taut waist. He stood erect, but limber, with both hands in his hip pockets. He announced at the last moment that he would speak ad lib. Now his eyes crinkled slightly as he watched for his cue. A man in earphones from the U.S. Information Service stood on a chair behind the red-eyed cameras which now zeroed in on Chase's face. The USIS man held a fist aloft, lowered it, opened it, and pointed a finger at Chase, who then began talking in a deep, sonorous voice which held traces of his native Virginia accent.

"Fellow Americans: Our country has suffered a tragic loss in the death of President Lepol. I express a deep sympathy for his family. Under the Constitution, I am his automatic successor. I ask the help of the Almighty God.

"You do not know me very well, my fellow Americans, and it is important that we become acquainted. You heard me ask for God's help. I am aware of a well-known precedent in November, 1963, when a President, who took office under similarly sad conditions, used the expression, 'I ask your help—and God's.' I do not criticize that order of priority. But it is not for me. You will find me a man who puts first things first. I put God first.

"There is a passage in the Scripture where our Savior was asked which was the greatest commandment. He replied: 'Thou shalt love the Lord thy God with all thy heart, and with all thy soul, and with all thy mind. . . .' He then added: 'Thou shalt love thy neighbor as thyself.' To me, that authoritative statement puts the things of God before the things of man. To me it means that morality and honor and reverence in the running of a great nation are of more importance than welfare and politics. Therefore, although President Lyndon Johnson appealed to the people first and God second, I deliberately reverse that order, and that is how I choose to introduce myself to you as your President.

"Next, there is the matter of the oath of office. My State Department advisers in this embassy urged me to take it more than six hours ago. I declined to move in unseemly haste, so soon after the mortal end of my friend Samuel Tilden Lepol, and at a time when his shattered body had not been decently recovered from the wreck and moved to a privacy where his grieving family and friends could gather.

"I have another reason for not taking the oath. The Constitution provides that the Vice President becomes President instantly upon the passing of his predecessor. This is the American version of the British saying, 'The king is dead. Long live the king.' It is the essence of the continuity of unbroken office. Does anybody imagine that the great office of the American presidency would not reside in the living successor until and unless he takes the oath? Nonsense! To assume that line of thinking would be to admit there is a gap of authority, between the quick and the dead.

To assume that is to forget that every Vice President is already under oath to uphold the Constitution. What would be the situation, for example, if conspirators prevented a President-designate from swearing another oath? Would the office then be vacant? Heaven forbid.

"The oath, then, is a formality—a sacred but not indispensable formality. As such, the oath may be administered at the time and place most fitting, not at the time and place that unhappy circumstance happens to offer. I think it fitting that the formal swearing should take place on continental American soil. Every American embassy is, in theory, American soil, but—let's face it—this is stretching a fanciful thread of thought to the breaking point. I shall not take the oath of office in a foreign country.

"Nor shall I hurry home. As you know, I am in Argentina to attend the Hemispheric Conference on Aid and Security. In a moment or two I shall say something about the importance of this conference, but before going into that I wish to comment on another related matter. The President of the United States is President of the United States wherever he happens to be. He is just as much the Chief Executive whether he is in Washington, Boston or Buenos Aires. And although he is the nation's Chief Executive, it would be a monarchical concept—unworthy of a democratic republic—to suppose that the President is the Keeper of the People. The people are their own keepers. They are their own sovereign. Let nobody say—when the cat's away the mice will play.

"Our country is a federation of states, a composite of many powers and delegations of power. The schools will keep, the mail will be delivered, the police will walk their beats, the banks will count the money, the businesses will seek their profits, whether or not the President is in residence. We are not a young country any longer. We are a mature country. I refuse to believe that panic and pandemonium will reign in America just because the President is necessarily absent.

"I am aware that the Attorney General has taken some precautionary actions. I find no fault with what he has done. I do not believe he has violated any civil liberties—such as abridging the rights of free speech and assembly. But I now order that all military commanders, federal and state, disband their formations and return to their bases. The Secret Service and Capitol Police of Washington are sufficient to protect the unoccupied White House.

"I am informed that two persons, one a Hale Society member and one an alleged Communist-fronter, have been journalistically fingered as the murderer of the late, lamented President. Obviously, both cannot be the missing pilot of the collision aircraft in question. If Miles Standish Smith is alive and within the sound of my voice, I ask him to make his whereabouts known. I ask Carlos Martinez to do the same. When we find an innocent man, or two innocent men, we narrow the hunt for the culprit—if there is a culprit. In any event, let us have no witch hunt—no guilt by association—no taking of the law into your own hands by threatening the members of any society or political group, whether left or right. We have trained police to track down suspects and courts of law to try their cases. Please do not take these duties upon yourselves.

"Let us now turn to the Hemispheric Conference on Aid and Security. The United States is represented here along with nineteen Latin American nations. The absentee and the enemy is Communist Cuba under the bearded dictator called Sanchez Barbaquito, the successor to Fidel Castro. When I came here to Buenos Aires, I was Vice President. Although I was the U.S. representative, I was not authorized to make policy. I had relatively little status. All that is changed now. I am President. I am the policy maker. If I should leave the conference at this point, it would amount to torpedoing this conference. If I stay, I hope to accomplish something that is meaningful in making this hemisphere too hot to hold the Communist stooges in Red Cuba.

"Some of my duties as President can be postponed; there are numerous documents that can as well be signed next week as now. But I do have a duty under the 25th Amendment which cannot be postponed. This duty calls upon me to nominate a Vice President for confirmation by Congress. Since Congress is in recess, it would have been pointless for me to make the nomination today. I shall make it tomorrow by courier. The man who will fly to Washington tonight carrying the sealed letter which contains my nomination is with me now. I wish to introduce him. This is Army General George Patton Rigor, Chairman of the Joint Chiefs of Staff. General Rigor is all that his name implies. George, will you stand up, please?"

Cameras swung to a stern, keen, soldierly countenance. General Rigor had held several command posts in Europe and the Far East. He was recognizable to most Americans.

The President resumed:

"My countrymen, I wish to send my personal condolences to the widow and orphan of today's tragic event. I assure them that the entire facilities of the United States Government are at their disposal for the planning and conduct of funeral arrangements for our departed chief.

"Finally, I end this talk as I began it, as a man with fundamental beliefs in God and country. May God be our helper. In God is our trust. Good night."

Attorney General Hannibal rose from the couch and switched off the television. The power that he had held and had exerted as a surrogate fell from him like the great weight of worry that it had been. The President had been superb. The country could go to bed in serene confidence that its troubled affairs were in good hands.

"To bed," murmured Hannibal stretching his arms and yawning, "is where I'm going. As soon as all those people get off the streets—"

The door opened and Secretary Knockery, man of politics, came into the room. He advanced with his hand extended.

"Erasmus, let's shake. I went off the deep end there just for a moment. Things like this happen under stress. I want you to know I have no hard feelings toward you."

"That's mighty white of you, sir," said Hannibal, taking the proffered palm.

"I'll show you how much I mean it," insisted Knockery. "When I was next door listening to President Chase I had a flash of clairvoyance. The President mentioned you favorably—as was right that he should. He's sending General Rigor here overnight with that sealed nomination for vice president. I don't have a doubt about whose name is there—yours, Erasmus Hannibal, yours. A very fine thing for the party."

Hannibal shrugged. "Right now I'm too tired to care. If the President wants me, I'll be happy to serve."

"You're forgetting. The President proposes—Congress disposes. You'll need a campaign manager on Capitol Hill tomorrow. It won't be cut and dried. There's a lot of prejudice up there. Unfortunate though it may be, you will have to run the gantlet of discrimination."

"Yes, Mr. Secretary—let's never forget. I'm a Negro. It's good of you to remind me."

"Yes. Good night, Erasmus. Get a good sleep. Leave your future and the party's in my hands."

When the obnoxious man had gone, Hannibal needed a drink. Coffee wouldn't do to get that taste out of his mouth. He sat down at his desk, pulled open the lower drawer and took out a bottle and a glass. The raw whiskey cut through his fatigue. He lay back in the swivel chair, judging that he might as well wait for the other caller who was sure to come. Presently there came a rap on the door and the gentle man of peace, Seth Phillipson, entered.

"Hello, Secretary Pax," said Hannibal, letting the whiskey do some of the speaking for him. "That's a great man—President Jerry Chase. Superlative performance."

"Quite," said Phillipson drily. "But you turned off your television too soon, perhaps."

"Did I?"

"NBC announced that Mr. Smith, the Nathanite, immediately gave himself up at Bridgeport. He's been there right along, sitting in the airport. It seems he was flying from Boston to New Haven this afternoon, but had to divert because of weather. Cal Borton has made a terrible mistake. Smith is not the assassin."

"Good," yawned Hannibal. "That's settled. Why must there be an assassin? Why is America so eager to believe in a conspiracy?"

"Not so fast," said Phillipson, still looming in the doorway. "What do you know about the other suspect—Carlos Martinez?"

"Never heard of him."

"Odd. He gave your name as the person to call in case of accident."

"Yes, I noticed that. Didn't seem important at the time. Odd, I'll admit. But I don't know him."

"Martinez has been captured. Not by your military patrols, however. A lady reporter stopped her car outside Greenwich to eat a sandwich. Her K-9 set up a growl. The girl let the dog lead her into the roadside bushes and there was a man semi-conscious under a parachute."

"Martinez—that Puerto Rican fellow?"

"A member of the Puerto Rico National Guard," declared Phillipson. "But actually an American citizen who happened to live in the Island. A man who has followed your career—an avid admirer, so he told Miss Eula Breck. It was she who appeared on NBC with the scoop of the day."

"Mr. Secretary, I'm very sleepy."

"This will wake you up," said the gentle statesman wickedly. "Miss Breck showed a flashlight picture of Martinez. He's an American Negro, Erasmus, just like you."

"There are many of us around these days, sir."

"I know," said Phillipson. "But this one has confessed to ramming FAA One. He says he did it for you. He wanted to make you President."

"Get out," yelled Hannibal springing to his feet. "Get out of here or I'll clout you."

Phillipson faded away beyond the door.

Hannibal stood swaying on his feet.

Chapter Nine

In New York at the Robert Francis Kennedy Sports Center (formerly Yankee Stadium), the four-man backfield of the Green Bay Packers (aggregate weight, 1211 pounds in the buff) wept copiously at half-time. In Houston at the Lyndon Baines Johnson Moon Port (formerly the NASA Space Center), sixteen nuclear scientists placed the rose called "Peace" in a Harris County ballot box to commemorate the dead President's conquest of the electorate and Space. In Minneapolis, a six-weeks old infant girl was distinctly heard to lisp, "Don't cry, Little Ike." And at the University of California stadium when Juno Lepol announced her husband's passing, hundreds in the audience quietly released the white doves which they had brought to the pageant.

From abroad the response was varied. In Scotland, the Prince of Wales immediately cancelled the grouse-shoot he was conducting with the Premiers of Upper Volta, Gambia, Ghana and the Crown Colony of Hong Kong. At the Kremlin, the Protector General of the USSR, Marshal Markov, head of the Soviet State, paid his respects to Princess Razzuzo, the late President's oft-divorced sister who served as American Ambassador, prepared to attend the funeral, address the UN and pay a State visit to Cuba. In Ciudad Castro (formerly Havana), Premier Barbaquito demanded a merger between the Commonwealth of Puerto Rico and the People's Republic of Cuba. In Peking the only official reaction was to call for the instant withdrawal of American forces from the Navy bases at Guantanamo Bay and Saigon.

As Thanksgiving Day receded into the past on the stroke of midnight in the five time zones from Washington to Honolulu, the long weekend of mourning commenced. Juno and Dwight D. returned on Friday to the White House. The widow brought with her from California the Great Seal of the President of the United States and set it up in the East Room where she conducted the sad details of arranging the last rites. These she announced in person, standing in flowing black, before a hushed group of reporters:

"First, in accordance with a cherished custom of memorializing the honored dead, with particular reference to the Lincoln Bed upstairs, I wish this room to be hereafter known as the Samuel T. Lepol Parlor. Second, the Library of Congress to be similarly renamed the Lepol Library."

An Associated Press reporter ventured: "Madam Pres—I mean, Mrs. Lepol, excuse me, will these renamings of public property require acts of Congress or executive actions?"

"There will be no question period at this conference. I ask you to respect my grief."

"Very well, ma'am."

"My husband's body will not return to the White House. I have thought it more fitting that he lie in state from Friday through Sunday in the room of the General Assembly at the United Nations. I have asked the representatives of the United Nations' member-states to act as honorary pall bearers. After funeral ceremonies on Monday at the General Assembly, the procession will pass by way of Columbus Circle, down Broadway to the Battery. There in Battery Park I have requested the U.S. Army to conduct cremation at a pyre of suitable size and dignity. The Navy will supply the music. The Air Force will provide a black-painted plane that will fly at a low altitude across the country, and will scatter my husband's ashes upon the land he loved.

"On Monday evening my son and I shall receive callers at a funeral supper here at the White House. I have invited all members of Congress, the Cabinet, the Supreme Court and the foreign embassies to attend. I understand that the Honorable Jeremiah

Chase will be engaged in other activities outside the country, but he is welcome to attend all of the ceremonies if he cares to do so. Thank you ladies and gentlemen."

"Thank you, Madam—Mrs. Lepol."

This historian refrains from describing the long weekend of national demonstrations of sorrow and respect, since this is essentially a book of politics. Suffice it to say that America behaved in keeping with past performance. The deaths of Presidents Lincoln and Kennedy affected the mass of the people much as did the deaths of Presidents Harding and Lepol. Millions had lined the railroad tracks to watch the funeral train travel from Washington to Springfield, Illinois, and millions did the same when Harding's body rode the rails from Washington to Marion, Ohio. Lincoln's assassin was shot to death, as was Kennedy's. A wide-spread conspiracy concerning Lincoln's death was attributed to the Southern Confederacy and, nearly a century later at Kennedy's death, to the city of Dallas.

The conspiratorial assumption is inseparable from presidential deaths. Rumors that Mrs. Harding had poisoned her husband were avidly received for many years after his death, despite the plain evidence that he was a 240-pound victim of heart attack brought on by overweight, overwork and worry. Hard facts do not convince people when they indulge in the orgy of mass emotion. Those who wanted to believe the Borton exposure of a right-wing assassin doggedly clung to that tenet of the creed after the contrary evidence was in. The believers in a Caribbean plot were not satisfied when it turned out that Martinez was a full-blooded American Negro and a registered Republican—they remained convinced he was an agent of world Communism. The disclosure that a colored man had piloted the fatal plane divided the nation into opposing camps of racism—those who could excuse a Negro for anything and blame his actions on social factors, and those who welcomed the tragic incident as proof of inherent racial savagery. Little was heard during those four days of ceremony and hysteria about the unimpeachable electronic testimony that FAA One had been hurled downward by natural and unpredictable forces into the path of the climbing jet.

And yet, there were elements in the normal atmosphere of 1975 that had not been present in the previous years of presidential demise.

The affection and reverence in which the American people of the last century had come to hold Lincoln were not transferable to the brave, earnest man who took his place, Andrew Johnson of Tennessee. The country would have to wait many years to find a new hero. Similarly, the love that was felt for the handsome Kennedy never quite passed over to the energetic, colorful Johnson of Texas. In both instances the people's genuine sorrow remained unassuaged. But while it cannot be written that the nation instantly opened its heart to Jeremiah Chase, a unique recognition was clearly indicated, as attested by contemporaneous reporting. In its Saturday editions the *New York Daily News* made this telling point:

> A coast-to-coast telephone poll, as well as a street poll in the boroughs of this city, reveals one consistent reaction by viewers to Mr. Chase's telecast on Thanksgiving evening: "I have seen that face before."
>
> The many who gave this kind of statement were usually quick to add: "But I never saw Jeremiah Chase—or if I did, I wasn't noticing." Followup questioning soon disclosed that the people meant Chase's features, his voice, his dignified confidence struck chords of memory beyond casual recall. When this editorial office began to collate quotations at large, we found that individual persons in each of the thirteen original states along the Atlantic Coast and persons in twelve other states had said: "He made me think of George Washington."
>
> This was such a remarkable coincidence of reaction that we set our switchboard to work and called back 1200 persons previously interviewed. When we asked, "Does Jeremiah Chase remind you of George Washington?" eighty-five percent of the respondents declared enthusiastically that this was true—that it was, in fact, the very comparison they had been searching their minds to make.
>
> We are not a journalistic mouthpiece of mysticism. We don't believe that General George Washington has been reincarnated in the person of this other Virginian. But in their subconscious minds, a large number of Americans do apparently have that fleeting impression. And, to be honest with our readers, this editorial board was superstitious enough to do a rerun of the Thanksgiving broadcast for another look at that broad, masculine, impressive, dedicated countenance of Jeremiah Chase. We looked from the television screen to the

reproduction of Peale's portrait of Washington which hangs on our wall. We tried to imagine how the first President's voice and manner might have made themselves felt to his associates. And, while we came to no conclusions, we were not in any mood to scoff at what the polls were telling us.

That was the first element of unusualness in the moral atmosphere of 1975. Another was very much like the first, in that both had an air of other-worldliness. One could feel this second phenomenon, and not be able to define it. A prophylactic ambivalence seemed to be working on the mind of the populace. People embraced whatever theory of conspiracy seemed most congenial and they whispered or declaimed about it to the martial strains of the funeral music and amid the pomp and splendor of the rites. But somehow these people who played at exhibitionism of their disturbed mentalities appeared to be half ashamed of doing so. "Damned right a Nathanite did it," yelled a man into Eula Breck's microphone on a street corner interview. "But I don't want to say any more." Phil Obermeister managed to meet Miles Standish Smith, the man who was made martyr by the false accusations. Mr. Smith said he was in more demand than ever as a spokesman for his Society, but that he chose not to capitalize on his ordeal.

Such reticence appeared to be the prevalent, sober second-thinking of the people, and it was reflected in the editorial comment of several leading journals. For example, the *Chicago Tribune* declared on Sunday:

Although we are in the midst of a tragic and perhaps an evil moment of history, it is worth remarking that extremism, while not absent, has quickly abated. Letters and phone calls to the office of this newspaper attest to a certain suspension of vengeful and illogical demonstrations. Our reporters here and in our bureaus around the country tend to confirm the impression that while intense feelings rage and wild deeds are contemplated, a mood of moral self-censorship has had a restraining effect.

How to explain this phenomenon? A consensus exists, for what it is worth, among the producers of our editorial page and news columns that President Chase's telecast is the influential factor. While we criticize Mr. Chase for his deliberate absenteeism and for his flagrant stubbornness in postponing the oath of office, we are forced to admit that the sum of his words and actions comes to this admonition: "Grow up, America."

The new President has put the people on their own. He has refrained from taking the center of the stage, from enacting a showy role that would enhance his recently attained status and would supply the people with a figurehead to worship. By what he has done and said, the President has chosen to treat Americans as grown-up men and women, and with some exceptions and uneven performances, they are behaving like mature citizens.

We take this occasion to compliment the new President upon another example of modesty and good sense. Rather than assume that the people knew all about him just because they had supported the ticket on which he ran, Mr. Chase introduced himself and spelled out some of his beliefs and characteristics. We think this was a fortunate way to begin his term. Of the Vice Presidents who have suddenly become Chief Executive, some were well known but others were not. Theodore Roosevelt and Lyndon Johnson needed no introductions. But was this true of Chester Arthur and Millard Filmore and Harry Truman? The question answers itself. Most Americans will hardly remember two of the succeeding Vice Presidents, and Mr. Truman's vivid personality required a whistle-stop campaign to make it fully appreciated.

In Jeremiah Chase we have met a man who is not a conformist, and who will require further time before he can establish his "public" personality. And while the question, "Who is Chase?" still puzzles many, we must concede that his first impression upon us was favorable, and that his distant appeal, "Grow up, America," has had a salutary effect.

Chapter Ten

When President Chase finished the telecast he stepped back from the electronic assembly out of the glare of lights. For a moment his broad, forceful face went blank with exhaustion. Then with a brusque shake of the heavy shoulders he seemed to send the fatigue scattering from him like a mastiff shaking off water. He threw back his head, stretched his long arms and indulged a yawn so cavernous, so relaxing, and yet ending so energetically, that those present heard his jaws click like the cocking of a trigger. But his manner seemed languid.

"Well, men," he said, "We'd better go upstairs and hold a huddle."

He led the way to a self-service elevator. He was followed by the Honorable Paul Hazleton, American Ambassador to Argentina; by the Honorable Robeson Burnbagge, Assistant Secretary of State for Foreign Aid to Latin America; by General Rigor and finally by Jim Flynn, press secretary to the man who had come to Buenos Aires as Vice President. That man halted at the small elevator and opened its door.

"Jim, you come with me. You other fellows give me a few minutes in my apartment to rest up before we talk. After that, I'll need a car to take me back to the conference."

The thin-faced, steel-spectacled Ambassador interposed.

"If I may say so, Mr. President, you shouldn't go back to the conference tonight. All those other delegates have had their siestas this afternoon. They've taken a long break over their dinners. You haven't stopped working all day."

"Have the car ready," said Chase.

"Sir, I'm told it will be difficult to obtain a quorum."

"Let me worry about that, Mr. Ambassador. Jim?"

Jim Flynn, a broken-nosed, ex-halfback for Notre Dame, followed the President into the cage. As soon as the door closed, Chase pushed the down button, although both men knew the VIP apartment was up two floors from where the telecast had been held.

"I need time alone with you, Jim. First, I want to apologize for what I've got to say. Make it a rule till we get back to Washington —don't ever be much further away than the sound of my voice."

"No need to apologize, sir. I'm glad and happy to be on this job."

The elevator reached the basement. Chase let it stand a few moments before he pressed the fourth-floor button, while he said:

"Jim, I even hate to see a man snap his fingers at a waiter. John Kennedy had Dave Powers on call wherever he went. Lyndon Johnson had Jack Valenti. No President ought to play the Almighty over any man. I hate it, but it's necessary for a few days. I bet you this lift is the only room in the embassy that isn't bugged. Take care."

"Yes, sir."

At the fourth floor, a Marine snapped to attention. Another stood rigid at the door of the VIP quarters. Chase went through into a pleasant living room. He walked to a window and looked out at the sparkling vista of the beautiful city of parks and towering statues.

"Like Sir Francis Drake, we finish the game of bowls, and then we finish the Armada. Flynn, I need a drink. Make it tall and dirty."

Flynn went to the door and spoke to the Marine. He returned to midfloor and waited for the President to speak again.

"When you think I'm curt and rude, try and forget it. A President's got to be a take-charge fellow if he's nothing else. Sometimes I'll have to behave like a plain son-of-a-bitch. People back home will say that about me because I may have to skip Sam Lepol's funeral. Some of these Latin delegates will say it when they find out how I'm going to run this conference."

"Yes, sir."

Chase still had not turned from the open window. All over the world tonight, thought Flynn, people would be asking: "What sort of man is Jeremiah Chase?" Men of introspection (which Chase was not, in Flynn's long observation of him) expended a great deal of navel-staring and printer's ink in self-inquiry. "*Cogito ergo sum.*" Thus Descartes had thought it necessary to prove his own existence. Flynn quoted Matthew Arnold from memory: "Weary of myself, and sick of asking what I am and what I ought to be." Such soul searching was not for Jerry Chase. If he was looking out the window—he was looking out the window, that's all, and probably getting his ducks in a row. This afternoon Flynn had come to the huge oval table at the conference hall where the Vice President sat with nineteen other delegates of the Americas and whispered:

"Sir, the President is dead."

"You couldn't be mistaken, Jim?"

"No, sir. Air crash. The Ambassador has just phoned, Mr. President."

Mr. President! Any man hearing himself thus addressed for the first time could be excused for mentally stepping outside his corporeal self and looking with awe on the majestic embodiment of the most coveted office on earth. Any number of reflections could come: *Fate has willed it. I have arrived. I must be worthy. I am overwhelmed.* Any number of visible reactions: surprise, shock, humility, the acceptance of a burden, the sudden ennoblement which great responsibility brings.

Jim Flynn heard the President murmur: "Poor Sam. Poor devil. It must have been a terrifying experience." Flynn saw Chase's blue eyes cloud for an instant with compassion for a colleague of the road and then glitter as he picked up what the Mexican delegate was saying in Spanish about the insidious mischief of the defunct Monroe Doctrine. Chase broke in, choosing to use English although he was fluent in Spanish.

"Let the record show that the United States strenuously objects to the unnecessary rudeness of the Mexican spokesman. I didn't come here to sit and listen to insults to my country."

Mexico: Yankee Colossus.

Chase: Just as I would not cast maledictions upon the smallest nation in the hemisphere, neither will I allow the largest nation to be maligned. The purpose of this conference is being subverted when we criticize our partners.

"Both objections are noted," said the chairman, a Venezuelan. "Let us return to the subject."

Mexico: We obtain and maintain security by collective action. It requires a majority vote of the Organization of American States, after which each State is free to do as it likes.

U.S.A.: That is the preachment of inaction. The Monroe Doctrine declares that it is intolerable for any European power to set up a system in this part of the Atlantic world. Well, we know Russia has kept a satellite in these parts since 1959, and has used Cuba as a launch pad for subversion. Dozens of resolutions by the OAS, some timid and some thunderous, have come to nothing—to wordy, preposterous inaction. Castro seized power, and a be-whiskered Communist mountebank who calls himself Barbaquito has succeeded him. The threat against our security remains and increases. There is only one military force strong enough to dislodge Castroism—the United States of North America. None other. Therefore, I propose a reactivation of the Monroe Doctrine. Our policy toward Cuba should be—throw the rascals out.

Peru: The delegate cannot speak for North American policy.

U.S.A.: You are wrong about that. If the chair will permit, I will make an announcement that is not on the agenda. President Lepol has been killed. I am President of the United States.

The Chair: This conference will stand in recess upon further call.

Chapter Eleven

Jim Flynn had been covering Capitol Hill for the *Richmond Times-Leader* when the Vice President took him on. Before that Flynn had known Jerry Chase around the Virginia courthouses where Chase had plead the big corporation and municipality cases—a brilliant advocate for the richest clients. He remembered covering Chase's first Senate campaign nine years ago—one of the first Republican statewide victories against the fading Byrd organization. Jim was there at the Chicago Convention when Chase was the surprise nominee over Erasmus Hannibal for the vice-presidency. Flynn was a news writer, not an editorialist, but he'd been asked to sit in at a luncheon of *Wall Street Journal* editors and to give an opinion on Chase, whom not many people knew well.

"He's got more brains in his ear lobes than most senators have in their heads," Flynn had said. "He can come to the heart of a subject quicker than anybody I ever knew. He's able to do this because he can size up men the way a cattle buyer can judge livestock on the hoof—and because he's a reader. I mean he reads everything and he keeps everything he reads—newspapers, legislative bills, judicial opinions, biography, history and high-class fiction. But he's got one fault—he's lazy. That sounds contradictory in a man who was All-Conference Quarterback at the University, a Navy fighter pilot in the Korean conflict and the highest-paid lawyer in the South. What I mean about his indolence is that Senator Chase has never extended himself. Nobody knows what he's capable of being or doing. Things come too easy to him—he's a man who's never gone all out."

Chase had stood up at the conference table and waited by his chair. One by one the delegates approached to shake his hand, and then eighteen of them bolted off to make contact with their home governments. The one who did not dash away was a debonair, mustachioed man of remarkable self-assurance. He lingered to speak to Chase.

"Mr. President, I am the Foreign Minister of El Salvador."

President Chase chuckled: "You do yourself scant justice, Colonel Ramon Antonio de Crevecourt Duños Marin. You are Foreign Minister, and also Prime Minister and also President of El Salvador, are you not?"

"In addition, a colonel of artillery, which I studied at your West Point. I am what is called a dictator, Mr. President. There is no need for me to consult with my government. One might say—*L'état, c'est moi!*"

"So much the better. It allows us to talk turkey, does it not, Colonel Duños?"

"It might, Mr. President. We shall see."

Chase said to Flynn: "We'd better get to the embassy. Put through a call to my wife, Jim. Send telegrams of condolence to Juno Lepol and that boy. Where's General Rigor?"

"Here, sir." The bullet-shaped little man stood ramrod stiff at Chase's elbow. The President took the arms of Rigor and Flynn, and ignoring efforts of the police to clear the way to the main exit, went out onto a balcony that was connected with the ground by an iron fire excape.

"This gives us a few moments together," said Chase as they descended. "General, you and I have discussed a certain plan in the abstract. You have said that two Army divisions, with a brigade of Marines, given Navy and Air Force support, could readily break out of the beachhead we hold at the Guantanamo Navy

Base in Guantanamo Bay and move into Eastern Cuba. I believe you spoke of capturing the two cities—they would be Santiago de Cuba and Santa Vercia."

"Correct, sir."

"It would be feasible to establish a government of East Cuba in Oriente province. We needn't look beyond that for some time to come. We won't move until Barbaquito gives us a renewed incentive. And we should not move until we have at least one Latin American ally. General, I want you to cultivate Colonel Duños. Do you agree with me that this conference is worth saving?"

"I agree, Mr. President," said Rigor, "that if there were no overriding reasons for you to return to Washington, you could make this conference into an event of surpassing importance and significant accomplishment."

"Bilateral treaties are the thing, General. Two words I don't want to hear for a long while are "collective defense." Action just can't be collective—because that means waiting for a majority vote. It can't be defensive—because to win means to attack. Make good use of your time. I'm sending you to Washington tonight."

"Yes, sir."

Flynn remembered all this. There was a knock at the door of the VIP quarters. Flynn admitted a swallow-tailed butler who handed through the door a silver tray that held an ice bucket, a tall glass and a decanter of liquor. Chase came over, lifted the stopper and sniffed it.

"Scotch. Or worse. Maybe knockout drops. Hazleton doesn't want me to go back to the conference. In my bedroom, Jim, there's a fifth of bourbon."

When Flynn had mixed a stiff highball, Chase took it from him, flung himself into the large armchair and in the same powerful motion heaved his glistening tan shoes to the edge of the table, settling back in solid comfort.

"I need to hear every report, see every piece of paper that comes from the States. Be sure these are brought to you, and that you bring 'em to me."

"Very well, sir."

Chase took a gulp of the liquor and smacked his lips appreciatively. He held up the glass to his eyes and appraised the volume and consistency.

"Nobody likes his hooch more than I do, Flynn. I don't think it ever did me any harm, but that's a chance I can't take. This is going to be my last drink so long as I'm President. Stand outside the door and let me enjoy this farewell to an old pal—John Barleycorn."

Alone in the room, Chase took a short sip. There at the window a few minutes ago he had been re-compartmentalizing his brain. Out went the speech he'd just made to the American people. In came the address he would make before bedtime to the Hemispheric Conference on Aid and Security. He filed that one away, and now over his liquor he was thinking of what he intended to do with his presidency. He murmured half aloud:

"First and foremost, to exorcise from the Republican party and the United States the last vestiges of Lepolism. Root and branch, the silly, perilous thing must go. How to beat the Finnigans—that'll come later."

He allowed the creeping warmth of the drink to stir the essential memories. His nostrils remembered the hanging stench of the Chicago stock yards upon the stale air conditioning of the GOP Convention. His ears recalled the offensive, nasal voice of the Platform Committee Chairman reading the Resolutions:

> *Fifth*—we assert that it is folly for this country to cling to the illusion that half a billion persons in continental China do not exist. We favor full diplomatic recognition of the People's Democratic Republic of China and the admission of that established government into the United Nations.
>
> *Sixth*—we pledge ourselves to the principle of Every Man, Every Vote. We shall make the Republican party the pioneer of total democracy by enactment of a law for compulsory suffrage.
>
> *Seventh*—

But here a page touched Senator Chase on the shoulder with a folded note. It read: "Jerry: Must see you immediately. Sam Lepol." Chase had left his seat under the banner of Virginia and wiggled his way to the aisle, proceeding thence to a room where he had been before. It was down under the stage. Sam and Juno Lepol were waiting for him.

"Jerry," said Lepol, "the voting on the platform is cut and dried. It will be over and done with in thirty minutes."

Chase said: "I'm going to oppose Points Five and Six. If I weren't a good party man, I'd walk out on the whole show."

Juno moved away from them, throwing a line of dialogue over her shoulder: "Get on with it, Sam."

Lepol plashed whiskey into an iced glass on a pineboard table. He knew the Virginian's weakness.

"Down the hatch, Senator. Listen—when the Democrats convene next week, they'll take Red China into the fold. It's unavoidable after all these years. Our party has got to keep pace with history."

"I will grant you one thing—the Reds have established a de facto government there. Maybe it's inevitable, but it's distasteful that we have to recognize them as a matter of being realistic. But if so, the resolution ought to be worded that way—full of distaste and reluctance."

"Senator, nothing says that you can't offer such an amendment to Point Five. I might even support it."

"You would?" exclaimed Chase. "What's up, Secretary Lepol?"

"You're up, my friend. Judge Hannibal—he's down. Down and out. You may not have heard about the latest Harris poll. It won't be published till next week, but we've got an advance. Erasmus would add only one quarter of one percent to my national appeal. On the other hand, what would happen if I yoke myself to an economic conservative and an Armed Services' senator with a strong nationalist image?"

"I don't know."

"Four percent," said Lepol. "I want you to run with me. If I'm nominated tomorrow, I will leak it to the press—Lepol and Chase for the people's race."

Juno slid back into the men's vision. In the fetid heat she was white-clad and cool as a statue.

"Senator Chase, my husband will go to the floor and second

your amendment to tone down the China Resolution. Is that enough?"

"No, but it helps some," said the Virginian. "I don't like Point Six either. Who ever heard such nonsense—compulsory suffrage! If a citizen doesn't choose to vote, why should he? And to take his Social Security card away as a penalty for not voting? I ask you, in heaven's name, what kind of freedom would that be, Sam?"

"We like the slogan—Every Man, Every Vote. It'll flummox the Democrats. They won't be able to top it."

"Flummoxing the Democrats isn't a good enough reason for the GOP to adopt a police-state gimmick."

"Oh, grow up, Jerry," said Sam, cheerfully. "If we ever get that plank through Congress, it'll only be a law. Nobody's going to enforce it. Offer an amendment to strike it out. I can't support you there. You'll lose."

"I hate losing, but I believe it's sometimes necessary. Otherwise I wouldn't be in the minority party."

Juno flicked a look at her wrist watch. "Senator, Sam will help you modify the China Resolution, and he won't object to your opposing the Must Vote. I suppose you realize you've been offered a chance to become Vice President. Is the price all right?"

Chase shook his head: "No, not yet. If I go on the ticket, I want a promise from you, Sam. I want it in writing, because if you ever break it, so help me I will read the promise back every hour on the hour."

"What is it?"

"A promise that never in your term or terms of office, for whatever reason, will you withdraw American forces from Guantanamo Bay and Saigon."

"Jerry, what's wrong with my given word? I wouldn't want to put such a thing on paper."

"Suit yourself. Luckily, I don't have to be Vice President. I'm not even sure Cora would let me be. Right now, I'm going back to the floor to fight those two points. Good-by, Juno."

Now, as President, Jeremiah Chase tilted the glass and thought of the many ways there were to become Vice President. Away back there in 1800, Aaron Burr manipulated the votes so that, under the laws then in force, he and Jefferson had ended in a tie—for the presidency itself. Martin Van Buren, the Red Fox, craftily latched onto the coattails of Andrew Jackson and had ridden from there to the White House—a maneuver that failed in the instance of Richard Nixon and another Old Soldier. John Tyler, a conservative Virginian like himself, had ridden in behind a soft-money man, William Henry Harrison, who obligingly died after a month in office. Poor Andy Johnson, a courageous anti-secession Southerner, came in with Lincoln's second term and was elevated by a pro-secession assassin. The bosses put Theodore Roosevelt on the McKinley ticket to smother the Rough Rider. Cal Coolidge ran with Harding mainly because no top-rated Republicans would take the nomination. Harry Truman proved the Convention's lucky choice to run with the dying FDR, and Lyndon Johnson took second place on the Kennedy ticket against the advice of his friends and Kennedy's too.

You had to be Destiny's Cinderella Man, mused Chase, to get to the White House by way of the chimney corner where the vice-presidency places you. No matter what anybody had said since, John Adams had been right about it: "The most insignificant office that ever the invention of man contrived." But, even so, there was some bargaining power when a presidential candidate needed a running partner as much as Lepol had needed him. Lepol's need for him had been instrumental in toning down the Red China Resolution and keeping the GOP on record as being anti-Communist. Sam hadn't budged from his support of the damn-fool Must Vote proposition, and it went through the Convention without alteration.

No wonder so many of his, Chase's, followers had cussed him up and down. Red China got its ambassador in Washington and the Compulsory Suffrage thing created hordes of card-carrying constituents who would go to the polls for cab fare plus a dollar. Every Man, Every Vote had cheapened the privilege of the franchise and lowered the quality of the electorate. Good men asked: "How could Jerry Chase stoop to help Lepol-for-the-People to the top?" Answer: because good men didn't always know. That written bargain had saved the two key Navy bases from being liquidated. The contract had been witnessed by two women who had equal but separate reasons not to talk about it. Juno and Cora, as different as two wives could be, had collaborated in a secret agreement which only they and their husbands knew about.

"Let history judge me," thought Chase over the final drops of his final drink. "I bargained for something before I would give my name to the Lepol ticket. It was a corrupt bargain, one might say, because I intended to tie the hands of the people's choice. But I did it on the excuse that has been called the 'last refuge of a scoundrel'—patriotism. I wanted the American Navy to hang on to those bases on opposite sides of the globe because they've turned out to be our last outposts. I ran on the Lepol ticket, not to help him, but in hopes I'd someday be able to help the country. It didn't seem to be much that I'd done. In all truth, there was very little that I could do—till now, by god, till now."

He swallowed the dribble that was left in the glass. He went to the door and said, "Gentlemen, please come in."

Chapter Twelve

The four men entered and he mentally catalogued them:

Ambassador Hazleton: looked like a chipmunk in a wire cage behind those steel-rimmed spectacles. Former Harvard professor of sociology, taken right out of the same drawer that had supplied the short-lived New Frontier with braintrusters. Appointed by Lepol, Hazleton was intellectually affiliated with Lepol's sloganized New Atlantis—which signified utopian concepts of brotherhood and of internationalism so rabid as to amount to anti-nationalism. A policymaker of Share America. A peacemonger. An addict of Giveawayism. An altarboy at the shrine of Juno—of the woman who made it her business to know everything about everybody else's business.

Assistant Secretary Robeson Burnbagge: a cruel-jawed, furtive-eyed man who belonged to the populous corps of Washington "fixers". He had come out of a Washington law office to do odd jobs for the Lepol Administration and had become an inside operative for Juno. Without a doubt, Burnbagge had been attached to the Vice President's mission to Buenos Aires for the chief purpose of spying on him. Burnbagge was part of the Dump Jerry clique in charge of digging up a scandal that could be used for ending the now-extinct Lepol-Chase ticket and for nullifying the agreement on the Gitmo-Saigon bases. A "fixer" who, rumor said, would be rewarded by a seat on the Supreme Court.

General Rigor: built like a keg of nails, and just about as tough. A professional soldier who knew all there was to know about military strategy and national security, but nothing about politics.

Jim Flynn: a blocker and linebacker on a pretty good Notre Dame team. Had never been a ball-carrier, nor a glory-hunter. A fact-finder in journalism, never a stylist. Good solid man to have around.

"Please, sit down," said Chase, taking the easy chair. "Jim, fetch me the briefcase that you'll find hidden under the mattress of my bed."

The Ambassador winced. "You should have asked me to put it in the safe for you," he said in an injured tone. "Don't you trust your own Ambassador?"

"I'm coming to that," replied Chase drily. "It's customary for a new President to decide who's going to represent him in foreign capitals, and we'll discuss that later. Thank you, Jim—" the President received the black, flat briefcase, took a key ring from a vest pocket and opened the container, from which he extracted two envelopes that were sealed with red wax.

"As you probably know, gentlemen, I worked part of the afternoon at personally typing out my first message to Congress. It is required by the Constitution that I nominate a successor to the vice presidency, and I have thought it proper to inform Congress of the reasons for my choice in more than the fewest necessary words. General Rigor, there is an Air Force plane waiting to take you to Washington. I charge you with the duty of handing my message to the Speaker of the House and to the President pro tem of the Senate. You are to meet with them as soon as possible in the Speaker's chambers at the House of Representatives and give them this document with my compliments."

Chase selected the slightly bulkier envelope of the two and passed it to Rigor who had sprung to his feet and saluted when he was first addressed.

"Two things more, General. Once this message is in the hands of the proper congressional authorities, there is no need for formal action until after the funeral of President Lepol. Out of respect to the departed, I suggest the Joint Session not be held till Tuesday morning. Second, I want you to seek out the Attorney General and give him my personal congratulations on his conduct during the crisis that followed the assassination. I would be glad if you would do this in the presence of one or more reporters, as I want the country to know the high regard in which I hold Erasmus Hannibal."

Burnbagge stirred in his seat and said: "Such an announcement, Mr. President, will certainly tip your hand. If you go out of your way to praise Judge Hannibal, everybody will know that you have picked him for your Vice President."

Chase ignored the interruption. "Very well, General, take off."

"Yes, sir."

Rigor departed. Chase reflectively tapped the remaining envelope on the table.

"It would be unsafe and unwise to entrust the only copy of such an important document to a single individual on a long flight. I had planned to send you, Burnbagge, with the alternate copy, on another plane. But if you're inclined to second-guess the President, I may decide on another messenger."

"Sir, I spoke out of turn. I'm sorry."

"Yes, and I'm sorry if I seemed rude. You'll find a reservation for you at the airport for the Pan American flight to Dulles. When you reach Washington go directly to the State Department and put this onion-skin copy in your personal safe. Inform the Speaker of the House as to its whereabouts. I don't want it lying around there indefinitely, but only so long as it's needed in reserve. Therefore, on the morning of the Joint Session, take it personally to the Speaker and say that I suggest he dispose of it in the manner he sees fit."

"Yes, sir," said Burnbagge. He reached—a little too eagerly, thought Chase—and received the lighter envelope.

"You may leave now."

When Burnbagge was gone, Chase once more delved into the briefcase and brought out a sheaf of some dozen typed pages. Their preparation and that of the message to Congress had occupied most of his time between the announcement of the assassination and the telecast to the nation. What was left of that crowded interim had been spent in telephoning Cora—actually in comforting Cora, who had deep personal reasons for not wanting to live in the goldfish bowl of the White House. Jerry Chase's mind was half on his wife's distress and half on the content of the papers which he now scanned while Hazleton and Flynn waited for him to speak.

"Ambassador, this is the address I shall make very soon at the Hemispheric Conference on Aid and Security. I intend to speak without notes on the well-known theory that if I can't remember what I've got to say, I shouldn't expect an audience to remember. But I want this address mimeographed in a hundred or so copies in English, Spanish and Portuguese. I want it distributed to the members, of course, also to the press and to any other interested parties."

"Very well, sir."

"But before we do that, Ambassador, we must decide whether you are to continue as Ambassador. As long as I was Vice President, you can attest, I followed the dictates of President Lepol. But it's hardly a secret that I did not agree with his policies, is it?"

"No, sir. I think your record in the Senate was one of skepticism toward what has been called the soft line."

"Hazleton, I'm a lawyer by trade. I was choosy about what clients I represented. I liked them rich, but I insisted they be ethical, too. I fought for their interests as hard as I knew how. My present client at this conference is the United States of America. Let us never forget, Mr. Ambassador, that you and I don't represent the hungry Indians of Peru, nor the proletariat in the streets of Rio or Caracas. Much as we may feel for those people, our central responsibility is our own country."

"But we must make concessions, Mr. President. If we don't, all those Indians and proletarians will turn Communist, if they aren't already. We've got to give them aid and let them spend it as they choose, or else we'll lose the battle for the hearts and minds of men."

"Oh, please, Mr. Ambassador, let's not talk hogwash. Most of the aid we give ends up in the hands of the bureaucrats down here. I realize that roads, schools, hospitals, dams and all the rest are needed. They cost more than they should because of the graft that sticks to a lot of fingers. I'll tell you where the Yankee dollar is best spent. It's best spent when U.S. corporations come down here and set up plants, pay living wages and reasonable taxes, and improve the communities where they operate. When private enterprise comes in, many of these other matters take care of themselves. The local facilities get built by those taxes, and the hearts and minds of men get won over because men can see that it's a good system. A damned sight better system than Communism, that's for sure. As to AID policy, if we have to give aid to the government, let's get our money's worth in other things."

"What other things?"

"The main thing at this time of history is to kick the stuffings out of Communism wherever it gets in our way. This gathering is called a Hemispheric Conference on Aid and Security. I intend to reverse that order of priority. I'd call it a Hemispheric Conference on Security first, Aid second."

Hazleton squirmed in his chair. Security first—Aid second? My god, he thought, if Chase was going to grab the ball and run with it in that direction, there'd go the ball game. The OAS was shaky enough already. The whole structure of the delicate relationship between the Colossus of the North and those excitable, suspicious—all right, Hazleton admitted to himself—those avaricious Latins, would come clattering down.

"Mr. President, may I offer a word of advice?"

"Yes, do."

"Sir, why don't you fly home tonight and let me handle this Conference? An abrupt change of policy would be most unwise—perhaps disastrous."

"You would carry on the Lepol policy?"

"Yes, sir—at least for some time to come."

The President shook his head. "Hazleton, as Vice President, I was second cousin to a fish peddler so far as prestige at this conference was concerned. As President, I'm bullfrog of the pond. I feel it would be an abnegation of opportunity not to try and make this hemispheric meeting into an event of lasting importance. Right or wrong, that's what I'm going to attempt. I am not going to fire you, but you now have a chance to resign. Just tell me, yes or no, whether you are willing to continue at Buenos Aires on my terms."

"I—" gulped Hazleton. He had his principles, but the dread of ceasing to be Mr. Ambassador and of hunting an ill-paid, obscure teaching job outweighed all else. "I think it my duty to remain at my post, Mr. President."

"I thought you would," said Chase. "Forgive me if I seem abrupt, but I'm anxious to get back to the conference. I want you to contact all delegates and tell them they needn't return for another meeting if their countries are willing to forego all North American aid. To put it bluntly, I shall cancel assistance to any nation that is not at the conference table when I show up there within the hour."

"Sir, are you forgetting? Those nineteen delegates are proud, sensitive men."

"So are you such a man, Hazleton. But you've just made a practical decision. You've decided to keep a job that thousands of professors would give their eye teeth to have. I want you to go downstairs to your office, get on the telephone and use all your diplomatic skill to impress the proper parties that it's very advantageous to be at that conference table when the President of the United States arrives."

Hazleton got shakily to his feet. Chase handed him the sheaf of typescript.

"Mr. President, some of the delegates may have gone out on the town. Some may even have gone to bed."

"Find 'em, Hazleton. Wake 'em up. Leave me alone with Flynn. I have a few more arrangements to make."

When Hazleton left, the President looked longingly at the bourbon bottle, which he could see through the open door of the bedroom.

"Flynn, one more won't hurt me, as the saying goes, and I hope you'll be around to see me take my next one when I'm not only ex-President but ex-son-of-a-bitch. I hated talking that way to Hazleton, for he's a good fellow—which is more than I'd say for Burnbagge. I had to convert Hazleton in a hurry from Lepol's ambassador to mine. What time is it in Washington?"

"Same time as here, sir. It's 10:30 p.m."

"Just time for a goodnight talk with Cora. Poor darling, she's upset about all this. Get her on the phone for me, Jim, will you?"

Chapter Thirteen

Cora Chase, rosy and plump, her white hair fluffy and her light blue eyes serene, had taken Thanksgiving dinner alone in the sunny dining room of Waverly Farm. A starch-coated brown butler had brought her consomme, and a cerise-aproned mulatto maid had removed the empty cup. The butler had set before her a breast of turkey, and the maid had passed dishes of boiled potatoes and cranberries. There followed a plate of home-made vanilla ice cream, a venetian-glass finger bowl and a small cup of rippling black coffee.

Cora thanked the butler, who drew back her chair, and smiled at the maid, who opened the door into the living room. Cora took a wool shawl which hung on a peg by the front door and went out into the bright autumn sunshine. The azure glory of the rising Blue Ridge Mountains lifted her spirits, which were a little droopy despite the pleasant smile that played on her lips.

She didn't mind being alone for a holiday dinner. She had never cared much for public festivals, though she put large store by family birthdays and anniversaries. Jerry, while he traveled much, had been away longer than usual this time. She might have decided to accompany him: a borderline decision, in fact. Campaign trips—never. State visits—not if she could get out of them. She knew that as an unattached male he could accept or decline the wearying social functions of a foreign capital, whereas if his wife were along the acceptance was obligatory. He would come home sooner, and less fatigued, because of her staying here, and that was as it should be. But—ah, she missed him.

The children, too, were absent and accounted for. Chi Chi was starring on Broadway in the new Andy Anderson vehicle, and there were matinees the whole of the holiday weekend. Granville (his mother couldn't help blushing even at the mental admission) had flown all the way to Berkeley with a Goucher girl, ostensibly to represent the family at Juno Lepol's pageant, but really just for a lark with that pretty redhead. Cora didn't approve of these crosscountry datings, but what could you do? You tried to bring up your children with the right set of ideas, but you didn't try to police their lives. She and Jerry agreed on these family formulae, and Jerry carried them into his political beliefs. He had conservative principles—but the fewer laws to force people into any sort of conformity, the better. The people had to learn, he said, and maybe they would someday.

Cora walked across the rough-cut lawn, through the iron gate of her flower garden. A few marigolds close to the earth had survived the frost. Under the shelter of the brick wall hung one brave bloom—the last rose of the past summer. She took clippers from a small tool box and snipped the rose. Indoors, perhaps, it would last till Jerry returned. The mountains, as she turned toward the house, had lost their azure and now hung jungle-green against the direct blaze of the high-in-the-heavens sun. She walked on—down past the clean, freshly painted stables where she stopped to rub the velvet nose of her mare, a little way down the lane between ducks, turkeys, chickens and round-shouldered bronze hogs. She turned back at the beginning of the apple orchard, and treated herself to her favorite stroll. It was the one—any one, in fact—which let her approach the beautiful white house, with red chimneys on its ends, and blue shutters framing the glistening panes. An enchanted life she had lived with Jerry in this house that his fine success in law had built. They had chosen this matchless site, set in the midst of rolling meadows, buttressed by the splendor of the glowing mountains—with the neighbors neither too close, nor too distant—a whole verdant Virginia valley that was filled, it sometimes seemed, with Jerry's relatives and her friends.

For a while she had feared that his entry into politics would change their life too much. She had heard men—and their wives, too—vow that they never sought public office, but she knew it was a rare, rare case when this was true. Maybe it wasn't true of any man in politics except Jerry. She remembered very well the evening when a committee of neighbors had called to ask him to run for the Senate. He'd tried to get out of it by saying he was a Republican and they were all Democrats. He'd called in Cora, who was dead set against the foolishness, and he'd even phoned his law partners, who also opposed it. But the committee had brought a petition with a thousand or more signatures. Finally, Jerry said he didn't see how he could refuse to do what the best folks in the Shenandoah Valley wanted him to do. He did extract the one condition—that his wife and children, under no circumstances, would ever be drawn into the campaign or publicity. Privacy was the one thing he wouldn't sacrifice for his country.

Jerry's life in the Senate hadn't threatened their privacy. He could drive to Capitol Hill in fifty minutes from the farm gate. His work on the Armed Services and Judiciary committees appealed to him, and even when he became Minority leader he was nearly always home for breakfast and dinner. But then there was that situation in Chicago. They were in their hotel room, away from all the clamor, when he broached the subject.

"Honey, they want me for Vice President."

"Whatever for? I thought it was Judge Hannibal?"

"So did I. But the party has made one of those in-depth surveys. It turns out the country is a lot more conservative than the newspapers seem to know. The Democrats will be split all which-a-way, and Sam says that he needs me to make a winning ticket. There's another matter, too. He's made me a couple of promises that are very important for the country. If you agree, I'll expect you and Juno to witness a bit of contract."

"Well, dear, whatever you think is right."

She entered the house, hung up the shawl and went up the

gracefully turning staircase to the bedroom. She hadn't done so for several years without blessing the names of Hubert and Muriel Humphrey. It was this previous vice-presidential couple who'd objected to leaving their comfortable suburban home for the expensive mansion that Congress had built for Vice Presidents on the Naval Observatory grounds. The Humphreys had stalled, giving one pretext after another, for not uprooting themselves and family. Muriel had set the saving precedent, thought Cora gratefully, as she unbuttoned her dress, put on a negligee and lay down for her afternoon nap. The mansion for Vice Presidents was used for entertainment, and for one of the three or four offices available to persons of that rank—but none had made it a home. Hence Vice President Chase and family still lived at Waverly Farm.

Vice President! Hardly an hour later, Jerry was President. The maid had broken an inviolable house rule and interrupted her afternoon nap. Cora felt the need of a warm bath with salts in it. She re-dressed and came below to listen to the radio—she didn't care for television—to the unfolding aftermath of tragedy. She knew that Jerry would call her as soon as he could, and certainly before making any public appearance. The call came through at about half-past four.

She hadn't noticed till she hung up—Jerry had warned her—that a strange man was sitting on a camp stool in the garden. She spotted his partner parked in a car down by the stables. She had planned driving about five miles to have supper with the Benjamin Sommerses, but now her breath came short as she thought of leaving the house and coming back after dark with strangers prowling the premises. She phoned Edith Sommers to say she couldn't come (hoping that Edith would ask her to spend the night), but Edith acted as uninformed persons usually do about the personal problems of their friends in public life. Edith said she understood. It was perfectly all right, she understood.

But Edith didn't understand. Perhaps nobody did, except Jerry, who had explained why he couldn't hurry home, and asked her if she could make out all right. She had assured him she could. She could be a convincing liar when it was absolutely necessary, and Jerry was easy to deceive. Jerry at least remembered what others had forgotten. There was a special reason for this secluded home, for her uninvaded privacy. The reason was buried deep in a psychiatric hospital where Cora had spent ten months during the fifth year of her married life.

Faces at the windows. Voices from the corners. Slinky persons in crowded places whose touch would poison her with loathesome disease. Men with knives to hold at her throat while raping her. Fiendish urchins to claw at her breasts and thighs. Fears that were whelped in a cold attic during long New England nights with a mad, muttering grandmother, and kept kenneled when she was sent to a school near Staunton for "unusual" children. Later, because she was poor and came cheap, a job as dorm-mother in a fashionable girls' school, and the trusting, handsome, strangely bashful young lawyer who came there and lived at the school cottage for two weeks while he was going over the school accounts to find out which one of the trustees had misappropriated ten thousand dollars.

She hadn't deceived Jerry about her past, as she might easily have done. She'd told him what there was to tell. But they were so much in love that neither cared about the past. Something went wrong when she had Chi Chi and went from bad to worse when she had Granville. The doctors were better at finding long-stemmed definitions than at working cures. She'd have been locked up yet, thought Cora, if Jerry hadn't signed a lot of papers, and taken her away. With the children farmed out among Jerry's numerous relatives, she and Jerry had driven clear to the West Coast and back, living in their trailer, rarely seeing the same person twice. They'd stood side by side at the edge of gaping canyons, and had knelt over almost microscopic wildflowers. They'd slept under blankets beneath the cold desert skies. When they returned East, they found the site at which they had cried out in almost one voice, "Yes—here. This is the place."

After nearly fifteen years at Waverly Farm, the unhappy past was buried if not entirely forgotten. In this familiar, protected, beloved place Cora made a complete recovery from that nervous breakdown. She and Jerry no longer even talked about it. She had returned to a wholly normal existence and she knew the reason why. It was because Jerry treated her as if she were a wholly normal woman. He was considerate and unfailingly solicitous of her general well-being, but he never behaved toward her as if she were or ever had been a mental case.

"That's all very well," thought Cora in her parlor, "so long as I can live this quiet life and see only those people I want to see. But—already the prowling Secret Service, and soon the White House. Oh, I can't stand it—I simply can't."

She would have flung herself right down there on the sofa and had a good fit of weeping. It would have relieved her, she knew. But—what would the servants think? And what a way for her to behave when Jerry had suddenly inherited the burdens of Atlas. No tears—no demonstrations. When Jerry got back he would soothe and help her as he had before.

She rang for the maid: "Kitty, I shan't be down for supper. I'll take a sandwich on a tray."

"Yassum, we heard it on the kitchen radio, Mrs. Chase. Would we be movin' in town to the White House soon?"

"Never mind. I won't want a sandwich. I must rest, Kitty. That will be all."

Move into town? Live at the White House? The thoughts pursued Cora up the stairs like furies. She fairly ripped off her outer clothing and dove into bed where, with the covers to smother her cries, she gave way to racking hysteria. It was by no means the good, comforting female cry that might have calmed her nerves. She gave way to muffled shrieks and then to deep, despairing sobs. This was how she had been many, many years ago. It made no more sense then, when she was a young wife with two lovely children, than it made now, when she was a mature woman with a loving husband who was, at this moment, the most talked-about man in the world.

Terror! With part of her mind, she knew how absurdly she was behaving. The two men outside the house were nothing new to her, really. She had known for a long time that the Secret Service kept a discreet watch on Waverly Farm. At Jerry's insistence they usually stayed out on the highway, a quarter of a mile away, except at nighttime when they sometimes moved in a little closer.

But the full moving in, the sense of being approached and watched, was what made the difference.

The hallucination of prying eyes and clutching fingers had driven her mad in the first place, and she had not improved for as long as she remained incarcerated in that gloomy institution. Only when Jerry had taken her on that year-long trip, keeping her about as remote from personal contacts as it was possible to be, had she turned the corner back to sanity. The part of her mind that didn't see how absurd it was to fly off the handle about nothing at all was seeing how horrifying it would be from now on to live as First Ladies in her memory had always lived—attending large parties among strangers, going among crowds where heaven knows what frightful creatures lurked, living in a house where tourists tramped and gawked for six hours on six days every week. These were unendurable thoughts, and they would drive her crazier than she'd ever been before.

She wept and shrieked some more, not so careful now to keep the servants from hearing, and for no more than a few moments she dropped off into a sleep of exhaustion. But in that sleep there was a blessed surcease, a short while when she had fallen into unconsciousness and had not known where or who she was. Coming wide awake, she sat up in bed and saw that the early winter darkness had come to the windows. The darkness, the sleep, the escape from all the haunting, panic-bringing thoughts suggested what had to be done.

Cora got off the bed and went to the medicine closet in the bathroom. There were three half-filled cylinders of sedative pills—round ones, flat ones, submarine-shaped ones. Cora dumped them into the toothbrush tumbler. She filled another glass with water and returned with these vessels to bed.

Chapter Fourteen

That Thanksgiving afternoon Chi Chi Chase was halfway through the final act of the matinee performance of *Hellcat in a Hurricane* when the director caught her offstage for an instant and whispered the news. She nodded her comprehension. She drifted back on stage in the final phase of transformation from a Southern slut into an English lady, which was what the part of Rozzie called for. The *Pygmalion*-derived vehicle was such a hit that close to five hundred people had been glad to catch the special holiday bill, and Chi Chi had welcomed the extra performance.

Chi Chi couldn't remember when she hadn't loved the challenge of putting her imaginative mind to the task of illuminating the myriad secrets of inner life that good playwrights could discover and express. Even a poor play, if it had so much as an ember of lifelikeness in the first or second female lead, entranced her. She took it as an adventure and as something of a duty to try to extend the wonderful communication of an invisible soul across the footlights to people she didn't even know and rarely saw when she was there on stage. The part of Rozzie wasn't the best she'd ever played, but it had what she liked—the emergence of a living character from a crusty cocoon into the colors and volatility of a butterfly.

She took the usual curtain calls and then the several encores without dropping out of the character she portrayed, and it wasn't until she was back before the dressing-room mirror, having scrubbed her face and discarded the silvery wig so that she could look at her own round, glowing face under its mop of tawny hair, that she fully realized the import of what she'd heard. The director knocked and stuck his head in:

"Dark house till after the funeral, Chi Chi."

"Thanks, Don. Be sweet. See if you can get me a flight to Washington while I'm dressing."

"Sure, darling."

Chi Chi got hurriedly into her street clothes and found that she had credit cards and enough cash to go straight to the airport. She kissed Don on the way out of the theater by way of thanks. The smart, tan autumn suit she wore carried on its lapel the entwined initials CC, which stood equally for Chi Chi or for the underground organization to which she belonged. In the taxi to La Guardia she reflected that Don, who had quite a name among the cast for being a loverboy, would lose interest pretty fast if he knew about that organization. At Radcliffe three years ago, Chi Chi had resigned in a careless moment from the Virgins Club but she had thought the whole thing over and decided to become a member of the V.C.'s alumnae group, the Chastity Club.

Prudishness didn't enter into it. Something like a moral conversion had been moving through the American campuses in the midst of times which seemed to be without any discipline at all. But maybe history, like the seasons, changed so gradually that only the closest observer could feel the first balm of coming springtime in a cold February wind or sense the breath of autumn in a smouldering August day. Look how the wholesome bawdiness of Elizabethan drama had soon shaded into the naughty wit of Congreve and Wycherly, and from that to the good clean fun of Sheridan and Goldsmith. Later Victorian prudery passed into the scoffery of Shaw and the boozy profundity of O'Neill, and soon from there to a stage where there was nothing between musical comedy and unbuttoned naturalism.

For the most part, Chi Chi thought, the people who were self-appointed to call attention to changes never could do so until the changes had already taken place. Anyhow, although rapes and interracial liaisons were rife, although most people over thirty were divorced and many over seventy had taken rejuvenation surgery, there was this counter-swing among the young educated classes, resulting in V.C.s and C.C.s—the Virgins Clubs for the simon pure, and the Chastity Clubs for the second-thoughters.

If Chi Chi's mind had been on sex almost constantly since hearing that her dad was President, that was not unusual. Death and politics, public matters and family matters, made her think of sex simply because everything made her think of sex. In fact, Chi Chi at twenty-three was pretty sure that there wasn't anything in the world except sex or, if you wanted to use the Shavian term, the Life Force. That is how she thought of Sam Lepol, dead and forever non-sexual, while her dad had become practically a rampant sexual symbol, a man who could create a whole new age that might just as well bear his name as she and Granville, his children, bore it.

Well—the planes were all off schedule, naturally. She went into one of the cubby-hole bars and ordered coffee, to the sniffy disdain of the barmaid and the amusement of a couple of cowboys who were looping over their liquor. Chi Chi impudently crossed her provocative legs to give the cowboys something to drool about, but she was thinking about the Age of Chase. She knew her dad as well as a doting daughter could know a progenitor; he wouldn't take long to galvanize the floundering nation behind his own Life Force. Dad Chase was an All Man, whereas Lepol was poor, pathetic, hen-pecked—a gelding in Chi Chi's estimation—and the country would soon find out what the difference was. She hadn't a clue of what Pappadoodle would come up with as a national program, but it would have a high morality in it, a conservative affirmation which would have more real vitality than all this loose-lipped liberalism ever had. Freedom was discipline—liberty was a kind of chosen chastity.

Over her second cup of coffee, Chi Chi noticed that the telescreen above the bar was showing a re-run of the Berkeley pageant. There was Dwight D., the lecherous lout, reciting his lines, or rather reading them, in a tinny sort of singsong that showed he didn't know what his yammering was all about. She had several times given Young Ike a chance to seduce her, mostly for the fun of turning him down. He was so conceited that the refusals slid off him like confetti, and maybe the only hope was for him to fall in love with a decent girl and to give up the pursuit long enough to stop and think what life was all about. It seemed a shame for a fellow who really had some charm and a fair amount of brains, and who very well might someday become President—but she broke off with a stifled gasp. She'd almost forgotten. Ike's political career had certainly been sidetracked now that his mother wasn't First Lady any more.

Juno appeared on the screen in the first act of *Liberty Unlimited*. No doubt about it, Chi Chi had to confess, Juno had an air of authority about her. Tall, graceful, assured, well spoken and thoroughly stage-trained, she was easily carrying a part that otherwise would have been as wooden as the boards. But there was one thing that Chi Chi, the young pro, perceived in Juno's performance. It never quite lost the telltale artificiality that clings to performers who aren't quite first-rate professionals. You never forgot that they were acting. They didn't have the verisimilitude that came when an actor deeply felt his part. "What's Hecuba to him or he to Hecuba?" Hamlet had soliloquized in wonderment when he saw an actor emotionalizing so deeply over a dead queen that the sorrow seemed utterly sincere. For all her competence, the girl discerned, Juno Lepol didn't emanate sincerity because the joys and sorrows and perplexities of the character she played weren't really hers. Then—

Suddenly, the scene changed. Juno had come back on stage to announce the death of her real-life husband. Chi Chi strained forward to watch. For now Juno would be playing the part she was herself—a suddenly stricken widow, a woman with the immediate passion of grief and shock in her breast. The beautiful face on the screen, adorned by those spectacular braids of shining hair, seemed to be right here in this stuffy, gimcrack little barroom. Juno was speaking:

"Dearly beloved, this is a moment for me that I would give all I have, never to have lived. My husband, your President and mine, has been taken from us."

Chi Chi gasped. For what she saw was horrifying to her. Juno was still acting! She might have been reciting a playwright's lines about a person she'd never known. Oh, the shame of it, the mockery, the cold-blooded hypocrisy! Chi Chi shoved a bill under her saucer and fled from the scene.

In the concourse, a loudspeaker was calling her plane. She hurried to it and felt a grateful release from the reality of earth as the craft rose in its takeoff. She must put that memory out of her mind, because its cruelty seemed unbearable. The plane's hostess bent over her:

"Aren't you Miss Chi Chi Chase? I had to ask."

"I'm glad you did, Honey. Yes, it's time I remembered."

Time to remember because the reason she was hurrying home was to be with another First Lady and, if Chi Chi knew her mother, there would be need for help on that front. Nobody had to tell this daughter the difficulties of the inner life of Cora Chase. Momma, poor dear, was one of life's benign parasites. There were some very beautiful parasites, orchids for example, frail and exquisite, but dependent for their very existence upon the sturdy growths to which they clung and on which they fed. Never to stand by their own strength, never to be an entity from root to topmost leaf. No more could Cora stand or thrive without Jeremiah Chase than an orchid without its supporting tree.

At Forrestal, Chi Chi rented a car and swept along the benighted freeway till she reached the exit that brought her into the Valley of the Shenandoah. In another half-hour she was turning into the Waverly Farm driveway. A lurid searchlight flagged her to a halt, and a rough masculine face poked itself through the car window.

"Where do you think you're going, Miss?"

"I live here if that's all right with you."

"Why, sure you do. Pass on, Miss Chase."

She used her own key and entered the dark house. The sound of her entrance brought Kitty and William from the kitchen.

"Mercy me, we're glad you've come, Miss Chi Chi," said Kitty. "I didn't like to disturb the missis. But she cried a lot, and then she became mighty still."

Chi Chi hurried up the stairs in alarm. She opened her mother's door and flipped the light switch. One glance told her all—the rigid form, gasping heavily for breath, and the empty toothbrush tumbler on the bedside table.

"Mother!" cried the girl. "Kitty! William! Bring me some ice and cold towels. Put on some coffee. Don't ask questions. Hurry!"

Chi Chi had played these scenes in realistic plays too many times to be ignorant of what to do. There was only one treatment—wake up the patient! Keep the patient awake! It took slapping. It took talking. It took ice and coffee and cold applications—anything to get the patient's attention.

"No—no! We mustn't call for a doctor. If it's possible, nobody outside of this house must ever know about this. Least of all must Mr.—President Chase ever know. You hear?"

"Yes, Miss Chi Chi."

After an hour of treatment, Cora was blinking bleary-eyed into the light and consenting to swallow an emetic.

"Brr-rurr!" went the telephone.

"Heavens," moaned Chi Chi. "It has to be an overseas call. It has to be Dad. Momma, can you talk?"

The poor woman shook her head in despair.

"Never mind," said Chi Chi. "I'm going to talk for you. I'm going to impersonate your voice. If I'm worth a hoot as an actress, I can sound like a loving, waiting wife—why not?"

In the VIP quarters of the Buenos Aires embassy, Jerry Chase hung up the phone after a very satisfying good-night talk with Waverly Farm.

"I feel better than ever, Flynn. I was a little worried how Mrs. Chase would take all this. Now, I guess we're ready for the conference."

Within a quarter of an hour he was back in his seat at the semi-circular table. As he had hoped, there was full attendance. Chase spoke slowly, in English, to the attentive group. He said:

"Mr. Chairman, the North American position has changed because, as you all know, the American presidency has sadly undergone a change. Briefly, as Ambassador Hazleton fully understands, my country will henceforth consider this to be a conference in which the matter of military security of the hemisphere comes ahead of economic assistance to the hemisphere."

He paused here and swung his glance to meet the liquid, sympathetic glance of Colonel Duños, that good-natured strong man of El Salvador. The President continued:

"General Rigor may have discussed certain matters with some of you, so that what I say will not come as a complete surprise. During the next several days, I will be available for the negotiation of bilateral treaties between the U.S.A. and the individual member-nations of this conference. In substance, each treaty will pledge instant military action against one specific country, Communist Cuba, in retaliation for the first act of aggression that follows the date of the signing. Make no mistake. The armed forces of the United States will join your forces in a combined attack by land, sea and air. We propose to install on Cuban soil a free government and we propose to support it, though we need not undertake to liberate the whole of Cuba at once. We will give the people there a chance to overthrow their oppressors and to join our forces."

Colonel Duños twirled his mustachios approvingly.

"It will be said that this action invites the peril of all-out nuclear war with either or both of the two major Communist powers. This is as good a time as ever to discuss that dread possibility. I shall do so in all frankness.

"As you know, certain changes have taken place in Soviet Russia since the late 1960's. The long-suffering people of that vast nation have been asked to bear burdens beyond their strength. One of these is the burden of internal tyranny, the dead weight of constant pressure imposed by the police state in a closed society. Another is the stultifying drag of a huge military establishment, costly to maintain and depressive to the spirits of the people. Still a third has been the immensely expensive and non-productive program of Space spectaculars—a circus which has had diminishing returns in its purpose of taking the people's minds off their troubles.

"Without these burdens it is possible that the talented and energetic Russian people might have solved the basic problem of producing enough food, household goods and services for their needs. But the monolithic regime of the Communist party has not allowed what the people most desire.

"Instead of relaxing its grip, the Kremlin gang has tightened it. In the most recent shuffle of leadership, a new kind of figure turned up at the top of the deck. It was thought that the people might be less restive if presented with an image that combined more color with more paternalism—a kind of glad-rag Big Daddy. And so, instead of Chairman of the Council of Ministers, the head of the Soviet state is now known as the Protector General of all the Russians. He is Field Marshal Dmitri Markov. In his veins runs a combination of European and Asiatic blood, a sort of symbolic cocktail that is supposed to make him kin to a majority of the people. Since they don't allow free elections in the USSR, Markov is supposed to be the next best thing—a barbaric token of democratic consensus.

"It's significant, however, that Markov likes to be known by a warlike nickname—the Tartar. He enjoys appearing in Red Square parades on horseback at the head of tanks and self-propelled artillery. He expresses, in short, the tired old cliché that the way to divert the people's mind from their woes is to give them something that catches the eye and stirs the imagination. If this cliché is carried to its ultimate expression, it says that foreign wars are the best cure for domestic unrest. Therefore, I do not believe that the nuclear-armed USSR is less dangerous here in the 70's than in the 50's and 60's. I believe it to be potentially more dangerous.

"But even if Marshal Markov were the Genghis Khan that he likes to appear to other nations, he would have no effect whatever upon the policy I am stating. The U.S.A. will not be frightened by force, it will not be seduced by false offers of peace, it will not agree to shameful conciliation with the Bear that walks like a man.

"It happens that Marshal Markov is planning to be in New York next week. He has asked that a conference be arranged between himself and me. I shall be glad to meet with the Tartar, whom I knew many years ago during his assignment at the Russian Embassy in Washington, but such a get-together must be secondary to my engagements at this conference. And if it takes place, I assure you that it won't be a summit meeting at which any Latin American interests are compromised. So much for Soviet Russia.

"The other Communist power with nuclear missiles to rattle is half the world away. But its agents are training and supplying the trouble-makers in Cuba. My country does not fear the threats and will not brook the intervention of Red China. I spoke this morning for the Monroe Doctrine. I intend to reinstate that Doctrine as a foundation rock of the United States policy in Latin America. In sum, my country now undertakes to reverse the invasion of Eurasians into this hemisphere, and to repel any further advances.

"We intend to do this with or without the bilateral treaties I have mentioned. But I wish to give fair notice. All aid voted by the Congress will be distributed by means of these treaties. No treaty, no aid. I repeat—no treaty, no aid.

"These bilateral treaties, of course, do not contemplate collective action by the whole of our American community. If one nation in South or Central America finds a fresh instance of Red aggression of any sort, the United States will go to war in alliance with that nation against the aggressor. If the other eighteen nations choose to sit it out, that is for them to decide. But the long-endured folly of waiting for a majority to vote on action, and then seldom taking any action, must be discarded.

"This, in brief, is my program. It will require ratification by the Senate of my country, and I know that it will require agreement by the governments of your own countries. These are important decisions, not to be made hastily or without due consideration. It is well for all of us to stay in this beautiful city and to determine if we can reach a meeting of minds. For myself, I shall stay here as long as there is any need to do so. Mr. Chairman, I think we should now hear from other members."

As Chase sat back in his chair, Flynn leaned forward and handed him a card on which was engraved the name Ramon Antonio de Crevecourt Duños Marin. On the card was the written word: "Bravo."

Chapter Fifteen

On Tuesday morning Juno awoke in the huge Lincoln bed. The act of coming awake had always been instantaneous for her. "I regard sleeping, like eating," she had once told Eula Breck in an interview, "as a necessary interruption in the work day, and I do not linger at bed or board. To do so would be to encourage habits of sloth which I abhor." Eula had been on the point of asking whether such dispatch might not make for a life too hurried for full enjoyment, but she thought it better not to press the question. Springing out of bed, the former First Lady rang for her maid. By the time Juno emerged from the bath and reappeared in a flowing morning robe of red taffeta, the breakfast tray had been set by an upper White House window which overlooks the south lawn. The maid awaited further orders which were soon forthcoming.

"Have my son waked and see that he comes to me as soon as he can," Juno said. "Tell the people downstairs I shall expect everything to be in order there. And tell my secretary that I'll receive Secretary Burnbagge up here as soon as he arrives."

These instructions encompassed preliminaries for what was sure to be a trying day. Last night Juno had presided in black at a lavish post-funeral supper. Juno herself might not care to linger over the ritual of eating, but Washington society did not feel that way about it. The 535 members of Congress with their wives, the entire diplomatic corps and Supreme Court, most of the state governors and all of the Cabinet had assembled at her command invitation to feast on plates of chicken, crab meat, and potato salad. It was a gigantic buffet, preceded by cocktails and followed by champagne. Queues of guests filled Executive Avenue between the White House and Treasury Department, entered by the East Gate, flowed through the lower floors of the mansion, spilled out into the gardens and lawns, and departed after midnight, leaving the house and grounds in a condition of litter that Juno could imagine through experience.

All had come to pay their respects to the widow, and she had moved majestically among them, mentally on the prowl for anyone of importance who had failed to show up. One absentee, in particular, she had marked for retribution—Cora Chase. Juno knew perfectly well that Cora didn't like large parties and often cut them, but this was the cut unpardonable. With Jerry still out of the country, Cora certainly owed it to every canon of sympathy and decorum to represent the family. But Juno, who long ago had learned that nearly every incident in life, if properly appraised, can be turned to advantage, had not gone to bed last night without confiding significantly to her diary:

> I now have very good reason to take my leisure about leaving the White House. Since Cora has not deigned to call on me at a time I set, I shall be in no hurry to set another time. It is well known that she prefers to live at Waverly Farm, and in this I intend to accommodate her to the fullest extent. Mrs. Jacqueline Kennedy, who was the acme of taste, required three weeks to make her arrangements for vacating the mansion to the Lyndon Johnsons. If I play my cards right, I can stretch my occupancy to a matter of several months. Cora won't push me. She doesn't want to relocate. Jerry won't push me because he's too much the gentleman. There's nothing like being in possession of the fort. If I can hang on till Dwight D. wins the New Hampshire primary next March, I don't see why I can't manage to stay put and run the entire '76 campaign for Young Ike right from this central place.

Last night, amid the festive solemnities, Robeson Burnbagge had managed to slip her a typed note which she had scanned behind her tear-moistened handkerchief and which she now perused again after ordering the breakfast tray removed. Burnbagge had used the departmental form of communication, and cryptic language.

> Memo:
> Subject: Confidential
> To: Recipient
>
> 1. Highly sensitive carbon copy document in bearer's keeping.
> 2. Probably choice is horse of another color.
> 3. Early a.m. contact desirable.

The missive was easily translatable to Juno. It meant that Burnbagge had brought to Washington the duplicate of Jerry Chase's message to the Joint Session of Congress, and that the Attorney General had doubtless been named as Vice President. Burnbagge wanted to see her about it before the session convened at noon.

There came a knock at the door, followed by the appearance of Dwight D. in robe and slippers. To her surprise another figure, but this one in a somewhat rumpled suit and a borrowed clean shirt that was too big at the neck and sleeves, followed her son into the room. The visitor was a blond, curly-haired youth who looked as if he had been up too late last night.

"Morning, Regina," was her son's familiar greeting. "I guess you didn't notice Granville in the crush last night. He flew back from the pageant with Pinkie Perkins and Cassie so they could all make their manners. We've got the girls stashed away in the sewing room on cots."

"Dwight! I hardly expected you to make a house party of this occasion."

"Don't be hard-hearted, Regina. You said you thought the Chase family ought to be represented, and here's Granville—a little the worse for wear, I'll have to admit. We bailed out of the mob scene last night and went to a key club for dancing. Nobody but members can get in, so it wasn't like going out in public."

"Good morning, Granville," said Juno, giving her hand to the attractive youngster.

"I'm awfully sorry about Mr. Lepol, I really am," Granville said with a natural embarrassment. "He was a real nice fellow. He sent me a book every birthday. The last one was *The Adventures of Huckleberry Finn*—only it had some of the pages cut out. I went to the Princeton Library and found out what had been censored, and when I told the President that one whole sequence about Nigger Jim was excised, he laughed and laughed."

"That will do, Granville. Tell me—is your mother well?"

He blushed. "The fact is I haven't been home, Mrs. Lepol. I would have gone, but Mother sort of disapproves of Pinkie, and when I telephoned it was Chi Chi who answered the phone. Chi Chi is a bug on certain matters that I don't think are proper to discuss. Say, how about Dad getting all those Latinos around a table and knocking their heads together? I know where he learned that stuff about cutting off aid because he used to cut off my allowance whenever I got out of line and—"

"Granville!" she broke in. Heavens, did the youngster always talk such a blue streak. Ah—but that might be useful, and her tone softened. "I want you to make yourself perfectly at home here, dear. Later we'll have a nice chat. Why don't you go wake up the girls? I must see Young Ike alone about the day's arrangements."

As Granville made for the door on the pleasant assignment of visiting the sewing room, the portal opened for him from the outside and the obsequious private secretary, Lutherina Jones, announced that Secretary Burnbagge was downstairs.

"When I ring, Lucy," said Juno, and turned to her son.

"Dwight, we have to work fast. In less than four hours, Speaker Krebs and Senator Nestorson will announce who's to be Vice President. I think I know, but I'll soon find out for certain. Whoever it is will be easier for you to beat next year than Jerry Chase."

"Aw, Mother, I don't want to run for President. For one thing, I'm having too much fun. For another, I think about poor old Pater. He was much happier before he took this crazy job. Why can't I loaf around Sacramento for a few years and then go after the old Lepol seat in the U. S. Senate? Wouldn't that satisfy you?"

"No. It would not."

"But I don't see any percentage in being in such an all-fired hurry. I can wait."

"Maybe you can wait, Dwight. You're young. But I can't wait. How can you be so selfish? Remember—this is your mother you're talking to. Have you no gratitude?"

He melted at once, as he always did when she pulled her maternal status. Leaning over, he kissed her cheek and was forgiven. Juno continued.

"What I'm getting at is that Jerry Chase is behaving like a maniac down there. Imagine treating those delegates as if they were schoolboys whose allowance he can cut off at will. Why, with all his blustering he's only got one of those bilateral treaties so far—with El Salvador, of all countries! And the threats he's throwing around. The Red Chinese Ambassador was very cool last night. I don't wonder."

"There's nothing we can do about it. Old man Chase is President, I suppose."

"Is he?" demanded Juno. "That's a question in itself. I spoke to the Chief Justice last night. He seemed very dubious that a man is officially in office until he takes the oath. We could easily ask for a Supreme Court opinion. Your father appointed three of the Justices, so we'd have that much to start on, and with the Chief Justice on our side, we'd need only one more vote."

"But the most you could accomplish is to force Chase to take the oath. We'd be no better off than before."

"I know that," said Juno, touching the bell. "The Supreme Court is not our best forum. I'll tell you what is—the Cabinet. All eleven of them are your father's appointees. Under the 25th Amendment, the Vice President and a majority of the cabinet can determine that a President is not capable of discharging his duties. As soon as we make certain who the new Vice President is, we'll go to work on him. Yes—come in, Mr. Burnbagge."

That person scurried across the carpet and almost genuflected as he received Juno's hand. Then, without a word, but with a look of furtive accomplishment, he unpocketed the wax-sealed letter handed him by President Chase five days before.

"Here it is, ma'am. Oh, hello, Dwight. I just noticed, however, that the envelope is not only waxed tight, but some sort of crest is set in the wax. It isn't the crest of the United States, so I suppose it's Jeremiah Chase's personal seal, done with his ring."

Juno went swiftly to a table in the center of the room, opened a drawer and took out a small instrument attached to a hand battery, and also a thin silver paper cutter.

"Seal or no seal, I intend to open it up. Don't think I haven't done it before when the State Department has sent documents that Sam didn't have time to read right away. Now, stand back. Don't walk. The floor is rickety and you'll make the table rock."

Burnbagge watched with fascination in his furtive eyes while Juno applied the heat, softened the wax and then deftly pried open the envelope flap. She took out the flimsy onionskin sheets with a firm hand and, still bending over the table, gave a cry of astonished joy.

"Dwight! My darling!"

Since he'd seen his mother open secret documents before, Dwight had not been watching the operation but now he became tense with attention. There was something very foreboding about the near-ecstacy in Juno's shrill cry.

"What's up, Mother?"

"It's all so logical," she exclaimed as her eyes swept once more over the pages that she turned. "Why, Jerry knows perfectly well that only one Republican ticket can beat the Finnigans next year. Lepol-Chase ran roughshod over the Democrats in 1972, and Chase-Lepol is the best bet to repeat in 1976."

Burnbagge yelped with excitement. "Then he didn't name Erasmus Hannibal, after all?"

"No—no. He explains it all in a lot of words, but here it is in the very last paragraph. He says: 'Having considered the cardinal need for continuity of office, and mindful of the heart-felt esteem in which the late, lamented President Lepol was held, I nominate to the office of the vice presidency, his son, Dwight D. Lepol of California.' "

Dwight D. gave a giggle of delight. "Good old Chase. He's got me off the hook. At least I won't have to run for President for nearly nine years."

Juno sought the sofa and sank down to let her pounding heart resume its normal beat. Why hadn't she guessed? Chase had made the only decision he could have made—as a politician.

"That's exactly why I didn't guess it," thought Juno. "Chase, the high-minded lawyer and statesman. Chase, the fundamentalist. Chase, the reactionary. Chase, the nationalist. In all those roles, I would recognize him and would know how to cope with him. But this is a new side of him, and it will take different tactics. Very well. So be it. He wants to play politics, does he? He'll have to get up early to beat me at that game."

Nevertheless, she admired the President's artful move. In one stroke he had eliminated Young Ike as a competitor for next year's race, and insured that race for victory against the Finnigans, for no Democratic combination could defeat Chase and Lepol-for-the-People, especially with her management in the background. But Jerry was a reckless man to put himself just a heartbeat ahead of an ambitious woman. Or maybe he hadn't read *Macbeth* lately. Mentally she recited the lines that prologued the death of King Duncan:

> *Macbeth:* My dearest love, Duncan comes here tonight.
> *Lady Macbeth:* And when goes hence?
> *Macbeth:* Tomorrow as he proposes.
> *Lady Macbeth:* O, never shall sun that morrow see.

Juno rose from the sofa, shaking her head. Too fantastic! America, with its dynastic houses vying for the presidency had moved back a long way into Old World ways when nobles schemed for the crown, but the country wasn't yet ready for the kind of thing that used to go on among the best people of England, France, and Italy. No, the times still required bloodless coups. Of one thing she was certain. She couldn't wait for Jerry Chase to serve out his normal term or terms of office. That would be too long—not for Dwight, but for her.

"Ike, this is an unexpected development. We must move faster than ever. In a few hours you'll be Vice President. That gives you the right to raise the question of the President's fitness to discharge the duties of his office. With a majority of the Cabinet concurring, you can easily prove that Chase's behavior in Buenos Aires is insane, and Congress will agree."

"But, Mother—"

"Be quiet. Mr. Burnbagge, I'll seal up this envelope and you must take it to the House of Representatives. Nobody will look at it because the original is already in the possession of the Speaker and Senator Nestorson. But give it to the Speaker. As soon as you do that, I want you to contact all the Cabinet members except Hannibal. They're all strong Lepol men. They'll be glad to get rid of Chase. Do you understand what I have in mind?"

"Yes, I do."

"Well, get going."

When he was gone, Juno caressed the pouting cheek of Dwight and, at the table telephone, pushed the call-button that was marked "speechwriters." When the phone was answered she simply said, "Front Man," in the manner of a hotel clerk summoning a porter. Talented writers had been used in a pool system at the White House since the Franklin Roosevelt days, but their status had sunk in recent years. The computerization of ideas tended to sap the pride and originality of creative writers. "You'll need an acceptance address, Ike dear. It won't be any trouble to deliver it because you can wear your father's audioprompter in your neck tie. I believe you should speak from the Truman Balcony with the Senate standing down on the lawn."

"Regina, I just thought of something. I'm only twenty-nine years old. Doesn't the Constitution say a President has to be thirty-five, and that the Vice President must have the same qualifications. Besides, wasn't I born in France when father was a staff officer under Eisenhower at the NATO headquarters?"

"Don't be silly. Nobody's paid any attention to those old rules and customs since Senators Robert Kennedy and Pierre Salinger picked out adopted states in 1964, and the Mexican-born George Romney decided he was eligible for the White House. The Constitution is still read in colleges, but I doubt if anybody in Washington has cracked open a copy in years unless it would be—oh!"

"What's the matter, Mother?"

She had turned pale at the thought, and grasped the table for support.

"I—I automatically started to say—unless it would be Jerry Chase. What a start it gave me. Of course Jerry reads and rereads the Constitution. He knows it practically by heart. On the other hand, he's nominating you purely as a political expedient. Politicians don't care whether they violate the Constitution or not, but I must say I'm rather disillusioned with Jerry. We'll have to be ever so careful in dealing with him, Dwight. He's become just as unscrupulous as the Finnigans. Yes, come in."

A dignified, gray-haired man, with erudition written plainly in his care-marked face, had entered. He was James Parton Lowell, several times a Pulitzer Prize winner in history and biography, but Juno paid no more attention to his arrival than if he had come to pick up some luggage.

"Something about twenty minutes in length," she said, without looking in his direction at all. "Jazz it up with some rhetoric, and don't forget that the quotable passages should be short enough for headline purposes. I'll need it promptly and I'll want it on microwire recording."

"Yes, Madam President." He used the term of address that had been customary among the White House staff and servants. When he was gone, Juno said:

"Get dressed, Young Ike, and look your best. I must do the same, for I'm going to the House Gallery at noon."

In the old-fashioned, chandelier-hung office of the Speaker of the House, young John Krebs sat reading the onionskin message which Burnbagge had recently left there. Nearby, in a big, velvet, spoon-shaped easy chair, the ancient Senator Arthur Nestorson was spilling cigar ashes over his brass-buttoned vest while reading the hardpaper copy brought several days ago by General Rigor.

Speaker Krebs, at 28, was one of the youngest and most brilliant members of the House, and he was the youngest Speaker since Henry Clay. Something that nobody well understood had happened to the national legislative body closest to the people.

Not only were the districts electing alert, attractive, youthful Representatives, but the House members themselves had snapped out of the lazy custom of letting mere seniority decide who was to be their leader and presiding officer.

Senator Nestorson, who had stopped counting his birthdays at eighty-five several years ago, could be said to represent a reaction in the states against choosing senators who were barely dry behind their ears. The people of his state were not insensitive to Nestorson's age, but they realized that elderliness in a statesman is actually an advantage so long as he has all his buttons—which Art Nestorson certainly did. He huffed at the cigar without removing it from his lips, sending another spray of ashes over the sporty vest which was already pocked with holes where live tobacco had landed down the years.

"Well, sir," said Krebs. "What do you make of Jerry sending us two different documents?"

"That young feller is sharp as a tack, Johnny. There ain't any doubt that he intended us to use this-here hardpaper copy, for he signed it and he didn't sign t'other one. I'd say he was settin' a trap."

"This onionskin copy has been opened and read before it reached us. I'm going to send it around to the FBI and see if they can make some identifications."

"Smart idea," Nestorson cackled. "Want to make a little bet?"

"Not against you, sir," laughed the Speaker. "It's time we went outside to meet the limousine and conduct Mrs. Lepol to the Distinguished Visitors' Gallery."

"You gonna read the message to the House or have the clerk read it, Johnny?"

"It's quite a state paper, don't you think Senator? I'm going to read it myself, but I'm going to keep an eye on the Visitors' Gallery, too. Come on."

A few minutes later, flanked by Capitol policemen, the young Speaker and the elderly Senator took the dazzlingly black-robed Juno to her seat. It was in the front row. She was the object of every gaze in the crowded chamber and other galleries, and she was playing to the hilt the double role of a stricken presidential widow and the proud mother of a Vice President, as she thought, soon to be. When the Senate, the Supreme Court, and the Cabinet and Diplomatic Corps had filed in to take seats on the floor, Speaker Krebs rose and said: "A message from the President of the United States."

Without further preliminary, Krebs began to read:

> Mr. Speaker, Mr. President, honored colleagues and fellow-Americans:
>
> As President of the United States it becomes incumbent upon me under the 25th Amendment to present the name of a person to be Vice President with the concurrence of both House and Senate.
>
> No more solemn duty could fall upon a man newly called to the presidency, and I wish to share my thinking with your honorable bodies.
>
> What should be the qualifications of the person I must choose? Let us dwell upon that.
>
> Primarily, his integrity of character and keenness of intellect should be of the highest.
>
> He should possess, equally with the President himself, the ability and knowledge to serve as Chief Executive.
>
> Special conditions should enter into this appointment. In the present circumstance, with a national election less than a year away, it is practical for a President to be aware that he may be appointing both his successor and his running mate.
>
> But I have felt that the matter of succession should take primary consideration over that of practical politics.

Speaker Krebs paused to take a sip of water, and to sneak a glance toward Juno Lepol. It was at this last-read paragraph that the hardpaper document began to differ from the onionskin version. Juno, he saw, sat like a rock. Krebs resumed his reading:

> Indeed, politics should not enter at all into this selection. The man chosen should be a stand-in. He should be an emergency appointment. I would not name any person who would use the office for his self-aggrandizement.

Once more Krebs sipped and peeked. Not a flicker of emotion had crossed that beautiful face. Krebs asked himself: "Could I have been wrong about her? Is it possible that she didn't come here expecting Dwight to be named?" He returned to the pages before him:

I shall be frank in saying that I considered several persons other than the one I finally decided would be best. Since the Speaker of the House of Representatives is chief officer of the nation's legislative body that is closest to the people, I weighed the name of the Honorable John K. Krebs of Nebraska. He is young and able. In fact, under the Constitution's Article II, Section 1, Paragraph 4, he is too young.

I weighed the name of every Cabinet member, beginning with the Secretary of State, who is ranking officer of the Cabinet. I gave special consideration to the Attorney General, who presided admirably over the short crisis immediately after the sad death of President Lepol. The Honorable Erasmus Hannibal is mature and able. But the recent tragedy has placed before the Justice Department the very delicate matter of determining guilt and punishment. I believe that the Attorney General should personally conduct that case.

I weighed the name of every Justice of the Supreme Court, beginning with the Chief Justice. But I have felt that my predecessors have injured the dignity and reputation of the High Court by using its membership as a source of political supply.

Other names passed through my mind. I believe that this country is richly endowed with persons capable of serving in the presidency. I would tremble for my country if I felt otherwise, and I completely reject the thesis of the indispensable man which was held in the 1940's when we ill-advisedly broke the two-term tradition.

Since it is entirely undemocratic, and a possible flaw in the 25th Amendment, that I and the Congress, rather than the people, should be picking a national officer, it behooves me to pick a man who will fill in for a few months and never, as I said before, attempt to use his office as a springboard to another office.

Again, in reference to the 25th Amendment, I note that the Cabinet officers may actually play a role in forcing a President to relinquish his power for an indefinite period of time, should he be judged incapable of discharging the duties of office.

While Cabinet officers may very well be able to judge the capacity of a President who appointed them, and with whom they have long associated, they cannot know much about a new President. Therefore, I require the resignation of all heads of executive departments, exclusive of the Attorney General, Mr. Hannibal. I see no reason why the next ranking officer in each department cannot run the department until further notice.

Now to return to the central theme of this message—the nomination of a Vice President. I have chosen a person in whose hands the country would be safe in war and peace. It is our nation's finest soldier, Chairman of the Joint Chiefs of Staff, General George Patton Rigor, whom I commend to your final selection.

Chapter Sixteen

One who watched the tableau presented by Juno's motionless behavior in the House Gallery that day was a butter-yellow, slant-eyed, portly little man, the ambassador from Peking, Lin Pang Phu. He found her performance to be superlative—just as good as the one he was giving himself. Juno's Nordic imperturbability and Ambassador Lin's Oriental inscrutability were hewn from the same adamant stoicism, an Hellenic term, but universal as that courage which Hemingway defined as grace under pressure.

Mr. Lin was not ignorant of the former First Lady's expectations. Robeson Burnbagge had been scurrying around town this morning with the misinformation obtained from the onionskin document. He had told ten of the eleven Cabinet members in utter secrecy that Dwight D. Lepol was to be nominated there in the House chamber, and in Washington you cannot tell three persons without the FBI, the CIA and the Communist apparatus finding out all about it.

President Chase's neatly sprung entrapment had been fully successful. Such was the decadence of Constitutional awareness in 1975 that no one clearly perceived the joker in the packet that Burnbagge had circulated. Young Ike wasn't thirty-five years old, therefore wasn't eligible for either top office. Had he been as brilliant as Alexander Hamilton, Chase would not have named him. But those who recalled this provision in the Constitution believed that Chase hadn't recalled it or that he was willing to ignore it and was confident that the Supreme Court, if called upon for a decision, would also ignore it. Ambassador Lin was among those who, like Juno, considered the American Constitution to be a dead letter—and both had been shocked to learn otherwise.

"Fine kettle of fish," mused the abassador of the People's Republic of China in the language he would later transmit to his government. "We are faced with an American President who is enamored of that bourgeois eighteenth century scrap of paper. He cannot be trusted to observe the socialistic and pacifistic precedents which have made coexistence possible."

Lin Pang Phu many years ago had been a student at the Johns Hopkins School of Advanced International Studies. He had traced the decline of the American Republic in the erosion of its fundamental principles, and in his mind he felt sympathy for Juno. Her dynasty, as well as the Finnigans', along with all the foreign adversaries of early Americanism, stood to lose face and position by the ascendancy of this throw-back to fundamentalism, Jeremiah Chase. Lin could feel for Juno, because he felt in himself the terrible conviction that Chase was not only a determined man but a wily one. In one sweep Chase had shaken the Lepol power structure by the removal of ten Cabinet ministers who might have connived against him, and he mortified the reigning queen of the House of Lepol by showing her that he could beat her at her own game of intrigue. In Lin's opinion, it took as much strength of character to stand up under mortification as under physical torture, and he had watched with kindred understanding the display of sangfroid in Juno's unmoving features as she received the avalanche of humiliation from the President's message.

Now he came to his feet with all others in the House Chamber and stood in respectful silence as Speaker Krebs and Senator Nestorson left the rostrum to appear in the Gallery where they ceremoniously escorted Mrs. Lepol from the scene. After that, as the Chamber emptied by a procedure of protocol, the crestfallen Cabinet members, the Justices, the Senators and the

Diplomatic Corps, Ambassador Lin began to think of what his own duties required. Within a half-hour, he was back at the Red China Embassy, formerly the University Club, which was conveniently next door to the Russian Embassy. He sent the message and soon received instructions by satellite communications from Peking that he was to protest vigorously against President Chase's conduct of the Buenos Aires Conference.

Back in his limousine, Lin had himself driven to the State Department where, having sent word of his business, he was pleased to be met at the steps by a young Foreign Service aide and taken at once to the fifth-floor suite of the Secretary of State. A polite, red-headed, high-busted receptionist took his hat, offered him a seat and then went blithely back to her typing for the better part of fifteen minutes by which time he felt it the part of dignity to remind her that he did not like to be kept waiting.

"I'm very sorry, Excellency," the girl said. "As you know, we don't have a Secretary of State. Mr. Phillipson came for his personal belongings immediately after the Joint Session recessed. We do have an Acting Secretary, Mr. Harvey Jones, but I'm afraid he's gone to attend the swearing in of Vice President Rigor."

"I have an important communication from the People's Republic of China."

"Yes, sir, I know. We've been instructed that the regular business of the Department is to go on as usual. No regulations have been issued about irregular business."

"Who's in charge here?" demanded Lin, drawing himself up to his five-foot-six-inch height. He was not really an officious person. In fact, he had a hard time forgetting that his grandfather had been a Chinese laundryman in San Francisco, and that his California-born father had admitted to being a little ill-at-ease in the presence of light skin and blue eyes. This pretty American girl did not exactly give Lin an inferiority complex, but the sight of her made him clutch hard for the hard-nosed training he'd had. In the Communist creed all the bourgeoisie, especially the American and British varieties, were objects of contempt and hatred. To buttress this party line indoctrination for looking down on Westerners, Lin had the distant ancestral assurance that the peoples of the Middle

Kingdom were intellectually and culturally a master race. Still, he couldn't quite shake loose from the knowledge that the British by seapower, and the Americans by corporate enterprise, had once fairly dominated the earth. He knew that these wayward and forbidden thoughts of his were vestiges of a "colonial mentality." His Communist educators had tried to drum such thoughts out of him and out of all the other Asians and Africans who were World Revolutionaries. Lin re-summoned the arrogance he'd been schooled to maintain. He again demanded:

"Who's in charge?"

Without breaking the rhythm of her typing, the girl answered, "I think it's President Chase, sir, although he's a long way off. I don't know how to explain it, but there seems to be an idea going around that we don't fly into a tizzie when something out of the ordinary turns up. I suppose you'll have to wait till Mr. Jones comes back."

Ambassador Lin could think of no answer, so he did wait, and in another ten minutes, a baggy, heavyset man with the air of a weary but practiced careerist came in from the corridor.

"Good afternoon, Mr. Ambassador," he said, shaking hands. "I'm Harvey Jones. It seems I've inherited the chair for the time being. Come on back to my private office."

When they were closeted in the large, well-appointed room, Jones said:

"Have a seat? No? Prefer to stand? What can I do for you?"

Lin again drew himself as tall as possible. He breathed deeply to discharge a long sentence, "Mr. Secretary, my government protests in the strongest possible terms against the irresponsible behavior of your President in re-activating the Monroe Doctrine, and in making a bilateral treaty with El Salvador which threatens the integrity of my country's friend and ally, the People's Republic of Cuba."

"I see."

"My government was willing to let the matter ride until the events of this day disclosed rising dangers to peace. I refer to the nomination of the militarist General Rigor to be Vice President. We cannot look with tranquility upon the cumulative evidence that the United States is willing to endanger the peace of the world."

"Very well," said Jones. "I'll convey your message through our usual channels to the President. He's pretty busy now. You'll be hearing from him in a few days."

"That isn't soon enough, sir," stormed Lin.

"No? How soon would be satisfactory, Mr. Ambassador?"

"I demand that the President be instantly informed of the attitude of my government."

Jones hitched at his sagging belt line. "Mr. Lin, I've had thirty years working my way up the ladder. I've seen a lot of things done in hell-bent haste because some country like yours makes loud noises. But the feeling I get from President Chase is that we don't jump through hoops any more when a Communist bellows. I could be wrong about what President Chase expects of us, but right now—well, sir, I'm not going to burn up the circuits to Buenos Aires to let Mr. Chase know that Red China is peeved at us—I'm sure he already knows that."

Lin could hardly believe what he was hearing. Could it be true that down in the second and third echelons of the State Department establishment there really were persons like this undistinguished, overweight, bureaucratic hack who didn't go into a flap the way the top-level intellectuals did? Was he discovering another reason for Chase's unruffled confidence in the American people in the fact that ordinary but competent persons can fill positions of trust in times of crisis?

Lin decided to report this disquieting thesis as soon as possible to Peking. Lincoln had said the Lord must love the common people, for he made so many of them. But it had been years since a government in Washington had really trusted government of the people to the people. Instead there had been the vast institutionalism which took care of how the people grew their crops, found their jobs, made their labor contracts, got their education and filled their declining years. The American press was divided between calling the system Liberalism, if it approved, and Socialism, if it disapproved. But the social structure had become so like Communism that the reasons for world conflict were fast disappearing—till now. Peace was possible in coexistence, so long as the American plan was collectivism and surrender. But this man Chase—his spirit, even in absentia, was turning back the clock.

"Mr. Jones," said Mr. Lin in sepulchral tones, "do you realize that there exists a grave danger of a nuclear holocaust? Do you have children? Grandchildren? Are you willing to see your government, through intransigence, risk the incineration of the earth?"

Jones, who had been standing till now, took a seat behind the massive desk and, vaguely waving the Ambassador toward the leather sofa, spoke quietly. "I wish you'd sit down, Mr. Lin. My feet hurt, and I'm sure you must be tired from all the strains of the day. It's half-past four and I'm going to have a snort. How about you? No? Well, here's how."

While Lin squatted on the edge of the sofa, Jones produced a bottle and a glass from a drawer and poured himself a generous draught. He threw the whiskey against his tonsils and his manner became more expansive.

"Yes, sir, I have five daughters, two of 'em married, and both of 'em blessed with daughters of their own. A big stake in the future, you see. But here's how I look at it—it's almost better to go ahead and have a nuclear war than be afraid of it. Not that I think we will have it, you understand. President Lepol would have run up the white flag before we ever got that far, and President Chase would throw the American Sunday punch before China or Russia got its fist cocked."

"Are you mad, sir?"

"Nope. Not very bright either. Not very diligent. I always knew I would go just so high in Foreign Service, but no higher. I'm a good administrator, but they'd never keep me in a policy-making position for very long. There's this to say for me, however. I don't scare very easily, and I don't think the American people do either."

Lin sprang up. "I demand to see somebody in authority around here."

"Take you to my leader?" yawned Jones. "The best I can offer is the Vice President. He told me at the ceremonies that you'd probably be coming around. He said he'd be glad to see you if you care to be his guest at the watch-in."

"What's the watch-in?"

"General Rigor and some of the top NASA officials are going to view the launching of the MOL, Mark III, at six o'clock. It's a closed-circuit viewing and we'll hold it on the top floor of the NASA office building on Independence Avenue. You have a special invitation to join us. Give you a chance to have a chat with General Rigor."

"Very well, Mr. Jones. At six."

The MOL—Manned Orbiting Laboratory—didn't interest the Red Chinese Ambassador overmuch, but he welcomed the chance to meet General Rigor whom he knew only slightly. Lin returned to the embassy, asked his military aide to bring him the MOL folder for a routine perusal. MOL, Mark I, had been launched in the Johnson Administration, and the Mark II version in the Lepol Administration. Both were reactor-propelled space vehicles with a small crew of Air Force personnel who practiced peaceful observation of space phenomena and generously shared the data with world scientists. Lin transmitted to Peking the hitherto unannounced plan to launch MOL, Mark III, and also word of his coming engagement with General Rigor. Then he called a staff meeting in what had once been the indoor swimming pool of the University Club. He lowered himself naked into the tepid water, signalled for the lights to be lowered and soon heard the giggles and splashing of the embassy girls who joined him in the pool with his male assistants. Americans made a naughty thing of nude bathing, but that was because the boys and girls liked to show off their bodies. The Oriental custom of not looking at other bathers was strictly observed here, and the Ambassador paddled around, conversing on routine office matters that had to be brought to everybody's attention. He noticed the fat form of his military attaché slip into the pool, and presently was told in Chinese that Peking wanted to know what he knew about the Mark III edition of MOL.

Lin and the attaché left the merry dip, dressed and went back to the main office. There they examined the super-secret folder again, and what he found upon closer reading caused Lin to say:

"Not so good, eh, Comrade?"

"It is a special project. Personal direction of the Chairman, Joint Chiefs of Staff."

"General Rigor."

"Himself."

"No more?"

"No," said the military attaché. "General Rigor is most close-mouthed. Runs a tight shop."

"Not so good," repeated Lin.

He was uneasy as he left the elevator at the top floor of the NASA building. Vice President Rigor himself made the initial greeting and introduced the Ambassador to the half dozen men there in the room with an ordinary television set. The close-mouthed man wasted no words, merely gestured for all to be seated, and thereafter fixed his attention on the screen which showed the altogether familiar scene of men in flying suits and helmets climbing into the nosecone of a Goliath missile, the latest in the American family of space launchers. At precisely six o'clock by the sweephand of the wall clock, there was a volcanic eruption of steam, and the huge, pencil-shaped object tottered upward into the Florida sky.

"Velly nice," said Lin, and was annoyed to hear his well-trained voice drop back into the pidgin English he'd learned from his grandfather. This sort of thing always put an Oriental at a disadvantage. He cleared his throat and tried to assume a menacing accent. "I am now ready for our conference, Mr. Vice President."

"This is it," said Rigor, beginning to fill a MacArthur-type corncob pipe. "Any questions?"

"I would prefer we be alone, sir."

"Sorry, I can't arrange that. These men are my staff experts. Three from Air Force. Three from NASA. If you have no questions, we can terminate."

"Please," said Lin quickly. "I wish to know about Manned Orbiting Laboratory, Mark III."

"Bruce," snapped Rigor at one of his staffers.

A young crop-haired man stood up.

"First, Mr. Ambassador, the initials MOL have a different meaning in the Mark III version."

"Yes?"

"Military Orbiting Liason," said Bruce. "Not Manned Orbiting Laboratory."

Despite his schooled phlegm, Lin actually stammered: "Mum . . . military?"

"Check," said Rigor. "Tell him, Jackson."

Jackson, also crop-haired, stood up.

"Mr. Ambassador, Mark III is now in orbit over Red China. It is being directly monitored by the American Navy station commander in Saigon."

"So?" cried Lin. "You have invaded the airspace of the People's Republic bloc?"

"Not the airspace, just the space," said Jackson.

"Tyler," snapped Rigor.

Crop-haired number three was on his feet.

"Military Manned Liaison will circle the Chinese landmass indefinitely. We are able to replace the crew with fresh personnel. And, of course, to re-supply the payload."

"Payload?"

"Bombload, to be precise," said Rigor as Tyler hesitated. "Mark Three has enough guided nuclear warheads to blow your country off the face of the earth, Mr. Lin. That, however, is at the discretion of two persons. One is the President. The other is the base commander at Saigon."

Lin almost screamed: "A field commander with his finger on the trigger? This is—sheer Goldwaterism."

"The Saigon base is, of course, equipped with detection systems to anticipate any nuclear preparation on the part of your country. At the slightest indication of a cocked fist—"

"General Rigor, I protest—"

"President Chase has passed the code word, Mr. Ambassador. The code word is Sunday Punch. It is not intended to be very subtle."

Lin was on his feet. He gesticulated wildly, but his voice failed him. One false move in Peking, one mistaken signal in Saigon, and the entire industrial, cultural, social structure of the People's Democratic Republic would go up in mushroom clouds! The crazy, trigger-happy Jeremiah Chase was the Headless Horseman of the Apocalypse!

Lin struggled and at last found his voice in the bottom of a very dry throat.

"I must inform my government," he croaked.

"You had better," said the laconic Vice President.

Chapter Seventeen

Two others who watched a closed-circuit showing of the MOL launching were President Chase and Colonel Duños, the jolly dictator of El Salvador. They had dined early this evening in Chase's VIP quarters at the Buenos Aires embassy, and dined well, as was attested by the flush of well being on each face and the row of six cut-glass wine goblets and an out-sized brandy snifter at each man's place on the lace table cloth. All of the El Salvadorean's receptacles were upright and still in use, but the North American's were downturned.

"Yes," said Chase as he received and read a note brought him by Flynn, who quickly retired to the bedroom where he was monitoring a hot-line telephone to Washington, "Ambassador Lin has watched the launching in company with the Vice President. It appears that the desired impression was conveyed upon the representative of Red China."

"Excellent," cried Duños as he flourished a glass. "I bet he was one scared Chinaman. I drink to the hope that MOL, Mark III, caused his pigtail to stand on end if he has one."

"I join your toast in spirit," laughed Chase. "I think that no free nation need fear Chinese nuclear blackmail so long as our vehicle is in orbit."

"Amigo, you are a man of my own heart," declared Duños as he quaffed another drink. "And now—on to Cuba, what?"

"I admire your spirit, Colonel. But—not so fast. The Senate has ratified our treaty. Your country and mine are comrades in arms. However, there will be no war unless the Red Cubans commit an act of violence."

"But that is oh-so-easy, my Presidente. Am I not Minister of Interior in San Salvador as well as everything else that matters? I will send a telegram. At any hour of the day or night which you care to specify, a bomb will explode in my Chamber of Deputies. What an outrage! What a dastardly assault against the very citadel of democraticia in San Salvador! My national police will instantly arrest well-known Communists and establish their guilt beyond doubt. No?"

Chase had been patiently shaking his head throughout this fluent description of the way things got done in a dictatorship.

"But, amigo, wasn't it Franklin Roosevelt who said he would hold hands with the devil himself if it got him across the bridge? Is it not often said by American diplomats of foreign despots—'He may be a son of a bitch, but he's our son of a bitch?' "

"That's true," agreed Chase.

"One must accept life as it is, my Presidente—as Carlyle more or less said, 'By gad, we'd better.' Where would the U.S.A. have been without Chiang Kai-shek on Taiwan? What happened to your interests in South Vietnam when the rug was pulled out from under the anti-Communist Diem?"

"Colonel, you are reminding me what a tough job it is to be the head of any country. I'm not a man who thinks he's solved the eternal riddle of always knowing the difference between right and wrong."

"Then let me bomb my own chamber of deputies. I guarantee to put the Communists in the wrong."

"Hitler did that when his Nazis burned down the Reichstag and blamed it on the Reds."

"I am smarter than Hitler. I won't get caught at it."

"No," said Chase. "We'll play this my way. We obey the treaty, in letter and spirit, or it's no go."

Duños laughed uproariously. "As you will, sir. In the end it will not matter much. The Communists will test us, rest assured. Within twenty-four hours there will be a genuine incident. I will not fake it or promote it, but it will take place. I only meant to hasten the inevitable and to have the advantage of timing it to our plans."

"Let us wait and see then." Chase stood up. The visitor understood that the meeting was at an end. He rose and with gracious thanks took his leave. Chase called.

"Come in, Jim. You might as well set up that apparatus in here. Lordy, I see what other Presidents have meant when they called this job one long headache. And to think that I was once a truly lazy man who never drove himself to the limits. Flynn, did you ever hear of the old stake horse named Exterminator?"

"No, sir." Flynn was stooping beside a small table in a corner of the room. He was putting some gadgetry in place there. "What about Exterminator?"

"Well, he was one of the great ones. He won half-a-hundred races in his day. But, you know, he usually won by a short neck. Exterminator was lazy. He liked to win, yet his horse sense told him that it was pointless to run any faster than necessary. I was that kind of lawyer. I seldom lost a case, but I never knocked myself out to flatten the opposition."

"This job is different?"

"Flynn, this job has got more angles than a diamond has prisms. If a President doesn't go at top speed, he'll find himself dropping behind. I can see that much already. Big matters and small ones, domestic affairs and foreign affairs. I had to change the tune of the conference, and I had to think up ways of outsmarting Juno. Very important to put the right man in as Vice President, but no less important to checkmate Red China and find the right kind of ally against Cuba. Duños is useful, and yet—I dunno, Jim, I dunno."

"Sir, if I'm not stepping out of line—what about Russia? You've stymied Red China, but how can you expect the USSR to stand still for an invasion of Cuba?"

"Good question. Fuzzy answer. If I tried to give it before a Senate committee or a jury, I'd soon be in the soup. First, I'm relying on the axiom that a dictator won't order a war while he's away from home. Too much chance that his subordinates would use the crisis to grab his job. Second, I'm playing the human equation. I used to know Dmitri Markov. It's too long a story for now. I'll tell you later."

Flynn stepped back from the table and the President inspected what was there. Literally, there were two buttons, and Flynn was now literally plugging them into a vast world-wide system by inserting a brass conductor into the floor socket. Each button was about the size of an upturned teacup. Each was made of enamel. Each had a symbol embossed on its curved surface, so that the President would know exactly what he was doing when he chose to press. One button was marked with the familiar mushroom cloud. The other was in the shape of an old fashioned icetongs with two handles and two spikes in a swivel.

"Power," mused Chase. "With one push of my finger, I can signal MOL to start shooting. If I press that button twice, our silo-based Minutemen will start firing eastward. If I press it three times, they and the Polaris subs will zero in on the USSR. Remarkably efficient."

"I hoped you'd like the arrangement, Mr. President."

"Then there's Operation Icetongs. Hand me some coffee, please." The President sprawled into the easy chair. "Pour yourself a drink, if you like, Jim. I'll be glad for your sake, when I'm back in Washington. You'll be relieved from the arduous duty of being my sole advisor. Tell me—have I gone too far with Duños?"

"Sir, I hope not."

"Duños is a good fellow. He's probably the best thing that has happened recently to El Salvador. Makes the buses run on time, and all that. But I look at him sitting there with the entire control of his little nation on tap, and the unlimited ability to do whatever he thinks will work. I look at Duños—and whom do I see? I see myself."

"Hardly an apt comparison, sir."

"Apt enough to worry me, Jim. The Constitution gives the President enormous authority, but it imposes limits that haven't been recognized for many years. The Congress and the people don't play their part in the scheme of things any more. I sent the El Salvador treaty to the Senate for advice and consent. The Foreign Relations Committee looked it over for a couple of hours, and the Senate rushed it through under a suspension of rules. I got what I wanted, but the question is—should I have got it so easily? Where are the safeguards when a President is on the honeymoon of a fresh term? Where are they when a President gets so popular that Congress doesn't dare question his programs?"

"But the restraints are always there if needed."

"Flynn, the restraints are rusty with disuse. When's the last time a presidential veto has been overridden? I wish it happened more often. It makes for good legislation. The Taft-Hartley Act is an example of how the 80th Congress felt the need of a labor law so strongly that it defied President Truman. That was good. It was the right thing for Congress to do. It's the American way of government."

"Truman didn't think so. He campaigned against the 80th Congress."

"That's also the right way. American democracy is working when the President and Congress are butting heads, and the people are getting into the brawl. But every now and then the system breaks down. Congress stood up to Truman and Kennedy. It largely collapsed before Johnson. The people saw something they didn't like about Dewey and Stevenson—a certain superciliousness, a lack of the common touch. But the people fell for Sam Lepol—a colossal fraud. It bothers me, Jim, it does. I tell you America is ripe for dictatorship. I don't want to be the man who mounts the balcony or the white horse."

"I think you're exaggerating, sir."

"No, I'm not. The Senate rubber-stamped my treaty. I can use it to take America to war tomorrow by pushing a button."

"Yes, if you think it's the right thing to do."

"Presidents always think they're right. They need to be reminded that they might be wrong. Sure, the U.S.A. needs a victory. Sure, Communism has to be stopped. The people know that, but they don't say that. There's that phrase in the Declaration of Independence—'consent of the governed.' A passive phrase, Jim. But the American Constitution called for positive assent by the people. Article One, Section eight, tells the Congress it has the sole right to declare war. If that means anything, it means that the country shouldn't go to war unless Congress says so. But Truman went to Korea, Johnson went to Vietnam, and I'm probably going to Cuba. It's wrong—wrong because that kind of executive action bypasses the Congress."

"The country backed Truman and Johnson. It'll back you."

"That isn't good enough. The country ought to participate in its wars. There ought to be decisions at home and sacrifices at home as well as on the battlefield. But what do we get when a President acts on his own? We get business as usual, and welfare as usual in the midst of warfare. Democracy is mocked when the people don't live up to the Constitution and take the consequences."

"But the people trust you."

"Forgive me, Jim, but you see what's happening right here in this room. My trusted advisor has become a yes-man."

Jim Flynn roamed the floor with the highball in his hand. He knew that the President was using him as a sounding board. As lawyer and Senator, Chase had said a great deal about the need for America to get back on a strict constitutional basis. As Vice President, he hadn't been his own man. He could say nothing in criticism of Lepol. But now Chase had come to the test of his own fundamentalist doctrines. He had, in effect, rigged up a small war by entering a shady collaboration with a pipsqueak dictator. The President knew that his aims were right, but that his methods were wrong. His conscience was aching with the knowledge that he was cutting constitutional corners and taking advantage of the lassitude that existed among the guardians of the Constitution back in Washington.

"Mr. President, why don't you ask Congress for a declaration of war tomorrow?"

Chase was staring into the bottom of his coffee cup as if the answer to his problems might come to him from there. When he looked up, the expression on his broad, thoughtful face seemed to be saying that men should know better than to believe in the easy way out. No good looking for omens, or trying to find a portent, or going to an oracle, or listening to roadside witches. If God gave you brains and equipped you with the powers of decision, that way your answers lay. It took endurance and discipline to think, and it took courage and skill to turn your deductions into action. But action itself had to be measured and timed. The immediate thing to do might not be for the ultimate good. Sometimes the progress had to be taken step by step.

"No," Chase answered Flynn. "For several reasons—no. First, I must stay close to the developments of this conference and not go home until it's over. To call for a declaration of war is a solemn act and would require a message that should be delivered in person. If I attempted to do it over television, it would look too much like a speech from the balcony. Besides, in one sense, I already have a mandate. Or at least an excuse. The treaty is self-executing. It declares in advance how we will react to certain specific deeds by the enemy. But, Jim, I think there is an even better reason why I should go it alone this one last time."

"Like taking that last drink before swearing off?"

"If it works out my way, Jim, the people, during this administration, will hear a lot about the Constitution. They're going to start to think—and then they're going to demand to know why the nation isn't being run by the rule book. To hell with consent of the governed. I want them to question the presidential power. I want them to call me to account. Tomorrow's too soon for any of this to happen. It's a terrible thing to say, Jim, but the American people have been so lax for so long that they aren't ready for self-government."

The President arose and stretched and announced he was going to bed. Flynn waited till the lights were out in the bedroom, and then he crossed the hall to his own room, leaving word with the Marine to be called if there was any message for the President. Jim had a full night's undisturbed sleep. He was in the shower next morning when the Marine stuck his head in and announced that Ambassador Hazleton was there. Jim emerged in a bathrobe and found the Ambassador pale behind his steely glasses.

"Flynn, there's been a coup in San Salvador. Revolutionary elements have seized the government, and Duños has been ousted."

"Right, sir. Let's go in and tell the President immediately."

"You don't seem very surprised, Flynn," said Hazleton as they crossed the hall. "Do you realize what's taken place? This isn't the ordinary Communist roughhouse."

"Tell the President, sir," broke in Flynn as he opened the door of the suite. Chase was fully dressed, enjoying the view from the window that looked out over the city. He turned and nodded to the incomers. Hazleton broke into words.

"The coup that has displaced Colonel Duños is authoritatively reported to be of popular origin. Democratic factions in charge of the revolution."

"Are there any Communists?" demanded Chase.

"Sir, there are a few minor Communist figures on the edge of it. That's inevitable, but my best judgment is that this is a liberal revolt against a strutting, megalomaniacal, militarist dictator, and we ought to support his overthrow."

"If there are Communists in it, it's a Communist movement," said Chase. "If they're not in command right now, they will be later. That's the assumption I'm going to make. Get word to Colonel Duños that we honor our treaty, but that I will expect him to restore order in San Salvador and to call for popular elections."

On that, Chase walked to the table in the corner. He put his thumb firmly on the button that was marked with the icetongs.

Chapter Eighteen

The broad, canted deck of the nuclear-powered super-flat-top U.S.S. *Pedernales River* (CVAV-70) was an immense ballet of scarlet, green, purple and ivory-white figures. They ran to and fro to the rumble of the ship's engines and the thunder of six F-109's that were warming up for flight. The screech of a siren sent the deck-crew flying for cover, and now the first jet moved into line for takeoff.

Phil Obermeister stood watching in a deck-level hatch. The vivid panorama of warfare lay for the first time before his dazzled eyes. This was only a part, though perhaps the most colorful part, of Operation Icetongs, but he envied other reporters who had drawn more active assignments and would get stories of personal adventure into their papers.

To be assigned to a carrier vessel meant that he would see little more of the action than the takeoff and return of the flights. The dark Caribbean stretched out of sight beneath the breaking of a bright December dawn. With a mighty whoosh the lead plane roared down the deck, found its buoyancy in a wobble of wings, and was off—the first armed aircraft going in against Communist Cuba.

The pilot of that plane felt the surge of a thousand horsepower under his buttocks as his craft lifted from the deck. He flew straight out for a thousand feet, gaining his altitude, winged over and headed east at five-hundred feet.

Swift and clean, he thought, as he and so many American pilots must have thought over the years in these wretched, brushwar strikes against the homelands of smaller nations. Do it—get it done with. Pray to heaven that you don't have to remember the flaming straw of native huts and the red gash of a stick of bombs across the heart of some village street. Sherman was right, and war was hell, and God forgive men who felt they had no choice except to order the deluge of death upon their fellows.

Had an American President ever been zestful in hurling his nation into conflict, as so many kings and dictators had done in the name of glory and conquest? The pilot tried to remember his history. Madison caught like a pigeon in a badminton match between Napoleonic France and Wellington's Britain, egged on by a war hawk Congress. Polk and McKinley swept into warfare by a Manifest Destiny that seemed beyond human and political resistance. Lincoln acting after the enemy had already struck. Wilson being dragged into it by his blundering policies. Roosevelt joining a World War that was already there. They all in a way had excuses for going to war, and Kennedy at the Bay of Pigs had found excuses not to go. Between the two extremes—the excuse for fighting and the excuse for not fighting—the pilot thought he would take the former every time. But better yet, when a President saw what had to be done, and did it without any mawkish apology to his contemporaries or to history. Harry Truman's decision to A-bomb the Japanese and get the war over was the classic example. Truman never looked back in remorse—not Harry. He did what he knew to be right, and to hell with it. What about this new man, Jerry Chase?

Down below the pilot saw the uneven line of the enemy coast, and there in the cockpit he saw the concentric circles that marked his target. He went into his dive, feeling the swell of his flying-suit as it filled to compensate for the G-force. Target: the SAM sites just west of the city of Santiago de Cuba.

He leveled off at fifty feet and went in, his cannon thudding in the wings, his bombs streaking in behind their heat-seeking noses.

Swift and clean! He heard the enemy groundfire bonging on his fuselage, and it made him feel better to know he was being shot at as well as shooting. He pulled up and climbed, and looked downward to see the other planes of his flight dash into the attack, and the high-flying debris of the bomb-strikes at the center of the SAM sites.

Then, as he steered out to sea, he made a wide circle to give room for incoming flights. Below him he made out a microcosm which seemed to describe the world situation of the moment. Lying at deep-sea anchorage was the mother ship of the Russian fishing fleet, the *Pushkin*, a quiescent but brooding alien presence here in the Caribbean Sea, which for years had been considered an American lake. And he spotted, further out from shore, the lumbering landingcraft, escorted by destroyers. They were making for the Cuban coast where at the turn of the century the U.S. Marines had landed to liberate the island from the Spanish. When would there be no war? No reasons for war? Any substitute for victory?

He climbed a little, circled the *Pedernales* and set his plane down on the deck. He threw open the canopy and began unbuckling his gear. As the first man in and the first man out of the new undeclared war, he was scheduled to be interviewed by the waiting press. How did it feel, Commander? What were you thinking about on "Bombs Away"?

Having watched the pilot land, Obermeister walked down one of the narrow, innumerable ladders of the carrier and threaded his way through the labyrinthian passages to the wardroom where the interview would be held. Seven hours ago, at midnight, Navy Public Relations had briefed him on Operation Icetongs. The tripod with its visual aids still stood at the front of the room. Curving arrows like tongs pointed at a map of Cuba and the sea approaches to the two assault areas. One was the city of Santiago de Cuba on the island's east coast, and the other the city of Santa Lucia on the west coast—both less than a hundred miles north of the Amercian base at Guantanamo Bay.

It was a modest undertaking for American arms. It was designed to get a foothold in Oriente Province. The Navy briefing officer had explained that the operation was undertaken in compliance with the bilateral treaty between the U.S.A. and El Salvador, where a pro-Communist riot had been staged two days ago. Phil sat alone at one of the dining tables and reviewed the notes he had taken at the briefing. They read in part:

"The United States is committed by solemn agreement to come to the relief of the Republic of El Salvador, which has been infiltrated and attacked by militant bands trained in Cuba.

"It is the intent of the United States, in a joint operation with El Salvador's armed forces, to effect landings of Army and Marine troops in southeastern Cuba in order to provide a buffer zone and a warning that no more intrusions of free territory will be tolerated.

"Operation Icetongs will commence at daylight, the purpose being to pinch off the lower peninsula of Cuba, liberate its population and establish there a freely elected government of Cubans under the auspices of the present allies. The mission of U.S.S. *Pedernales* is to reduce resistance in the area of Santiago de Cuba and thereby facilitate the landing of forces."

Phil riffled his notebook to a blank page. Yesterday he had gone out to the Pentagon with a group of accredited reporters, which included Eula Breck, and drawn his assignment from a bowl. Eula had been luckier than he. She had drawn the assignment to cover the assault of the beaches near Santa Lucia, and right now she was probably among fighting men who were storming the enemy defenses amid a rain of bullets and glory. The pang of anxiety he felt for the Mechanical Maiden was mixed with a thrust of disdain for his own safe and distant post. Besides, Phil had mixed feelings about this deviously contrived method that President Chase had used to get a foothold on Cuba. Practically everybody back home was bursting with pride at the way Chase had nullified the Red Chinese nuclear threat by launching MOL, Mark III. But the El Salvador bilateral treaty, concluded with an absolute dictator, hadn't been so well accepted. It didn't seem quite the instrument for spreading democracy. Still, with the popularity of the absent Jerry Chase at its zenith, both Houses of Congress had shouted through resolutions of concurrence and the thing was under way.

Phil looked up at the sound of dragging footsteps. The pilot, still in the heavy flying gear but wearing a blue baseball cap in place of the helmet, had entered the wardroom. The man was not young. His large, somber face was grizzled with a gray growth of beard, and his silver hair was damp on his forehead. On the cap he wore the gold leaf of a lieutenant commander. A man of those years and relatively low rank had to be a Naval Reservist. Then Phil looked again.

He sprang to his feet: "Sir?"

"At ease, young man."

"Mr. President."

"Yes," said the officer as he sank down at the briefing table. "I've seen you at a few press conferences, Mr. Obermeister. Please be seated. How do you like the war?"

"Why, sir, I—"

Jim Flynn had entered with two cups of coffee, which he placed on each table and withdrew.

"No comment?" said Chase. "Well, you're the questioner. First, I have a statement, if that's all right . . ."

"Please, sir."

The President blew ripples across the fuming surface of his coffee cup.

"There's only one thing worse than war," he said, speaking slowly, "and that's defeat. There's only one justification for war, and that's victory. The American people probably know these truisms by now, after so many years of bloody and inconclusive engagements, but it's time they heard a President lay it squarely on the line. I'm not going to give them any of that guff about 'I hate war' or 'I love peace'. Action always speaks louder than words. I flew the first mission of this operation. That's how I regard this undertaking."

"Sir, how did you feel when you—?"

"I felt very much as I hope all the others are feeling as this operation gets under way. Let's make it swift and clean. There's a line in the national anthem that says, 'Conquer we must, when our cause it is just.' "

"Sir, there's bound to be some comment—well, criticism, about the Commander in Chief doing what you've done."

"Yes, I know that. I anticipate it. First, I am not in any sense taking over for the military leaders. I assert no control over the running of this ship, and have not attempted to be the tactician of Operation Icetongs. That's up to the professionals. On the other hand, there's precedent for what I'm doing. President Washington, during a border uprising in his administration, appointed the Governor of Virginia to lead the troops. But Washington added that this appointment stood only if he felt that he himself couldn't be spared from the seat of government. Washington retained the right to decide whether he could do more good at the front or back home. I thought I could do more good by leading this first sortie. There's a lot to be said for a President's personal involvement in a battle. As I have indicated, it speaks for itself."

"Yes, sir. I think it does."

"Any more questions?"

"No, sir."

"I have a couple of my own," said the President. "Did any of you columnists take exception to the way your President razzle-dazzled your country into war?"

"Only one of us that I know of," smiled Phil. "He's not one of the heavy-calibre, influential columnists, and what he said will have little effect. But he raised the question, if you'll pardon the familiarity, sir, of your methods. 'Will Success Spoil Jerry Chase?' was the title of that column."

"Tell me more, Mr. Obermeister."

"This columnist noted that a small number of people in Congress and elsewhere were saying that President Chase incited the Communists to attack El Salvador, much as Roosevelt incited Japan to attack us somewhere in the Pacific. Both Chase and Roosevelt were itching to get us into war, for reasons which they thought good and sufficient, but which were not laid before Congress for approval. The Constitution was ignored."

"Does anybody care, Mr. Obermeister?"

"A few people care, Mr. President. A few more are very dubious about your tricky use of Colonel Duños. In nineteenth-century Europe it was common practice for chancellors and kings to find a pretext for conquering some small enemy country, but it doesn't seem becoming in an American President. However, the main point raised by the columnist was something else. He has held you in the highest admiration, Mr. President. He sees you using questionable and uncharacteristic methods. As an American he can't help but hope they will succeed against the Communist foe. At the same time, he wonders what the effect will be on you, sir. He thinks you can get away with anything so long as it works. Other Presidents have done so. But this columnist questions whether getting away with it is good for you and the country."

"I see. Well, off the record, Mr. Obermeister, I like what you've told me. A few people care what's happening to the Constitution. At least one writer doubts that success automatically justifies the means. I like that. I like it very much. Good morning."

When Chase left, Phil sat still to let the experience sink in. At first he felt that he had muffed the opportunity that all newsmen regard as the best there is—a personal interview with the President. Why hadn't he probed? Surely there were other questions he might have asked. Writers always said of statesmen that they were "complex men" with hidden depths and complicated thinking. A reporter's task is to get into these crevices of character and to find the hitherto buried reasons for statesmen doing what they do. A President who had deliberately provoked a military action which might have the gravest consequence, who had performed an historical "first" of leading off a battle, who had offered himself for virtually unlimited questioning—there must have been the chance here for extensive, penetrating examination.

But was there? It was easy to overestimate the need for profound interpretation. Why must it be assumed that, in the cliché phrase, a President is inordinately "complex"? Wasn't it a better service to truth to take Jeremiah Chase on face value?

The President seemed to be a forthright, action-taking individual. He seemed to know that he had cut some corners. He seemed to be inviting criticism of himself that would lead to improvement.

A man whose purposes were so clear wasn't very complex, after all. There was a lucidity about him, a rugged simplicity. If you were going to compare him with other Presidents, you wouldn't say he had the arrogance of Roosevelt or quite the flat-footedness of Truman, who never admitted a mistake. Chase didn't have the bookish intellectualism of Wilson and Kennedy, nor the corn-ball manner of Johnson, nor the gloomy depths of Lincoln.

Chase had an air of his own, one that called up memories. He looked as if he could just as well have dismounted from horseback after a battle as from a jetplane. He hadn't asked for praise, but about the behavior of the people in this crisis. He seemed pleased to hear that a few people were justifiably dubious about some of his doings. The way Chase had asked questions made Phil recall, for some reason, the story of how Washington had asked about the Battle of Bunker Hill: "Did the men stand and fight? . . . Then America can be saved." Chase had almost duplicated this: "If some Americans find fault . . . then there is hope for the country."

The young man thought: "I've had quite an experience, all right. I don't mean just covering a battle or interviewing a President for the first time. I've been in the presence of greatness—and it's a very wonderful thing."

When Chase left the wardroom after the interview with Obermeister he was joined by Flynn in the companionway. The President and his aide went aloft by elevator to the comfortable Flag Cabin which had been placed at the disposal of the distinguished visitor.

"You'd better rest, sir. You look very tired."

"I flew one sortie and I'm ready for the sack. Others will fly all day. That's one trouble with war, Jim. A young man's game. It tends to kill off the bravest and best, and bring about the survival of the unfit—the tired old men and the draft-dodgers. Do I have a pipe?"

"Here, sir."

Chase sprawled in a chair, filled and lighted the English briar.

"Keep an eye on the clock. Meanwhile, give me a fill-in while I catch my breath."

Flynn sat down with a clipboard of notes: "The Russian ship that you may have overflown inshore to Cuba is the *Pushkin*. It's called a fish factory or the mother-ship for the Soviet fishing fleet in these waters. The *Pushkin* is 2600 tons, speed better than 12 knots, built in East Germany, has a helicopter deck on the stern, light arms and no armor."

"Markov's itinerary?"

"Yes, sir. The Marshal attended the Lepol funeral on Monday, then flew to Cuba for a state visit with Barbaquito. Yesterday they were together in Ciudad Castro or, as the Russians call it, Castrograd. Your note was delivered to Markov through the Swiss Embassy there and he agreed to fly incognito to the *Pushkin* for a secret conference. We have reason to believe that he witnessed our American attacks on the Cuban coast."

"Could he have talked with Barbaquito in Spanish?"

"No, sir. English is his only foreign language. He learned it at, pardon my halting pronunciation, Veonnaia Akademiia Krasnoi Armil im. M. Frunze."

"Yes—the Military Academy of the Red Army, named after General Frunze. No, I don't know any more Russian than you do, but you recall that I used to know Markov."

"That's an advantage."

Chase laid down the pipe and took a turn of the cabin, beating his right fist into his left palm.

"Let me tell you the story, Flynn. When Captain Dmitri Markov was a young military attache in Washington, he often vanned a horse down to the Virginia hunting country and rode to hounds with us over the weekends. He was there as a guest on diplomatic courtesy. We were polite, but we never liked him. He twirled his mustaches at our girls, and he let it be known that he was a trained boxer and duelist. Jim, did you ever play football against a rather flashy performer who you suspected was a fraud and a show-off?"

"No, sir. Football separates the boys from the men at a very early age. I have never underrated a player who delivered the goods on the field."

"Well, there's a difference between the body-contact sports and the ones performed on horseback. We Virginia youngsters, boys and girls together, my many cousins and our friends, were a tally-ho-in-front crowd. Our elders called us the Beeline Bunch. That's the way we went—straight cross-country and never turned our horses' heads from any fence or obstacle. We were pretty brash and full of ourselves in those days, and this Russian was equally brash. He had no horse of his own. He rented mounts, or borrowed them, and he rode more like a heavy-seated cavalryman than a foxhunter. Still, we knew it was greatly to his credit that he usually managed to be in the first flight, on horses that were strange to him and slower than our thoroughbreds. He knew this too. He boasted about it. He let us understand that his superior horsemanship, his cunning and his daring, made him a very remarkable fellow. We had a feeling that he was waiting for the opportunity to show us that he was the best rider in the field."

"But you had your doubts about him."

"Yes, Flynn, I did. If he'd been English or even French, I think I'd have taken him at his face value. If he'd been a Russian refugee—an aristocrat out of Tolstoy—I'd have thought him genuine, if obnoxious. But a Bolshevik—I couldn't equate that with cross-country skills. I felt he was using his slow horses as an excuse, and was getting by on luck and brass. I kept waiting for the day when he'd have a clumsy accident, or do something gauche, or lose his nerve."

"He never did?"

"No, I underestimated him. It's a bad mistake to make with an enemy, but I'm glad I made it twenty years ago. One day—it was a big holiday hunt with lots of people out—we jumped a fox that simply loped in front, out from the hounds, for two hours over the tallest fences of our country. The MFH and the older folks got left behind. The Beeline Bunch had the run of their young lives, until the fox and hounds wiggled through a large, barbed-wire fence and brought us to a standstill."

"You didn't care to jump over wire?"

"No, it isn't done. The most fearless, hardest-riding Virginian won't do it. We've been taught that a horse can't see wire as he sees timber. If a high-strung thoroughbred falls into barbed wire, he'll thrash about and be cut to pieces. We drew rein, like the well-trained, well-bred young people that we certainly were. We weren't counting on the Tartar putting us to shame."

Chase went to a mirror on the wall. He seemed to be searching into the stubbled, middle-aged face for the youthful memories he was probing.

"We sat in our saddles, and watched the hounds disappear, and along comes Dmitri Markov on a big, heavy-footed mare that he had borrowed from somebody in Embassy Row. He booted her into the wire fence, made a clean jump and left us stranded. By the time we found a gate in the fence, the hunt was gone from us—only Markov had made it to the end."

"Nothing wrong with his nerve."

"There was an explanation, but we didn't know it at the time. The mare's name was Waltzing Matilda, and Markov had borrowed her from an Australian diplomat who'd brought her up from Down Under. I expect that Australia is the only place in the British Commonwealth where horses are especially schooled to jump over wire. The Tartar's feat wasn't as heroic as it seemed to be, but he'd beaten us at our own game."

"With a secret weapon."

"You begin to see the profile of this adversary, Flynn. Overbearing. Aggressive. Crafty. A taker of the calculated risk. Knowing what we now know of Communist discipline, I must assume that he had both a personal and ideological purpose. He had set about to humiliate our little cadre of aristocrats, as he saw us. Back at our clubhouse, after we'd dressed for dinner, he became insufferable. Have I described him?"

"No, sir."

"He was of average height, but stocky, strongly built. His round face just missed being swarthy, and wasn't quite an Oriental yellow. His eyes didn't match the complexion—they were quite blue. You will wonder, as I did, what the girls saw in him. He had his own theory about that, and he spoke it on this evening as the highballs passed. Here is what he said in the presence of mixed company: 'We, the Tartars, are swordsmen in more ways than one. Men have fallen before us, and women, too, if you take my meaning. In your language, you have a word that explains it, and the word is virility. We populated every land that we conquered—and will again, with enthusiastic cooperation of the childbearing sex.'

"I said: 'That's enough, Dmitri.' He said: 'You would not tell me that, Chase, if we were alone.' I said no more, but turned and walked away. I went upstairs to the men's locker room where I locked the door and waited. He soon followed, knocked and said: 'It is I, Dmitri.' I let him in, and relocked the door.

"He said: 'You are one big dam'fool, Chase. You are keeping me from a rendezvous in a car where I have left the heater going. Never mind. I shall not keep the lady waiting long.'

"He took off his coat and shirt," the President resumed. "I must tell you, Flynn, that his alacrity surprised me. I had thought that, if he came at all, it would be to palaver, to find grounds for excusing himself as one who was a stranger and didn't know our etiquette. Mind you, this was the time of the Berlin Blockade, and the Russians had been obdurate but hadn't fired a shot in anger. When had they ever fought well except up to their chins in snow before the walls of Moscow and Stalingrad? They'd been beaten by the Japanese at the turn of the century. They'd have lost to Hitler without our Lend Lease. They'd obtained atomic formulas only by stealing them from the West. They'd copied their aircraft and missiles from our models and from captured German documents. Even their Communism was invented by the Prussian, Marx. I was the creature of my patriotic and provincial prejudices. I expected this Russian to offer to negotiate. I was not unwilling to hear him say that we'd both had too much to drink, that he'd decided to take his sport hereafter at some other hunt club. But when he stripped to the waist, I did the same."

"Did you wish that you'd done so first?"

"Yes, I wished that I had. He had scored a point against me by showing that initiative. And while I got out of my dinner jacket and the starched evening shirt, and hung them carefully on a chair, Dmitri affected bored impatience. He lighted a cigarette, turned his back and examined some old hunting prints which were there on the walls. When he turned back, finding me ready for action, he balanced the cigarette on the window sill, as if he intended to reclaim it very soon. Jim, have I told you how these affairs are conducted?"

"No, sir."

"Well, somebody below had undoubtedly explained to Dmitri. An altercation between any two young men of our set called for the challenger to do as I had done—walk conspicuously to the locker room, lock the door and wait. The contest would take place in private, so as not to disturb the social function below stairs, and not to attract the attention of our elder members who, no doubt, knew all about it, but left us to our own devices for satisfying honor.

"Very well, then, Dmitri and I squared off. Having kept him waiting this long, I felt obliged to strike the first blow. It glanced off his forearm, and my follow-up went past his chin as he expertly moved it a fraction of an inch. He was no fake. He was well-trained at boxing. Next, I felt the smash of his fist against my temple, and the sickening pain of his knee as he jerked it into my groin."

"A dirty fighter."

"Yes, but again I'd underestimated him. His every move, from the wire-jumping to this below-the-belt stroke, caught me by surprise. He stepped back, and calmly unlocked and opened the door. He said: 'Shall we talk it over, if you please? I think our time is limited. In order to spare you needless punishment, I have tipped my servant to come to me with a message that I should call my embassy instantly. I must, of course, obey.'

"Again, you see, Jim, he had out-maneuvered me, and I had only the one recourse. With the door open, I went at him, and for a few furious moments, I took more blows than I gave. Then—with his servant shouting at the open door and people running up the stairs—I got inside his guard. I beat him in the face, with blood now running over my knuckles, until his knees gave way and he sank to the floor at my feet."

"You whipped him. Thank God for that."

The President picked up the discarded pipe, found a match and relighted it before resuming.

"Jim, who's to say? He won the first round, and I won the second. The third was never fought, because the Master of Fox Hounds himself had arrived to intervene. He couldn't ignore, and could not countenance, such an unseemly rumpus with men and women, boys and girls, crowded into the locker room. Dmitri demanded his right to continue, but the MFH ordered him off the premises never to return, and gave me a tongue-lashing. After so many years, it hardly matters who won at fisticuffs. Dmitri was sent home. I never saw him again. What matters, now, is how much I learned about the Protector General of all the Russians, and how it will stand me in the next encounter. What time is it, Jim?"

"It's time to go, Mr. President," said the aide.

President Chase departed from the Flag Cabin, escorted by two Marines, and Flynn descended alone to the wardroom which had been set up as a press center for the lone reporter. When Flynn arrived, he saw Obermeister punching slowly at a typewriter and scowling furiously over the slow-moving copy.

Flynn did not disturb the correspondent. He knew well enough the symptoms of a writer in the throes of difficult composition, so he sat down at another machine on the central table, fed in a sheet and set about to bring his own thoughts into presentable array. They were at first sight ready and obedient, for all he wanted to do was to synopsize the narrative that the President had related a few minutes before. The record of a youthful fracas between two present heads of hostile nations, given in the President's own words, would make valuable reference, both for continuous official scrutiny and for history still unwritten.

But when Flynn, his typewriter making a metallic and uneven duet with that of Obermeister's slower pace, had consumed nearly a half-hour and had reached the moment of truth as the contestants squared off to fight, his thoughts exercised a mutinous disorder and refused to stand in the ranks and files as he desired. Flynn's pace lagged, and the silences lengthened between the phrases he meant to set forth. The same thing appeared to be happening at the other machine, and Flynn looked up to see Obermeister's delicate, aesthetic face in torment.

"I'm stuck. You, too, Phil? Let's see if the galley will give us some coffee."

"It wouldn't help me," groaned Obermeister. "The way I've tried to write this piece, I feel like a spastic one-armed paperhanger. In six hundred words, I've got to combine a battle yarn with a breath-holding essay on simplicity in greatness. I need to write action like Breck and belles-lettres like Borton, but the helluvit is I can't stop vibrating. Right in this room I talked with the President."

"My heart bleeds," Flynn replied unfeelingly. "When I read your stuff in the papers, it runs so smooth I think you must have poured it out of a cream pitcher. What's all this jazz about simplicity? Every man is complicated, and I do mean Jerry Chase. That's what's got me hung up. How do you say that the President's mind was officiating in two time zones that are twenty-five years apart?"

"You tell me your dream, Jim, and I'll tell you mine."

A ship's steward, hearing the writers talking instead of writing, did the right thing and brought them two cups of coffee. Flynn gave Obermeister a cigarette, lighted that one and his own, and hitched both legs over the back of an adjacent chair.

"With me, there's no excuse. I'm the faceless chronicler for the White House files. This goes no further, understand, until I get permission to spring it some day or another. So . . . neither of 'em was a barefoot boy, but instead they were young bucks, booted and spurred, and they needs must wrangle till they fought, which is not hard to understand."

"Luckily, I'm clairvoyant," said Obermeister, "so I have no doubt you're talking about two youths who subsequently made good. The yarn has a little dust on it, because lots of people still can give a garbled account of how Jerry and Dmitri mixed it up in a gym over a girl—half a dozen middle-aged ladies of Virginia now claiming the honor. My facts are fuzzy, but it's public knowledge that our guy beat the tar out of the other one."

"Now, don't jump through the overhead when I tell you this, Phil. You'll learn it soon enough. The President left in his flying suit nearly an hour ago to 'copter over to a Russian fish factory. He's holding a very private summit meeting with Markov. You're right . . . they did fight long ago, and when it ended, young Markov was flat on the floor. The President told it to me modestly enough, and my original viewpoint was strictly that of a dumb halfback. 'Atta boy, Chase,' I came into this wardroom thinking. 'You did it before, and you'll do it again. This time you won't be trustful enough to let Markov foul you. He knows that you took the worst he could give, and then you flattened him out.' Consequently, I thought, till I tried to write it all the way through, 'there's nothing to worry about, because Chase cannot lose to the man he's already licked.' "

Obermeister, sitting on the table and coddling the warm coffee container, had kept nodding while the other man talked. "Jim, you think out loud real well. If there must be summit conferences, let's always send Americans who've knocked their Russian opposite numbers for a loop. Where's the problem, then? Chase is a simple, two-fisted man at heart, and the story he told you goes to prove the one I'm trying to write. The youngster of the fisticuffs is father to the presidential jet pilot and to the man of action who goes to the summit in his flyboy togs."

Flynn pulled thoughtfully on his jagged nose. "If that's true, then the saints preserve us. Does the U.S.A. send Peter Pan to do a job on Ivan the Terrible? That's what happened at Vienna in '61. If you don't believe it, read the Kennedy-Khrushchev dialogue that took place there. Even the friendliest biographers, Schlesinger and Sorensen, couldn't help but make JFK look like a lamb at the slaughter when he tried to sweet-talk big K. When the conference was half over, Kennedy turned to Ambassador Llewellan Thompson and asked: 'Is it always this tough?' When the conference ended, Kennedy couldn't do any better than make the sophomoric quip: 'It's going to be a cold winter.' Why, Jesus, Obermeister, I hope the simplicity is in you instead of in the man you're trying to write about. If Chase thinks he's up against nothing more than the grownup rider of Waltzing Matilda, there's hell to pay."

"I see it from a different slant," insisted Phil earnestly. "There's been too much over-intellectualizing toward the Russians. Too many of our American diplomats have figuratively put on their striped pants and kid gloves and academic gowns for these showdowns. I'd rather send the village blacksmith than a Fancy Dan to hammer out our positions. Strong and simple does it better."

Flynn would buy it that way.

"No, when the President was telling me about the fracas, I think he was looking before and after. He'd whipped Dmitri in the locker room—it wasn't a gym—but he'd made a lot of misjudgments coming up to the act. He'd been out-smarted all the way, and he left an unnecessary amount of his own blood on the floor. But today I think he was master-minding on two planes, Phil. He's transposing both himself and Captain Markov from the early 50's to the middle 70's. Himself, who'd been catapulted into the presidency only a few days ago, Markov, who had schemed and clawed his way through the Communist echelons to the top. That's a dual transformation, and it's difficult to express, yet I believe it's in the President's mind, and it ought to be included in the record I'm trying to transcribe. If anybody ever reads what I put down, I want him to get the interior message."

"Both of us had better assume the well-known posture," said Phil: "The seat of the pants to the seat of the chair."

They sat down again at their separate typewriters. They haltingly recommenced the path-finding in words toward the fugitive and indistinct ideas in their heads: Obermeister, that Chase, when all was said and done, went to his objectives like a bullet-simple projectile; Flynn, that the President went to his objectives like a sophisticated missile which could change course in mid-flight. Neither writer had achieved the state of creative rapture, and both were merely pecking away when a Marine sergeant stuck his head into the wardroom and stage-whispered: "Tenshun! Here's the man."

Flynn and Obermeister sprang to their feet, as the figure of their weary and stubble-faced Commander in Chief entered and said:

"You fellows go on with your work. Flynn, I'll need to get something down before I fall down. Is there another machine?"

"Yes, sir." Flynn lifted a portable Navy-issue typewriter off the floor, set it on the table and placed a pile of yellow copypaper beside it. The President sat down, inserted a sheet in the rollers, rubbed his bristly cheeks briefly and began to type rapidly. Soon there were three instruments of clatter in the room, one giving a steady staccato against the unsure intermittent clickings of the other two. The President wrote:

U.S.S. *Pedernales* at sea
2 December, 1975

TOP SECRET—HOLD FOR APPROPRIATE RELEASE

My fellow Americans: at 0840 hours this date, I flew by helicopter from this carrier to the flagship of the Russian fishing fleet. The *Pushkin* had the look of a clean ship, but the fishy smell arose to the flight deck where I was deposited. The 'copter churned away and left me among stocking-capped sailors who wordlessly stared at me up and down. I must have been in this uncomfortable situation for ten minutes when a bow-legged man in a visor cap came leaping up the ladder, scattered the sailors and saluted. I asked him if he were the skipper, to which he assented with a jerk of his head and said: "Plizz to follow."

We went belowdecks. The *Pushkin*'s interior was air-conditioned, but the fishy smell persisted and I already began to wonder if I would ever get the odor out of my nostrils and skin. The skipper halted before a brass-bound oaken door marked with a large red star. He knocked, whirled on his heel and left me there—again to wait, this time for about five minutes.

The door was opened by a barrel-chested, thick-necked man in the smart uniform of a Russian field marshal, including several rows of medals at the chest. I instantly recognized Dmitri Markov, for the years rolled back to when I had known him as a dashing young attache of his embassy in Washington. In good time you will have a chance to read an account of my previous acquaintance with Markov and to know why I did not regard him with admiration or affection. He had aged, as it were, in toughness, for the same brute strength was in his solid frame, the same craftiness in his strangely blue eyes, now narrowed with crowsfeet, and the same contemptuous arrogance in his mien. He had planned, I feel sure, to humiliate me by leaving me to wait on deck and outside the door. His first words had the same intent. I give the dialogue while it is fresh in my mind:

Markov: You don't show me the respect to have shaved for this meeting, Lieutenant.

Chase: I did not come here to indicate my respect for you, Protector General. It was arranged that we both appear in plain uniform so as to attract as little attention as possible. I did not bother to shave as I'd been up all night with preparations for an early morning flight. I believe you witnessed some of our air action.

Markov: I saw your planes strike the peaceful villagers of the coastline with typical imperialist brutality.

Chase: We bombed the SAM sites, but I won't quibble. I'm glad you saw the action. It saves explaining our new American foreign policy for these parts.

Markov: I demand instant cessation of hostilities, and one billion dollars indemnity to Premier Barbaquito of the People's Republic of Cuba, Lieutenant.

Chase: This talk of ours will begin to make sense when you do. It strains my credulity to hear that a marshal of the Red Army can't read American military insignia.

Markov: Very well, Lieutenant Commander. Let us take seats, if you like.

The cabin contained a heavy-duty table and two swivel chairs, all bolted to the floor. We sat down, and he said: "If this table were a chess board, I would like my chances better than yours. You're not very well positioned to give me provocations."

"No," I said, "I'm on a Russian vessel and badly outnumbered. On the other hand, we're two minutes flying time from the carrier. If I'm not on deck within an hour, waving my baseball cap at the helicopter, I can promise you a boarding party of Marines."

At this, the trace of a thin, new-moon crescent of a smile appeared on Markov's face, and he remarked:

"You are said to be a reckless adventurer, Mr. President. Take care not to prove it."

"I needn't prove myself to you, Protector General. We've met before."

He did not answer to this, but the smile enlarged itself perceptibly into a quarter-moon. I must tell you, fellow citizens, that this very moment was the crucial one of the conference. For in that hard and serried countenance, I was seeing two men, of different vintage, of different antecedents. One was the grown-up associate of years gone by. We had not been friends, and yet the renewal of an old acquaintanceship carries sentimental influence. It tends to plead—let bygones be. There on that rough visage was the beguiling smile that invited me to come to the halfway house where old adversaries might forgive and forget.

The other man in Markov, the other antecedents, had nothing to do with personal memories. Dmitri Markov was the lineal descendant in the political line of Russian rulers. He once liked, and still does like, I understand, to call himself the Tartar. Well, the tracings of my imagination found the tracings of Genghis Khan in his physiognomy. I could read there the lineaments of the sixteenth-century Czar who once proposed marriage to Queen Elizabeth I as a means of extending the empire. That smile—it was a proposal of union between himself and me in our national capacities. Much closer to the surface in Markov's countenance I could see the impassive mask of Stalin and the lively image of Khrushchev. The invitation in the smile said: "Come, coexist with me, America."

So, which of these men was I dealing with? A mere opponent of ordinary human clay and frailty whom I had reason to hold in little regard, or the diabolical result and embodiment of a vast hierarchy of Czarist and Soviet despots? For centuries this hierarchy has been schooled in treachery, dedicated to the black arts of power, existent in time and space for the avowed purpose of overthrowing whatever throne or state stood in the path of conquest.

You may say to yourselves as you read my lines that I had a sorry choice, but a manifest one. Reject the illusion of youthful memory. Accept the challenge of grim reality. Dmitri Markov is the successor of Stalin and Khrushchev. Of that, I am sure the American people would advise their President—and their President sought to anticipate their advice.

Yes, but what then? Do not call it easy. Subconsciously and by the strongest bonds of precedent, the American President is as much the mental and moral offspring of his predecessors as is the Russian dictator. I ask you to remember the names and connotations of former summit conferences. What is brought to American minds by the recital of Yalta and Potsdam where Roosevelt and Truman met with Stalin? What is conjured up when we recall the genial Eisenhower in a grinning match with Khrushchev and Bulganin at Geneva? Have you recently examined the photographs of Khrushchev's jovial, cat-and-canary greeting of Kennedy at Vienna? I am saying that it is owed to the veracity of history to remember that every President before me had approached his Russian counterpart as if it were, in fact, possible to reach some rational and binding agreement when, in truth, no such outcome is ever attainable. It is unattainable because there is not even a common language, however translated, between our side and theirs. Peace does not mean to us what it means to them. To us the status quo means stability, and to them it means the continuing progress of their World Revolution. To us liberation means the freeing of an enslaved nation to seek its own form of government. To Communists wars of liberation mean the subjugation of peoples to a Marxian dictatorship.

You will see, I think, that I had to break away from any concept that Dmitri Markov was little more than an old acquaintance with whom I might strike up a rapport. I had also to break from the dead hand of the past which had governed all U.S. relationships with Soviet Russia. I had prepared myself for this meeting by a re-reading in depth of the dialogue in Vienna, where, even in the kindly account of Kennedy's devoted biographer, Arthur M. Schlesinger, Jr., President Kennedy was verbally hung, drawn and quartered by Premier Khrushchev. This atrocity happened, to use Schlesinger's own words, because Kennedy opted to approach this tough, terrible butcher with the featherduster of "reasonableness," whereas Khrushchev elected to set upon the gentle, naive Kennedy with the dagger of "intransigence." In a matter of months after the Vienna meeting, Khrushchev had slammed the Berlin Wall into our faces. In hardly more than a year he was shipping nuclear missiles to Cuba.

There in this small cabin of the *Pushkin*, while Markov was slowly turning up the breadth and warmth of his smile, I made the readjustment and the determination of mind that I thought vital to American interests. Markov had resumed talking. He admitted with a shrug that the SAM's destroyed this morning were not of Russian origin. The People's Republic of China, he said, had sent them to Barbaquito. He, Markov, was not deeply offended at the reduction of Red China's armament in Cuba, for it was greater than suited the Soviet Union. Markov hinted that he did have some technicians in Cuba, and that he would agree to bring them home if I would bring home the American garrison in West Berlin. Furthermore, he beamed, he would recall the Caribbean fishing fleet if I would recall the Sixth Fleet in the Mediterranean. Upon hearing these absurd and insulting proposals, I judged it to be the propitious moment for taking charge of the conversation, which renewed itself as follows:

Chase: The Berlin garrison and the Sixth Fleet are positioned to prevent the Soviet Union from extending its ill-got gains. Any time you Russians go back where you came from, be assured that we Americans will do the same thing.

Markov: Do you wish to enrage me? I cannot turn back the advance of Communism into Eastern Europe or anywhere else, even if I wished to do so. Communism has replaced capitalism just as capitalism once replaced feudalism. Communism is the scientific inevitability of the future.

Chase: Then I don't know why so many millions of refugees have risked their lives to leave East Europe, Cuba and Red China. I would be willing to stake everything on free and supervised elections in the areas under dispute. Capitalism, as you call it, is an integral part of democracy. People go to the markets of commodities and of labor. They vote their preferences by what they buy and by where they work, just as they vote for candidates at the polls. Your people have no such choice under Communism, which is a modern industrial feudalism.

Markov: My aim is to secure a lasting peace. But I cannot guarantee its continuance if the American imperialists try to extend their system into places where people live happily under their socialist regimes.

Chase: I do not think peace is as important as freedom. We will always fight for it, and will sometimes assist other peoples to do the same. There is no use in continuing this discourse if you don't understand that.

Markov: Be careful that you don't make a miscalculation. I am willing to overlook the event of this morning. But any further adventurism will bring grave consequences.

Chase: I want to assure you that if Barbaquito makes another move in Latin America, we will make another move at him. I do not ask you to control him, for I intend to control him myself. If you should come to his aid, you will find out I am not fooling.

Markov fell into silence at this point, and I rose to leave, but he motioned me politely to remain. He said we had come to become reacquainted and should not hurry to depart. He then referred to the occasion when Napoleon and Czar Alexander had met on a raft in the Neman River to make a truce and divide Europe into shares.

Markov: Your MOL is over China, and my armies are standing on the Sino-Russian border in Asia, the longest land-border on earth. I can see the advantage of a neutralization of continental China after which, my dear fellow, you and I would be in the roles of the French Emperor and the Russian Czar.

Chase: You understand very little in offering that analogy. No American President is an emperor, and my country has no interest in dividing up the world into shares. We think that the spread of free systems is inevitable, and that your grandchildren will live under democracy.

He was much taken back by this statement and switched the subject to disarmament. He thought we should send representatives to Geneva and agree to a *quid pro quo* on the dismantling of bombers, submarines, missiles and nuclear stocks. I remarked that American and Russian representatives had been yammering around tables in Geneva for years with no results because the Soviet Union was only looking for results that would disadvantage the Free World. If disarmament ever came, I said, it would be from causes that did not relate to weapons.

Markov: What do you mean by that?

Chase: I have already told you what I mean. When your grandchildren live under democracy, there will be no more need of troops and armor in Europe than there is today on the American-Canadian border.

Markov: But the late President Lepol was at the very point of taking the lead in disarmament. He intended to lay down American arms as an example to the world.

Chase: Mr. Lepol is no longer President of the United States, and this President wishes to get back to his ship for a warm bath and nap.

This ended the shortest summit conference of them all, and I have now ended this summary account of my part therein.

J. F. Chase

The President finished his stint at the typewriter, but the two professional writers who were respectively trying to explain his simplicity and complexity still hadn't finished theirs.

The motor boats that put away from the APA found themselves in rough water. Eula Breck, weighted with cameras and sound equipment, crouched between two frightened boys, one from San Salvador and the other from Omaha. One of them began to cough as a prelude to vomiting. The other was murmuring prayers as the shells from the shore batteries plopped about them in the heaving water.

Eula didn't feel so brave herself. The scrambled eggs she'd had aboard ship were threatening to come up. The geyser of spray from a near-miss in the sea brought salt to her lips and it tasted suspiciously like her own tears. At a time like this, it was better to do something—practically anything. She swung a camera up to her eyes and sighted it on the beachhead with Santa Lucia in the background. The distance was too great for a good picture, but she thumbed the lever anyhow. Might as well do something.

It was a picture she would never see. Four plops to starboard and four more to port were convincing proof that some gun-crew on the shore had bracketed a target. The next salvo came in just below the waterline and the boat began coming apart in a screech of metal. Whether she jumped or was heaved overboard in the general confusion, Eula didn't know, but she was grateful for that last gulp of air which she held in her lungs. She felt grey waters closing about her and the weight of her gear taking her deeper. She fought at the straps and buckles, but they were hopelessly snarled in her clothing, and somehow the inflated Mae West life preserver had pinioned her elbows so that she couldn't reach for the buckles at the back of her belt.

She ripped the beltline and let her slacks fall off, and then she wrestled her elbows free. In the process the Mae West was gone, and so was her blouse. She never did account for the rest of her clothing, but when she rose gasping to the surface, Eula was as naked as Eve.

She was among floating debris. She clutched at a green canister of CO_2, got it into her arms and clung to it, wheezing and sick from the brine that she'd swallowed. The spreading flotilla of boats seemed almost out of sight between her and the shore. She was too weak to call out, even if that would have done any good. A sodden object brushed at her bare flank. She tried to kick it away, but it clung to her despite her efforts. She gave up kicking, gave up watching the distant boats, did nothing except hug the green bottle and fight for breath.

After a while she noted that the water was no longer rough. The sun was higher, and its warmth became soporific. She dozed . . . may even have slept. She felt wonderfully refreshed and somewhat amused at the predicament she was in. The object that persisted in clinging to her turned out to be a six-by-four American flag. She took an edge of it in her teeth, partly for good luck, partly for the practical purpose of having some covering if she ever reached land again. The calm water told her that she must have been carried by the tide below some promontory that served as a breakwater. She tried letting down her feet. Unbelievably, she felt sand beneath her toes.

Low tide, a strip of land not a quarter of a mile away. When she could stand, she discarded the bottle but kept the flag. She waded to the beach, draped herself in the Stars and Stripes and commenced walking toward the sound of the battle.

Chapter Nineteen

A week after the battle of the Caribbean Sea, a cheerful, full-bellied man walked whistling up the windy sidewalk of Wisconsin Avenue and turned off that central thoroughfare into the village atmosphere of Georgetown with its bookstores and antique shops in every block, with its uneven brick sidewalks and the whole contrived air of quaintness that was attractive for all its artificiality.

The man continued walking and whistling till he stood before a four-story, red-brick mansion that gleamed of polished brass and scrubbed white paint. Whistling still, the cheerful man rocked back on his heels to check the street number, although that was hardly necessary. He was a follower of the newspaper society pages and the Sunday features. He'd seen whole pages of text and full spreads of color photography which described the outside and inside of Calvin Borton's splendid home, the elegance of his furniture collected from all over the world and the selectivity of everything pertaining to Borton—friends, books, servants, clothing, cuisine.

The whistler did not go to the forbidding front door, but dropped down three stone steps to a basement entrance where he tapped on a pane and turned the iron knob. He was faced with a tidy office of regimented filing cabinets, wall maps, writing and dictating equipment, and a pleasant hearth where a subdued fire was glowing amid the pleasant aroma of fresh coffee. In the center of the room stood a rather dainty, inlaid desk at which was drawn an embroidered teakwood rocking chair. In the chair reposed the great man himself—haughty-faced, fierce-mustachioed, gleaming teeth and all, although looking a little seedy, which was disappointing to the visitor.

"Mr. Borton—"

A handsome, dark-haired woman of middle years and stern efficiency confronted the invader.

"Yes?" she asked.

"My business is with your boss, ma'am. I'm Joseph Markey from the Circuit Court of the District of Columbia. I've got a paper to serve."

Borton rose and came toward the door. "It's all right, Naomi, I'll take it."

Markey plunged a hand down deep into the folds of overcoat and suitcoat and searched about in that invisible recess, and then brought forth a sheaf of material held in place by a broad, black elastic band. He selected a folded document which he handed to Borton, saying:

"Nice place you got here, sir. Must stand you quite a bundle. Always thought that someday I'd get me a little place in Georgetown. Fix it up myself. Say, Mr. Borton, that was quite a war, wasn't it? Short and sweet. The way I like 'em. No flies on Jerry Chase, right?"

"Is there anything else I can do for you, Mr. Markey?"

"Nope," said Markey, his good humor unabated. "I'm glad I had a chance to drop in. I don't work these high-class parts of town much. See you around sometime, maybe."

When the door closed on the visitor, Borton carried the document back to the desk and sat down heavily. He unfolded the stapled sheets, three in number, and scanned them with a groan. Complainant: Miles Standish Smith. Action: libel. Damages asked: five million dollars.

"Put it somewhere," he said, holding the sheets above his head to Naomi Nathan. "My god, it's almost a relief to have it happen. It had to come."

"Maybe there's a way out."

"Hopeless! Hopeless! There couldn't be a more open and shut case. I'll never know what possessed me that night. Did I ever write such a story before without checking it out? I'm ruined, Naomi—ruined in every way that counts. My god, I'd rather be dead than have to live through what lies ahead—bankruptcy, disgrace, the end of all that matters."

"Mr. Borton, it can't be that bad. You've been in lawsuits before, and never been scratched."

"Let me alone. I must work—if I can work."

He bent over the desk where for three hours he had been trying to set down in outline the kind of column he could ordinarily dash off in half that time.

All he wanted to say was that the outlook for the nation was far blacker than it seemed—a theme that was second nature to him by this time. His congenital pessimism, lighted by gloomy insight and stoked with facts, figures and historical analogies which nobody else seemed to perceive, had always found the lurking dangers, the misread signs of optimism, the writhing worms in the apples of bland, chuckle-headed contentment. Today, more than ever, there ought to be crepe hanging in place of the pennants and bunting. What looked like a cheap victory in the Caribbean was an illusion. Wait till the costs came due. Our side hadn't begun to know the deficit in world opinion.

Then there was Chase's new Cabinet, appointed and confirmed while he was still away: monstrous. The new executive heads were nothing but paper-pushers, efficiency experts, hardly men or women of ideas (in the sense of Henry Wallace whose ideas had revolutionized agriculture for Roosevelt) or of excellence (the Kennedy-Johnson criterion). What was Jeremiah Chase up to on domestic policy? By heaven, thought Borton, the new President seemed to be trying to de-emphasize Federalia, to give the country back to the people, to revive local sovereignty and private enterprise, and all such nonsense.

There, in digest, was the black lining Borton envisioned inside the silver cloud on which the fatuous nation was floating in its silly hero worship.

But why, moaned Borton, why couldn't he say just that? Get it down on paper in his inimitable style and impenetrable complexity? He knew why. He leaped up from the desk. He put his hands to his head and shrieked.

"Naomi. My god, I'm finished. I'm washed up. I can't write. You've got to do one for me today. Just this once. Take this outline. Take some damned book and review it for me. Anything."

"Yes, Mr. Borton."

He rushed out of sight through the door that led into his living quarters.

Naomi had been with him for thirty years, had weathered many a crisis in which his temperamental, over-worked genius tossed on the cruel seas of this demanding, highly-competitive profession. She had seen him in anguish when a deeply-researched prediction got knocked down by unforeseeable quirks of history or unpredictable changes of policy. She had seen him go into rages when some lesser journalist scooped him on a story that Borton already had in his notebooks under seal of secrecy. She had seen times when he misjudged a public mood and found himself swamped with hate-filled letters and threatened with multiple cancellations. She had even known him to make mistakes in fact and grind his teeth over a typewriter as he sat down to acknowledge them with a bad grace that made him unbearable company for weeks on end.

But she was an unmarried woman whose natural affections attached to the nearest object, and after her fashion she loved this irrascible, lonely, distinguished man of letters. He returned her devotion with fitful spasms of trust and informality, and with matching periods of rudeness and disdain. She had watched with apprehension the hardening of his attitudes as age and fame, privilege and vanity, made inroads upon his encyclopedic mind and uniquely independent personality. How he despised contrary opinion and loathed any opposition to the fixed ideas that composed his political philosophy. He still called himself a reporter, but he had become an atrophied repository of prejudice and arrogance.

This latest crisis wasn't like any in the past. Yet she had seen its shadow marching on ahead of the actuality. He'd become purblind to other viewpoints. He'd become very much like persons on the other side, she reflected. If she'd been on hand that night when Borton leaped to the conclusion that, if murder was done, a Nathanite must have done it, she might have stalled him off, slowed up his reactions, cooled off his hot copy. She might have. She couldn't be sure. For as a devout and well-read Jewish woman, she knew that Borton was putting on nothing less than a personal pogrom against a hated cult of persons who were different from himself. He loathed those he thought of as reactionaries. He had picked on somebody named Miles Standish Smith the same way that the French officer corps had picked on Dreyfus.

The door burst open. Borton was back.

"Naomi, never mind the outline. Don't write a book review. There's something I've got to do. You know it. I know it."

"Yes, I think so, Mr. Borton."

"But you must do it for me. Write a retraction on that Smith piece. I made a mistake. I had faulty information from the Federal Aviation Agency. Say that I—that I—"

"That you're sorry. That you made a mistake. You offer an apology."

"No, I can't apologize. Not that. But get me off the hook somehow. A five million dollar libel suit. Naomi, I'll be impoverished. A ruined man."

He dashed again from the office, through the inner door to the house proper, and up the spindled staircase to his bedroom. He flung himself down on the canopied bed with the silken counterpane. Sleep. Rest. If he only could forget that ghastly blunder for a few hours. If he only could.

But that was out of the question. Nothing had been right since Thanksgiving. Everything had gone wrong. He thrust from his mind for a while the dreadful climax, the five million dollar libel suit that would finish him as man and writer, and took his thoughts back to where it all began. There on the flight out of Boston, just before hearing of Lepol's death, he'd bickered with that boy and that girl. They'd dared to dispute with him, to jeer at him. His irritation at them had carried over into a subsequent conviction that guilt attached automatically to anybody who took sides against the liberal cause. From there, how wantonly his prejudice had led him to self-slaughter, to the egregious assumption that the anti-liberal nearest to Lepol's plane must have rammed it.

Pavlovian reaction! The same conspiratorial slavering that had manifested itself immediately after the Dallas tragedy! Many an instinctive liberal that day of JFK's death had felt instantaneous conviction that the same reactionaries who had mobbed the Lyndon Johnsons and spat upon Adlai Stevenson must have produced the killer of Kennedy. Even after Oswald had been caught and guilt affixed by the high authority of the Warren Commission, there flowed from printing presses that indictment-for-murder of Dallas itself. Collective guilt! That city of hate! Fit company for Sodom and Gomorrah.

"But I—?" moaned Borton on his bed of anguish. "I—Calvin Borton—? It's one thing to have such thoughts in mind, and something else to rush them into print like a—like an amateur sleuth. No, worse than that. Like the very thing I most despise—an emotionalist—by god, like an extremist."

He got off the bed and roamed the room, prowling it like a criminal in his cell. He was, in fact, immured. Since Thanksgiving night he hadn't left his house. Not since the moment he learned that Carlos Martinez, the true killer, had been caught. Caught, too, by that damned Mechanical Maiden who was out doing what a good reporter ought to do—out and hustling for concrete evidence. Even the despised Obermeister had poked around into records and put something factual into print about Martinez while he, Borton, had lunged from bare guesswork into as bad a piece of writing as ever got published. How could he show his face after that? How ever again could he sit as the pundit of the refectory table at the Professional Club? Or go out to parties where once he was the focus of admiring eyes and inquiries? How dare he even send out his column through a syndicate that regarded him as a million-dollar meal ticket, and to the desk of 574 editors who thought of him as a seer?

His pacing took him into his thick-carpeted, silk-curtained

dressing room where ordinarily his valet would lay out his daily wardrobe of sculptured suits and severely tailored waistcoats and shirts. But today and yesterday, many yesterdays by now, Borton had shooed the man away and snatched up the first clothing that came to hand. He saw himself in the mirror, wearing a rumpled pair of slacks that hadn't been pressed for weeks, a soiled shirt without a tie and a velvet lounging jacket—evening wear, at that—the sackcloth and ashes he had subconsciously donned in his shame and dismay.

He flung himself into a padded rocking chair and snatched up the *Standard* which he'd begun to read while taking breakfast here. Gad! When would papers get tired of saluting Jerry Chase for leading a two-day victorious war? "Swift and clean" was the subject of another nauseously laudatory editorial. That drooling column by Obermeister called "Greatness in Lucidity" was being quoted everywhere, it seemed, and newspapers couldn't be put to bed any more without tucking in a cheesecake photograph of the luscious Eula Breck, draped in that silly flag, as she reported the surrender of Santa Lucia over a borrowed microphone. It was too much—too much.

Borton turned to his own column in the *Standard*. It was a lame piece of house-bound pontificating that labored the tired situation of a President still out of the country and the widow of a former President still occupying the White House. Juno had importuned the Supreme Court to declare the offices of the presidency and vice presidency still open because Chase stubbornly postponed the oath-taking till he returned to American soil. It was stale material for a column: indoor thinking instead of outdoor writing. This self-imposed sequestration would put the kibosh on his career even if the ghastly, libelous false witness against Miles Standish Smith didn't. Strangely, thought Borton, there hadn't been any indignant cancellations in the three weeks since that monumental blooper. If editors cared about accuracy, readers didn't. On the same page as his column was another of those zany letters from a leftist lunatic who praised Borton for the misdirected assault on the Nathanites. My god, what a commentary on the kind of people he wrote to please.

The housephone tinkled on the table. Naomi announced that another visitor was below. Who? A Mr. Harold Bardson, purporting to represent the libelled Mr. Smith. Borton was on the point of shouting, "See my lawyer," when he remembered that he hadn't engaged one yet. What for? A hopeless case if there ever was one.

"All right. Tell Harold I'll come down."

Waiting in the office was a pleasant-looking man, strong-faced despite seemingly genial manners and the general appearance of circularity—head, stomach, arms, muscular shoulders and small, white hands all asserted a roundness, as did the man's reputation for versatility as Borton remembered it. As Harold Bardson, the man wrote excellent though conservative-oriented history books, as Hal Bard, he was a popular fictioneer, as a lecturer and organizer he represented the respectable right.

"I hadn't known you were an attorney, too," growled Borton when they were seated. "What's there to talk about? I suppose you'll offer an out-of-court settlement for my total wealth. It won't reach five million, I'll tell you that."

"Let's not begin by quarreling," Bardson said gently. "My client is far from being a vindictive person. He has pity for you."

"Pity. Thank you. I don't care to be patronized by a kook."

"You know nothing about Miles Standish Smith."

"I know his association. He's a Nathanite."

"That tells nothing, Calvin. My man is a high-principled gentleman. He believes in God and country. He's felt the United States has been in danger for many years from its collectivist leadership. Has been, I said. The emergence of President Chase may make a difference. Mr. Smith is in a mood to be charitable."

Borton grasped at the floating straw. "You want a retraction of what I wrote? Would that be satisfactory?"

"It would be gratifying. Satisfactory, no. But if you're willing to talk this thing out at length, I can see a possible solution."

"Such as?"

"A mere admission of factual error is not enough. If you've seen the error of your thinking, that would be a substantive matter in our minds."

"What are you saying, Bardson? You want me to recant my

convictions? To do a public brainwash? I never would—no, never."

"Don't be arbitrary, Calvin," Bardson said. "My client anticipates something like an Era of Good Feeling under President Chase. Mr. Smith wishes to make his own contribution. If you'll make a public apology, he will drop the suit which was initiated in a moment of understandable anger."

"I'll make an admission of factual error. I had bad information. I'll admit to that much—nothing more."

"You called my client an aerial assassin. The idea of violence is so far from anything that Mr. Smith stands for, that he'd like you to understand this. If I can bring the two of you together for an honest discussion, I feel that you'll be convinced. If convinced, we would like you to say so in print."

Borton shook his head. "Harold, for me to concede anything good or even innocent in a right-wing individual or organization would be impossible. I don't care to meet your client. I might like him. Imagine that—my liking a Nathanite. Why don't you let me admit to a factual error under great stress, and see where we can go from there. I don't want to lose my fortune. I will make a reasonable settlement in cash."

Now it was Bardson who shook his head. "That won't do, Calvin. To be frank with you, I have never practiced law although I'm entitled to do so. If I go into court, I'll try to show how wrong you are in your estimate of the right wing. My client won't touch your money. In fact, it offends his religious principles to consider getting something for nothing. He isn't acquisitive. He believes in 'Vengeance is mine, saith the Lord,' and that bread should be earned by the sweat of the brow. Not one cent of yours is endangered, Calvin. We want your friendship, not your fortune."

"Do you mean that?" ejaculated Borton. "This suit is nothing but a way of dissociating the Nathan Hale Society from its public image? I remember in 1964 that the Democratic platform actually grouped the Birch Society with the Ku Klux Klan and the Communist party. I thought that the association was deserved. I feel the same way about these Nathanites. I don't want to change my mind. But—you're sure Smith won't accept any damages?"

"Take my word on it, Calvin. Now, be a little generous yourself. Treat yourself to an open mind for a change."

"What you propose is out of the question."

"Very well," Bardson rose and departed quickly, and Borton almost shouted:

"Naomi, did you hear? There won't be any damages. The suit is nothing but a plea for restitution of character."

"Yes, sir. I'm very happy for you." She approached with a typescript. "Would you like to look over what I've written for you. It says you made a factual mistake and you're sorry."

Borton gestured it away. "Tear it up," he commanded. "I was a sick man when I told you to write it. Now I'm well. I'm quite myself again. Fetch me some coffee. I shall write my column as usual."

For forty minutes, without lifting his head, he made the electric typewriter sing. He didn't use the laboriously constructed outline. He wasn't writing today about the hidden dangers of the Chase regime. He was ripping off a seering diatribe against right-wing extremism and the evil that it had brought upon the country.

He finished it, scanned it, and handed it to Naomi for re-typing.

"Ring up my valet, please. Have him hurry to my dressing room. I need to be clothed again and in my right mind. I'm going to luncheon at the refectory table in the Professional Club."

Half an hour later, clad in a Saville Row set of razor-edge slacks and a dark blazer, a choker shirt collar and a pale-blue tie, Borton emerged on the dining floor where the exclusive table stood, frequented by the kind of men whose company he chose. It was already peopled with fifteen or more important personages: a shady foreign ambassador and an unseated United States Senator, an unfrocked Episcopal bishop, a nuclear chemist who favored unilateral disarmament, a wealthy banker, a four-star retired general who worked for ADA, a fellow journalist, a clever lobbyist and others. They looked up at Borton's approach and he had the intimation that they'd been talking about him—about his nationally published blooper, his unrepented slander of an innocent man.

For a moment Borton hesitated to approach. These prominent

clubmen might very well snub him for what he'd done. Not that they were men of sensitive ethics. Among them were scratchers and biters in the Washington rat race, the givers and takers of money that wasn't theirs, the borrowers and stealers of wives, the smashers of covenants and commandments that got in the way. If they rebuffed him, it wouldn't be from offended virtue, and if they received him, it wouldn't be from personal fondness—Borton had few friends.

Yet, while he stood for an instant in doubt, Borton saw something he hadn't expected to find in their faces, and he guessed it had been in their conversation about him too. It was a fear—fear of unnecessarily offending, lest in his newly demonstrated recklessness he might strike at them, without restraint, without compunction, without truth. The mistake he'd made about Miles Standish Smith had marked him as a dangerous man to cross. They didn't like him but they'd never snub him, thought Borton, because they didn't dare, and this was attested in their forced smiles of welcome as he stepped to join the table.

A new power was his—greater than he'd had before. Into Borton's mind came a couplet written by another man of letters in another century, a man of virulent hate, unbridled ruthlessness, scathing wit and savage thrust. It was Alexander Pope who had written the lines:

> Proud? Yes, I am proud. I must be proud to see,
> Men not afraid of God, afraid of me.

Chapter Twenty

Another walker this blustery morning, though not a whistler, was a short, thin, walnut-skinned man who paced a small circle on the sidewalk in front of the White House. The sandwich board that hung from his narrow shoulders carried a legend in front: "WHY WASN'T HANNIBAL MADE VICE PRESIDENT?" and a legend in the rear that read: "HANNIBAL FOR PRESIDENT IN '76." A solitary, well-wrapped policeman watched disinterestedly from the curb, and the few pedestrians who hurried past scarcely bothered to take more than a casual glance at the picketer. He had been on the beat for three weeks, and was no longer a curiosity even though his name was Carlos Martinez.

Had the passers-by looked more closely they would have seen his bitter lips curl with scorn at every repetition of neglect. He wanted to talk. He would have welcomed hostility or sympathy with equal appreciation. He yearned to tell his story—tell it again—with the unchanging statements that were its seal of truth. But by now, it seemed, everybody knew all about him. The newspapers had told many times of his birth and childhood in the wretched Chicago ghetto, in a measure created by his own people's sloth and crime, from which Carlos had been liberated by determined bands of white people in what was called the War on Poverty.

He had been born Charles Martin, but a civil rights militant had once told him it was a slave name and persuaded him to "latinize" it. From Latin America, said the militant, the Western hemisphere would find true brotherhood through mixture of the races. The agitator also persuaded Carlos to accept the white people's offer to educate and train him for a job. An educated, job-skilled revolutionary would be that much more useful to the cause and a Negro Republican was better positioned than a Democrat. At the University of Michigan, Carlos had taken Air Force training and later was accepted for commissioning in the National Guard.

Several television documentaries had shown him as a page boy during the last GOP Convention at the stock yards. When not on duty, he had joined the demonstrations in the aisles for Erasmus Hannibal, and he had been one of the noisy Negro band of hecklers called Mothers' Sons ("every mother has a right to know her son may become President"). Further documentation depicted Carlos as a district salesman in Guayama, Puerto Rico, where he worked for an Indiana oil company. He had made speeches, some of them taped and rerun, demanding the impeachment of Samuel Lepol for the high crime of having passed over Hannibal, thereby offending against the "equal protection" clause in the Fifteenth Amendment. There was no secret about his membership in the Pan-Caribbean People's Unity Party, but a brief try by the Senate Internal Security Subcommittee to suspend his commission had been foiled by the American Civil Liberties Union which upheld his right to free assembly under the First Amendment.

As to Martinez' story since the fateful Thanksgiving, the news media had given it saturation treatment. Soon after being discovered under his parachute by Eula Breck and Bosco, he had been taken into custody and flown late that night to Washington. No less a personage than the Attorney General himself, almost green with fatigue after his ordeals of the day, had been present at the special session of Federal Court which assembled shortly after midnight. A bleary-eyed judge, who plainly resented being drafted for duty on a national holiday no matter what the circumstances, declared the court to be in session for the specific purpose of arraigning one Carlos Martinez. The court would make him aware of the charges against him and would appoint counsel to advise the prisoner of all his rights.

"May it please the court," Attorney General Hannibal interposed at this place in the proceedings. "I speak for the government. We recognize the peculiar horror that attaches to a presidential death, and we propose to use all caution to prevent anything going wrong with our case against the accused."

"Make your points, and let's get on with it, General Hannibal," chided the Judge. "I was about to remand the accused to prison, pending grand jury action."

"Your Honor knows the precedents established by my distinguished predecessor, former Attorney General Robert Kennedy. Mr. Kennedy declared many times that it is unfair to send a man to jail before he's had a trial. How can he collect witnesses and information for his own defense when he's behind bars? Knowing the Supreme Court as I do, your Honor, I will not put my case in jeopardy of being thrown out when it comes up for appeal. I request the release of this man, Martinez, until I can obtain his indictment."

"I understand your concern, General," said the Judge, "and at your request, I will set bail for the prisoner at $50,000. Is there a bondsman in court?"

A bondsman stood ready to put up $50,000 in cash upon receipt of $5,000 for the service, but again Hannibal demurred.

"Once more citing the precedents of Attorney General Kennedy, who still has a tremendous following in the liberal precincts of jurisprudence, I would protest against the setting of excessive bail."

The sleepy judge was irritated.

"But the money's available, General. I agree with you that we're now forced to treat poor people better than rich people, but this man is not indigent. We know him to be employed and to be a commissioned officer of the armed forces. I don't believe I'd be picking on an underprivileged person if I held him in a bond of this size for a case of this seriousness."

"If the Court please," said Hannibal, "I think I know our appellate apparatus better than your Honor does. Martinez is a Negro. I beg the Court not to prejudice my case at this early stage by holding the man in bond. The Supreme Court is very partial toward minorities."

"But, General, this man has confessed to murder."

"Sir, you know what happens to voluntary confessions when they go to the Supreme Court. How can we be sure that the confession was obtained without all the due process? What if there is police brutality alleged at the trial, and my case is thrown out? I am under a deep obligation. I must get a conviction if I possibly can. I entreat the Court to turn the man loose. We have no evidence of previous convictions or arrests."

The Attorney General's excessive caution and solicitude for the prisoner had been such a subject for exhaustive discussion and editorializing that by the end of a fortnight it was a stale subject. Martinez was offered counsel by the American Bar Association but he declined, and the Justice Department decided it was proper to wait until after New Year's for presenting its case to the regularly drawn grand jury.

The whole dilatory procedure irked nobody more than it did Martinez, the man it was supposed to protect. Now here he was on daily exhibition in front of the White House, and he drew less attention than the bronze equestrian statue of Andrew Jackson across the avenue in Lafayette Park.

"Why don't you go somewhere and lie down," snarled Carlos as he passed the lone policeman this time. "Maybe some Jack Ruby will shoot me and get me off your hands."

"This isn't Dallas," returned the cop. "You can get me out of the cold anytime you want to stop picketing. Why don't you go back to the hotel and get warm?"

"Maybe I like to suffer."

"That's no joke, buddy. I know you do. But only in public. Who's paying your bills at the Statler Hilton? Is it the Party?"

"Shut up."

"I will," said the cop. "If I don't mistake the evidence of my smilin' Irish eyes, here comes somebody to cheer you up."

From the West Gate of the White House appeared a stately figure in flowing sable furs—Juno. She carried a silver tray on which was set a china pot and china cup and saucer. Behind her trudged twenty or more reporters who had been alerted by the promise of a newsmaking event on an otherwise dull day. The delicious odor of steaming chocolate was wafted from the tray that Juno bore. She halted where Martinez stood waiting.

"To err is human—" Juno began, against a sudden howl of the wind.

"Madam President," yelled a reporter. "Louder please. What's that about Harry Truman?"

"To forgive divine," continued Juno at a higher pitch.

"Dear lady," shouted Martinez, in order to be heard on the outer rim of the press circle, "I had no malice in killing your husband. I did so because it was necessary to call attention to the injustices done to my race and to all minorities."

"I have brought you something to warm you up," said Juno. "There is enough suffering in the world already, and I have had more than my share."

With steady, stage-practiced hands she held the tray aloft and poured the chocolate so that the act could be well televised. She lowered her hands and passed the saucer and cup to the picketer. He took it, allowed himself a ceremonious sip only, and returned it to her.

"If my mother is listening," yelled Martinez into a handmike that somebody held to his mouth, "I want her to be proud of me. I am going to be executed in the electric chair so that no little Negro boys will grow up without the equal chance of living in this house yonder."

"You are innocent until a court finds you guilty," intoned Juno. "In my heart I bear you no ill will. I'm sure that my husband doesn't either."

When she withdrew and the crowd dispersed, Carlos felt that his day was made. Nothing else to match this breakthrough into the news was likely to occur. He ducked out of his harness, turned the sandwich board inside out and walked to the curb. In a short while a cruising automobile, driven by a fat, purple-cheeked man, drew to the curb. With a wink at the policeman, Carlos tossed his paraphernalia into the back seat and joined the driver up front.

"Did you catch the act, Braddock?" asked Martinez. "Just by luck I added what I did about other minorities."

"That was good," nodded the fat man. "I'm going to make a check-out on who was on that plane you bumped."

"Shut up," snapped Martinez. "I don't want to hear any more of that."

"More of what? Getting the death penalty? You're a real buccaneer, you are, Carlos. You want to die the martyr. But we've got to watch out. Wait'll you see what that crazy cat, Obermeister, has got in his column today."

When they had turned over the car to the Statler Hilton dispatcher and arrived in the ninth floor suite, Carlos grabbed the *Washington Express* from the table where Braddock had left it. Under a heading, "The Scientific Proof of Innocence," the Obermeister column began:

> The Justice Department has done well to move slowly in its prosecution of the case against Carlos Martinez. Its reasons for choosing a deliberate pace have changed from a grim, studied desire on the part of Attorney General Hannibal to get his man to a grim, studied doubt that Martinez is their man after all.

Carlos looked up suddenly. He had felt the small, flesh-buried, almost colorless eyes of Braddock upon him while he read. Now, Braddock dropped his gaze to a menu in his lap and pretended to be choosing what to order for luncheon. Carlos knew nothing of Donald Braddock except that Braddock had turned up at the arraignment that night and afterwards had driven him to this hotel where evidently the suite was a permanent convenience for one or more organizations which Braddock represented. Carlos hadn't been there very long before he realized that he was a prisoner. Plastered into Braddock's yielding stomach by a shoulder holster was some sort of heavy-caliber hand-gun. Every day Braddock took him to the White House pavement, cruised the nearby streets and brought him back to the hotel.

The column continued:

Justice Department lawyers have spent many hours over the flight records of the Federal Aviation Agency, which followed the FAA One from takeoff to impact, and today there are some reconstructed records concerning the collision aircraft that came up from Otis Air Force Base. The examiners are finding it more clearly evident than ever that the rendezvous of these planes was made possible by an unpredicted onset of clear-air turbulence (CAT), and could not reasonably have been caused by human navigation or piloting. Although Martinez has confessed that he took off for the purpose of overtaking and ramming the presidential craft, he could not possibly have planned to catch FAA One over Connecticut at the time it was separated by weather from the Air Force security planes. If Martinez had come anywhere near FAA One at any time except during the CAT incident, he would have been shot down in flames. The Justice lawyers, anxious as they are to win a conviction and avenge the death of President Lepol, are a long way from being able to prove that the crash was a premeditated killing.

Again, Carlos lifted his glance. This time he thought that Braddock was waiting for him to comment on this first half of the Obermeister piece. So Carlos said:

"You warned me not to change my story in any detail. You were right. This article could be a Justice Department plant to mix me up. They'd like me to jump at the chance of pleading to a lesser charge. Despite all that's said, the government is half afraid to execute me. They know they'll have riots from Harlem to Los Angeles if they put a Negro to death."

Braddock nodded. "That's right, Carlos. But stick to your story. Nobody except you knows what went on in your mind and in your cockpit. They'd like to make you say something screwy because then they could go to not guilty by reason of insanity. I'm going to be your defense counsel. I suppose you've guessed that."

"This is the first time you've said you were a lawyer."

"Yes, I belong to the National Lawyers' Guild. We provide aid for persons like yourself. I'm also a member of the National Council for Equality and Mobilization—called NECKEM."

Carlos went back to reading the column, which continued:

Another puzzle for the Justice lawyers is Martinez' behavior since his release from custody. He had been offered protection; the government would be glad to send him to some out-of-the-way military establishment where he would be in no danger. But his persistent exposure of himself as a White House picket raises the question of whether Martinez is inviting the fate that befell Lee Harvey Oswald. If a death wish is indicated here, it throws some shadow of doubt over the confession, which can also be regarded as a desire for fatal punishment. In these days and times, the public would not accept the conviction and execution of an insane person, least of all a Negro and an avowed leftist.

Behind this weird conglomoration of contradiction and mystery lies the predicament of a conscientious man, Erasmus Hannibal, who now for the third time seems to be in line for the vice presidency, but only if he can make a creditable showing in this most puzzling case.

Carlos threw down the paper.

"What do you want to eat?" asked Braddock. "I knew that cat would upset your appetite. How about just a bowl of vegetable soup?"

"Anything. I don't care. They're trying me in the newspapers, aren't they?"

Braddock talked to room service, ordering a steak with French fries for himself and soup for Carlos.

"It isn't fair," said Carlos. "Reporters don't interview me any more. They don't ask me why I'm picketing. This morning when Mrs. Lepol came out was the first time in a week that I've had any say. Does it make me crazy because I carry a sign for the only Negro who had a chance to make a national ticket? I was for Hannibal before Chicago. I'm for him now. Is that insane?"

"Don't get excited," said Braddock. "If you stick to your original story, nobody can shake it. You knew Lepol was going to fly to Boston and back on Thanksgiving. You got yourself assigned on t.d. at Otis. You gave Hannibal as the one to notify in case of accident because you knew you were going to be in an accident. You had a well-established motive for killing Lepol. You are willing to pay society for your crime. That's all."

"I didn't know it was going to take this long."

"The longer the better, Carlos. Think of what others have gone through, and think of the good they did. The American conscience hasn't been the same since Sacco and Vanzetti, nor since Julius and Ethel Rosenberg. You made up your mind a long while ago to give some meaning to your life. Don't get the idea you're a failure just because they haven't killed you yet. We'll get a lot of mileage out of this thing."

A waiter arrived with the meals. Braddock ate heavily and went to his room for a nap. He was soon snoring lustily. This was the first time Carlos had felt completely unguarded during daylight hours, though he had an idea that there were scanning devices in the suite so that he could be watched by somebody elsewhere in the hotel. If he should go through the door into the corridor, for instance, Braddock would probably be waked by a phone call and come lumbering after him.

Carlos wasn't sure of the details, but he knew that one of Braddock's organizations—now identified as NECKEM—was spending a lot of money on his case and intended to keep him in sight. Today, for the first time, it had dawned on him that Braddock and he had the same purpose: a capital conviction. It was an idea that took some getting used to; namely, that your self-appointed counsel was trying to get you electrocuted. Even when you had the identical idea for yourself, it was not a good feeling to know that your supposed benefactor was serving also as vicarious executioner. How could he consider Braddock a friend?

Carlos again picked up the *Express*. President Chase was reported back in Buenos Aires and said to be pressing every advantage of the lightning victory in eastern Cuba. There was a story out of San Salvador to the effect that Dictator Duños had promised to hold elections and would even accept OAS supervisors. Other Latin countries seemed to see some gains in signing up for bilateral treaties that promised both aid and protection against Communism. Things didn't look so good, thought Carlos, for the revolution that was going to sweep away the American white power structure. Maybe it would have been better to let Lepol live.

His turning of the pages brought him back to Obermeister's column, and he noticed what he hadn't seen before. In small type at the end of the column was the announcement that this was one of a series on the Martinez case, commenced now that the columnist was home from covering the war. Strange, thought Carlos, this Obermeister had been the first to put the name of Martinez in print as the possible assassin, and yet there he was writing in a vein that seemed to throw doubts upon the murder. There could be a lot of explanations, such as double-cross and entrapment, but it did seem on the face of things that Obermeister was more friendly than either Hannibal or Braddock. And Carlos, who hadn't thought it would take this long to die for a presidential killing, was feeling the need for friendship.

He picked up the telephone directory and found Obermeister listed on 25th Street with a phone number beginning 333. It was impractical to ask the newsman to come here, and very difficult to get out of the suite to go there. But why—for a man who wanted to die—was there any reason to be timid about taking some chances? Of course, he wanted to die in a certain way, a way that would hasten the revolution, but Braddock had that same intention for him, and wouldn't be likely to shoot him in cold blood. Some boldness was indicated.

Carlos went quickly to the door, opened it and stepped sidewise into the corridor. As he anticipated, the telephone brayed in Braddock's bedroom. The fat man came charging out in his shirt sleeves, clutching at the hunk of metal that was sunk into his belly. Braddock made straight for the elevator well, Carlos ducked into the fire escape staircase. He raced down five flights, walked through the hallways to the opposite side of the building, and found steps leading to the lobby. He was soon in the street, just in time to step aboard a bus which was headed westward. He rode five blocks and got off at 21st Street. It had been easier than he thought.

Carlos thought he had forgotten the street number of Obermeister's home, but it came to him quite clearly as he walked along—Number 922, which would put it between K and Eye, N.W. He crossed Pennsylvania Avenue near Washington Circle and came into the area called Foggy Bottom. Here the dwellings clustered between the Potomac and the far-flung stone ranges of the State Department. A few high-rise apartments intruded but the general architecture went to small, two-story houses which somehow gave a personality to the neighborhood, each being of a different color, from uncompromising red brick to subtle pastel shadings in pink and blue.

Unlike Georgetown, Foggy Bottom lacked both grandeur and

contrived quaintness. There were no stately mansions, no cozy restaurants and not one antique shoppe, only one beauty parlor and not even a book store. In midafternoon Carlos found the streets nearly deserted. Most of the inhabitants worked downtown at newspapers or in government offices, or attended or taught at George Washington University. The house which Carlos settled upon looked what it was—a fixed-up workers' dwelling that had stood for fifty years where the Washington Gas Company used to build brick homes for their employees, who over-filled them with happy Irish and Italian children. Now the area had been taken over by single tenants and childless couples, and there was an air of space and relaxation.

Carlos knocked on a glass-paned door, and was surprised that it fell open to his touch. He went into a small, well-appointed living room. He could see, past the glittering-brass kitchenette, a shady patio under a huge mulberry tree. Though the day was cold, there seemed to be two persons sitting under the tree, but they hadn't noticed his entrance into the house. Before he had made up his mind what to do, Carlos was charged by a sleek-haired monster of foaming jaws and terrifying ferocity. The animal leaped straight to his throat, but somewhere in mid-air relaxed and fell back at the feminine command of "Down, Bosco."

Drenched in the sweat of terror, Carlos froze in his tracks. Two merry faces, male and female, showed through the door that led to the patio.

"Looking for somebody?" inquired the young man.

"If you're Philip Obermeister, I am. Please call off this beast."

"Come here, Bosco," the young woman said, and then cried out: "For heavens sake, it's you, Captain Martinez."

"Yes." Carlos advanced carefully into the patio where the dog eyed him with familiarity and no sign of forgiveness. "We meet again, Miss Breck. It's you I came to see, Mr. Obermeister."

"Have a seat, then." Phil gave him a straightback, perforated metal chair, like the other two in the garden, which were drawn to a similarly designed table. "Here's a blanket for you. Eula and I don't mind sharing one. We've been studying, of all things, presidential assassins." He slapped a set of notebooks on the table. "And in you walk."

"Yes, I saw by the paper that you'd be writing about me some more. Have you come to any conclusions?"

Phil and Eula exchanged glances. The girl did something to a microphonic instrument which she picked up off the ground and placed on the table. She nodded to Phil.

"We'd both welcome your comments," said Phil. "We've been curious as to where you fit into this particular branch of criminology. By the way, are you armed?"

"No, I'm not."

"We have no reason to take your word, but it would seem a little melodramatic to search you. Just be careful. Don't get any ideas."

"You're the idea-man around here," said Martinez. "From what you published today you seem to think I'm no worse than a reckless pilot."

"We can tick you off closer than that," Phil said, taking up a notebook. "Let's see what kind of company you seem so anxious to join. Of the nine men who have tried to kill Presidents, five were foreign-born and four were natives like yourself. They were Booth, Guiteau, Czolgosz and Oswald. Booth and Oswald ran away from their crimes, and both were killed before coming to trial. Guiteau was hanged and Czolgosz was electrocuted."

"All four died for their crimes, you say. Then why are you trying to prevent my dying, Obermeister?"

"Hold it," said Phil. "Guiteau and Czolgosz were definitely demented by modern standards of psychiatry. There was insanity in Booth's brilliant family, and Oswald was certainly a loner and a psychopath in some degree. That puts you pretty deep in the madhouse, doesn't it? Of the other assassins, along with the two Puerto Ricans who tried to kill Mr. Truman, there's Schrank, who fired at Theodore Roosevelt. He died in an insane asylum. Zangara, who fired at Franklin Roosevelt, was a very mixed-up man, and probably insane. Richard Lawrence, who fired at Andrew Jackson, was acquitted on grounds of madness. In the whole study of presidential assassination, the scholars like Robert Donovan haven't been able to find one who was clearly responsible for his deed."

"You are going to try to get me committed instead of executed?"

"Yes, I am," said Phil. "Unless you can change my mind."

"The National Guard medical records would state my sanity."

"No, they would only show that nobody there knew you were deranged. Why did you want to kill Mr. Lepol?"

"I did it because he sidetracked Judge Hannibal."

"Are you a Communist?"

"No, I am not."

"Do you have Communist associations?"

"I think it is beyond doubt that Donald Braddock, my counsel, has been sent me by Communists who want me to die as a symbol for their cause."

"Are you willing to die for that cause?"

"No, I choose my own cause. The cause of minority races against the white power structure."

"Have you ever heard of Francis Scott Key? I don't mean as an anthem writer. He was District Attorney of the District of Columbia under Andrew Jackson. When the man named Lawrence fired at Jackson, it was to Key's benefit to get a capital conviction. Instead, Key acted from conscience. He made the Court aware of a similar case in Britain where a demented man had fired at King George III and missed. In possession of this British precedent, the American court found Lawrence not guilty and confined him to an institution for the rest of his days. I cite this case because Judge Hannibal is in much the same situation that Key was in. He is a prosecutor with a conscience. In the end, I think, he will give the Court every opportunity to rule on your sanity."

"There may be a similarity between Hannibal and Key," Carlos said. "There is no similarity between myself and any of the crazy men you have mentioned. Look at me. See for yourself. Do I talk like a man who is demented?"

"No, you don't," admitted Phil. "I'm not sure you are as anxious to die as you pretend. You carried a chute. You tried to escape. But perhaps you hoped to live long enough to play the martyr. I would say that the presumption of insanity goes with any man who wants to kill as good a person as Sam Lepol was, but I will leave that to the courts. Still, wanting to do so isn't the same as doing so. You did kill Mr. Lepol, but it wasn't murder."

"I tell you I was climbing," said Martinez. "I saw FAA One in front of me. I smashed into its tail assembly."

"Why didn't you use your guns?"

"What?"

"You were flying a fighter plane. It was armed for target practice with .50 calibre machine-ammo. Have you forgotten? The investigation proves you didn't fire."

"I guess I didn't at that. I just wanted to bring him down, and to be able to say that I did it."

"Your chances of surviving a mid-air collision were slim. It would have been easy to shoot down an unarmed plane. I think it's beyond a reasonable doubt that you blundered into the tail section. You may not have been sure it was FAA One. It could have been any airliner for the length of time you had to look."

"Then why did I hide?" asked Martinez.

"Because you felt guilty. Or because you soon ascertained that you'd hit the presidential plane by accident. I will leave the subject there, and go to another point. The books that Miss Breck and I have covered tell us that there are two acts to every royal or presidential assassination. Act One is the murder. Act Two is the almost inevitable proclamation. John Wilkes Booth shouted: 'Sic semper tyrannis!' Every one of the assassins, whether effective or not, freely asserted the glory of his guilt. Here is the documentation. Booth said: 'God simply made me the instrument of his punishment.' Guiteau said: 'Let your verdict be that it was the Divinity's act, not mine.' And so forth. Of them all, only Oswald denied it with his last words, and we'll never know about that. But the preponderance of evidence is that Act Two of the assassination is the proclamation."

"Very well," said Martinez. "I have proclaimed."

"You proclaim too much," said Phil. "Did you really perform Act One? Are you really fit to be the martyr that you yearn to be? How about it, Carlos?"

Carlos looked across at the other two, huddled there comically under a single blanket. He spread his hands in appeal.

"I should tell you, Mr. Obermeister, I came here because I had need of friendship. I have felt very bereft of it in the past weeks. I was not flung into a cell. I was not attacked by mobs. There is no hurry on the government's part to rush me to my death. So who feels sorry for me? Who visits me in prison? Who tries for the salvation of my soul? You are not really trying to save my life, are you?"

"No," said Phil, "I'm concerned with preventing the country from performing a barbaric revenge. An insane man should not be executed. An accidental killer has no right to the dignity of trial, conviction, sentencing and last minute heroics."

"Miss Breck?"

"No, Captain, I am an automatic recorder of news and views. I have no opinions. But I'll be very glad to take any closing statement you wish to make." She pushed the portable sound recorder toward him across the table. "Go ahead."

"Will you put my statement on the air just as I give it? Mr. Obermeister, will you put it in your column?"

Phil nodded. "Miss Breck will run it verbatum. I will run it with my own comments. What I say will depend upon whether I believe you."

"If I were dying, would you accept my deathbed statement as true?"

"I would not believe a Communist on his deathbed," said Phil, "but I don't believe you're under Communist discipline."

The reply seemed to satisfy Martinez. He hitched his chair closer to the table. He spoke slowly and distinctly into the instrument.

"I, Carlos Martinez, swear on my mother's name to tell the truth. I thought if President Lepol were to die, that President Chase would certainly appoint Erasmus Hannibal to be Vice President, within one heartbeat of the White House. Mr. Hannibal should have been made Vice President before now, but Lepol passed him by in 1972. I had this reason to hate Lepol, and I planned to kill him. It was my intention to overtake his plane and to shoot it down in a diving attack as it descended for a landing in Washington. At that time it would be most vulnerable. The Air

Force escort planes, which were flying high cover, would have been least likely to intercept at the end of the flight.

"Suddenly, while I was climbing out of Otis Air Force Base, a large airliner showed up on a collision course. I tried to avoid it, but struck its tail assembly and immediately ejected. I had plenty of time, both before and after my chute opened, to read the lettering and to see that I had rammed FAA One. I saw the big plane disintegrate in the air. I knew that I had accomplished my mission in a way I hadn't planned.

"I had given the Attorney General's name for notification in case of my death, because that was the way to become known and remembered as the Negro who gave his life helping another Negro to become Vice President and possibly President. I desired this measure of fame. My plans were rational from beginning to end. The fact that they miscarried does not reflect upon my sanity. I do not regret the death of Lepol, but I am sorry for the others in the plane who died and whom the press has scarcely mentioned. I want it known, never to be forgotten, that the only lie I told was in proclaiming myself an assassin. If I had said would-be assassin, it would have been the whole truth. Good-by, Mother. I want you to be proud of me."

Martinez stood up, and so did the dog.

"Down, Bosco," said Eula. "Thank you for the interview, Captain."

"I thank you for the opportunity, Miss Breck. Now, everyone will know that I'm not crazy."

Carlos Martinez departed through the house into 25th Street. One block away, on 24th, there was a crossing where a bridge offered pedestrians a passage across the rushing traffic of a tunnel where K street plunges beneath Washington Circle. A body falling into this rushing channel of vehicles would be hit and smashed by several of them before anybody could drag the remains away.

This was what happened to Carlos Martinez a few minutes after he had given his dying statement to Phil and Eula. The police ambulance soon came screaming to recover the suicidal remains.

Chapter Twenty-One

In those waning days of 1975, the American people and their new leader, Jeremiah Chase, showed their resilience under the stress of death and war. Congratulations were due the populace, and they were not stinted. American newspapers praised their customers for not giving vent to riots and panic as so often happened in lands beyond the seas. By the time the ashes of the slain President had settled to the ground, business as usual was the order of the times except among the few in Washington who sought to gain something for themselves by usurpation and intrigue. By and large, the people demonstrated a homespun ability at self-government—which is to say that, left alone, they displayed a remarkable competence for getting along without the politicians and, most notably, without the paternalistic presence of their Chief Executive, who remained abroad for nearly a month in the public interest.

The same praise was due President Chase, who established himself as a well-nigh flawless master in the clutch of a critical circumstance. It was written many times of Jerry Chase (as soon as the editorialists began to comprehend his style) that he brought out the best in all the people. He made them understand the difference between the mere hocus-pocus of governance and the solid reality of it. He was, as he said, the automatic successor to the presidency, and the formality of taking the oath could better be postponed than hurried, since he was already pledged to do his duty. That duty kept him out of the country, and he did not expect the mice to play—did not, in truth, expect the people to behave like rodents. He had set a precedent by becoming a Commander in Chief who led the first ranks into battle, and he broke a long precedent set by Commanders in Chief who behaved as if there were something sinful in the frank use of force to implement the nation's foreign policy. But he made it understood that he hadn't flown the first-strike mission in any spirit of ostentation or braggadocio, nor had he refrained from sententious remarks about "hating war" or "loving peace" in order to make his predecessors, notably Roosevelt and Johnson, look bad. He intended to bring about a changed attitude toward the disagreeable necessity of asserting American might to attain American purposes. He believed that this assertion required no apology, and certainly no obeisance in the direction of the myth called "world opinion."

In many ways, during these trying weeks, Chase had been lucky as well as plucky, and somehow he made the country comprehend that these adjectives rhymed in more than diction—that they were in consonance through the laws of life. Fortune made favorites of the man and the nation who were brave, and made fools of those who hesitated on the brink of enterprise. The President conveyed these creeds of his by acting upon them, and the nation felt that his bravery was their own, since he was acting in their behalf.

So much for the interlude of tragedy and battle, during which all went so well. But excitement does not sustain itself for very long. Chills and thrills are not the regular fare of personal or national life. The humdrum of diurnal existence had to return, and with the arrival of the New Year both the country and its President must meet fresh tests.

No one who has awaited the arrival at an airport of the presidential transport ever outgrows the thrill. Veteran reporters who witness the spectacle several times a day in campaign seasons never turn blasé. First there is the fly-by as the huge, graceful, glistening craft descends from the sky and makes its run across the vision of the thousands with their upturned, expectant faces. Then the plane disappears in a wide circle and comes to view again in its let-down to the concrete. The roll-up is a magnificent sight, for now the aerial vessel with its august voyager becomes a chariot of blue and silver, its proud length an astonishment to the most accustomed watcher and its majestic size a wonderment in lightness of smooth, slow motion on the earth.

When the mammoth ship has come to a halt, a few persons of no importance to the onlookers may descend in haste by the rear stairway. Nobody notices anything except the trundling up of the disembarking apparatus to the front door of the plane. Now there is the interminable delay—so it seems—when nothing happens. A few persons may have recognized faces in the windows—governors and other eminent guests who could have mattered on any other occasion. But there is only one face and figure that will satisfy the waiting welcomers. He appears, nearly always with a hat in hand above his head (Jack Kennedy would instantly discard the headpiece), and comes down the steps at a gait just right for dignity, masculine vigor and eagerness to be among his people.

This was the scene, oft-repeated but forever new, as President Chase stepped onto Forrestal Airport at the end of his flight from Buenos Aires in the big, new Boeing that would now be called, as in the Kennedy-Johnson era, Air Force One. Christmas was only five days away and on this morning the whole Potomac basin glistened from a snow that had stopped falling only an hour before.

Thousands cheered—standing on the galleries of the passenger terminal, packed a half mile deep amid auxiliary television boxes behind the fences, hanging precariously from the windows of Laker's Acres—as the President walked in his knee-length tweed overcoat, pinched felt hat still aloft, to the two-foot platform where at the stem of a single microphone a big, white-haired man in a black cape and holding a book stood alone. The President passed his hat to Jim Flynn, took a longer stride that lifted him effortlessly, without need of using the steps, to the platform. He did not immediately greet the Chief Justice but simply put his left hand on the Bible, raised his right hand and without prompting recited the words prescribed in the Constitution:

> "I, Jeremiah Fielding Chase, do solemnly swear that I will faithfully execute the Office of President of the United States and to the best of my ability, preserve, protect and defend the Constitution of the United States. . . ."

He added words not prescribed in the oath:

> So help me Almighty God, ruler of this blessed land.

He now shook hands warmly with the Chief Justice, but it was plain to see that this was not the greeting he yearned for. Then a dumpy, fleecy-haired little lady skipped up the platform steps. President Chase's long arms stretched wide open in an unbelievably enormous span before they went around her in a hug that took the breath out of the watching multitude. It brought an involuntary "Ah-h," heard round the world that day over electronic devices—no doubt the most homely, human, heart-reaching sound that ever traveled through the heavens.

The big man's arms were full of Cora, but a moment later they opened to receive a lithesome beauty of Cora's own height who had jumped to the stage with a flash of silken knees. Anyone would have thought that a man with such an armful of family love could hold no more. But—wait. A slim, not very well-kempt youngster in corduroy pants and a half-zipped wool windbreaker hung on the edge of the group, a little gawky at being before so many people, a little hang-dog, as if not sure of his welcome. For a moment the family group separated, but only for as long as it took Chase's long stride and lengthy arm to cup a hand around the boy's neck and bring him to Cora and Chi Chi. All three of them, wife, daughter and son, literally disappeared from general view in the President's all-encompassing embrace.

He did not prolong it beyond decorum. When he stepped to the microphone, his eyes were misty, his voice throaty at first and there was unmistakable lipstick on his chin and cheeks.

"Fellow-citizens, fellow countrymen—"

He had to pause for the roars of cheers came like an ocean wave that began at the depths, mounted to prodigious height and broke of its own weight with a crash that reverberated into tumult, dying slowly in the distance, echo upon echo. He continued, restraining further demonstrations by his raised hands.

"I am reminded of these moving lines:

> Breathes there the man, with soul so dead,
> Who never to himself hath said,
> This is my own, my native land!

You must believe me when I say that I would not have been away so long—almost a month—if I had not been about our country's business.

"Now I am home—not empty-handed. By grace of the skill and valor of men at arms, I am able to welcome a new neighbor into the community of the Americas. The nation of East Cuba is a small one, but there are those who love it. Thousands of escapees and refugees of Castroism are already its patriots.

"I have in my briefcase bilateral treaties with the fifteen of the nineteen other Latin American nations that have decided never more to put up with Communist incursion. We have shown that we mean business. Another wrong move by Communist Cuba will mean that we liberate another area of the island by allied arms and that we annex it to East Cuba.

"In due time and detail I shall give a formal account of my stewardship to Congress. Meanwhile I am going home for Christmas at Waverly Farm in the historic Valley of the Shenandoah. To all of you who have come to greet me, I can wish no greater happiness than that you return to your homes with the same joy that I return to mine. Good-by."

With his family and the faithful Flynn, Chase was soon in the official limousine behind a flying wedge of motorcycles. Granville and Jim Flynn sat in front with the chauffeur, the President sat in the rear between Cora and Chi Chi. Granville turned around to say: "I was kind of worried, Dad. I 'speck you know the dean has me on probation. I've been hellin' it around a bit with Dwight Lepol and the girls."

"I ought to give you a kick in the pants to straighten you out.

But maybe I'll let you do it for yourself. You're a good boy, son. Just don't talk too much around the Lepols."

"I'll behave, Dad."

Chi Chi sniffed. "I've got a hand-painted picture of Granville wearing his halo."

"No more of that talk," said the President sternly. "Cora, dear, it will be wonderful to have another Christmas at the Farm. Would you feel up to moving into town after that? We must get rid of Juno. My domestic policy demands I live in the White House. You must help, Cora."

Cora did not answer, but buried her face against his shoulder and cried a little. The President chose to believe her tears were only happiness at having him home. They had a jolly dinner, except that Cora seemed more subdued than the occasion warranted. Shortly after the meal she said good night and went to her bedroom, leaving the President in front of the living room fire, regaling son and daughter with anecdotes from aboard the *Pedernales* and among the temperamental Latin diplomats. But the adventures of a father are not of a vintage to intrigue a son for very long. Granville grew restless. He squirmed in his seat on the floor, turning first one side, then the other, then his back upon the cheerful blaze. He took surreptitious peeks under his cuff at his wrist watch, stiffled a few yawns, tried with creditable attention to follow the account of a carrier strike and the far more intricate game of treaty making. The ring of the telephone energized Granville into a headlong dash for that instrument in the hallway, but the reliable Flynn had already answered and was saying:

"No, this is not your fuzzy-wuzzy, and I don't know anything about Doug the D at the Gas Light Club."

"Gimme, man," hissed Granville, snatching the phone away. "Couldn't you be faithful confidant and intimate advisor in some other room for a while?"

Flynn phased away. Somebody, he thought, should have arranged to have the phone off-listed and changed. He sat in the deserted dining room, well within call of the President, and checked his notebook for tomorrow's engagements. The Cabinet had to be greeted, the National Security Council had much to impart, the Congressional leadership would expect a consultation and there were scores of official papers requiring signatures.

Flynn heard the boy return to the sitting room, making elaborate excuses, heard him crash through the front door and soon heard the spurt of a hot motor car leaving the estate.

Jim stole a look into the living room to see that all was well. The President was bending forward with the tips of his fingers resting on his daughter's chair, his face a study of the deepest concern.

"She's telling him," thought Flynn, who had learned the whole story from the Secret Service guards, "that Cora simply doesn't have the stamina to be a President's wife. This is the first crisis of Jeremiah Chase's domestic program. How can he ever run the country if his wife can't tell Juno Lepol that it's time to vacate the White House?"

Only the Adamses, father and son, had kept presidential diaries as frank as Juno's. She never counted upon its being discovered (what female diarist ever does?) and much less upon its use in this history of her own life and times. For all her own venality, the woman never guessed at the cupidity of a son whose high cost of living made him an easy mark for a certain young journalist who took her facts where she found them. On the last few days before Christmas, 1975, Juno Lepol, in her overblown style, wrote several items of interest to the chronicler of this volume:

> *Item:* Granville Chase, whom I have permitted to make a love nest of my sewing room, at least has rewarded my hospitality. Knowing that his father, a disciplinary presence, returns tomorrow from Buenos Aires, Granville has become extraordinarily (even for him) communicative about his family affairs. I think he must have learned more from the Waverly Farm servants than from his sister or from his own observation, but suffice it to say I am possessed of a valuable fact—Cora Chase is emotionally an invalid. I always knew she was shy and nervous, but not to the degree it now appears. Her psychotic sensitivity renders her incapable of First-Lady duties. She would rather die than live at the White House. Granville bubbled something about an overdose of sedation when his mother heard of her husband's elevation to the top office.

Item: Burnbagge brought me today, shortly after I watched Chase's landing at Forrestal, the hitherto useless file titled "Dump Jerry Movement." How hopefully I had compiled all that Federal sleuths could collect on the Chase career! How often I had combed the reports for derogatory evidence in some of his law cases where he defended his robber-baron clients, or where he fought for southern communities to find some loopholes in the statutes that voided their peculiar institutions. All unavailing. How many hotel registers were searched to learn if he kept romantic rendezvous, and what expense was incurred by tax-paid agents of the FBI, IRS, Secret Service and all the others to find a bankcheck that would lead us to the incriminating clue. All the scents were cold. The blameless man is blackmail-proof. Yes, there were those bills he paid for his wife at Dr. Calloway's Nursing Home, Richmond, Virginia, long ago. But nervous breakdowns of wives seemed too commonplace to suggest any political vulnerability. How could I know that Cora had never recovered? That she has been hardly better than a mental out-patient committed to her husband's care?

Item: Oh, dear, the-might-have-beens that taunt us to the last. If my fingerprints hadn't been found on that onionskin ruse, I might dare to run next March in the New Hampshire primary as Senator Maggie Smith did years ago. But Speaker Krebs would expose me. If Operation Icetongs had proved a Bay of Pigs, the Supreme Court might have followed the battle results and ruled the presidential office to be open. If Colonel Duños had welched on his promise to hold free elections—and if he hadn't been overwhelmingly re-elected—there might have been a case of impeachment against Chase. If Martinez hadn't taken his own life, rather than stand trial, there might have been riots to rock the ship of state, and perhaps Young Ike could have answered the Lepol-for-the-People call, the Constitution notwithstanding.

Item: Christmas Eve. Cora writes a note which says that she will pay the long-delayed condolence call upon me this afternoon. Take tea in the Green Room, will she? She implores that I meet with her quite alone. I don't think Cora knows how easy it is to open the White House gates to the rag-tag of the town. Has she forgotten how in Johnson's Administration those slimy beatniks came in with the tourists and pulled a sit-down in the halls? Does she know what dregs of café society Young Ike can round up for me in the dives of the Gas Light clubs? And along Skid Row? I do not ask myself what the profit will be if I send the President's wife into a public fit of the screaming meemies. All I know is that it will hurt Jerry Chase in his softest spot—his heart, his pity, his life-long love of this frail creature who is his wife.

At four o'clock that afternoon of Christmas Eve, a snow-haired lady alighted from a limousine at the rear White House porch, the one fronting on the gardens. It is out of sight of the several public entrances on Pennsylvania Avenue. She had come alone, for that is how one's enemy is best faced. But the symptoms of jangled nerves were evident, even to the avuncular butler who bowed his venerable head and murmured sympathetically:

"Won't you come this way, Mrs. Chase? Madam Lepol is expecting you in the Green Room."

The dumpy little lady thanked him timidly and mounted the graceful stone stairs. One could see that she had somewhat overprepared herself for the encounter. Pallid cheeks had been given the color of courage by too much rouge. The shy, drooping eyes had been shaded to an unbecoming purple by eye-shadow. One could guess that on the unnerving drive from Waverly Farm she had squirmed so much in the lonely back seat that the pretty blue suit, perhaps a little too young for her anyhow, had lost its fit. The skirt was a trifle awry and the coat was buttoned wrong. The white gloves showed from their wrinkles that she had been wringing her hands, and any woman would have known from the frumpish sag of the stockings that the visitor's girdle was out of alignment.

At the far end of the upstairs parlor, she paused in the doorway of the Green Room to clutch for something in her handbag. Out came a balled-up handkerchief and a pair of dark sunglasses. She daubed with the handkerchief at the base of her nose, put on the glasses, nervously removed them and made her entrance where Juno waited.

"My dear Cora," said Juno, not rising from behind the silver service, "Are you well?"

"Why, yes, of course. Why do you ask? Have I changed so much?"

"Only a good friend would notice," said the hostess, giving a hand above the table setting. "If I were on the verge of tears, I'd certainly put on dark glasses. Why don't you?"

"Thank you, Cora." She put them on with trembling fingers. "You are always thoughtful."

"How do you take it?"

"Usually with cream. Today, however, strong, if I may."

"You certainly may." Juno poured. The hot biscuits were passed by the hostess who remarked: "You did say you wished to be alone. I've sent the maid away."

"How considerate, Juno."

The women had their tea and biscuits. It did not take long, and conversation did not flow easily. With a murmur of apology, Juno said she must have the maid take the used cups away. She rang a handbell. There was a lengthy wait. When the double doors came open, the maid admitted what no visitor could have anticipated. It could only be called a rabble of wretchedly clad children, of ill-shaven stew-bums and of squalid old bags of women. Behind this horrid assembly came the White House press with their cameras, microphones, pads and pencils. Juno stood up now.

"Christmas Eve, Cora. Sam always said it was a time of open house."

The startled little lady jumped up so hastily that her glasses fell off and one of the urchins made a grab for them.

"Give those back to Mrs. Chase," said Juno imperiously. "Hand them to her personally."

The visitor seemed to shrink with mortal terror as the wretched brat approached. The camera flickered and the pencils flew to work.

"Hand them to her!" thundered Juno at her stage-trained best. "No! Stand on a chair, you ninny. Place them on Mrs. Chase's face."

"On a chair?" said the tremulous caller. "Not in my house, Juno. Here you are, sonny."

Juno gasped as the caller bent and lifted the stinking boy in her arms. She gave him a warm hug and set him down.

"You may keep the glasses. I don't want them. Have a biscuit. Juno, surely there's more to eat. If ever I invited the multitude to my house, I'd have whole tables loaded with goodies on Christmas Eve. You people hear that? When Cora Chase takes over as First Lady, she won't play dirty tricks like this. Go to the State Dining Room. The maids will bring you chicken and ham from the cellars, and cake and ice cream from the pantry. Tell them I said so. Go on. The maid will lead the way. There's a new mistress of the White House now."

Juno could hardly stand. She had clutched at her chair for support.

"Cora Chase—you're out of your mind. You can't do this to me."

"That's what you thought, didn't you, Juno? Now, then, you press people, I'll tell you what this is all about. I have come to take over the White House."

"Mrs. Chase?" asked a scribe, "do we understand that you are ordering Mrs. Lepol off the premises?"

"You needn't put it as bluntly as that. I give her forty-eight hours to move out. We Chases expect to enjoy Christmas at Waverly Farm. But on the 27th we'll start moving in. I'm sure it won't be necessary to call the paratroopers to move Mrs. Lepol out. That's all for now."

The snow-haired little lady picked up her handbag and left the room. She departed from the White House as she had come, down the stone stairway to the limousine, stopping to shake hands with the attendant butler as she wished him "Merry Christmas."

The family driver bowed as he opened the limousine door.

"Back to the Farm, Miss Chi Chi?" he asked.

Luckily no reporter was close enough to hear him use Cora Chase's daughter's name.

"Please," groaned Chi Chi, "and keep your eyes front. I've got to get out of this damned stuffed girdle and clean my face. It was my finest performance, if I do say so myself."

Chapter Twenty-Two

Jim Flynn, the broken-nosed halfback, was back in his natural element. He hadn't cared for his all-over-the-landscape job of being the President's counsellor and sounding board on every problem that came up. Flynn didn't want any part of shaking the world. He just wanted to be around to report how and why the shaking took place.

In his days as a correspondent Jim passed his news along to editors and readers. As the new White House press secretary, the job was superficially different in that he didn't write for publication, but it was essentially the same in his large concept of journalism—he made it possible for others to write the news, and to do so with all the information he could procure, none of it falsified, none of it slanted, none of it planted and none of it withheld except on the highest level of national security and for that frankly given reason.

The President had promised Flynn this set of criteria, and Flynn had plenty of reason for regarding his own little cubbyhole in the White House west wing to be just as much a citadel of truth as the spacious Oval Office of the President himself. Other presidential press secretaries, he supposed, had absorbed some hero-worship of their bosses, and had been willing to do anything, including the telling or acting out of lies, for the sake of making a good show. But Jim's own relations with Chase were not so much man and master as that of ball-carrier and blocker. Both men had the same purpose, and that was to put points on the scoreboard of truth.

If this was a somewhat simplistic way of looking at his job, Flynn was content to have it so. He was no sophisticate. Chase was his quarterback. He knew how to mix up the plays, when to pass, to punt, to pray, as well as when to grind down the middle of the field on weight and muscle. Flynn had never played pro football. He still believed in a certain amount of rah-rah for the Varsity, and he believed in the whole Code of Play Up, Play Up and Play the Game. So did Chase. Lots of words described the President, but the coverall description in Flynn's mind was: decent.

If Flynn had needed any convincing, which he didn't, the few days at Waverly Farm over the Christmas vacation would have furnished proof positive. The First Family was sitting around after dinner on the night that Chi Chi had returned from the ousting of Juno. Jerry's laughter came in bursts as the daughter did many encores of mimicry in describing the inside details of the encounter. Cora joined in the fun, for her husband had relieved all the pressure upon her by saying she didn't have to move to the White House at all. She could live at the Farm and come and go as she liked. He would commute by helicopter, a mere twelve-minute hop, on whatever nights he could get away from his work. Granville for once seemed resigned to spend an evening at home, and in fact announced that he had a statement to make. The President calmed the gaiety and said:

"Go ahead, son. What's on your mind?"

"Chi Chi thinks she's pretty superior with that Chastity Club of hers," said the boy.

Chi Chi shot back: "You'd never qualify, that's for sure."

"A man's honor and a woman's honor are two different things," declared Granville loftily. "You go ahead and keep your pure, white body in its immaculate condition. A man looks to higher things, doesn't he, Dad?"

"A gentleman should be brave, true, clean and reverent," said

Chase solemnly. "That isn't the whole catechism, but it's the shorthand of it."

"I belong to a secret society, same as Chi Chi does," the boy went on. "I'm a charter member of the Princeton chapter, and I don't want anybody to laugh. We call it the Hatchet Society."

"For chopping up nightclubs?" jeered Chi Chi.

"Dad, I did a terrible thing," said Granville, "and I want to say I'm sorry. I especially want to say it to my mother. I let Mrs. Lepol find out that something went wrong here the night Chi Chi came home from Broadway. I didn't exactly know. I guess she guessed. Anyhow, I let Mrs. Lepol give me lots to drink and put me up in the sewing room. And—I blabbed. I certainly am ashamed of myself, and I'm going to stay away from Pinkie and Cassie and Young Ike and all those rotters—if I can. I'm going to straighten up and fly right—if I can."

He went over and kissed his mother who cried a little as she caressed him.

"Son, I'm proud of you," said the President. "I've always been. You've been a scamp, but you could no more tell a lie than bite your own nose off."

"Hey, kid," said Chi Chi, a little chokey over the family scene. "Don't be so stingy with those kisses. Come over here and give your big sis one."

When brother and sister had embraced, Granville blew his nose a time or two and continued to address the family circle:

"This Hatchet Society has chapters at men's colleges all over the country." He turned back his lapel and showed a little emblem in the shape of an axe head. "You can laugh if you want. We take our name from what George Washington is supposed to have said:

> I chopped down the cherry tree, father.
> I did it with my little hatchet.
> I cannot tell a lie."

"I don't hear anybody laughing, kid," said Chi Chi.

"We don't pretend to be good boys," her brother went on. "Some of us are real hellions, I'm afraid, and our girl friends would never make the CC's. We don't sing and shout about our sins, but it's part of our pledge that we don't give or take any help on exams, and that we play fair in sports and cards, and that we never crawl out from a fix by telling lies."

Flynn was sitting in the dining room, getting a little homework done. He couldn't avoid hearing this conversation and nobody had to tell him that the son and daughter were the kind of young people they were because of the father they had. As for Cora, in any other kind of household than one so truthful and loving, she might have turned into a total nervous wreck. As things were, though she was a semi-invalid, Cora lived a pleasant and enjoyable life despite her frailties. A man like Chase, thought Flynn, could bring qualities to the presidency that might well do for the country what they did within his own family.

At this point, a Secret Service man entered from the pantry and told Flynn that a reporter had driven to the gate and was asking to speak with Mrs. Chase. Flynn went outside to find Eula Breck and her paraphernalia in custody of the security force.

"Turn her loose, boys. Any girl who walks into battle with no more armor than the American flag is bound to be welcome at the President's home. What's on your mind, Eula?"

"Truth," said the Mechanical Maiden. "I've got to give a morning broadcast on the casting out of Juno Lepol. Everybody else is reporting that Cora Chase faced down the goddess of know-it-all. I decided to go to the source and check my facts. That's why I'm here."

"Come in."

Flynn left Eula in the pantry and consulted briefly with the President before ushering her into the living room where Chase stood waiting.

"I'm proud to shake your hand," said the President as they all rose to greet the girl. "I think you've met Mrs. Chase and Chi Chi. This is Granville, my son. Have a seat and have a drink."

"No, thanks," said Eula, "but I'll have a question or two, if I may. Somebody around here put on a superlative performance in the Green Room. I wasn't there. I studied the pictures. I'm not quite convinced.

Flynn said, "Mr. President, you have a perfect right to say—no comment."

Eula turned on a microphone at her belt. "So far as the world knows, it was a personal triumph for Mrs. Chase over Mrs. Lepol. As the story stands, it would make a stupendous publicity image for the incoming Administration. Ever since Eleanor Roosevelt, the people have loved the idea of a forceful and colorful First Lady. More than half the population of the country is female, and women hold a very high percentage of the nation's corporate wealth. Much of President Lepol's strength was in his wife. The Finnigan Clan has its mastermind in a matriarch. It's greatly to your advantage, Mr. President, to claim that your First Lady is a match for any of them.

"All you say is true," nodded Chase. "What's your question?"

"What member of your family went to the Green Room today?"

Chi Chi gave her brother a rough shove. "You and your damned Hatchet Club."

Cora sighed. "If you must know, Miss Breck, I haven't left the Farm all day."

"And I," said Chi Chi, "ought to get an Oscar for that performance. So long as you're such a sleuth, Miss Breck, I hope you'll interview Juno too. I have a hunch she didn't see through my makeup until the big scene when I hugged and kissed that smelly urchin. By then she was too late."

Flynn said: "Satisfied, Eula?"

She thanked them all and went her way. Next day Eula's broadcast completely demolished the popular impression that the country had a First Lady who was a fit mate in dash and cunning for Jeremiah Chase. Instead it became known to the detriment of the Administration's prestige, or at least to the delight of its political opposition, that Cora Chase was pretty much what she seemed to be—a shy recluse who would never take her place among the White House wives who were coadjutors of their husbands, valuable getters of public attention and votes.

Rumors went around that Cora couldn't face the responsibilities of White House hostess-ship. There was also a splurge of gossip about Chi Chi and the sinful life she must lead in show business where she portrayed very immoral heroines, and much more well-founded stories about the escapades of Granville, who seemed to be known by every barkeep and B-girl in the night club circuit.

Flynn thought it was part of his job to worry about the First Family's image, and he did worry until he had a long talk with the President during Christmas week. This talk was the basis of a speech which Flynn made on New Year's Eve before the local chapter of the Sigma Delta Chi fraternity. Since the address set forth an important policy of the new Administration, it was closely noted:

"Gentlemen: I can give it to you from the horse's mouth. The White House press secretary is no longer to be regarded as a press agent. I'm a journalist, not a p.r. man. I know that you who have covered the White House in recent years will take this as a revolutionary announcement. For the first time since Herbert Hoover there will be no promotion of the presidential image.

"Now that peace has broken out, people are beginning to ask if Jerry Chase can live up to all the razmatazz of his first month in office. I want to tell you that he's not trying to live up to himself or to any predecessor.

"The same applies to his family. Mrs. Chase won't be giving any lavish parties, and she won't be out in public oozing charm and sympathy as others in her position have done. Chi Chi will go back to Broadway, and Granville back to college.

"In the past you've heard a lot about managing the news. It's easier in the White House to do that than to do the opposite. Under Roosevelt and Truman there was an unwritten law against direct quotation—that was a form of management. Both Eisenhower's Administration and Kennedy's got caught in public lies—one about the U-2 over Russia, the other about the raid on the Cuban air force prior to the Bay of Pigs. This Administration won't get caught because it won't tell lies. Kennedy used his press conferences as public shows in which he was the star performer, and Johnson used his to make speeches over the reporters' heads to the people at home. We will not perform and will not speechify at press conferences.

"We are going to avoid both management and showmanship. The press conferences will not go out over radio or television, although microphones and cameras are at liberty to record what the President says and how he looks. But our idea is to communicate directly to the news media, and let the news media give the information to the public, with or without comment.

"The President will never decline to answer any questions, except speculative items about the future. He will never give anything but a truthful answer about any event that has already taken place. This puts the responsibility on you to respect the national security. I think you'll find that when you give him the chance, he'll begin every response with a simple yes or no, and then go into some further explanation.

"Now, honesty doesn't make for mystery and glamour, and it may get pretty dull. But tomorrow—the anniversary year '76—will find us a mature country, 200 years old, and the President is going to treat the press and the public in an adult way that befits an adult nation."

Two days later Jim followed the President into the crowded East Room. There was no podium, only a desk and chair against the wall. The President started to take the chair, but changed his mind and sat on the edge of the desk. Flynn stood by his side and said:

"Ladies and gentlemen, the President won't waste time by reading any announcements. He's ready for your questions. We have no time limits and no ground rules. Use your own judgment. Cover as much ground as you like."

Q: Mr. President, this room, as well as the Library of Congress, was proclaimed by Mrs. Lepol as being henceforth named for her husband. Are we, in fact, meeting in the Lepol Memorial Parlor, and is the book depository at Third Street and Independence Avenue, South East, the Lepol Memorial Library?

A: I'm sorry to contradict a lady, but—No.

Q: In general, what do you think about renaming national sites for departed Presidents in a time of emotion over their deaths?

A: I'm against it. A decent, thoughtful period should pass. I'm still not sure that Cape Canaveral and Idlewild Airport should be called by their adoptive names.

Q: On somewhat the same subject, do you believe the presidency has been—or is becoming—a prize for family dynasties?

A: Yes. I believe that the Constitution wisely forbids the youthful sons of Presidents to follow their fathers into office.

Q: What about a brother-act, Mr. President? It's been said that Mrs. Nellie Finnigan has an ambition to place Senator Finnigan, Governor Finnigan and Mayor Finnigan in the White House in that order.

A: Something has gone wrong with American democracy when the presidency is up for grabs by ambitious family groups. We have had Adamses and Harrisons and Roosevelts in the White House, but never in direct or very close succession. I do not regard these as examples of royal families on the make. But I'm suspicious when wealthy fathers and mothers set out to capture the presidency for their sons. It's not the American way.

Q: Mr. President, won't these remarks be taken personally by Mrs. Finnigan and Mrs. Lepol?

A: Yes. I wouldn't make the remarks if I didn't have the Finnigans and Lepols in mind.

Q: Sir, do you have a choice for your running mate in the next election?

A: No. Except that it won't be General Rigor. I chose a military man as a one-year stand-in. That's the only way military men ought to get into politics—on a short, limited, emergency basis.

Q: Mr. President, off politics into diplomacy, it used to be said that the two great nuclear powers would get into war through miscalculation. President Kennedy laid great stress on this point in his talks with Khrushchev. Do you feel there is any danger of miscalculations on the part of yourself and Marshal Markov?

A: No, I do not. I told Marshal Markov that I regarded freedom as more important than peace. I'm sure he had reason to understand me. As for my miscalculating his intentions, I think it's unlikely. My attitude toward all Communists is to expect them to behave like Communists, and to act accordingly.

Q: Mr. President, again changing the subject, have you picked a slogan for your Administration?

A: Try that one again.

Q: Well, Theodore Roosevelt had his Square Deal, Wilson had his New Freedom, Franklin Roosevelt had his New Deal, Truman had his Fair Deal, Kennedy had his New Frontier, Johnson had his Great Society, Lepol had his New Atlantis. What's your slogan?

A: Mr. Borton, you've forced me to think. . . . I hadn't contemplated a sloganized Administration. At the risk of having my remarks misconstrued as puerile and lacking in sophistication, I'd say I'm calling upon the people for a renewed oath of allegiance, such as most of us gave in our childhood: "I pledge allegiance to the flag, and to the republic for which it stands: one nation under God, indivisible, with liberty and justice for all."

Q: Sir, when you announced undeclared war for the purpose of Operation Icetongs, the Senate and House instantly voted their moral support, along with a bill titled Billions for Defense. Why haven't you signed it?

A: Because I intend to veto that bill. My message will be delivered in due time.

Q: Can you tell us what the veto message will say?

A: Yes, Mr. Obermeister, it will say that Billions for Defense is a misnomer. The bill provides billions for the pork barrel. It establishes a number of military bases and facilities of no military necessity whatever. I consider it a mercenary measure to pour federal money into states and congressional districts so that senators and congressmen can take credit for their service in Washington. When senators and congressmen do this, they are little better than bagmen. When a community elects and reelects such legislators, it is hiring procurers and not statesmen.

Q: Aren't you setting up a feud with Capitol Hill in using such forthright language, Mr. President?

A: Perhaps. But I believe that frankness is indicated. Private enterprise brings prosperity. Public enterprise brings higher taxes and debt. Candidates who boast, "I can do more for Massachusetts," are saying in effect, "I can do the federal government for more."

Q: Mr. President, you have talked of reducing the size of the federal establishment. Do you have any specifics?

A: Yes. When I address Congress later this month on the State of the Union, I shall announce several executive actions. One will issue a moratorium on federal hiring. For a full year, this Administration will not hire any federal employees to replace those who die or retire. We will also offer bonuses to employees who care to retire early. If our extrapolation statistics hold, this will reduce the government payroll by 100,000 persons and by $800,000 in the first year. We won't fire, but neither will we hire.

Q: Doesn't this plan require congressional approval?

A: There is no law that forces the executive department to spend.

Q: Any other economies, Mr. President?

A: Yes. I have in mind a major consolidation of executive departments. For example, I shall appoint a single cabinet officer to preside over the Departments of Agriculture and Interior. In effect, these departments will be combined. Their overlapping functions will be reduced.

Q: Any other consolidations, sir?

A: Yes. The Departments of Labor and Commerce will be merged, with a single secretary in charge. The Federal Bureau of Investigation will be merged with the Central Intelligence Agency. That is only a beginning. We are going to introduce a Spartan regime into the federal establishment.

Q: Sir, won't the Senate, which has the duty of confirming Cabinet officers, feel that it is being deprived of a prerogative?

A: Very likely. It can't be helped.

Q: Mr. President, do you recall that in 1868 President Andrew Johnson was impeached and nearly dismissed from office for something of the sort?

A: I recall that Andy Johnson was nearly thrown out of office for trying to do his duty. I also recall that he won. If called upon to fight an impeachment, I would also expect to win.

Press: Thank, you, Mr. Pres—

Q: Sir?

A: You have another question, Mr. Obermeister?

Q: I'm afraid it's speculative, sir, but I'd like to try. You said you would fight and win against impeachment proceedings, which are most unlikely, considering the consensus you've established.

Where do you expect your opposition to come from—from Democrats, from Republicans, from Communists, perhaps?

A: As you say, Mr. Obermeister, that's very speculative. I expect that Democrats will support me some of the time and Republicans will support me most of the time, but I'd feel mortified if such Communists as there are in the country support me any of the time.

Press: THANK YOU, Mr. President.

Upon this familiar signal, the press conference ended, and reporters streamed out of the East Room. Phil found himself with Eula and Borton. The latter sneered.

"What a fool question you asked, Obermeister. Don't you know there aren't any more Communists in America? It was sheer McCarthyism even to bring the subject up."

"Speak for yourself, Calvin," said Phil shortly. "Hi, Eula, what are you doing tonight?"

"Hello, Phil. I hope you're asking me for a date, but I'm driving to Albany to take a fix on Mrs. Finnigan. From there I'm off on a cross-country trip to test the Zeitgeist."

"The what?" In the shuffle and chatter of reporters he'd missed the word. She repeated it more loudly. "The spirit of the times! Are the American people really ready for—what'll we call it? —Mr. Chase's New Allegiance? That'll make quite a yarn, Eula."

"Coast to coast interviews," said the girl. "Like to come along?"

They paused under the tall Ionic columns of the White House portico.

"I would, Eula. I can't. That last question of mine wasn't as dumb as Borton seems to think. There're bound to be some Communists in the woodwork, and I'd like to find out what they're doing these days."

Borton had heard his name mentioned and turned to look at the other two.

"The imbecilic young!" he pronounced scathingly, and then strode on alone toward Pennsylvania Avenue.

Chapter Twenty-Three

Back in his snug living quarters in Foggy Bottom, Obermeister set up his typewriter on the small dining room table and tried for a column. He wrote:

The legend is that St. Patrick drove all the snakes out of Ireland, and nobody has ever disputed it. But who was it that drove all the Communists out of the United States of America?

It is unclear from an answer during his press conference this week whether Mr. Chase believes that Communists still exist in our land. The liberal dogma is, of course, that they do not. If I understand the liberal thesis, it is that domestic Reds vanished at or about the time that Senator Joe McCarthy was censured and later hounded to an early death by ridicule and despair. Joe hadn't found any real Commies, had he? Ergo, there were none.

By a strong act of wish fulfillment in the 1950's, the Liberal Establishment not only concurred in the proposition that domestic Communism existed solely in McCarthy's mind, but took the viewpoint that whoever had destroyed McCarthy had also exorcised the Red figments of Joe's fevered imagination. From this postulate, it was logical to reach the next assumption—namely that whoever was chiefly responsible for getting rid of the senator from Wisconsin had also pulled a St. Patrick—had cleansed the land of Communist reptiles.

The accredited historians, however, have never fixed upon a single extirpator. Some gave the credits to a fusty old gentleman, Senator Ralph Flanders, who had made a dirty speech on homosexuality which allegedly was handed him by a respectable lobby called Committee for

> an Effective Congress. Others awarded the accolade to another rather ineffectual nonenity, Senator Arthur Watkins, who presided at the hearing which recommended the censure. Later, when the search for a hero became intense, a worshipful biographer of Lyndon B. Johnson, William S. White, employed the hindsight of panegyric to proclaim that the 36th President, when a Senate leader, had engineered McCarthy's downfall through secret agreements, secretly arrived at in the Senate cloakrooms.
>
> By the 1970's all these claims had become dormant, but the general idea remains—there is no such thing as domestic Communism. This situation offers real difficulties because I plan one or more off-beat columns with the working title: "What do our Communists think of the New Allegiance?"

Phil stopped writing at this point—as well he might. He had painted himself into a corner. The column, so far as it went, was no good. It was desultory rambling with a too-fancy beginning, not much of a middle and no end in sight. Phil did the only thing he could do, which was to wad up the sheet and throw it into the empty fireplace.

After that, as columnists in this sort of fix sometimes behave, Phil allowed both his feet and mind to wander. He went upstairs and sat cross-legged on his bed, looking at the dazzling Bachrach portrait of the honey-haired Eula in her Inaugural Ball evening gown. She had given it to him as a Christmas present and signed it: "Affectionately, your colleague and competitor, Eula."

His critical inspection of the picture soon set off another train of thought. He admired both gift and giver, but he'd never been able to overcome some difficulties in making love to Eula. In the first place, they'd been constantly on the move since Thanksgiving, running down stories on separate beats, and finding few opportunities for dates. Then, despite the pictorial proof that she did sometimes wear pretty clothes and look like a woman of romance, Phil seldom encountered Eula when she wasn't encased in the gadgetry of her trade. It was difficult to hug a girl who was literally encrusted with bits of glass and steel. She did shed her prickly paraphernalia when they were together in her apartment at Laker's Acres, but those hanky-panky buttons on every wall were not conducive to passionate approaches. On the several occasions when she came to his place, or when they strolled along the Potomac waterfront, that damned dog—the protective Bosco—was always there as an abominable chaperone.

Phil reached for the phone and dialed her number.

"Say, darling, won't you have time for dinner before you leave?"

"Oh, Phil, I've made my sandwiches and I'm practically out the door. One of my editors has a hunch that the Finnigans are making contact with the Cabinet officers whom Chase fired, and I've got to snoop something out. Do you have any fast reactions on the press conference?"

"Only that the President was in great form."

"I'm not so sure that he didn't lead with his chin," said Eula. "Goldwater was the last politico who promised to cut down the size of government, and look what happened."

"Chase is different, Eula."

"Yes, but is the American public any different? Well, I won't know till I've been to California and back to test the Zeitgeist. Good-by, now."

Phil hung up in something of a huff. Eula was a liberal at heart. Could there ever be a true marriage of minds between left and right? To ask that was a double question: could he and Eula ever be fully in love, and could America itself ever resolve its ideological differences and become a contented, united country? Jerry Chase had found a fleeting consensus by his dashing leadership, but he'd already risked it by threatening to cut off the modern spoils of war—the huge federal spendings on unnecessary military contracts.

Phil sat and pondered. The President might find both Democrats and Republicans against him if he persisted. Many members of House and Senate stayed in office by preaching economies, but by practicing the ancient rites of log-rolling for expenditures in their own states and districts. Maybe Chase, as a Republican President, could count on GOP support, but the Democratic majorities in Congress weren't going to stand still for losing their pelf. The liberals always regarded themselves as the first beneficiaries of a giveaway government.

Phil had let his mind take him far from the column he'd hoped to turn out tonight. Never mind! He could always write something early in the morning, and put it on the wire to his syndicate. Right now, sex and ideology looked at him from the saucy, green eyes of Eula's portrait, and the effect was disturbing. He went below, put on a jacket and went out to the patio under the cold, starry night that had fallen.

Eula still lingered in his thoughts. He remembered she'd been here in this garden when they did joint research on a story that related to domestic Communism. Carlos Martinez, while denying his own Communism, had mentioned that fellow Braddock . . .

"Braddock!" Phil ejaculated. "Why didn't I think of that name before? Martinez as good as called Braddock a party worker. Let's see—the papers said Braddock went back to New York. But the D.C. police knew that Braddock and Martinez had stayed in a permanently rented suite at the Statler Hilton, and it wouldn't be hard to get the number of it."

The suite was numbered West 999, and its permanent tenant of record was a tax-free foundation called Lobby for a Lovable World. This much Obermeister ascertained by phone from an obliging police lieutenant at Central Headquarters. Well—what next? By now it was nearly eight o'clock. What with making a false start on his column, racking his brains for a better idea, talking to Eula and poking around, he'd forgotten to eat and was feeling dispirited as well. First thing tomorrow he'd go to the Hill and see if the Lobby for a Lovable World was registered for lobbying and, if so, who its officers were. Meanwhile, the thought of opening cans in the kitchen was distasteful and he knew that all his married friends at the National Press Club would have finished their drinks and card game and gone home by now.

With nothing better on his mind, Phil took a cab for the Statler Hilton and went up to the ninth floor, carried there by the sheer inertia which moves a journalistic body toward any object of interest or curiosity. As he turned into the 9th corridor, West, he saw the door of Room W-999 swing open and emit a well-shaped, chiffon-bearing figure on black spiked heels. She wore neither hat nor coat, indicating that she couldn't be going very far, and the bright little face under a bouncy supply of jetty hair looked as lonesome as Phil was feeling. He let her come toward him and said:

"I was taking a chance on finding Mr. Braddock in his suite."

"You lost," the girl said. "No Mr. Braddock. Nobody else. Just me. I've had to work late. I've got to work some more, but I'm famished."

The common ground of hunger established, Phil introduced himself and invited her for dinner at the hotel. She introduced herself and accepted.

"Osa Lubov?" Phil repeated her name in the self-service elevator. "That's the Russian word for love."

"Obermeister—that's a name in newspapers. I have to buy the late editions."

In the lobby he purchased for her the *Standard*, the *Examiner* and the *Express* and carried them to the dining room. They had cocktails and steak, red table wine, and green mint for a finisher. By this time Phil was well informed about Osa Lubov, why she was working alone in the suite and why she needed the newspapers. He suggested that an extra pair of hands would make the work lighter. Why not allow him to return upstairs and help out for the evening.

Loneliness is the best aperitif for new friendships. Osa was a language major at George Washington University. Her parents worked as clerks in the Russian Embassy and her heart had been left behind her in Minsk. For the girl this tryst was nothing but a lark. For Phil, who missed Eula, who believed that a journalist could get lucky just by being at or near places of interest, the evening provided solace and the opportunity to learn something from her and from Braddock's files. Yes, there still were native Communists in the United States.

Next morning over his typewriter, Phil postponed the remorse which he knew would come for being untrue to Eula. He concentrated on the story he'd found. He didn't know where it would take him, but he knew he was on his way into areas that had been unexposed for many years.

He fished the rumpled page out of the fireplace and slightly revised what he'd written yesterday. Then he added the ending that had been missing till his adventure with Osa:

> Communists, once called by J. Edgar Hoover, the "masters of deceit," have now become the hidden pastmasters of political disruption. You will seldom find them brazenly taking 5th Amendment dodges before Congressional committees, or bothering very much to heist secret formulas and designs of nuclear constructions. They may have run out of mischief to make in the race movement, where they once were infiltrated, and they no longer have much credence as organizers of the campus teach-ins which once threatened to subvert the war effort in Vietnam.
>
> But the Communists have not folded their tents as is commonly assumed. Their ambitions have not lessened, far from it, but have mounted to the topmost level of intrigue. From the moment of Samuel Lepol's death, and increasing with the tempo of President Chase's pace to reform this country's foreign and domestic policy, the homegrown Communists have been at work on a special project. Their purpose is to get Mr. Chase out of office as quickly as possible.
>
> Since no news story about Communism is much good without names in it, and since a writer ought to holler Red when he sees Red, let us go no further in this anonymous vein. One of the pro-Communist leaders in a cabal to unseat President Chase is the Honorable Seth Phillipson, whom Mr. Chase himself unseated as Secretary of State.

Chapter Twenty-Four

Whether or not this provocative Obermeister column would stand up to the attacks it was destined to bring, the Honorable Seth Phillipson could credibly be numbered among those few Americans who were dismayed at the victory of the Battle of the Caribbean.

He had not waited even that long into the Chase Administration to express his displeasure with the train of events. On the afternoon which saw the nomination of General Rigor and the simultaneous removal of all the Lepol Cabinet officers, Phillipson went straight from the Joint Session to the State Department.

In what appeared to be precipitous haste, he called for his personal papers to be brought him from the files and safes, and packing these into two outsized dispatch cases, quit town by private limousine. He left word for his agents to close and dispose of his gabled house at Oxon Hill, and for the next several weeks he was publicly known to be sequestered with his invalid wife at his other home at Surrey-by-the-Hudson, a gloomy heap of granite called Maison de la Paix.

Not publicly noted in those stirring days, when general attention was focused upon Washington, was the arrival one afternoon at Maison de la Paix of a bug-like compact car from which there alighted a spritely but elderly lady who was so well bundled in an expensive overcoat as to be difficult to recognize. But when she doffed that fleece-lined covering and the slouch-felt hat, handing them to the butler inside the former Secretary's hall, she stood there in a neat gray dress with a dark rose at her shoulder and did not need to identify herself to the servant.

"I wish to see Mr. Phillipson."

"Yes, madam. He's expecting you, Mrs. Finnigan."

Ushered into the tall, sumptuous, oaken library, Nellie Finnigan glanced appraisingly at the full-length portrait of the owner of this house, which occupied one of the wall panels. He had been younger when the picture was painted, but the resemblance was perfect. Very tall, very thin, very pale, Phillipson had been all of his life. The gentle face had a curving nose and the softest eyes likely to be seen in a man, and this ensemble had a lot to do with the acceptance he had received by those who had occasion to describe him. Nearly always, the editorialists or the chairmen of committees or the toastmasters at banquets would feel moved to refer to Phillipson as "that gentle man of peace." The dove-like motif of beak and eyes almost demanded this sort of apostrophe, and the famous diplomat's long career attested to it.

"The gentleness is there," murmured the shrewd old woman, "but the guilt is there too. How many of the descendants and beneficiaries of the old buccaneers have that same look about them, and spend their lives trying to rise above their backgrounds! Right here in New York State, the son of a ripsnorting old railroad baron has been governor and been one of those globetrotting peace-mongers—Harriman was practically midwife to the Moscow Treaty for the Nuclear Test Ban. And the grandson of a petroleum-smeller, he's been a bleeding-heart governor too, and would mighty well have liked to be a peace-on-earth President like Sam Lepol. My boy Andy's the governor now, and he wouldn't be if I hadn't made my bundle at manufacturing those gadgets for the Kennedy-Johnson Space programs. Andy can act mighty pious—a man's almost got to if he plays for the main chance in politics these days. But I hope my boys ain't ashamed of how I made us a fortune when I'm gone."

Seth Phillipson, she reflected, was probably seething inside with double guilt. He'd not only inherited oil money that his forebears had pirated all over the Middle East, but he'd taken the economic precaution to marry a Pittsburgh steel woman who was some relation to the Krupp family. Seth's portrait, done in Germany between the wars, actually had a haughty look. Counteracting the face's gentleness, an iron-gray military cloak rested upon the shoulders, a medallion that looked like an iron cross was suspended about the neck over the dress shirt, and one hand that rested lightly on a table fingered an object that resembled a mace.

"What's it with these soft, finger-itchy fellers?" ruminated Ma. "They ain't much like the horny-handed old political bosses and robber barons of our granddads' days. The guilty feeling must make men like Phillipson yearn to be forgiven and to be loved, and yet the yen for power—by jiminy, it's in 'em. It must be they understand that you can't whack people around as it used to be done. Things are such these days that the old dream of strong men to conquer the world can't come true by powder 'n shot. Pshaw, they'd blow terra firma sky high if they went traipsing around like Napoleon and Bismarck. So there's got to be 'nother way to do the same thing. You conquer people with kindness, and you rule 'em by committees, but it could come to the same end. I don't care for this Phillipson kind. I don't fancy doing business with his sort. But there's a law of life that don't often get written down in the books. It's the ole law of Got To. Jerry Chase was following it when he buddied up with that peacock dictator in El Salvador. And for a while, I've got to buddy up with Phillipson. It could be a way to throw Jerry Chase out of there, and make my Andy the President next year."

She was seated on a brocade sofa when Phillipson entered. She let him do one of those European heel-clicks that he had learned around the chancelleries and she said:

"Mr. Secretary, it stands to reason you're mighty peeved to be flung out of office by that bourbon-drinking, war-mongering, dictator-coddling evil ole Southerner."

"I'm sorry, Mrs. Finnigan, that my dear wife can't appear. You know her sad condition."

"I hear she's not drawn a healthy breath for thirty years. If it was me I'd get out of bed and die with my girdle on, but everybody to his choice, as the old lady said when she kissed the cat."

Phillipson smiled wanly.

"Jeremiah Chase is a bull in a china closet. I know of no victory since the one at Asculum by Pyrrhus to compare with the mad venture of Operation Ice Tongs. I have issued just that statement to the Associated Press."

"I'll come to the point, Mr. Secretary. How'd you like to resume your rudely interrupted career?"

"As head of the State Department?"

"You can have the job back if my Andy beats Jerry in November. You can be Secretary of Peace."

"Mrs. Finnigan, I don't know that I would choose your terminology. However, if you mean that I would return to my life's work of solidifying world relations—"

"That's good enough," said Ma. "You mark my words—Jerry's riding for a fall. I don't know how, and I don't know when, but he'll come a cropper because he just isn't in what those fool Republicans still call the mainstream of American thought. Jerry just plain don't give a hoot for what's in the hearts of the Great Unwashed. People want their bread buttered and their beer chilled—that's domestic policy. They want something they can call peace—though it don't exist and never will. But that's foreign policy, Mr. Secretary—and it's your particular dish of tea."

"What do you want of me, Mrs. Finnigan?"

"I want the same as you want, mister. I want to cut down Jerry Chase. Got any idees?"

The tall man perched like a crane as he took his seat on the edge of a gilded chair. He knotted his long fingers and produced a bony crackle.

"There are ways to begin," he nodded to his visitor. "Mind you, I am not driven by personal ambition—"

"No, of course not."

"I seek only to put a spoke in the wheel of his war chariot."

"Yes, indeedy."

"I am in need of rest. I leave for Yalta tomorrow, to vacation by the Black Sea. I shall be going as a private citizen, of course, but if I am fortunate enough to have an informal conference with Marshal Markov, you may be sure I shall plead for peace. When I return, you and I must talk again."

"Very well," said Nellie Finnigan. "I'm driving over to Albany to stay a while with Governor Andy, and I'll tell him what we've said. But, Mr. Secretary, I've got one question to ask you."

"Very well."

"Are you a Communist?"

Never did the gentle smile seem more benevolent, and the dove-like sweetness of the beaked-face so forebearing as when Phillipson received this question. It had been a familiar one to him throughout his career. He had been asked it by hecklers at open meetings, by letter-writers of such outlandish groups as the Daughters of the American Revolution, the American Legion, the Free Society Association and the Birch Society, as well as by senators before whom he went for confirmation to the many appointive offices he had held. His reply was always courteous and explicit as it was now to Mrs. Finnigan.

"No, ma'am, I am not now and have never been a member of the Communist party."

This wasn't exactly what Ma Finnigan had asked him. She hadn't been around so long without knowing that there was hardly such a thing as a card-carrying Communist party member any longer. But to be a Communist could be to adhere to the party without belonging to it, to support its fronts with contributions and to back its political purposes with influence as well as money. To be a Communist might be to be so liberal as to be a leftist, and so much a leftist as to be in favor of making America over into a socialist state with pacifist tendencies that would not resist the loss of its sovereignty.

Nellie Finnigan didn't have—and seemingly nobody ever had had—documentary material to prove anything like this about Seth Phillipson. Without the proof in hand, there was no point asking further questions, for they would only put the questioner in the position of being a latter-day McCarthyite. Besides all that, in

Nellie's case, she was a practical politician. Phillipson could be useful to her in overthrowing Jerry Chase, and now that she'd satisfied her conscience by asking the question, she didn't feel inclined to antagonize the man.

"I'm very glad to have your answer," she said, rising from the sofa and giving her hand. "I'll pass it on to the Governor. You understand how careful we must be. If somebody should—" she paused.

"You were saying, ma'am?"

"If somebody should ever get the goods on you," resumed the old lady firmly, "there would be pluperfect hell to pay for anybody in politics who was associated with you."

His pale eyes seemed to flicker, and she thought their glance had gone involuntarily and barely perceptibly toward the portrait of himself on the wall. She was accustomed to noticing these subconscious giveaway reactions in persons who had something to hide. Why had his eye muscles flickered spasmodically toward the portrait? Nellie formed a quick opinion, but tried to conceal it by giving her farewell a little extra exuberance.

"Now, you have a good trip and a good rest, Mr. Secretary. Happy landings and all that. Toodle-oo."

"Good-by, Mrs. Finnigan."

When she had gone Phillipson closed and locked the library door. He didn't trust the servants, although he'd had them for years and caused their backgrounds and associations to be periodically checked by Braddock, who was useful for that sort of thing. The butler, the cook, the two downstairs maids, the upstairs maid and the practical nurse who looked after his wife were all immigrants with relatives behind the Iron Curtain. They had good jobs and light duties, since he was rarely in residence at Maison de la Paix, and poor Pauline never left her room any more. Just the same, it paid to be suspicious of everybody these days, and he didn't want anybody to see what he was going to do.

"That old woman is smart as a fox," he was thinking. "She caught me stealing a look over there. She must have seen a play or a movie where there's a wall-safe behind a portrait, and she thinks that's where I've got my papers stashed away—and she's right."

He moved to the ornate mantlepiece, pressed a button in its inlay and watched the splendid portrait swing on its hinges. A moment later he had twirled the dial on a safe-deposit lock and, extending his long arm into the deep recess within the wall, Phillipson brought forth the over-sized dispatch cases which he had brought from the State Department.

He carried the cases to a table, opened them and laid their contents before him for inspection. They represented exactly what Nellie had meant when she said "the goods." There was a great deal of correspondence with Braddock about the activities of the National Committee on Economics and Mobilization (NECKEM) which supplied funds and organization for sit-down strikes, campus teach-ins, racial disturbances as well as legal defense expenditures for operatives who fell into trouble with the law. There was a batch of letters concerning the activities of the Lobby for a Lovable World. This outfit went in for periodic ban-the-bomb demonstrations, and was particularly active in supporting the campaigns of senators and congressmen who voted for unilateral disarmament measures, as well as for measures like the Billions for Defense Bill which sapped the American economy by maintaining obsolete military facilities and by constructing new camps, bases, laboratories and test sites which were of no use whatever for modern war.

There were letters on plain stationery, in code, from members of the Russian and Red Chinese embassies whose duties were to keep him informed about possible concessions that would lead to fruitful negotiations. There were miscellaneous memoranda that related to the subsidizing of authors and book reviewers with the correct slant on world affairs, and a typed list of organizations to which he had contributed enough money to have a say in their policies to some extent. These included: the American Civil Liberties Union, the Congress of Racial Equality, the League for Soviet-American Friendship, the American Nazi Party and Americans For Democratic Action. Two yellow envelopes bound with elastic bands contained canceled checks from a blind bank account, and a small envelope contained a doorkey that would admit him to Room West 999 at the Statler Hilton where he sometimes made discreet visits to consult with Braddock and other functionaries of these groups.

Having assured himself that the papers were in order and had not been tampered with, Phillipson replaced them in the dispatch cases, let himself out of the library and went up the broad, poorly lighted staircase to his wife's room. As he anticipated from the time of evening, which was suppertime for the servant staff, poor Pauline was alone. He entered the high-ceiled, heavily-draped room with his eyes averted from the skeletonized, wrinkled, yellow-skinned figure on the divan.

He could scarcely bear to look at Pauline any longer. Forty years ago she had been a shy, slender heiress with all the advantages of expensive education, and not inconsiderable charm.

Fortune, at Pauline's birth, seemed to have upended the cornucopia of blessings and poured them over her, but the shower of material and personal advantages had one effect that was not good. She had a craving which is universal in kindly, normal girls. She wanted to be loved, but because this desire was so great, so was the anxiety that made up the other side of the coin.

The young Pauline feared that men would court and flatter her for her wealth and, if not for that alone, then for her deliciously soft and lovely body. She developed, as her psychiatrists cautioned her, an obsession for the ideal husband, one who was not likely to be found. Despite these warnings, Pauline dawdled through her youth, turning down a number of imperfect admirers, none of whom had as many millions as she did, and many of whom were undisguisedly passionate. Not till she was thirty, and becoming a little desperate, did she meet Seth Phillipson. He could match her wealth, million for million, and his gentle detachment, his highly trained diplomatic reserve, his deep concern for the fate of the world, dispelled any suspicion of passion.

They were married at a hunt club outside of Pittsburgh (Seth, a professed atheist, was not admissible to any church) in a six-digit saturnalia of imported caterage with entertainment by several famous orchestras and the entire cast of a Broadway musical comedy. Pauline didn't truly care for pomp and display, but she had so many friends, and had been bridesmaid so many times, and had waited so long, that her parents insisted upon an unforgettable gala, to which Pauline consented.

It was five years before she began to understand the man she had married. His outward calm, his savoir-faire and cool efficiency in all things were a complete disguise of the inner person. She had thought him as hungry for love as herself, and so he was—but the kind of love he craved was public adulation and forgiveness. He wanted to be known as a statesman-savior and wanted to wear the fame it brought him as a mantle of martyrhood. For people to say of him: "How arduously Seth Phillipson has labored to bring peace upon earth, how graciously he has put aside the temptations to be idly wealthy and to be a collector of art treasures or of mistresses, how bravely he has borne the stupidities of other men whose passions and ambitions would take every generation through the hellfires of war"—that was his heart's desire.

It was another five years before Pauline came to see in this seemingly passive man the same lust for power and might that had come to Pittsburgh from the Ruhr with her Krupp forebears, and had made international merchants of death out of mere steel mongers. Seth wanted to rule as much as they did, but to rule from a different power base. There must be a World Government, himself as its Grey Eminence, before there could be world peace, and before there could be Universalism there must be a total absence of nationalism.

After the first ten years of marriage, Pauline realized that the vast struggle in Europe between nationalism and Communism, passing in 1945 from hot war to cold, was taking place on a minor scale inside her own household. Seth had subdued and occupied her personality, much as Stalin had overcome and denationalized the ancient peoples and cultures of Eastern Europe. She had traveled with Seth many times to Moscow for his consultations at the Kremlin in the interest of coexistence, and had been with him in Warsaw and Prague, in Bucharest and Sophia, where he met with the trained proconsuls of world Communism who reigned in those capitals. In the faces of the people of the satellite states, she began to see her own face—that of the personalized captive who was being conditioned like a Pavlovian dog to accept the slavery as something that was imposed by a wise and benevolent system, and even to love the slavemaster.

For she did love Seth—he had not asked or earned her affection, but had commanded it out of her enslavement. She knew, whenever he entered the bedroom with his dispatch cases, that he loathed to look at her wrinkled, feeble ugliness, but her own glance followed him with canine adoration as he went to the sliding door of her clothes closet and pushed it open. In the days of long ago that closet had stood like an inanimate fashion parade—gowns so wonderfully wrought, fabrics so skillfully blended in vivid and subtle colors, so daringly designed to glorify her young body that they seemed indeed to be many incarnations of herself as she had appeared at many brilliant parties.

But no gowns hung in that moth-proof, moisture-proof treasury now. For fully twenty-five years of her forty-year marriage, she had had no need for clothing beyond the negligees in which she sat all day and the hospital shirt in which she slept at night. She saw Seth examine the closet shelf where her gay hats used to await her daily whim, and saw him place the cases there and push them back out of sight before he closed the sliding door.

"My dear," he said, "it is time for our sherry."

"I don't care for any tonight, Seth. Who was your visitor?"

As was typical of his mastership over her, he smilingly ignored both her statement and her question. From a wall cabinet he brought a decanter and two glasses, filled them and handed her one as he pulled a chair close to her divan, smiling gently still, yet still not looking into her pathetically worshipful face.

"I leave tomorrow aboard the S.S. *Cavour,*" he said. "It is nuclear-powered, and I wish it weren't. Even the leisurely Italian Lines try to set new transatlantic speed records. From Athens I make it in a short flight to Yalta."

"I think you had a lady visitor," Pauline said coquettishly, for she knew he liked being teased about his imaginary conquests. "I managed to stand up for a peek out the window, and I saw her—a very shapely young thing in slacks, accompanied by a big dog."

"There now," he patted her thin, limp, knuckly hand. "Those hallucinations. They're part of your illness. My caller was a little old lady who left the house in a heavy overcoat."

Pauline started to speak again. She was certain of what she'd seen from the window. But Seth raised a long, admonishing forefinger, and no longer was Pauline certain about the witness of her eyes. If Seth said the female figure was old instead of young, bundled in a shapeless coat instead of in weather-proof slacks, and stepping lightly with her police dog toward the garage, then Seth was undoubtedly right and the whole thing was hallucinatory.

They drank their wine, and he parted with a kiss upon her forehead. All unaware that Eula Breck had electronically eavesdropped on his conversation with Nellie Finnigan, and gone to the garage to bug his limousine, Phillipson waited in the library until the butler sounded the muted Chinese gong for dinner. He dined alone and next morning entered the limousine, which appeared on schedule at the door of Maison de la Paix. The driver was a trusted servant of Polish extraction, and the enormously obese passenger in the back seat was Braddock.

"I'm glad we've got this brief time to consult," said Phillipson. "I dread to turn on the radio or open a newspaper. Everywhere I must read another triumph for Jerry Chase. How will it end? He's named a dangerous Vice President, signed a treaty of aggression, won a two-day war and has returned amid the plaudits of his countrymen. Meanwhile you've carelessly allowed Martinez to commit suicide, but not before he'd practically admitted to that damned Obermeister and that damned Breck woman that Lepol's death was an accident. We should have bribed the American Nazi Party to kill Martinez if the law wasn't going to execute him. Things have gone from bad to worse, Braddock."

"Yes, sir. I know it seems that way. I've arranged for a girl from the Russian embassy to make a digest of every news story about President Chase and to keep you informed by radiogram on shipboard and in Yalta. The reason I'm doing this is that I'm sure Chase can't keep on being lucky. He'll begin to make mistakes. He'll slip. When he tumbles, he'll have a long way to fall."

"You're more optimistic than I am, Braddock."

"Wait till Chase has to deal with domestic issues, Mr. Secretary. Wait till his honeymoon with Congress runs out. Wait till he offends some of the vested interests. His popularity will drop like the bottom falling out of a barrel."

"Will it? I hope so. What then, Braddock?"

"Why, sir," grinned the fat man, "I fully believe that certain Democrats named Finnigan will redouble their efforts to tear him down so that he can be beaten this year. I wouldn't be at all surprised if some of our friends arranged a protest march on Washington. I should say it's entirely within possibility that a nationwide transportation strike could be arranged through the Teamsters. They have been ready for new leadership ever since Jimmie Hoffa retired, and leadership is our business, if I may say so, Mr. Secretary. Our purpose is to try for impeachment proceedings, of course."

The men continued their talk until within a few blocks of the Italian Line pier. Then, at a stoplight, Braddock stepped from the limousine and Phillipson went on alone. The men often met, but rarely were they seen together.

On the five-day nuclear-speeded voyage to Athens aboard the *Cavour,* Phillipson received daily summaries of the President's progress in popularity.

After the flight from Athens, Phillipson took up residence at a dacha—a country estate—that lay between the dark cypress forest and the dark, murmuring waters of the Black Sea.

The long sea voyage under warm skies had refreshed him. He was better able to sustain the continuing evidence of President Chase's rise in power and prestige. He could conjure a wishful belief that it was brought about by something like an intoxication with the derring-do in that man and by a befuddled state in the nation. Intoxication makes for recklessness and bemusement, Phillipson reasoned. It is not a permanent condition, and could not last. Braddock had to be right. Soon Chase must miss his footing. He would begin to topple, and that would be the time to conspire in his fall, and to bring him down forever.

On the third morning after Phillipson's arrival, a single horseman on a white steed emerged from the forest and stood there with his gold-and-gray jacket silhouetted against the dark wall of the trees. The distant sound of a brass bugle rang down the valley that sloped toward the sea. It was a signal which Phillipson had awaited. He ran to the balcony of the dacha where his own tall figure made a lean exclamation mark against the brown shingles of the wall.

"Prepare the espresso coffee that I brought from the Italian liner," called Phillipson over his shoulder to his house-manager. "Set out the doughnuts I bought in New York. I remember how the Marshal liked them."

"Excellency, we are not prepared for a troop," said the swarthy Armenian manager.

"The Marshal comes alone," Phillipson told him. "Send out one of the peasants to take his horse. The troop remains in the woodland."

"Yes, Excellency."

Markov looked well in the saddle. His gallop down the slope showed him sitting ramrod straight, his hands well down at his thighs, his gray lambs' wool cap aloft on a high-held head. Phillipson, who had descended to the gravel driveway, waited and watched in the admiration that he knew was expected of him. But the peasant at his side gasped in dismay as the horseman put his steed at a low stone wall and landed him plump in the middle of a small plot of winter wheat.

"Curses on him," muttered the peasant in Russian as the hooves smashed a path through the tender shoots of standing crop. "I mean the horse, of course. There goes my quota, and the commissar won't take an excuse."

"Silence, dolt. I will take the bridle. You hold the Marshal's stirrup."

Thus the Protector General dismounted in the style of a regal landlord of the czarist days. His own dacha lay beyond the woodland, and he had had a stimulating ride of five or six miles. The foaming steed was led away. The two men entered the rustic living room where just enough of a small fire glowed to give an air of welcome without too much heat in the mild weather. The room's only decoration was an idealized picture of Markov himself above the fireplace.

"Capital," said the Marshal when they were seated and a curtseying woman in broad skirts had set the coffee and doughnuts on a table between them. "Have you been well, Seth Phillipson?"

"None the better for Jeremiah Chase," grumbled the Secretary.

"Must we have the devil so soon?" exclaimed the barrel-chested, bull-necked horseman savagely. "But what's the difference? I suppose he is never out of our minds, what? I tell you, friend Seth, my patience is not inexhaustible. I shall demand concessions for what he did to my ally in Cuba. Kennedy dismantled the Jupiter missles in Italy and Turkey as a price for Nikita's cessation of arms in the Caribbean. Shall I tell you what demand I shall make over the hot line?"

"Please do," said Phillipson, holding a powdery doughnut up to his benevolent gaze. "Only don't make it too stiff. The man is unpredictably rash."

"Well, I'm no shrinking violet myself," exclaimed Markov, puffing out his purple cheeks to blow on the espresso. "He has mistaken a small episode of long ago for something it was not. A braggart, he thinks me. A show-off, before his Virginia belles. Must I bring off a world cataclysm to prove him wrong?"

"Careful, Markov. You and Chase are not two young cossacks riding in a match to throw each other down. What shall you demand of him?"

"The American Sixth Fleet in the Mediterranean. It must be withdrawn as the price of the land he seized from Barbaquito."

Phillipson wagged his thin head dolefully. "Too steep! Too steep! He'll never do it. There will be a nuclear shooting match if you prod him too far. It's quite unnecessary."

"Yes. Because he'll back down. He knows better than to dare me to the brink again."

"Perhaps he does," said the diplomat soothingly. "He's a brinksman who cannot fail to recognize intrepid brinksmanship in others. I said the risk is unnecessary because the American election is only ten months off. There are plans in the making to have Governor Finnigan defeat this daredevil."

"How many ballot boxes have the Finnigans? There hasn't been a stolen election since 1960 or thereabouts. You see, I know my American history. There was Duval county in Texas and Cook County in Illinois, and before that there were the city-hall gangs in

New York and Philadelphia. But the Tammany Halls and the Pendergasts and the Crumps are gone with the snows of yesteryear. No longer is political bosshood in flower. Don't pull my leg, old friend. Chase can't be defeated in an honest election."

Phillipson sighed.

"The political crooks are few and far between, that's true. But don't underestimate our demagogues. Besides, the womanly wiles have entered our politics, Markov. Juno Lepol was a cunning vixen, but Nellie Finnigan is as clever as one of your aging she-wolves. Chase has nothing like that going for him. Here is one thing I have to tell you. Ma Finnigan has promised to put me back in the State Department if Governor Andy wins."

"Ah—so?"

"You wish to demand withdrawal of the Sixth Fleet. Very well. Pick your time with care. Press the demand. But no ultimatum. Give me a chance to return to the State Department."

The Protector General of all the Russians sank his teeth into another yielding doughnut.

"You see, friend Seth, there is the blood of the Tartar in me. I am a man for conquest. In Russia, we haven't yet learned how to produce enough wheat to feed the people. The Supreme Soviet put me in power to take people's minds off their stomachs."

"Possess yourself with only a little Oriental patience," urged Phillipson. "We may not have to wait for the election. There are other methods of deposing a President."

"But if Chase were assassinated, General Rigor would take his place. I'd almost rather deal with Chase. At least I know him."

"Rigor is pledged not to run for election in any event. I wasn't thinking of assassination. We must sink the Republicans without a trace. How? The President's removal by impeachment."

"What? Surely Chase is too popular by far!"

"With the people, perhaps," nodded Phillipson. "But not necessarily with Congress. We have a heavily Democratic House and Senate. Even the most high-minded politicians, like young Speaker Krebs, are intensely partisan in a presidential election year. . . . Pardon me, Marshal. I think the post has arrived."

Phillipson had seen his house-manager on the porch receiving an envelope from a dispatch rider on a motorcycle. The Secretary rose and tapped the window, which he opened to receive the missive. With another apology he tore it open and read.

"Congress furious. Chase vetoes gigantic pork-barrel defense measure. Purges bureaucrats in merger of four executive departments into two. Lubov."

Phillipson read the message twice to make certain of these stupendous tidings.

"Marshal! What was I saying? Chase has hit our Democratic Congress right where it hurts the most. He has struck at the prerogatives and the sacred cows. These are the grounds for impeachment that I was referring to."

"Are you sure?"

"Read for yourself," replied Phillipson, thrusting the slip into the Russian's hands. "Now we have him hollow!"

Chapter Twenty-Five

"Naomi," said Borton, raising his voice above the hum of her typewriter, "if you don't mind."

There was an edge to his voice that told her he was repeating himself, though she hadn't heard him in the first instance. Naomi, his patient servitor and the forgiving butt of a thousand temperamental sulks and tantrums, switched off the electric machine and swung her chair to face him across the comfortable office-room they had shared for thirty years.

Borton sat there in his English tweed at the imported teakwood desk, and in the visitor's chair beside him, his fat haunches filling it as lard fills a jar, sat the gross, pig-eyed man called Braddock. Some of Naomi's fierce concentration on the column she was copying related to Braddock's presence. He wasn't here for the first time, and she hated to have him here at all. Not that she knew anything about him, except that he wasn't the type of person with whom her boss had associated down the years. It didn't take a long or deep acquaintanceship with Braddock to know that he was a low-life of some sort.

"Sorry, sir," she said. "I didn't hear you at first."

The edge roughened on Borton's voice.

"If you don't mind," he repeated, "I'd like to be alone with Mr. Braddock. Why don't you take a walk before your lunch hour."

She felt her cheeks flush. In a diversionary fluster she looked at her wrist watch: eleven o'clock. But the time of day had nothing to do with it. It was a time of life! The striking of an hour she never expected to live, one when Calvin Borton didn't trust her to be near him in his work. She had been in this room while he talked in confidence to the great men of the land, and she had been on telephone extensions to record his conversations with all sorts of strange characters—defectors from the Iron Curtain, mad scientists with plans to blow up the world, gratey-voiced operatives of the CIA who would spill state secrets in cryptic language that Borton would later translate to her in utter surety of her discretion. But—now. Incredible! Excruciating! He didn't want her around for his discussion with Braddock—as if she'd deign to listen without orders to do so. As if she'd ever tell anything she learned of her boss's business under any circumstances.

She went numbly to the closet for her coat, and stumbled in her daze to the door while the men sat in impatient silence to have her go. Out into the biting chill of Washington's uncertain February weather, the woman went, her heart more heavy than the dragging footsteps which took her into this banishment. Down the uneven brick sidewalk of the Georgetown street, made almost sacred to her because his house stood upon it, into the windy hillside boulevard of Wisconsin Avenue with the quaint shops for buying spicy delicacies from abroad, as well as household hardware, picture frames and rare books, Naomi made her way. In front of a famous restaurant she paused, looking downhill at a patch of the yellow Potomac into which many a lovelorn woman had thrown away a life that was no longer worth another sob or tear.

Not feeling the fangs of the searching wind, Naomi walked on toward the river. She wasn't going to jump in, for she was too religious a person to defy Jehovah's prohibition of self-slaughter, but she was also woman enough to feel that it would serve Calvin Borton right if she did so. Love—it was a multi-faceted wonder. Several times in youth and middle years she might have married some fine fellow of her faith, and raised a family in its spiritual comforts and glory. But on every occasion of such contemplation, she came to confront the insurmountable truth that her heart was where her work was. She was bound with adamant hoops of loyalty to Borton and his career, and his act of dismissal this morning was one of cruel and callous infidelity on his part.

At the foot of the street, she turned upstream and allowed her vagrant feet to carry her toward the city. Borton and his career—how abruptly both of them had altered since the death of President Lepol. Borton had felt the tragedy deeply, though more, she thought, in peeve and indignation than in manly sorrow for the loss of a friend. Lepol had stood for what Borton considered the final triumph of liberalism—a Republican Chief Executive who seemed to insure that forevermore the country would have a bipartisan monolithic position to the far left of center. Lepol's death and the sudden elevation of Jeremiah Chase had made a different man of Borton—a lesser and a desperate man who could do the unprofessional, despicable deed of charging an innocent Nathanite with murder.

"But if only he'd been punished for it," the woman thoug t. "If only he had been made to pay until he felt the enormity of what he'd done, and had sought atonement. He was on the verge of repentance when he thought the libel suit by Miles Standish Smith was the real thing. He was facing ruination in reputation and purse, and it was good for his soul. But from the very moment he learned that the suit was only a formality, he began to change—and, oh, what a change it's been."

Naomi found herself nearing Washington Circle where the General with drawn sword rode in firm superlative grace upon a handsome, foot-lifted charger. She came into the little park there, surrounded by traffic, and sat down on a bench to rest. Lunch hour! She never went out till one o'clock or after, as Borton well knew, so that her banishment still had two hours to run. The windswept plaza was not conducive to loitering, but its discomforts suited the malaise of her spirits. Only one other person had paused here. He was a lean, willowy fellow in a carelessly unzipped wool jacket, no hat on his light-haired head—Phil Obermeister—and he was shuffling sidewise around the equestrian statue, apparently studying the strong-jawed, majestic but remarkably human features of the rider's face.

"That poor boy," thought Naomi. "He looks distracted. What would a busy newsman be doing here in the middle of a working day, staring at an image of a dead President when there's a live President and plenty of news all over town?" Then she remembered. Phil also had been caught in the jaws of a libel suit by Phillipson, an action that could crunch Obermeister as man and writer. "Is he out of his mind?"

But Phil just then saw and recognized her, and the flash of his warm grin dispelled her gloomy diagnosis. He strolled over and seated himself on her bench.

"Hi, Naomi. What do you think? Will they throw a lasso around George Washington's neck and drag him from his pedestal? It wouldn't be any more incredible, would it, than this effort to impeach President Chase?"

"Oh—that?" she answered vaguely. "I'd almost forgotten that it's going on, although I was just typing Mr. Borton's latest piece on the subject."

"What's Calvin going to write next?" Phil asked. "No, you'd never tell me. I'll have to wait and read it in tomorrow's *Standard*. But, Lordy, Naomi, Cal has been gunning for Mr. Chase. He's supporting the impeachment movement as if we had a criminal in the White House instead of a new father of the country."

Naomi shook her head. She couldn't comment, but she put a kiss to his glowing cheek. Phil, always the hero-worshiper, ever since she'd first known him. He'd once thought Borton to be the greatest—now Chase was the object of soaring admiration. Well, the President wasn't a national father figure, but wasn't the nation-wrecker that Borton had been attacking either. She didn't pretend to understand politics—that wasn't any part of her duty. Yet the malice and irresponsibility of some of Borton's diatribes were very much on her mind, for the viciousness that had come to possess him was where her troubles lay.

"Phil, dear. Don't ask me what I'm doing here instead of in the office. I will tell you nothing. But don't make me cry. I beg you."

"Old friends like us? Can't we talk a little?" He took off his gloves and closed his warm hands over her frigid ones. "I'm going to take you to the Circle Restaurant yonder, and get you some hot coffee."

"No. Leave me to my misery. Just this—do you know a man named Braddock?"

Phil arose and pulled her to her feet. "Now that settles it," he said and took her arm. "I'm going to get you out of the weather. You needn't tell me your troubles, but I'm going to tell you mine."

Over a checkered tablecloth in the pre-noon solitude of the restaurant, Phil became almost garrulous on clear tea while she sipped coffee.

"I did a wrong thing, Naomi. I two-timed a girl whom I love a lot. You know, I never thought that a bachelor need have any biological morals, but there is such a thing as being true to one's true love, even if the affair is still in its platonic stages. She went away, and lonesomeness had something to do with why I strayed, but professional amorality came into it still stronger. By sleeping where I did, I found out a lot."

"This was your libelous column on the former Secretary?"

"The truth is no libel, Naomi. I'm convinced and I wrote the facts. Phillipson has close connections with Braddock, whose party assignment was to get Martinez executed as a martyr. Braddock's a Communist handyman, and he's up to odd jobs on this crazy impeachment movement. Why did you ask me about him?"

She kept on shaking her head. She would tell him nothing. But when they parted, Phil played the hunch and walked to Georgetown. He stood for an hour in a doorway across the street from Borton's home. He was rewarded. The man who eventually emerged from there was Braddock.

Having lunched and wined well in his home dining room, and awaited the return of Naomi, who arrived shortly before two o'clock, Borton caused her to phone for a taxi and was whisked to the House of Representatives.

He was well known in the House press gallery, but he ordinarily went there only for grand occasions such as joint sessions. He had a contempt, which he didn't hide, for the daily reporters who did the drudgery of following the regular meetings of the House, and when he took a seat on the bench overlooking the chamber, a couple of scribes nearest to him got up and found other positions—whether out of deference to him, or out of dislike, Borton did not know or care. He was here because he wanted to hear the opening round of the impeachment debate, and he had phoned for an interview with Speaker Krebs when the debate should end for the day.

That young, bright and promising official, John Krebs, was now in the well of the House, having come down from the presiding rostrum in order to declare the Democratic policy. When Borton arrived Krebs was saying:

"Mr. Chairman of the Committee of the Whole, I wish to declare before going any further with my remarks that I do not relish the duty I have undertaken. I could wish that the House never had to face a decision that could lead to the removal from office of a President of the United States. Our predicament is the more unpleasant because, in late December, less than seventy-five days ago, the Honorable Jeremiah Chase was the toast and enthusiasm of the entire nation. He had proved a peerless leader in time of foreign crisis. Democrat and Republican alike honored his name.

"But power, my colleagues, is a heady intoxicant, and I fear that the President drank too deeply of it. At his opening press conference in January, he threatened a veto of the bill we rightly call Billions for Defense. He carried out that threat in a scathing veto message which offended every member who voted for the measure. We re-passed it over his veto by a vote of 335 to 100—"

Up jumped Underthorn, Republican of Iowa: "Will the gentleman yield?"

"Yes, I yield for a question," said Krebs.

"Referring to the overriding vote of 335 to 100, is that not precisely the partisan ratio of the House? There are 335 Democrats, are there not, and 100 Republicans? Did not the vote to override the veto fall exactly along party lines?"

The Speaker said caustically: "The gentleman from Iowa must draw his own conclusions."

Congressman Underthorn shouted: "Yes—I conclude that there is a Democratic plot afoot to dismiss and disgrace a Republican President."

"I form a different conclusion," said Krebs, with a strange lack of conviction in his voice as it came through the loudspeaker on the lectern before him. "I assert that the party of Jefferson, Jackson, Cleveland, Wilson, Roosevelt, Kennedy and Johnson stands for representative government."

A bray of laughter broke from the Republicans on the floor, and Borton frowned. It was a sign of weakness in Krebs to fall back on a recitation of those honored Democratic names, which had nothing to do with the issue. Young Krebs' earnest, intelligent face showed itself in profile as Borton strained over the railing. The Speaker was pale and drawn, with the look of a man being driven to a duty that did not fit his conscience. He shuffled the papers on the lectern and continued:

"After this House and the other body had overridden his veto, President Chase compounded his original error by impounding the money we had voted. He refused to let his Administration dispose of one cent of what he unfairly called—Billions for Boondoggle. There is no way we can force him to spend the appropriations, but we can punish him for this high-handed tyranny."

"Yes," yelled the Democrats, while the meager band of Republicans shouted, "No."

"Mr. Chairman, I continue. Following this outrage to the dignity of the Congress, the President carried out another threat. He reappointed his Secretary of Labor to another post, and ordered that the Secretary of Commerce become Acting Secretary of both Commerce and Labor. The President then attempted a similar consolidation of the Departments of Interior and Agriculture. But when he sought to remove Agriculture Secretary Quarles, Mr. Quarles balked. He barricaded himself in his office, and there he stayed while Congress passed the Tenure of Department Bill, forbidding these consolidations. Again the presidential veto, and again the overriding vote by both chambers of Congress. But President Chase has worked his will against our consent. He has refused to submit new names for Secretary of Agriculture and Secretary of Labor. Again, I say—we cannot force him, but we can chastise him."

"Yes!"

"No!"

"Mr. Chairman, the President has more recently proposed to merge the CIA and FBI. He has sent us such a bill, which met the fate of the other disputed bills. I do not know what his next move will be, but certain members of this House decided not to wait and see. A bill of impeachment was introduced. It was referred to the Committee on Rules. There it was solemnly considered for twenty-one days, and today it has been reported to this floor with a recommendation of passage. Mr. Chairman, before I make my opinion known, I move that the clerk read the articles of impeachment so that we will have them fresh in mind."

There was a general disturbance on the crowded floor as members, having already heard the articles read and discussed many times, left their seats and milled about or drifted from the chamber. Borton deserted his own seat and retired to the press lobby for a cigarette. He had earlier studied the five articles that made up the bill of impeachment, and had written several columns about their merits. The first four articles denounced the President (in this order) for: refusing to spend the appropriated funds for military bases and facilities; attempting to merge Labor with Commerce; attempting to merge Agriculture with Interior; allegedly risking national security by a plan to merge the CIA with the FBI. But it was Article Five, as Borton knew, on which the impeachment would finally stand or fall. It charged that President Chase by his actions and public remarks "did attempt to bring into disgrace, ridicule, hatred and contempt and reproach the Congress of the United States."

Somebody in the lobby shouted: "Krebs is up," and Borton went back to his gallery seat. He could see Krebs leaning wearily against the lectern as members reappeared from various doors to return to their places.

"Mr. Chairman of the Committee of the Whole," said Krebs, "I now address myself to the matter at hand. Very rarely have I, as Speaker, attempted to advise you how to vote. I have never aspired to be the Czar of this body. But, then, I never thought I would face such a fateful decision. We Democrats have more than the two-thirds majority required to impeach President Chase. I do not like to call it to a partisan matter—for that implies enmity, and I feel no personal hostility toward Mr. Chase. But if our opponents wish to call it a party matter, so be it. On this highest level of responsibility, we Democrats must act in unison—just as we do when we organize the House into committees, just as we do when we meet in convention to nominate our national candidates. This is a national crisis. We are dealing with a national officer. We must not break into splinter groups and fail, by disunity, to do what must be done. I ask all Democrats to follow me in this most solemn act. Today we shall continue in debate. Tomorrow we will vote. I shall vote for the impeachment."

Up from the floor rose a tumult of cheers and catcalls, whoops and boos, as the Speaker turned and climbed back to the rostrum. Borton had heard enough. The rest of the debate would be meaningless, for Krebs would never have put his authority on the line if he weren't sure of tomorrow's outcome. That young man's career was at stake, and his ambition would not allow him to throw it away.

Borton went into the hallway and walked down the broad marble steps to the third floor where he entered a chandaliered, red-carpeted parlor that was set with several desks, behind which sat elderly, veiny figures—the highest echelon of House staff members, those who attended upon the Speaker himself. To one of those old men Borton gave his name and asked to see the Speaker.

"I'm afraid he's presiding, sir."

"Borton's the name," repeated Borton loftily. "I'm confident he'll leave the chair if he knows I've come earlier than expected."

He turned his back, found a seat and left it to the ancient functionary to decide how to treat the peremptory summons. Soon the old fellow, having consulted with others of his vintage, trotted away and in five minutes returned to beckon to the caller. Borton followed to a door that led into a smaller room which, like the outer and larger one, had the antique air of the gaslight era. John Krebs was seated and did not rise as he nodded for Borton to sit down.

"I am," said Borton in his most disagreeable tone, "overwhelmed by the warmth of my welcome, Mr. Speaker."

"To hell with all that," replied Krebs distinctly. "I don't feel one bit cordial, and I won't pretend that I do. When you've finished here, I wish you'd go down into the cellar where I keep my personal mailroom. There's just about enough space to squeeze in among the bundles of letters and telegrams that forced me to do what I did today."

The strained, youthful face changed, before Borton's eyes, into one that was yellowish from rising spleen and desperate in anger long suppressed. Krebs leaned forward to crash his hand upon the desk.

"Borton! I was never so ashamed of an American politician as I was today of myself. Political courage—I read about it in books. I hear it praised at gatherings. But I wonder where it finds a lodging place? Not inside of us who get to care more for our offices than for our consciences. If I'd had the guts of a cream-puff today, I'd have taken the other side—the Republican side, Jerry Chase's side."

"You're raging like a drunken man," said Borton drily. "How'd you like me to write this scene?"

"Drunk! I wish I were! You'd never write what I'm saying, else I'd never say it before you. You're hot for the impeachment—bring down Chase! Exile from public life the only man in a generation who has what it takes to restore the Republic. At least you've got the convictions of your malice and folly. I have nothing but the compulsion of a cheap ambition that won't let me do what I should."

"You brat!"

"Yes, I haven't grown up enough to be hardened to the game. You're right. I should send my conscience for a walk."

"Your conscience—your still, small voice of ignorance," Borton taunted him. "How much does your conscience know? More than the Democratic party? More than the dozens of party officers and hundreds of party workers out in Nebraska who put you in office? More than the older members in this House who allowed you to become Speaker?"

"Those damned letters and telegrams—"

"Damned important letters and telegrams," Borton corrected

him. "I don't have to ask where they came from. I know. From state chairmen, county chairmen, district chairmen all over the country. From every level of the Democratic political hierarchy. You're not just a congressman from Omaha. You're a very high-up Democrat and that means you're beholden to the politicians who put you there and keep you there. Those politicians who have written and wired you know what keeps the party together. It's patronage. It's pork, if you like. It's the old matter of doing-more-for-Massachusetts. If you don't get rid of Jerry Chase, your party will wither and die."

"That's what they tell me, Borton. We're held together by the cohesive power of public plunder. We pass these big appropriations so that we can bribe the people with their own money. I always took it for granted. I never had occasion to stop and think until a Republican President caused me to do so. I wish Chase were a Democratic President—and that's the gospel truth. I'd a lot rather follow that man than fight him."

"If you dared."

"Yes," nodded Speaker Krebs, "if only I dared to follow. I am young enough to break historical records if I remain Speaker. I am the top legislative leader of the nation, and I like it better than being an executive leader. I don't have the nerve to kick my ambitions in the teeth."

"Go to the cellar yourself and reread those messages," said Borton, getting to his feet. "They're the voice of your party demanding impeachment."

"I'm aware of that, you pompous pundit," the Speaker growled. "But they're not the voice of the people."

"Oh, you'll hear from the people, never fear. The people don't want their pap taken away. The funds that build yacht-basins for Navy defense, and dig tunnels through mountains to keep the Army Engineers busy—those funds spill over into community jobs and contracts. The people approve of that. They also approve of having an Agriculture Department bureaucrat for every family farm, and all the rest of it. The people always have an Uncle Ned or Aunt Nellie on the federal payrolls. The people won't mind if you impeach the man who wants to shoot Santa Claus."

"You're more sure of that than I am, Borton. We haven't heard from the country yet."

"In due time. You'll see. There will be anti-Chase demonstrations as this removal excitement heats up."

Krebs got out of the chair. "How the hell do you know there will be demonstrations? Spontaneous ones, of course."

"It's my business to know everything, Mr. Speaker. Good-by."

But in the taxi on the way home Borton wished he'd withheld those last two remarks. How did he know there'd be demonstrations—spontaneous ones, of course? Well, Braddock had assured him that such things could be arranged, and Braddock was someone that Borton didn't care to have any known connections with. If he met again with Braddock, it had better be somewhere else than in Georgetown.

The cab followed Pennsylvania Avenue and passed before the White House. By now the winter darkness was falling and the mellow lights in the fine old mansion were coming out like stars. The place had a lived-in look, he thought. Word was that Cora Chase, somewhat overcoming whatever ailed her, was spending a few nights a week there now. The First Family attended worship every Sunday at St. Paul's just across Lafayette park—no more of that LBJ skipping around for the church vote—and then drove home for Sunday dinner at Waverly Farm. The young scamp was sticking to his lessons at Princeton, but the daughter paid her own way down from Broadway after every Saturday night performance to be with her folks. A fetching family portrait, Borton mused, one that was earning popularity after an uncertain beginning.

The people . . . ? That was a bothersome thought, all right. Thus far the entire uprising against Chase had been here in political Washington—and Washington, even after Home Rule, wasn't America, any more than an impeachment proceeding, confined to House and Senate, was anything approaching a popular recall. Good Lord, there'd better not be shilly-shallying on Capitol Hill. The motion to impeach was sweeping like wildfire, but a gust of popular disapproval could blow out the blaze in a jiffy. The columnist recalled the anguish of moral dismay he'd seen in the face of the young Speaker. Despite that address he'd made to the House, Krebs was being internally swept with stormy doubts. Despite the certain passage of the House bill by tomorrow night, there was a rough road ahead before the President could be dismissed. A committee of House managers must take their bill before the Senate, where the Chief Justice would preside. There would be a court-like trial at which the President would be defended by legal counsel and an immense amount of publicity would be generated before the deed was done.

The cab had reached Washington Circle when Borton changed course.

"Go back to the Statler Hilton Hotel."

"All right, mister."

There was risk in going into Room West 999, but he knew no other way of reaching Braddock immediately and in person. The columnist pulled his muffler up around his face as he plunged through the lobby to the elevator. He rapped sharply on the door that he wanted to enter, ignoring the bell which might be connected with some alerting device set by spies or counter-spies who, you had to assume, were all over the place these days. A dark girl let him in. Yes, Mr. Braddock was taking a nap. She'd get him.

The fat man lumbered into the parlor of the suite, rubbing his slitted eyes.

"Had to see you," said Borton shortly. "I've been with Krebs. He's wobbly."

"We have different reports on him. Steady as a rock."

"I've been with him, I tell you, man. It's not tomorrow I'm worried about, but the days ahead. Krebs would feel better if he heard from the people."

Braddock gave way into a big chair, reached beneath it and was soon wrenching off the top of a bottle of beer. His coarse, heavy throat barely wrinkled as he poured the brew inside. He wiped his mouth with the stained palm of a hand.

"I promised you demonstrations, Borton."

"That would help. But Krebs is suspicious of their spontaneity. This man's a key figure in our endeavors. The mail from politicians doesn't altogether satisfy him."

"Osa," rumbled Braddock. The girl appeared from a back room. "Look in my file under L for Letters. Bring me what's there."

Osa was back in a moment with a folder which Braddock opened on his knee, grunting syllables while he searched: "L for Letters, and N for Nebraska. Let's see. How would five thousand do? I could get ten thousand, but that would be going outside our central membership. Why don't I set up for four thousand from NECKEM, and another three thousand from the Lobby for a Lovable World?"

Borton nodded in awe, as the fat man gave the dark girl orders to put out the telegrams of contact. Pushbutton pressure mail. Cal knew it existed but he'd never seen the automated process begun on short and easy notice.

Braddock belched. "Mr. Speaker will soon be hearing from his constituents, Cal. This is nothing more than what the Constitution calls the right of petition. Anything else on your mind?"

"You leave me flabbergasted," laughed the columnist. "I have to work hard at molding opinion. You speak the word—it's done."

"What else needs doing?"

Borton pondered for a moment. "I suppose it's out of reach," he said. "When I came past the White House, I couldn't help but think that Chase would be easier to remove if he and his family hadn't begun to get through to the people better than at first. It's not that Cora and Chi Chi and whatever the boy's name is are known the way the people know Juno and Lady Bird and Jackie and Mamie and Eleanor. But, if I'm right, there's a certain effusion of goodness and normality coming from the White House. When it appears that Chase is in serious political trouble, there will be much good will in reserve for him."

"Yes, it's a problem," Braddock agreed. "I'd like to have a solution in the files, but I'll have to look further."

"All right. Good night."

Again Borton headed home by taxi. A subdued Naomi had laid out the finished copy of tomorrow's column. Borton scanned it briefly, gave it his initials and tossed it in the action-box. Naomi came to pick it up. "Mr. Borton, when there's time, I'd like to talk with you."

"We talk every day, Naomi. What can you mean?"

"I—I may wish to give notice, sir."

"That's nonsense, of course. You're tired. Tomorrow you'll feel differently. If not, I'll be glad to hear what your complaints are. Good night now."

"Good night."

Until Borton went up to his dressing room and heard the valet running a bath, he'd forgotten where he would be dining tonight, for his social engagements were made far in advance. Evening coat and black tie laid out for donning told him it would be less than a formal outing. But he had to go to the dressing table and put on his glasses to read the notation of the evening which the valet always stuck into the crevice of the mirror. He read:

> "Dinner at eight. Semi-formal. State Dining Room.
> The White House. By President and Mrs. Chase."

To dine at the table of the man he was trying to destroy! To break bread and sip the wine of friendship in the home of his foe and putative victim! Calvin Borton smiled the smile of savoir-faire. He must be at his charming best tonight.

Chapter Twenty-Six

On February 15, 1976, the House of Representatives passed all five articles of its Bill of Impeachment. The vote was firmly on partisan lines. Three hundred and thirty-five Democrats voted aye, while one hundred Republicans voted no.

Until it actually happened, the American nation was hardly aware of what the action implied. The country was entirely unfamiliar with the impeachment process which hadn't been employed for 110 years—at the forgotten imbroglio over President Andrew Johnson in 1868.

The television newscasts and the news columns of the daily papers could not bridge the yawning gap of popular ignorance. People had come to know the Constitution by name only. They were only confused when newscasters and newswriters gabbled about Article One, Section two, Paragraph 5: "The House Representatives shall . . . have the sole power of Impeachment." Or about Article One, Section three, Paragraph 6: "The Senate shall have the sole power to try all Impeachments." Or about Article Two, Section four, Paragraph 1: "The President . . . shall be removed from office on Impeachment for, and Conviction of, Treason, Bribery and other high Crimes and Misdemeanors."

All this, and much more, including what was said in and reported about the House debate, got the people more mixed up than usual. They could understand an aircrash. They could comprehend a military victory. They thought it was wonderful the way Jerry Chase had stepped into the presidency, and that it was dandy the way he'd gone about twisting the tail of Communism. But for months they'd been reading that he was throwing his weight around in Washington, kicking officials out of office, feuding with Congress over the pork barrel or something, and the whole affair was very fuzzy in the minds of most citizens who had a living to make or a house to keep.

What they wanted to hear was whether this fellow Chase really was the real McCoy or whether he was another of those political frauds. In short: was Jerry Chase a good guy or a bad guy? The people, as always, preferred their public characters to be clearly labeled.

Thus it happened that the people turned, to a greater extent than ever before, from the news columns to the opinion columns. The historian of this volume hesitates to over-simplify. Yet it is a fact that in the period following the House action, the writings of Calvin Borton and Philip Obermeister were conducting something like an artillery duel for the winning of the public mind.

Calvin Borton, his pieces prominently displayed in all the large metropolitan dailies, was the first to score. President Chase was a bad guy, if you followed Borton, because Chase was a throwback to the past. He was a gunboat diplomatist who didn't understand that there was no such thing as victory any longer. He had gotten away with some tawdry gasconading in the Caribbean, but if he stayed in office much longer, the havoc would fall. American cities would be incinerated by nuclear war. Men would be sterilized by noxious fallout. The few women lucky enough to find mates would bear two-headed children.

Not only was Chase a trigger-happy warmonger, but he was a hater of the lower classes, a tool of the monopolists whose cases he had argued as a lawyer and a man gone mad with power, said Borton. The President was out to tear down the federal structure which, since the days of Franklin Roosevelt, had been the friend and benefactor of the poor. If Chase got his way, wrote Borton, the farmers would be reduced to the peasantry they'd once been, the workers would return to ante-bellum slavery and grass would grow in a thousand streets because when welfare didn't come from Washington it didn't come at all. Who "cared" about the American people? Your congressman cared, your Agriculture Extension Service agent cared, your patient and under-paid bureaucrats in the National Labor Relations Board, the myriad cells of the Department of Health, Education and Welfare, the Department of Housing and Urban Development, the Fish and Wildlife Service, the Bureau of Reclamation Land Management and in the civil activities of the Defense Department—they all "cared." Take away this paternalistic infrastructure of the national government—as Chase was scheming to do—and the American nation would collapse.

For these reasons, wrote Borton, Chase must go. The hard-hearted, medieval-minded, megalomaniacal dictator must be removed by Congress as provided in the Constitution, else mankind would never again stand straight and fearless and free.

Despite the occasional word they didn't understand—what's "infrastructure"?—his readers got the message that Calvin Borton knew how to put across. The people were sovereign. Like Caesar at the amphitheatre, they turned down their thumbs. The gladiator of Waverly Farm must die. Like the mobs around the guillotines, they howled for blood. That autocrat at the White House must leave his political head in the basket.

But the columns of Philip Obermeister, appearing for the most part in smaller newspapers or less prominently displayed in the larger dailies, subsequently began to take effect. President Chase was a good guy, if you followed Obermeister. Chase was, indeed, a throwback to the American past—and what was wrong with that? He was a figure of history and of universal size. He was a reincarnation of the greatness in the Founding Fathers. A man of action, he had proved that there was such a thing as victory in battle for America's vital interests. His exploits in the Caribbean, and over the landmass of Red China, and in an eyeball-to-eyeball encounter with Marshal Markov had not advanced the risks of nuclear war, but had defied nuclear blackmail and had halted a drift toward surrender on the installment plan. Chase was a life-loving extrovert who knew no fear of death. He had in a very short time breathed some of his own sense of valor and honor and hearty decency into the American people.

Like King Lear's youngest daughter, Cordelia, Jeremiah Chase didn't go around fawning on the monarch—the people are the monarch in America—and slobbering about how much he "cared." He was a man who let actions speak out loud and clear. He believed in the people—was a democrat in the highest sense. He felt that the people had lost much of their freedom to the paternalism practiced by the federal government. He knew in his heart that a leader who loved the people best governed least. Chase was trying to make the people take back some of the vast amount of responsibility that had been delegated to Washington. Surely, by this time, the laborer and the farmer, the merchant and the entrepreneur could conduct their affairs without a federal monitor looking over their shoulders. Surely, by this time, the home communities of city and town, suburb and farmland knew how to take care of their own. If they didn't know, they'd never learn by letting everything be done for them in the marble palaces of Federalia.

Chase thought it right, wrote Obermeister, that the people should stop being gypped by their own government. Government had become the biggest business of all, and it was an unproductive business. It earned nothing—it only taxed. It squandered the tax money that was extracted from the sweat of the people's brow. Chase wanted much more of that money to stay at home. Let it be invested in local goods and services that yielded profits and raised the living standards rather than taken to Washington for distribution among the drones. Let the money be freed from Federalia so that it would be available for state and local taxation, and spent in the same communites which had contributed it. Far from collapsing, the American economy would rise like a phoenix from the ashes of deficit and debt if only the full energies of the people were released.

For these reasons, wrote Obermeister, President Chase must be purged of the impeachment. This warm-hearted, universal-minded, democratic leader must be exonerated. To remove him on the specious charge of "high crime and misdemeanor" would make a mockery of the Constitution, and would cause government of the people, for the people and by the people to perish from the earth.

Borton had fired the first volley. Obermeister's artillery began to stir the people for a sober second thought on the subject.

Still, it was not the people who would pass upon Jeremiah Chase's continuance in office. The House had indicted him in mid-February. The Senate had scheduled its decisive hearing of the case for early March. The ordeal to which the President was to be submitted would take place in a closed arena of politics where the partisan odds were stacked against him. Did it really matter what the people thought? They would not go to the polls until November. By that time Chase might not even be on the Republican ticket.

If it didn't matter much what the people thought, Eula Breck had wasted her time. In January she had set out by car, accompanied only by Bosco, for a lengthy, intensive grassroots tour—taking the southern route to California and the northern route back to New York City. She had gone forth to explore the Zeitgeist—the spirit of the times in the early months of the anniversary year, 1976. But when she reached Radio City, a few days before the Senate was to sit in judgment on the President, the program manager of "Between Us Girls" was dubious about putting her on the air, as scheduled.

"There's a basketball game at the Garden that would fetch us a higher rating," the manager grumbled. "I think we ought to scrub your show, Eula. Put it on some other time. You don't mind, do you?"

"Who—me?" ejaculated the Mechanical Maiden. "All I did was log 10,000 miles on the seat of my slacks; interview practically every Tom, Dick and Harry from Laker's Acres to the Golden Gate and back to Harlem. Why should I care if my work goes to waste? I'll tear up my contract and see if somebody'll hire me as a disc jockey."

"Now, Eula, don't be like that."

"I know. You've got your viewers to think about. They'd rather watch a basketball game. I'll just take my show and put it on National Educational Television without a sponsor. How do you like that?"

The program manager shrugged. He couldn't imagine many viewers settling down in their homes and taverns to hear about something called the Zeitgeist, so he reluctantly paid Eula a cancellation fee and let her go. She had to hustle around to collect a panel, but people said of Eula that she was quite a hustler, and the three women she came up with proved that this wasn't an empty compliment. When the NET stations went on that Sunday night, only thousands instead of millions were tuned in, but the announcer was able to say:

"Stand by now for Miss Eula Breck in 'Between Us Girls.' The Girls tonight are Miss Chi Chi Chase of Broadway, who speaks from Waverly Farm, Virginia, Mrs. Nellie Finnigan, who speaks from her son's home, the Governor's Mansion in Albany, New York, and Mrs. Juno Lepol, who is in Concord to study the New Hampshire primary. They will question the famous Mechanical Maiden."

EULA, *in a silver, sleeveless dress, sat before a bare table with folded hands, and the program began:*

CHI CHI, *seated on a straight chair in a smart suit, showing her shapely legs:* Of course, I'm prejudiced. I'd like to hear that the people of America are heart-and-soul behind my father in his ordeal next Wednesday, and that they have let their senators know. Have the people made up their minds, Miss Breck?

EULA: No, I think the people's jury is still out on President Chase. They have heard from Cal Borton. They have heard from Phil Obermeister. If they've decided, I haven't been able to learn their verdict. As for letting their senators know, the people simply can't compete these days with the organized pressure groups. In every city, on every campus, I found persons willing to sign petitions, but seldom bothering to write individual letters. Mass opinion in America is not born, it's manufactured. It is a weakness of our democracy and perhaps the source of its eventual corruption.

JUNO, *in her familiar flowing robes:* My dear, I admire your industry, but didn't you waste your time going opinion-chasing at the grass roots? Didn't you find that people like to be told what's true by their chosen and trusted leaders?

EULA: There is something in what you say, Mrs. Lepol. But frankly, I found the people more influenced by what their leaders *are* than by what they *say*. People tend to be impressed by whatever family lives at the White House. This is not so strange when we recall that a whole age was named after Queen Victoria, who stamped her seriousmindedness and her prudery upon a nation. Without giving other historical examples, I think I have learned in my reporting that a marked change has taken place from coast to coast since President Lepol, yourself and Dwight D. have been replaced by President Chase, Cora, Chi Chi and Granville. Would you like me to expatiate?

JUNO: Certainly.

EULA: Well, you asked for it. Specifically, I was amazed to find that several voluntary groups, which were more or less underground movements a year ago, have come into the open and are flourishing. One is the Virgins Club, of which I am a member. We began with chapters only among the intellectuals—that is, in the universities and among their alumnae. Today, I find V.C.s in the high schools, among the drop outs and even in the Poverty population. Where girls have slipped, once, twice or many times, they still seek voluntary redemption—in the Chastity Clubs, which are also booming. I think it no small matter that Americans are exerting self-discipline. It is conducive to good citizenship and intelligent democracy, to the economic virtues of thrift, prudence and restraint. Where women are fastidious, men are likely to follow the examples of their mothers, sisters, cousins and aunts, and all of them follow the example of what they see in the White House. The spurt in applications to the Hatchet Club is not unrelated to the ingenuousness of Jeremiah Chase in his televised press conferences, and to the example of Granville, who is known among campus cut-ups as the scamp who cannot tell or act a lie. Therefore, I feel that my interviews have received valid answers. The people are truthful.

NELLIE FINNIGAN, *in her grey dress with its rose:* I doubt if people are much impressed by Mr. Chase's Honest Abe press conferences, which are extremely dull. People want to hear cleverness, rhetoric and quips.

EULA: No, we are in the twilight of the bunko artist, Mrs. Finnigan. Not only political campaigners, but also salesmen and evangelists, humbug novelists, hokum playwrights and slanted journalists have had their day. I found people very inclined to resent phony advertisements, and to boycott merchandise which is guaranteed to cure the incurable, glamorize the unromantic and turn geese into swans by use of toothpaste, lipstick, hairsprays, and stick-out bras. People who used to give themselves nervous breakdowns by trying to live up to the Joneses have come to notice that Cora Chase doesn't try to live up to Jackie Kennedy or Lady Bird Johnson, neither of whom she could ever match. People who used to get ulcers from striving after perfection are recalling the testimony of Mr. Chase's old friends, who said he was a man who never extended himself until the presidency was thrust upon him.

CHI CHI: And yet you say that the people are not deeply aroused about the impeachment proceedings.

EULA: People are fascinated that columnist Borton can see the President as a bad guy, and columnist Obermeister can see him as a good guy. After all, the President has not hesitated to take controversial positions in war and peace. He evokes discussion. He has continually asked that he be judged and criticized. People look upon the Senate trial this week as a sort of shootout. In olden days, men took their grievances to the dueling ground and knights had to prove themselves in the lists. There's a feeling that Mr. Chase has asked for this confrontation with Congress, and that he'll just have to put up or shut up.

JUNO: You're giving the impression that the American people

have undergone some sort of rebirth into a higher state of mind and soul.

EULA: If so, I have been overstating my impressions. The American people are not reborn but are being reawakened. There is still plenty of sin and sloth, but there is beginning to be an awareness that these need not be the norms of life. Their values are up for readjustment, that's all. The people are ripe for inspiration and also ripe for disillusionment. If they find in time that virtue has no reward, and that it pays just as well to be sluts and sluggards as to be honorable and energetic, they will fall all the harder for having tried to climb a little higher. But make no mistake—there is something on the move in this land of ours. People's hearts are lifted, and their heads are up. For how long, I do not know. I am a shoe-leather reporter and not a pundit like Cal and Phil.

NELLIE: Before you leave us, honey, will you give us some criterion by which we may judge this Zeitgeist, as you call it. If Jerry Chase gets flung out of office next week—and I won't shed any tears if it happens—that will be entirely a political action. It will be something done to a politician by other politicians. But is there some upcoming event to which you might direct our attention, so that we might see for ourselves how the American mind is changing—if it truly is?

EULA: Yes, ma'am. I think democracy is going to get a workout in two libel cases that are coming to trial. You've got to say that the common court system, whether it's represented by judge or jury, is the litmus test of democracy. It tells more than elections whether the public apparatus can produce wisdom and justice. The two journalists we have frequently mentioned will go on trial for their work. It's more difficult to reach a verdict than to choose between political candidates. Let's see what an ordinary city court says about Cal Borton and his charge against a member of a small, unpopular, ridiculed minority sect. Can a man of prominence and popularity get away with that?

ANNOUNCER: You have one minute left, Miss Breck.

EULA: The other journalist is Phil Obermeister. He has asserted what he calls the right to holler Red when he sees Red. He has chosen not only to challenge the national attitude of disbelief in domestic Communism, but also a powerful and sacrosanct individual, the Honorable Seth Phillipson. If this country can produce a random panel of jurors or a trial judge with the wisdom of Solomon to resolve such cases, well and good. If not, then I shall feel that I have misinterpreted the Zeitgeist.

And here, although a skilled professional, Eula Breck burst into tears before the announcer could bring the program to an end.

Chapter Twenty-Seven 

Chi Chi, ever the showgirl, gave the camera a final shot of her curvaceous legs and went to where her father and mother waited in the Waverly Farm livingroom. Cora rose to carry a tall vase of chrysanthemums from the mantel to the window ledge, where she stood back to view the effect. The President in his large, red armchair was pulling contentedly on a brair pipe and had just gathered some work sheets into his lap. Chi Chi walked between them to mix herself a whiskey and soda on the low table.

"How pretty you are on TV, darling," said Cora. "I couldn't go before all those people for the life of me. I'm downright ashamed for not accepting the invitation to address the League of Women Voters. I feel I've let your father down."

"Fiddlesticks," said Chase. "It was a last-minute invitation. Flynn says it was cooked up by someone named Braddock just to embarrass you—and me. Served 'em right for you to refuse."

"Dad, what does Jim say about your chances on Wednesday?"

"Jim Flynn's a congenital alarmist."

Chi Chi sat herself down and poked her pugnacious little chin at the man whose finger could signal Doomsday. "Now you listen to me, Poppa President. Jim's right. There's a very good chance that the Senate will dump you. In the first place, you've practically dared this Democratic Congress to do it. In the second place, you haven't prepared your defense as well as I've seen you bone up to defend some embezzling corporation high-binder. You remind me of Granville the time he lost two front teeth peddling down a girl's front steps on his bike with his hands in his pockets. He was showing off."

"Chi Chi!" exclaimed Cora. "You mustn't talk that way to your father."

"It's a free country. I've got a right to criticize the President."

"Sure you have," agreed Chase. "Let's admit I am pretty confident of acquittal. I don't deserve dismissal. I have a good lawyer. What's there to worry about?"

"You have the Attorney General to conduct your defense, but where's he been for the past four weeks? I don't believe Judge Hannibal can be memorizing Constitutional law while ploughing around the New Hampshire snowdrifts after primary votes. Even if he has, he's not the best lawyer in the country. You are, Dad. I'd feel safer for you if you were your own attorney."

Cora came and kissed them both good-night. "You two wrangle as usual," she said. "I'm going to bed."

"Good night, Mother."

"See you later, Cora." The President fastened his work sheets on a clipboard which he handed to his daughter. "Quiz me."

Chi Chi riffled the sheets with his notes on them. "This isn't law. It's history. All right—how many attorneys did Andrew Johnson retain to defend him from much the same charges that you're facing?"

"Four. Their names were Curtis, Stanbery, Evarts and Groesbeck—finest lawyers of their day, but too many for one case."

"How many House managers were prosecuting that case."

"Seven. Congressmen Bingham, Boutwell, Butler, Logan, Williams, Wilson—and Thaddeus Stevens. Only four House managers will come in against me. Their leader, John Krebs, isn't as vindictive as Stevens was. In fact, Speaker Krebs doesn't have his heart in it."

"Did Andy Johnson appear at the trial?"

"No. He stayed away—and won—although he had a larger majority of senators against him than I have."

"He won by a single vote, Dad. You may not be so lucky."

The President stretched and yawned. "Let's hit the hay. We'll get up early and take a ride."

"You're riding for a fall, that's what," declared the girl. "Jim says Obermeister warned him there'd be street demonstrations. You heard what Eula Breck said about the organized mail that can be fired at the senators. The Finnigans will stop at nothing, and heaven knows what other forces are working to get rid of you. Oh, Dad, I'm worried."

Chase yawned again and rose. "Leave the worrying to me, honey. The Finnigans are deadly politicians, but this aging progenitor of yours is no slouch in that department. Don't think I haven't been making some plans. If they work out, I'll carry a Republican House and Senate in November. If the plans don't work out—well, nobody can say I didn't give this job the old college try. Good night. I'll call you in the morning."

Chi Chi went up to her bedroom, got into her filmy nightclothes, but found herself too agitated for sleep. In all her life she'd never known her father to fail at anything. But the odds against him here seemed insurmountable—the way they seemed in a cliff-hanging play when the solution was only in the playwright's mind. Yes—but this wasn't fiction. Those sixty-seven Democratic senators would vote as a bloc, they always did, and that would be curtains for Dad. She needed comfort—someone to tell her there was an out for him somewhere. That horrid Cal Borton had been to dinner at the White House, smirking—Chi Chi's mother had told her—and licking his white mustache like a cat who'd been in the cream. Nobody knew more of politics than Borton, and there were rumors that he was part of the ouster movement. That faithful secretary of his had left him over some quarrel about the methods he was using. Chi Chi took the telephone directory, and looked up Nathan, Naomi, but changed her mind. Instead, she dialed long-distance for the NET station from which Eula had done her broadcast. An attendant said that Miss Breck had already left. Well, then, Philip Obermeister—and she found his number and dialed it.

"Phil?" her female treble fooled him.

"Darling," he shouted. "I hoped you'd call. I should have called you, but there was a reason."

"Hold it," she said soothingly. "I'm not your darling. It's Chi Chi Chase."

"Oh!" He had to be a lovelorn youth to express such disappointment at hearing from the President's daughter. He recovered. "Hi, Miss Chase."

"I can't sleep from worrying about Dad. Does he have a prayer on Wednesday?"

Phil's voice deepened with feeling. "Don't ever sell that man short. Tell me—is he a poker-player?"

"Why, yes," the girl laughed. "He used to be. I sometimes think he's risking his office so he can go back to whiskey and cards with his cronies in the backroom of the courthouse. I don't mean he overdid it, but what a man's man he is."

"You should have seen him where I did. The time he'd just finished his flight from the S.S. *Pedernales River*. Gee Whiz, Miss Chase, they don't make 'em like that any more. Your old man—I mean the Pres—"

"He's my old man. Go ahead."

"All right. I was going to say that he may seem reckless—but there's a method in it. He conducted that little war in person, knowing it would invite criticism. He told me he wanted to make people think—so they'd begin to take charge in self-government. I believe he's provoked this hassle with Congress with the same thought in mind. If they—the people—ever think—good-by, Finnigans!"

"Phil! Dad said he had plans. He said if they work out, he might have a Republican Congress next year."

"Then you'd better believe it, Miss Chase. I don't know what's up the President's sleeve, but I bet it's muscle. There's a report out of New Hampshire that the Attorney General will have an announcement at midnight. It's supposed to have something to do with the impeachment hearing. I'm going down to the *Express* to see what it's all about. Shall I call you back?"

"No," said Chi Chi. "I'm getting up early. You've cheered me immeasurably. So long, Phil."

After that, she slept and knew nothing till she heard her father knocking to wake her. She got into jodhpurs and a turtleneck sweater. He was in boots and his tweed riding coat at the front door when she reached there.

"Let's be quiet and not wake your mother. I didn't say so last night, but the gossip about her has been stirred up again. Somebody is smudging up the First Family portrait. Who the hell's this Braddock?"

He went out the door as he spoke, not expecting her to know, but she made a mental note to ask Obermeister if he knew. The big man strode like a lion, powerful and lithe, down the back road to the stables. He could have ordered horses brought saddled to the door, but—she knew—he didn't like bossing people around, even stable grooms. Besides, he had a horseman's love for the ammonia smell of stables and the leathery tang of the tack room.

"Yorktown," the President boomed at the big, mahogany bay horse that whinnied at him from the stall. "I've been neglecting you, you galloping lummox. Slap a saddle on your mother's mare, Chi Chi. We'll let 'em roll this morning."

Such a man! How could she have brooded? He wouldn't recognize the threat of failure if he'd met it in the middle of the big road to Richmond. She heard the jingle of bridle bits as he began bringing what was needed from the tack room. She was pulling on the mare's girth when whistling and merry yells broke from the nearby tenant house where the Secret Service was billeted. Other Presidents had chafed, or pretended to chafe, at the surveillance, but her dad took it, like everything else, in his stride. They mounted and walked their horses, then trotted and cantered them in the approved manner of warmup that all good horsemen observe. But once in the meadow below the house, Chase urged Yorktown into a gallop and they swept up the hill with the distant azure of the Blue Ridge Mountains breaking across the horizon.

Even now he did not extend the big horse into a flat-out run, as he might have done with one of his hard-riding companions of the past, but suited Yorktown's reaching stride to that of the plump mare which came behind. Chi Chi saw men running to open the gate at the hilltop. Otherwise, Chase might have set sail and jumped the fence, as he'd done before to the distress of the Secret Service. They galloped till the mare panted, and Chi Chi drew rein and let the man go on alone into the next field, which he circled at a faster clip.

It is imaginable from objective descriptions of those few who had seen both Marshal Markov and President Chase on horseback that the difference in performance was marked. For the Tartar rode stiff and long-stirruped like a passenger, like a policeman, while the Virginian rode as his ancestors rode. He was the big, bending controller, using enough knee-grip to manage the animal without the need of bit and rein. As man and horse rushed downhill through the gate again, Chi Chi saw the fierce look of command which usually lay dormant in his eyes and saw how he brought Yorktown down to a trot and a walk by nothing but relaxation of his own frame.

He motioned and they turned toward the stream, splashing boisterously through it, and on into the woodlands. There, on a path, they jogged side by side, and she joined his lusty baritone in the hunting song she'd often heard resounding upstairs to her childhood bedroom when he entertained his friends below:

> "Drink, puppy, drink. Let every puppy drink,
> That's old enough to lap and to swallow.
> And we'll pass the cup around,
> While he grows into a hound.
> For merrily we whoop and we halloo."

For an hour the man and daughter rode, this Monday morning. Soon she would be on a plane back to New York, and he would go to his own work at the White House and around the capital city. She was accustomed to his hearty outreaching ways, and she could guess at the repressions which a life of business and politics, and a not-quite-congenial marriage, had set upon him. With no difficulty at all the girl could imagine how, if he threw all discipline to the wind, Jeremiah Chase would rogue it and range it, with liquor, love and fights, a man to be remembered for prodigious masculine feats. She pulled the mare behind him as they neared the stables, and her eyes were streaming from all that she felt for everything that he was and might have been. The pettiness of daily existence contained him only because he willed it that way. Bigger than life. Like some of those outsized heroes of Shakespearean plays and Wagnerian operas. But, my god, how must he feel to be so insufficiently mated and companioned in his giant's estate? Who, except her, appreciated him, came close to understanding him? Not his wife. Not the newspapers. Not his political associates. Not the country. She dashed an arm across her face, and cried:

"Oh, the cold air. It's made my eyes run."

Grooms waited for them and Chase flung himself from the saddle, becoming, she thought, like those around him, a mere mortal, though the leader of his peers. Jim Flynn came running from the driveway with the morning paper he'd brought out from town, but Chase waited for his daughter to dismount and join him.

"Flynn! All right?"

"A bull's-eye, Mr. President."

The front page of the *Standard* stood tall and black with its headlines, and Chi Chi read:

> HANNIBAL ASKS N.H. TO WRITE IN FOR CHASE
> SEEKS VOTE OF CONFIDENCE IN PRESIDENT
> OUTCOME COULD BLAST IMPEACHMENT

Her tears came surging back. She went to her father's arms and wept like a child.

Chapter Twenty-Eight

When Eula left the studio that Sunday night after the broadcast, she drove to Surrey-by-the-Hudson where Seth Phillipson, who was still in Yalta, had his estate. Her trip was motivated by both love and money. She was worried at the thought of Phil's being ruined by the Phillipson libel suit. But if her intuition was sound, the proof of the ex-Secretary's complicity with Communism would be found, if anywhere, among his private papers. Not only would the proof clear Phil but it would be a revenue-producing scoop for herself.

Snuggling with the mute and companionable Bosco, the happy girl sped up the Hudson turnpike. Eula had crossed the Rubicon of the female mind. She had decided to give away that one possession which, she felt, makes a woman richer in its loss. When she returned to Washington, bringing the means of Phil's escape from the toils of the law, she would make the sweet surrender to him, but she would of course not become promiscuous. She would have only one lover—only her Phil. And when the November campaign was ended, and when she'd finished her book titled *People's Choice '76*, she would listen for his proposal of marriage, knowing it was sure to come.

"Bosco, you must learn not to bite every man who comes near me—do you hear? You must lick the hand that undresses me. I will get you a mate, and the four of us will keep house together."

When she reached the estate of Maison de la Paix after midnight, she parked her car in the shrubbery as before, and went with the dog to the garage. The miniphone she had planted in Phillipson's limousine was put there because of her journalist's knowledge that secretive men often discuss matters of import in the fancied safety of their cars. She fished the little instrument out of the domelight of the tonneau, and tiptoed with Bosco on to the main house.

To her astonishment the still night became filled with raucous laughter and gay music as she approached. What? Had Phillipson returned ahead of schedule? Could it be that his bedridden wife had decided to end her long invalidism with a spree? It would serve the old rotter right if Pauline had. But—no. The sounds, and now the mellow glow of curtained lights, emanated from the servants' quarters. It was the billionaire's hirelings who were living it up on his premises and probably on his best victuals and distilled spirits.

Eula knew little about the houses of the great, but a great deal about human behavior. Since it wasn't likely that the butler, maids and nurse were gallivanting with the mistress's permission, it was highly probable that the unhappy invalid had been left alone and unattended in the only upper room that was lighted. A recorded interview with Pauline Phillipson would be a bonanza, and the lady might be just vexed enough to tell where her vagrant husband had hidden the papers he'd taken from the safe.

Eula tried the front door first. In her experience this was the one portal most carelessly left unlocked. And if locked, it was probably equipped with a doormat under which unimaginative persons, rich and poor alike, invariably hid the key. As she anticipated, the key was there. If she got apprehended for burglary, she'd not be charged with breaking and entering. Shushing the dog, and hugging her paraphernalia so that it didn't clink, Eula mounted the wide stairs and cracked open the door at the top of the steps. There, solitary and helpless, lay the lady of the house, clad in a hospital nightgown with tie-strings at its back. On the bed were those two oversized dispatch cases that Eula had hoped to find, and spread on the counterpane were many pieces of paper, in addition to the one in Pauline's trembling hand.

Eula, finger to her lips, fully opened the door. "Easy does it, Mrs. Phillipson. I'll do you no harm. Down, Bosco."

The saddest and homeliest, the most pathetic and withal the most disillusioned female face that Eula had ever seen turned toward her. There was recognition in the droopy but still alert brown eyes as they added the dog and the shapely girl together.

"Yes, I remember you," said Pauline. "You wore slacks then instead of a skirt, but I read personalities by their figures. Down in the driveway, the night before my husband left—"

"He had talked with Mrs. Finnigan, and I was snooping," said Eula, drawing near. "If I don't mistake what's on your bed, it's what I want. How beastly of your servants to desert you like this."

Pauline gave the laugh of a ghoul. "They have an example of desertion in my husband. From sheer boredom I raided his papers. Will you believe it—I never knew till now how abominably he has betrayed me. It's written here—right here."

"You just keep on talking," said Eula, going to the bedside and unslinging her microfilm camera. "I'll make some reproductions and I'll listen with an open voice-mike to whatever you've got to say."

In hardly more than an hour, Eula had a double scoop—the private papers of Phillipson and the private life of Phillipson *et ux*. It was the family biography, listened to while she was snapping microfilm of the documents, which affected Eula so deeply that she bent and kissed the withered cheek.

"Mrs. Phillipson, you should make yourself free of him. Divorce the slinky skunk and start again. It's never too late."

"What a sweet thing you are," exclaimed the old woman. "No one except you has kissed me for love in forty years. It gives me hope. I'm not so ill I don't have anger, and perhaps I can rediscover other emotions. Good-by."

"Good luck, Mrs. Phillipson."

Back in her car, Eula drove to the highway and soon found a picnic pullout where she turned out the lights and went to sleep in the perfect security of Bosco's company. The same Monday dawn that heard Jerry Chase rapping on his daughter's door saw Eula bathing like a nymph at the drinking fountain after which she shared rations with her protector and caught the morning radiocasts.

A sickly cheerful voice was speaking: "And a hi-hidee-ho and a good-good morning. This is Eddie Eli with the top o' the news. At midnight in New Hampshire, Attorney General Hannibal withdrew from the Republican primary and entreated all Hampshiremen, whatever their party, to write in their votes tomorrow for President Chase. Here is the Attorney General as he gave a statement that must go down in history as one of the cleverest political parlays of all."

A pause and then: "Republicans! Democrats! Countrymen! Lend me your attention. You all know of the dastardly attempt to expel President Chase from the office of President. The House has voted, and on Wednesday the Senate will vote on whether to confirm an impeachment of the victorious Virginian. Here in New Hampshire, you have a chance to make the mountains ring with the voice of the people. Only you of all Americans can speak this month at the polls. Other primaries come later, and in November the entire nation will have its say about Jerry Chase. But you can stay this senatorial execution. Whatever your registration, simply write Jeremiah Chase across the ballot, so that tomorrow, the eve of the impeachment, the voice of the people will be heard in the land."

Eddie Eli was back on the air: "Hi-dee-ho. We take you now to Washington."

Another voice: "I am your toothbrush lark and not the nightingale, Happy Johnny Jorgins, with a profound analysis of the news. There is building up a people-to-people message on the impeachment action which was supposed to be wholly for the grandees of the Senate to decide. You have heard Attorney General Hannibal's appeal, and meanwhile in Washington the streets are filling at this early hour with demonstrators coming off buses that have been moving throughout the night. They are unfurling banners. Some read 'Chase Jerry Chase.' Others read 'Crazy Cora

—Back To The Nut House.' Still others read 'Chi Chi—the Floosie of the Footlights' and 'Granville—the B-Girl's Buddy.' A completely inside and confidential source quoted exclusively in this broadcast has predicted that the streets of Washington will run red with blood unless the Senate votes to unseat the President."

Eula switched off the commercials that followed. News was where the action is, and soon she was racing southward for Washington at about the time that Chi Chi and her dad were galloping up the hillside. To Eula, it made little difference who won or lost these partisan struggles. The conflict, the factual reportage from both sides, was all that concerned her. But she knew that the long, wheeled journey across the country and back again had revealed matters out of the ordinary coverage of big events. Something was a-march. The American people were up in arms against the long-existent order of apathy and venality, of slothful unconcern for morality and responsibility. Jerry Chase had spoken to the plain American people who had in common an idealism that answered to certain valid shibboleths that no reader for many years had enunciated.

Eula wanted to be the discoverer of this indefinable groundswell, and the exposer of those inimical and subversive trends that worked against it. By great good fortune, her findings coincided with the credo of the man she loved. She would be bringing to Phil the confirmation of his heart's desire for a conservative reaction against the long-persisting liberal line. And she would be bringing him, too, the little packets of film which were the substantive proof of what he had dared to write against Phillipson.

Never was she so happy as when she hurtled through the tunnel between Baltimore and Washington. She would go straight to Phil's lodgings in Foggy Bottom and offer these gifts from her hunting grounds—and offer herself too. They had been in love from November till March, and carried the pounding pulses of their passion in a continence that would make the physical consummation all the more welcome by both. For no girl of her attraction could travel alone on such a long journey without meeting temptation from demanding males, sometimes interviewed under seductive circumstances along the way. Just as, she conceded, no young man of Phil's charm could go about his business without meeting temptresses of many wiles and opportunities. How sure she was that he had been as much exposed, and as much resistant as she herself, to the lures of loneliness. How eager she was for the meeting.

"No, you must stay in the car," she told Bosco as she parked up the block from Phil's abode. "When I come back it may well be more a woman than a girl who returns."

Then, using the key that Phil had given her in exchange for a key she had given him, Eula opened the door of his house. Nobody was on the first floor nor in the patio, as she saw at a glance, and she heard with a thrill the shuffle of footsteps up above. She stood there waiting. Down the steps on satin slippers and in silken hose came a jetty-haired young woman who stared with an impudent Slavic quizzicality, and inquired:

"Who might you be?"

"I'm—," but Eula identified herself no further. Down the steps behind the interloping jade came Phil in slacks and shirtsleeves.

Not another word escaped the three of them as Eula wheeled and bolted back through the front door into the street. She sprinted to her car and soon was swallowed into the traffic, the city's digestive tract: her astonishment, anger, heartbreak, all.

One cannot conveniently emote while operating a vehicle amid crowded conditions. Her internal turmoil called for Eula to fling herself down on a flat object and drum fists and feet, to take down her hair from its pins and wail, to break china and to tear up photographs. All this had to be postponed till she reached Laker's Acres—except that she did, while crossing Memorial Bridge into Virginia, unhook the cylinders of microfilm that recorded Phillipson's limousine conversation and his private papers. She flung these sidearm into the Potomac, thereby destroying the evidence that would surely have cleared Phil of libel. Let them put him through the wringer! Let him be impoverished and discredited!

With Bosco kenneled, with her equipment taken off and hung up in the apartment, Eula then performed all of the postponed ritual of the woman scorned. Face down on the living room floor she hammered with hands and feet, jumped up to rip off her dress, which was not one of her favorites, anyhow, to heave two already-cracked saucers against the wall, and to tear Phil's picture from its frame and shred it into confetti.

Then, in a pretty slip, frilled panties and bra, she fell upon the bed, smothered her face in the pillow and sobbed. What delusion! Oh, she would take her revenge upon the human race by entering a life of sin—no, better than that, she would become a tease and cultivate frigidity in order to torment as many men as possible. Some individual punishment, cruel and calculated, must be meted out to Phil and his paramour. Acid in the face would not be bad enough for the jetty-haired tart of the staircase, and as for the traducer himself—

Eula sat up, startled. She had heard the sound of a key in the apartment lock, and a moment later she saw the pale, repentance-stricken face of Obermeister above her. He sat beside her on the bed and began the litany of the forgiveness-seeker.

"Darling, I'm so sorry."

"Do tell!"

"I can explain everything."

"Oh, sure."

"She doesn't mean a thing to me. It started—I didn't know how to stop."

"That's for certain."

"But it would have stopped as soon as you came home."

"How touching."

He had turned her over. He was adding kisses to his pleading. She was responding. The slip came off. She did not resist his hand that found the tiny buckle of the bra between her shoulder blades, but forced him to wait a while, as he attempted to remove the garment that shielded the virgin breasts. Then she sprang the trap into which she had ruthlessly led him. She pressed the hanky-panky button at the head of the bed.

Laker's Acres reverberated with shattering bells and wailing klaxons. These signals were a rarity, but so are fire alarms, and they will bring a crowd in very short order. Hanky-panky is far more exciting than a conflagration, so that in no time at all the corridors of the huge apartment complex were ringing with delighted and scandalized female shrieks, giggles and slippered footfalls. Phil, his own clothing mostly on the floor by now, sprang from the bed, and Eula sprang up too, winding herself in a sheet.

"Eula, how could you?"

"You had it coming!"

"I'm in one hell of a fix."

"Serves you right."

Amid the other sounds, they heard the heavy running steps of the janitor and the baying of a mastiff on its chain. Phil had only one leg in his trousers and was hopping toward the living room when that door burst open and the burly janitor arrived with the ravening beast. Behind him flocked the tenants, some in curling gadgets and negligees, some bearing such assorted snatched-up weapons as pressing irons and kitchen ware.

"Caught in the act," the janitor bellowed. "I carry a deputy policeman's badge. You're under arrest for assault."

"Shut up, you ape," growled Phil as he finished putting his trousers on. "Get those cackling hens out of here. Miss Breck is my fiancee."

"A likely story, mister. You can tell it to the magistrate."

Eula, the sheeted picture of threatened innocence, waited till Phil had completed his dressing in front of the scornful onlookers. She had her limits in revenge, and they were reached.

"No, Mr. Berlingback, I don't want him arrested. Let him go. Oh, Phil—I'm sorry—sorry, dear."

The blushing, mortified Phil thrust his way among the jeering G-girls and hurried away from Laker's Acres.

Chapter Twenty-Nine

One hundred senators answered to their names in the chamber on that historic noontime, Wednesday, March 11, 1976. The full attendance was unusual, it not unique, and it attested to the managerial ardor of Senator Barney Finnigan, who was leader of the Democrats, and Senator Lyle McJay of Minnesota, the well-regarded GOP floor leader.

Nothing yet had shaken the partisan formations: 67 Democrats for confirming the impeachment motion, 33 Republicans for opposing it to the bitter end. Two physicians sat on a leather couch at the rear of the chamber, one a heart specialist, the other an internist, their duty to be on hand if illness struck any participant, and especially if the angel of death should show his wings anywhere near the thin, drooping, tottering frame of the ancient Arthur Nestorson.

That old man rose with the others as the chaplain prayed, but his filmy eyes seemed to register nothing but incomprehension as the Vice President nodded to Caleb ("Catfish") Bates, the famous doorkeeper, who now bawled:

"Mister Pres-i-dent of the Senate, a delegation from the House of Representatives."

In marched Speaker Krebs at the head of the House Managers of Impeachment, and the four of them took seats to the right of the rostrum.

"Mister Pres-i-dent, the Attorney General of the United States."

Erasmus Hannibal, looking gray-green and weary from his campaign in New Hampshire, entered and took a seat to the left of the rostrum.

"Mister Pres-i-dent, the Chief Justice of the United States."

The broad-shouldered, snow-capped jurist, wearing his robes, marched up the center aisle and mounted the rostrum, where General Rigor ceremoniously handed him into his chair and said:

"The Senate is now in session for the pending business. Speaker Krebs and Attorney Hannibal are you ready for the prosecution and for the defense, respectively? With all in readiness for this solemn procedure, I turn my gavel over to the Chief Justice."

Chief Justice Thurgood Rustin, fleecy-headed Negro giant and the appointee of the late Sam Lepol, accepted the gavel and touched it to the wood.

"Senators, you are now in effect a court of law. You will try this case with diligence and objectivity, and you will render a verdict to be written upon the scrolls of time. Clerk will read the Articles of Impeachment."

Up in the press gallery, Phil Obermeister groaned: "Not again. I've heard that rigmarole so many times it puts me to sleep like our Rip Van Winkle down there."

Senator Nestorson, to be sure, had calmly settled himself in his chair for a noontime nap.

Calvin Borton, at Obermeister's side, gave a snort: "Let the old geezer sleep if he likes. Barney Finnigan needs only to wake him up five times to answer aye to each of the Articles. This trial has all the punctilio of a formal execution. The vote will be a safe two-thirds majority of the 100 senators present—67 to 33."

"After New Hampshire?" exclaimed Obermeister. "The President's write-in count is still going up and up. He'll show 200,000 votes from Republicans and Democrats alike when all the ballots are counted. Cal, there never was such an endorsement as Mr. Chase got in that primary."

"So what does it prove? New Hampshire is for Chase. The state has two Republican senators. Not a single vote will change. The primary doesn't speak as loudly as those demonstrators do. Have you seen the Avenue today?"

Phil nodded glumly. Still shaken by his rejection and humiliation at Laker's Acres two days before, he'd been up early to stand in Lafayette Park and watch phalanx after phalanx of marchers, representing every state, tramp from their mobilization centers and pack Pennsylvania Avenue across the whole front of the White House, extending several blocks both east and west.

Phil had seen their insulting placards that taunted the entire First Family. He'd heard their rhythmic chants of "Jerry Chase—He Must Go. Congress—Yes. Jerry—No!" And then the vile doggerel: "Crazy Cora—Chi Chi, too—Granville, buddy—down with you." It had sickened him to look and listen, and even while he'd watched, by some unrecognizable signal or by rehearsed timing, the mobs to the east and west of the White House peeled off from the center group and began marching south. Phil had followed with a flying squad of foot policemen who carried riot sticks and gas masks but no firearms. The marchers, under mysterious orders, reached Constitution Avenue in two columns and headed for Capitol Hill. Here, police helicopters with loud speakers hovered over them.

"You won't be allowed on the Capitol grounds. You must halt when you reach the foot of the Hill. It is illegal to demonstrate on the Capitol grounds."

They did not halt till they reached the parapet of the Capitol itself—and only then because National Guardsmen, with drawn bayonets, double-timed over from Union Station and deployed between the mob and the sacred building. The chanting rose again, and many a senator, hurrying to the session, heard the ominous demands: "Jerry Chase—He must go. Senators, listen—CHASE MUST GO!"

Borton laughed at Obermeister's serious mien. "The country will survive. Chase won't be missed. I should say not. He's a stupid man. Otherwise, he'd never have challenged Congress at the pork barrel. I hear he's called a press conference for tomorrow morning. Farewell address, I suppose. Did you hear about poor Cora?"

"Mrs. Chase? No—! What?"

"It seems on Monday the poor thing came downtown to shop, intending to lunch with the President. She hadn't heard of the demonstrations—everybody keeps things from her, y'know. Anyhow, Cora drives to the White House south entrance, and there's a batch of these marchers hanging around. They recognize her in the family car, and they halt it—and open the doors and pull her out—"

"My god!"

"Didn't hurt her, Phil. Gave her a scare. Yelled at her, 'Crazy Cora! Crazy Cora!' That was all."

Obermeister whirled on the older man. "I suppose you don't know how these demonstrations were arranged, Cal. You wouldn't have any idea whether a Communist handyman named Braddock happened to be behind this March on Washington? You wouldn't dare write that the Finnigan brothers and their ma think they can play ball with the Reds and then dump them—would you now?"

"I haven't an inkling of what you're talking about," said Borton. "Be quiet. They're ready to begin."

The five articles having been read, Chief Justice Rustin gaveled once more for attention, and got it from all in the crowded galleries on the floor with one exception—Senator Nestorson slumbered on.

"Senators, you have heard the reading of the Impeachment. Speaker Krebs is recognized for his opening remarks on the prosecution."

But Erasmus Hannibal had beaten Krebs to a standing position and said quietly: "If it please the Chief Justice, I move that discussion begin with Article Five. This is the catch-all indictment. It accuses the President of offending the dignity of the Congress. Once we dispose of Article Five, whether the Senate votes it up or down, the other articles will follow in a more logical order."

John Krebs arose and said. "The Managers of the Impeachment have no objection, your honor. We stake our case on Article Five."

"Without objection in the Senate, Article Five is pending business. Go ahead, Mr. Speaker."

"I thank the Chief Justice," said Krebs. "This matter has been so widely discussed in House and Senate, that I shall be brief. The Senate has been called the citadel of our liberties. It is here and here alone that a President may be brought to book for overstepping his powers. I charge the Honorable Jeremiah Fielding Chase with the high crime of demeaning the legislative branch of this government. He has used intemperate language in his veto messages. He has held us up to shame and ridicule in a press conference by saying that a member of Congress who seeks favors for his constituency is little better than a bagman. He has defied us by taking away our patronage, by daring to reduce the size of government without our permission and against our will. He has refused to spend our appropriations. He has appealed over our heads to our constituencies. All of this comprised an attack upon the dignity and integrity of the Congress. I move the adoption of Article Five."

The galleries rumbled, and the Chief Justice warned against any show of feelings of whatever sort. He nodded in recognition to the Attorney General.

Hannibal rose and said: "Senators, I also shall be brief. I do not intend to unsay a single word for my distinguished client, the President of the United States. I do not explain for him. I do not apologize for him. I simply quote you from the First Amendment to the Constitution, where it decrees that Congress shall make no law abridging the freedom of speech. The President is like every other citizen, except that he is our First Citizen. He is entitled to the same freedom of opinion and utterance as any person in the country. If you pass this part of the bill of Impeachment, Article Five, you will be abridging one man's rights to speak as he likes. Do not ask for whom that bell of censorship tolls—it tolls for us all. I thank you."

Again the Chief Justice used his gavel, more vigorously this time, for applause had started in the public galleries. "If there are no further arguments from the floor, the clerk will call the roll of the Senate. All in favor of adoption of Article Five will answer Aye. All in opposition will answer No. Proceed."

The clerk intoned the first name: "Mr. Akers."

"No," answered that Republican stalwart from Kansas.

"Mr. Andrews."

"Aye," answered that undeviating Democrat of Pennsylvania.

Borton whispered: "There it rolls. Party-line vote."

And so it seemed to go. Bilkins, Brookings, Bukers, Democrats, Aye. Calkins, Republican, No. Dobbins, Esters, Faber, Democrats, Aye. Down the alphabet. As soon as Barney Finnigan had answered to his name, he rose and hurried to the side of the all-but-recumbent Nestorson. Finnigan shook the old man gently as the roll call proceeded. Gambrill . . . Hastings . . . Inglehart . . . Jenkins . . . Knox . . . Lutherton . . . McJay . . . Nestorson . . .

Here the clerk paused. Senator Finnigan was shaking Senator Nestorson—not so gently now. He gestured wildly for the physicians, who dog-trotted down the aisle to Nestorson's seat. One using a stethescope, one applying reflex tests to the old man's gangling knees, they sought to find life in the lolling form.

The Chief Justice seemed perplexed. "The Senator must answer to his name if he's able. Clerk will call the name once more. Louder please, Mr. Clerk."

"Mr. NESTORSON," the clerk shouted.

That did it. The old man sat bolt upright. He pushed away the attendant hands and came to his crooked legs.

The Chief Justice said: "How do you vote, sir?"

"Present," said Nestorson. "*Adsum*, in the Latin, for the clarification of the Court."

"The Senator must vote Aye or No."

"No such a-thing," said the old man shrilly. "You may know court procedure, but you'd better look up the Senate Rules. I may answer Present, and that's what I do answer. I've never yet busted the party line, and I'd as lief sleep with a skunk as vote with the Republicans. But I won't have any part in ousting Jerry Chase, and I'll tell you why—"

"The senator from Arizona is out of order."

"No such a-thing," repeated Nestorson more querulously. "Since you insisted on gettin' me waked up, I've got a parliamentary right to explain my vote, as every senator knows. I ain't going to vote against Jerry Chase, and I'll tell you why. I've got to run for re-election this November. The people would turn me out of office if I voted for impeachment, and they'd be right. You Democratic fellers think that one over. I was in the Senate before any of you came, and I'll be here after you've been defeated for what you're going to do today. Call my name again."

"Mr. Nestorson of Arizona."

"Present!"

Obermeister barely suppressed a whoop of joy. Borton groaned like a soul in agony. Both knew the party line was broken on Article Five and that a vote of 66 to 33 would not make a two-thirds majority of those present. Amid dead silence, the clerk proceeded. Norris . . . Owens . . . Parker . . . all the way to Zimmerman at the end of the alphabet. The clerk then read the names of senators voting in the affirmative and of those in the negative. The scroll was handed to the rostrum, and the Chief Justice announced.

"Article Five having received 66 votes in the affirmative and—"

"Mr. Chief Justice!"

It was Andrews of Pennsylvania, Democrat. "Like the senior senator from Arizona, I am also up for re-election in November. If I may be pardoned an innocent pun, he is the Nestor of us all, and I bow to the wisdom of his years. May the clerk call my name once more for reconsideration of my vote?"

"Mr. Andrews."

"Present!"

The Chief Justice began anew. "Article Five having received 65 votes in the affirmative and 33 in the negative, a two-thirds majority is not achieved, and the Article fails of adoption."

Obermeister got to his feet. "That's it, Cal," he whispered in husky exaltation. "The other four articles don't have a prayer, and lots more Democrats will decide to take the easy way out. I'm going where the action is."

A few moments later he was on the steps of the parapet among the National Guardsmen who held back the mob. Many of the troops were carrying transistor radios. The news of the break in the Senate was already widespread. Obermeister sought out a captain with a walkie-talkie.

"Help me out, won't you, Captain. I'm a reporter. What's happening on Pennsylvania Avenue?"

"They've broken into the White House lawn. It's against the law. They've flopped down there. Gone limp on the grass. Thousands of 'em. The Colonel has flown over 'em in an eggbeater and warned them to get out or take the consequences. He's warned 'em all, here and there both—either get out or get gassed. I reckon they don't believe it."

"Look!" Phil pointed. The mob around the parapet had received some orders. "They're flopping too. Going limp."

"All right, Lieutenant," the captain bawled at a subordinate. "Pass word through the sergeants. Gas masks! Gas masks!"

"Did you get an order from the Colonel?" demanded Obermeister. "Give it to me straight. I've got to write it."

"Not from the Colonel, bud," the captain said. "Here. I'll give you my extra mask, and you better put it on as soon as you see what I'm looking for." He shielded his eyes and scanned the sky. "It'll be a Navy plane. A carrier-type dive-bomber, if you know what I mean."

"Captain, don't give me riddles. I need news."

"Bud, I'm a company commander, and not the info officer. All I know is that the Colonel is taking orders from the top—and I do mean the top. Do you know your history? Didn't President James Madison take personal command of troops in 1814 when the British marched on Washington?"

Phil thought it over and said: "Yes, Madison did. And President Chase flew that first mission in the Battle of the Caribbean. He flew a carrier-type dive-bomber, too."

"Yonder." The captain pointed skyward. A Navy jetplane streaked across the town at building-top level. "Masks, all."

The plane made two swooping passes above the general vicinity of the White House, and now it headed for the Hill at tree-top altitude. From its belly rained a shower of pellets that fell among the mob. The plane banked sharply and came again, showering pellets into the prostrate mob. A brownish haze enveloped the scene, and the mob burst apart into running, tumbling, rising, stumbling, falling figures.

"Sub-lethal stuff," yelled the captain through the mike inside the mask. "It would take the fight out of a wildcat. Next thing we do is herd 'em up, and get 'em to their buses with tickets-of-leave. Bud, you've just seen a one-man winner in the Battle of Washington."

Jim Flynn pulled on his broken nose. The President, looking hollow-eyed and sorrow-hit, sat on a straight chair there in the cubbyhole that was the White House office of the press secretary. Down the hallway in the East Room, the press corps was gathering for the Thursday morning conference.

"It's a mighty useful phrase, Mr. President. I know you've never employed it before. Today, I think you should duck certain questions with—no comment."

The President cupped his tired, sunken eyes with his palms. He dropped his hands to his knees. A prodigious sigh filled his broad chest and was slowly expelled.

"Jim, you are my chosen advisor on press relations. It is your field. You're the expert. I'll hear you out."

"You will get questions today that touch your intimate life. They are not within the public domain. No comment you can possibly make will be helpful. You will only distress yourself."

"Jim, the man I think of is Old Hickory. He was made a widower by the smears and slanders that killed his wife. I have reread the story of her torment and death in the fine biography of Andrew Jackson by Marquis James. Rachel Jackson, I think, simply lost the will to live when her husband's election meant leaving home in Tennessee and moving into the target area of the White House. How bitter Jackson was, and how tormented were his days in this very mansion."

"Yes, sir."

"Flynn, my case is like Jackson's. I concede that. But does it give me the right to do what you advise? No. I hope those questions won't come up. But if they do, I'll answer. I will not evade. The whole thrust of my service in this office is to level with the American people. Let's go, Jim."

They walked down the hallway with Flynn a half-stride to the rear, picked up Secret Service and entered the packed East Room. Chase went to the desk between the wall pictures of George and

Martha Washington. He stood there, his face gaunt with strain, not seeking the advantage of the subtle lighting that would have put protective shadows on his face if he had sat at the desk. Flynn said:

"There are no announcements. The President will take your questions."

Q: Mr. President, yesterday the Senate vacated the Impeachment against you. On the final vote only Senator Finnigan persisted in supporting it. Will you comment?

A: Yes. I am gratified by the Senate action which I take to be a vote of confidence. Senator Finnigan is entitled to the perversity of his lone dissent.

Q: Sir, will you continue your Spartan regime in cutting the size of government under the New Allegiance?"

A: I will. I intend to show a record which the American people may judge in November.

Q: Mr. President, a Navy bomber took off from Andrews Air Base yesterday and saturated two concentrations of demonstrators with sub-lethal but incapacitating nerve gas. The Defense Department has declined to give the pilot's name. What was his name, sir?

A: His name was J. F. Chase, Lieutenant Commander, Navy Reserve, also President of the United States. I undertook the strafing of the mobs on the White House lawn and at the Capitol parapet for two reasons that have been in my mind since the beginning of my term. First, I believe that the more disagreeable the duty, the more it is the President's task to perform it in person. Second, I want it well known that this country will never be governed by mob rule.

Q: Mr. President, the morning papers' editorials are highly critical of that action, coming as it does just when the Senate was purging the Impeachment against you. The tenor of criticism is that you should have exercised restraint and patience in the hour of your triumph.

A: Yes, I know. It is said that I employed the Napoleonic whiff of grapeshot to clear the Tuilleries. I make no denial. I stand by my action.

Q: Sir, a very personal question?

A: Yes.

Q: In conducting the strafings were you motivated by personal hate and revenge?

A: Yes, I was.

Q: Can you say anything beyond that, sir?

A: Yes. I had already decided that the streets must be cleared if the demonstrators became uncontrollably lawless. I had ordered a particular plane from the U.S.S. *Pedernales River* for that purpose. But events occurred which stirred my anger and indignation. Yes, I admit it. I took personal satisfaction in gassing those demonstrators.

Q: Why, Mr. President?

A: Please rephrase your question in a more substantive manner, Mr. Borton.

Q: Is it true that Mrs. Chase was rendered so distraught by a personal experience, and by the posters and chants which taunted her as Crazy Cora, that she suffered a collapse?

A: Yes. Mrs. Chase has been stricken with a traumatic nervous breakdown. She is now in the Paca Psychiatric Clinic, Johns Hopkins Hospital, Baltimore. Like Rachel Jackson, my wife has become the victim of scurrilous attacks by her husband's enemies. I cannot anticipate that she will ever share my public life again.

Q: Then, sir, you did act in part from vindictiveness?

A: I did.

Q: Mr. President, it used to be said by Senator Fulbright that every revolution in our times attracts Communists to its ranks, but that we should not call it a Communist revolution for that reason. Do you consider yesterday's March on Washington to be Communist in nature?

A: I am told by the Director of the FBI that many participants had Communist connections. Not that they carried Communist party cards. But their associations were with the only organization on earth that is dedicated to the overthrow by force and violence of the United States. I think it is high time that the American people got over their skittishness about using the adjective "Communist." Never mind the dictionary or the legalistic definition. Let us use words that express thought rather than conceal thought. Yes—yesterday's March on Washington was part of the Communist World Revolution, and I am glad it was repulsed.

Q: Sir, can you name a single well-defined Communist who participated?

A: All right. I name Donald Braddock. He goes by other pseudonyms. He was the organizer of yesterday's disorders and of much other mischief. I will take the FBI's word that he is a Communist.

Q: Will he be arrested and charged with crime?

A: No, I regret that he probably will not. It is not unlawful to be a Communist. It used to be unlawful not to register as such if that was the fact, but Supreme Court decisions have rendered our Communist-control statutes almost null and void.

Q: What can we do about Braddock, sir.

A: The American people, on whose wisdom I have based my entire service in this office, can take care of Braddock and all others like him. By that, I mean, they can treat him as a pariah. They can shun his every approach. They can eschew his company. They can scorn his advice. I call upon all loyal persons to give this man the absent treatment.

Q: Mr. President, to change the subject—

A: I'd be very glad to do so, Mr. Obermeister.

Q: Yesterday saw the breaking of the Democratic party lines. Actually, in the final vote the Republican floorleader, Senator McJay, who didn't altogether approve of what you've done, merely answered, "Present" to his name. The issue had been decided by then, and it didn't matter. My question is—do you see the possibility of a crack-up of blind partisanship in yesterday's events at the Senate?

A: I will have to speak more wishfully than factually to that question. Yes, I do believe that the party system of Democrat vs. Republican has become ossified and obsolescent. It would make far more sense if we divided between Liberals and Conservatives.

Q: The long-looked-for political realignment, sir?

A: Yes, there are many Democrats who are conservative at heart, and many Republicans who are liberal. I might as well take this occasion to make an announcement. I do not approve of Every Man, Every Vote. But it's on the books. Between now and the national conventions, I shall ask the Census Bureau to conduct a national compilation of conservatives and liberals. There will be voluntary compliance, of course. But I am going to invite all who affirm themselves conservative to consider themselves Republicans and those who affirm themselves liberal to consider themselves Democrats. If we get a large-scale participation, the expected result, I think we may have started a realignment of the party system in America—and it's time we did.

Q: May we ask if you have any other announcements you'd like to make, Mr. President?

A: Yes. If you'll look in the Fish Room on the way out, you'll find that this conference chamber has been fitted with a large round table. I intend to meet there periodically with selected persons, in and out of active politics, to take direct action on many problems that don't yield to legislative remedy.

Q: For example, sir?

A: All right. I doubt if we can ever outlaw poverty, or discrimination, or the insolence of office, or the law's delay and other woes that human flesh is heir to, but I'm going to seek other ways of setting the crooked straight.

Press: THANK YOU, Mr. President.

As reporters drifted down the hall to take a look at the refurbished Fish Room, Borton came to Obermeister's elbow.

"Who the devil does Chase think he is—King Arthur of the Round Table?"

Obermeister let the sneering remark go unanswered.

Meanwhile, the President led Flynn into the latter's office and sat down to discuss the conference.

"By heaven, Jim, they asked practically every question I didn't want to answer—except one."

Flynn nodded in relief.

"Mr. President, if you'd had to answer that one, the press would have had its biggest headlines since Sam Lepol was killed."

Chapter Thirty

What was the shape of historical patterns in this anniversary year of 1976?

Harold Bardson understood and wrote American history better than anybody since Charles Beard. He was first to call attention to the appearance of a Chase Cult. It had seemingly sprung full-born into being as a result of the President's military and political victories. It was there before anyone could say, "Look what's coming." Writing in *National Review,* Bardson declared:

> Although I do not consider the time well spent, I have devoted some recent weeks to the collection and perusal of a rabbit-like proliferation in Chaseiana. There has been a publication explosion of quickie presidential biography that threatens to surpass in sheer profusion, and often in bad taste, the rush of prints that followed the death of John F. Kennedy.
>
> The phenomenon is remarkable—one is tempted to write ominous. I learned that publishers of all sorts have hastily cancelled books and articles about the late, lamented Samuel Tilden Lepol and have commissioned some dozens of hacks to grind out instant works about Jeremiah Fielding Chase. Remarkable, I say, because we are far more accustomed to hearing of dead men prematurely hailed as martyrs, saints and heroes than to behold the near-deification of the living. Ominous, I contend, because this absurd practice is just as dangerous to the dignity of the nation as it is to that of the President himself.
>
> My count shows that there are already in print or under contract

six hardcover books, hastily composed, fifteen paperbacks, twenty-two Sunday features, twenty-three magazine cover stories and countless other pieces that relate, often with very insufficient authenticity, to the present occupant of the White House. At the cost of some embarrassment to myself, I present selected titles in the rough chronological order of Mr. Chase's life to date.

We start perforce with *A Nanny Looks at Jerry*, by the President's nurse, moving to *A Rat Makes Good*, which is an account of his first year at the Episcopal High School in Alexandria, Virginia, from thence to *Belles and Foxes*, his sportive youth, *Thunder Under the Rotunda*, his college days at Charlottesville and *The Socko Heard Round the World*, a non-observer's account of Chase *v.* Markov in a very brief fist fight.

Then there is *Chase and Jefferson, Chase and John Marshall, Chase and Patrick Henry*, by a professor emeritus who conducted some history classes for which the future President submitted some rather average papers. This is followed by *Chase's Mistress*, which fortunately refers to his practice of the law, *The Matinee Idol of the Court Rooms*, which tells of his winning ways with juries, *Jerry and the Juggernaut*, relating his victory over the Democratic organization in Virginia, *The Man in the Magic Toga*, his senatorial career, *The Divine Fire of the Smoke-filled Room*, the alleged story (written by an absentee) of how heaven intervened in the formation of the Lepol-Chase ticket of 1972.

There follows a splurge of miscellaneous trivia which includes *The Laughter of Jerry Chase, The Sorrow of Jerry Chase, The Chase Riddle, The Chase Syndrome, The Pater Familias*, relating to his home life, *The Man Who Dared, The Man Who Did, The Man Who Walks Like a Titan, The Man Who Saved a Nation, The Man Who Saved the Free World* and finally—I foreshorten the list out of sheer exhaustion—*Chi Chi's Daddy, Granville's Pop*, and *Up in Cora's Room*.

These and other titles are already finding scads of buyers at bookstores, newsstands, pharmacies and supermarkets. I have pursued the subject matter by conversations with authors and editors of the hardcovers yet to come. I think I'm sufficiently drenched in the drivel to hazard a prediction that by election day in November there will be a full-blown mythology—or the makings of one—unique and altogether unsettling.

Certainly, we have had periods of adulation and even hysteria relating to beloved public figures during their lifetimes. Mostly, these distempers have been parochial in extent. The admiration for Douglas MacArthur was intense in conservative and patriotic circles, while that for Adlai Stevenson was confined to groups that ranged from ultra-internationalist to pseudo-intellectualist.

These displays of worship were interesting but unimportant. Neither

MacArthur nor Stevenson had any power base, and could not be regarded as a menace to our democratic institutions. On the other hand, Huey Long, although his following was parochial, did manage to turn his Louisiana State Police into a semblance of power. Many observers of the day looked upon him as a dangerous prototype of dictatorship. Then there was Franklin Roosevelt. He used the camouflage of war-crisis, economic upheaval and the absolute control of his party to create the nearest thing we ever had to a monarchy in this country. Once Roosevelt broke the two-term tradition, it was inevitable that he would capture a lifetime presidency and would die in office like a king. Unfortunately, very few Americans were fully aware of what had taken place. Anybody who had successfully warned them would have deserved well of the republic. In that context, I depose the following:

The Chase cult has sprung to life with bewildering rapidity and in multiple dimensions. It is not a parish enthusiasm, nor a movement devoid of political and physical force. Though no demagogue, Chase has a charismatic appeal to the masses, an affinity with big business, a close connection with the military, a kinship to the aristocracy of birth and intellect, an unmatched propaganda machine which is all the stronger for being propelled by the profit system of the publishing industry. Chase has proved himself first in war, first in peace, first in the fluttering hearts of his countrymen. There is still opposition, to be sure, as there was to Long and Roosevelt. The fact that Chase is quite unlike either of those men makes his rise to power, and the dangers therein, all the more insidious.

He is brave, good and just. There are no signs as yet that he is overweeningly ambitious, but we have proof that he is immensely talented and overwhelmingly strong-willed. Single-handedly, he reversed a foreign policy that was State Department orthodoxy for four decades, bearded a Communist dictator in the latter's own den, challenged and disciplined a hostile Congress, chose his successor without prior consultation with anybody and apparently set about to realign the two-party system.

There is no question that these reversals, reforms and innovations are salutary ones. There is evidence that the President employs harmless shock-treatment solely to induce the country to think for itself. In solemn truth, virtually everything he has done meets with my personal approval, and I may be in the category of the Athenian who opposed Aristides and spoke out against him in pique at hearing that great man always called the Just.

To put the matter another way, it is the Chase cult and not Chase that sets my intuitive watchdogs to howling. It is not an inflated presidential ego that I am prepared to puncture—for truly he is a modest man. No, I am attempting to poke a hole in the rosy balloon of public infatuation.

For when all is said and done, the American populace, or what Hamilton once called "a great beast," is two hundred million strong—much stronger than Jeremiah Chase. It has more hands, more feet, more hearts, more heads, more lives than he has. Compared with America itself, Chase is small and weak, and brief of breath—not to be compared in importance with the nation that produced him. I do not count myself a jealous person, and yet I feel tempted to look upon him as a potential but guiltless Caesar. I am almost ready to cry with the jealous Cassius:

> Ye gods, it doth amaze me,
> A man of such feeble temper
> So get the start of the majestic world
> And bear the palm alone.

Bardson's criticism fell into the pond with a small splash. It produced some concentric eddies but it failed to inundate the shores of opinion. Bardson himself later acknowledged that another historian, Arnold Toynbee, had stated postulates which were more appropriate to the American story of this era. According to the Toynbee school of thought, the U.S.A., like all other major concentrations of peoples, contained the genes for producing a hero mythology. The ancient Greeks demanded heroes who were sons of the gods. The Romans enjoyed the legend that Romulus and Remus were suckled at the fierce udders of a she-wolf. Lofty but mysterious ancestry, the possession of an emblematic and all-conquering sword, are the preface and the myth that lead into the Arthurian tales of the man who brought unity and glory to the English crown.

Hence, one may discern both pattern and precedent for the legends which gathered about Jerry Chase at the summit of his career. The raw material had to be indigenous, and historians of the Toynbee school found it quite in keeping with past examples that Americans in some numbers became bemused over the relationship of Jerry Chase to George Washington, the founder and father-image of the nation.

Chase's distant and collateral kinship to Washington was, of course, well known to those many Virginians whose addiction to genealogy is bred in the bone. But it was the indefatigable Eula

Breck who somewhat inadvertently launched a fable soon to be popularized out of all proportion to the facts. The heartbreak of her shattered engagement to Phil Obermeister would not allow Eula to attend the Thursday press conference. She feared an encounter with her ex-fiancé there. As a substitute in presidential research, she drove off with Bosco into the Shenandoah Valley, the gateway to which is Harper's Ferry, West Virginia, where the Potomac and Shenandoah rivers meet, and where in 1859 Colonel Robert E. Lee captured John Brown.

Some twelve miles along the valley lies Charles Town, where Brown was tried and hanged. But its better claim to fame is that this whole area was surveyed and laid out into streets by the young George Washington, and that the town was founded and named by one of his brothers. At the far side of town, Eula found the first clue that she'd come to examine. It was a road-marker at the entrance to a grey-granite, compact and classical dwelling called Harewood. The marker told her that Harewood had been the home of Samuel Washington, brother to the General.

When she had taken a snapshot, Eula climbed the fence and went through the meadow and the apple orchard till she found the inevitable family cemetery of southern estates, this one located in a grove of willows. Some who lay there were slaves, and some were masters, such being the structure of ante-bellum families. The gravestone which Eula photographed was dimly chiseled on. Its greening tablet read: Abram Fielding Chase, beloved grandnephew of this home, 1800-1845, son of Fielding Lewis and our sister, Betty.

Eula returned to her car and driving southwestward, crossed the border into Virginia. She proceeded another twenty miles, reaching the village of Colby, where she entered the churchyard of Grace Episcopal Church. Here the stones were in better repair, and the one that she photographed had the clearcut markings: Captain Jeremiah Washington Chase, CSA, son of Abram Chase, died in the honor of God and country at the Battle of Winchester, Virginia, 1862. Nearby lay Elisha Chase, son of Abram (1860-1910), and Ezekiel Chase (1900-1945), the last stone erected by his beloved son, Jeremiah.

The girl noted: "A line of men with the names of prophets and patriarchs. Jeremiah, son of Ezekiel, son of Elisha, son of Abram the second, son of Abram the first, whose mother was George Washington's sister."

When Eula came to write her story as a regular contribution to the *Reporter*, she gave the complicated genealogy with precision, having doublechecked it through the church records. She reproduced her pictures of the various gravestones to dress up the article. But neither Eula nor her publishers had any control over second-and-third-hand renditions of her work. In her lonely quarters at Laker's Acres a few mornings later, Eula heard the nauseously cheery radio voice of Happy Johnny Jorgins, the "toothbrush lark":

"Wake up! Brush up! Here's the latest, highly confidential scoop. Have you noticed the striking resemblance of President Chase to the George Washington on your postage stamps? Have you had the feeling that these two men together are first in war, first in peace, first in the hearts of their countrymen. No wonder. It has now been revealed from top secret sources that Jeremiah Chase not only comes from a long line of prophets but is also the direct descendant of General George Washington, who hitherto was supposed to be childless. Now, for a telegenic smile like the Finnigan brothers, place one-quarter inch of Shino on your toothbrush and—"

It would be a distortion of history to imply that Americans of 1976 took any of this seriously. They no more believed that Chase was the reincarnation of Washington than the Greeks believed Homer's yarn that Helen of Troy was really the daughter of Zeus and Leda, or that Achilles was the son of Peleus and Thetis, the sea-nymph. But it was a pleasant convention to swallow these poetic fantasies. It paid a rich compliment that cost nobody anything to accept Helen as part goddess, and Achilles as part god. The Romans, inheritors of the Greek literature, adopted the same mock-credulous attitude. Ovid, writing in the sophisticated Augustan Age of Rome, spoofed and charmed his audiences by repeating the Greek myths, but did so with a knowing wink:

I prate of ancient poets' monstrous lies
Ne'er seen, nor now or then, by human eyes.

All would have passed off smoothly enough if certain dead serious, literal-minded monitors of public taste hadn't barged in. The *New York Times* disapproved of Chase as well as the Chase cult. It could not distinguish between them, and was completely taken in by the fanciful delight that people took in pretending to believe the charming nonsense about Chase's being a reincarnation of Washington or a modern replica of King Arthur. Toward the end of March there came this thunderation from Times Square:

> Hardly a Republican speech in the current West Virginia primary has failed to allude to the obscure incident after the American Revolution when George Washington was offered, and indignantly rejected, the proposal that he be crowned king of America. Flimsy as such material is, it has proved sufficient for undisciplined GOP politicians to lay claim to a "royal" descent for Jeremiah Chase. And the mere coincidence that the President uses a circular piece of furniture in the White House Fish Room to meet with a dozen unofficial advisors has prompted allusions to the Round Table of King Arthur of Camelot.
>
> All this is most unfortunate. True, the configuration of legendary history does somewhat match our recent national experiences. In mythology (and in 1976?) a majestic figure (Mr. Chase?) arises in time of crisis to save his people from disaster and to set them in the paths of salvation and grandeur. In the short view, Mr. Chase may have done this for America, but let us not hyperbolize. Mr. Chase in truth is all too human. He has very often been absent from his duties lately, and seems to spend an unwarranted amount of time at the Paca Clinic in Baltimore with his stricken wife. This itself, along with the fact that he is neglecting his official chores in guiding Congress, shows him to be an erring statesman if a devoted husband.

This testy contribution by the *New York Times* brought Chase widespread sympathy and approbation over the care he showed for the incarcerated Cora. It did nothing to discourage the fanciful enjoyment of modern legendry. There followed a widely reprinted column by Obermeister in defense of the President. Phil gave too much credence to the mythology, too much importance to the

Times and too much reference to a pair of historians, Bardson and the late Toynbee, whom his readers had barely heard of. The column did, however, justify in lofty terms the President's aloofness from public affairs, and it did predict that the President would eventually come back into action as a greater leader than ever before. Obermeister wrote:

> The *New York Times* ponderously objects to the mass worship accorded to President Chase, but does not come down upon the right chord. The only valid reason for deploring the adulation is the one previously put forward by Mr. Bardson—namely, that we are a democratic nation, and in no need of an Indispensable Man. Mr. Chase has said so all along. He has no part whatever in stimulating a hero aura. The opposite is true.
>
> Yet the critics who chide him with too much conjugal fidelity in withdrawing from public sight to visit an ill wife are unwittingly calling attention to another phase of the mythology à la Toynbee. Withdrawal of a legendary hero from the company of his compatriots is in perfect alignment to the much-discussed configuration or shape of the hero-myth. There must be withdrawal so that there can be return. Moses absented himself into the mountains and, farther back, a number of the Greeks made a descent into Hades. Toynbee himself discusses this phenomenon as follows:
>
> "The withdrawal makes it possible for the personality to realize powers within himself which might have remained dormant if he had not been released for the time being from his social toils and trammel. Such a withdrawal may be a voluntary action on his part, or it may be forced upon him by circumstances beyond his control; in either case the withdrawal is an opportunity and perhaps a necessary condition. . . . The return is the essence of the whole movement, as well as its final cause."
>
> I am suggesting that we must more patiently await Mr. Chase's return to the center of activities—at which time he will prove himself a still greater American than we presently know.

There came a discreet knock on the door of Cora's bedroom. A female attendant entered with the breakfast tray. Except that the door had a fake knob that didn't allow the door to be fastened, and that the single window was shatterproof and sealed, the room was like any other in a good hospital or small hotel. It was the best that the Paca Clinic could offer, and it was on the corridor called Seven-East, where patients were allowed to wear their own clothes.

Cora and the attendant exchanged "Good mornings." The bed was wound to a position for sitting, and the tray was placed on a table that fitted across the bed.

Cora partook sparingly of the sliced fruit, toast and coffee. She had slept well under mild sedation, and she thought of herself as "happy"—that relative, resilient word which fits itself to extraordinary circumstances. Here in her sanctuary, she was shut away from the fears and horrors that were beyond her understanding.

> Stone walls do not a prison make,
> Nor iron bars a cage;
> Minds innocent and quiet take
> That for an hermitage.

The attendant returned to remove the tray and to hand Cora the morning paper, the *Baltimore Banner*, its pages already searched and excised of stories that related to crime and violence, especially those that related in any way to suicide. But the national news was there, with reports on the President's doings, and so was the Obermeister column and other notices which dealt with the cult of worship that was building up around Jerry Chase. A perusal of these items fetched from Jerry's wife a merry laugh. Immediately, she heard the hustling footsteps of the floor nurse in the corridor called Seven-East. That solicitous warder seemed to pause outside the door to test whether the laughter was no more than a normal exclamation of amusement or would escalate into hysteria. Cora, knowing the signals, contained her mirth into a dimpled smile. But she thought:

"Imagine! Jerry—a reincarnation of George Washington! I'll bet he laughed much louder than I did. But I bet—I bet, after he thought it over, he was perfectly furious at such nonsense."

Then, she settled back against the pillows, and indulged a little in something she wasn't supposed to do, and wasn't allowed much solitude to do, that is—to think about herself. Cora was somewhat amused by the hospital rigmarole, and not at all mystified by the scientific jargon. During the morning she would be taken to the assembly room for the physical therapy class, then she would be allowed to go out with a nurse and visit some shops or one of the art galleries. Sometimes, instead of going out into the town, she would "go to clinic," as they called it, which meant sitting in a room with three psychiatrists who questioned her, and then talked aloud among themselves as if she were not there.

That was when she would hear the jargon, but she never let on that she comprehended. One doctor would name-drop her type. Schizoid: a personality in which the libido is directed more to the inner life than to the external world. Another would use the initials D.P. She knew them to stand for dementia praecox. There was always a lot of gabbling in prefixes, like acro-, myso- and xeno-. When they were attached to the base-word phobia, Cora knew the prefixes indicated that she had fears of high places (the White House), of dirt (on the hands of persons like those impeachment demonstrators) and of strangers (those millions of faceless citizens who were Jerry's constituents).

Her fears being what they were, this place was where she belonged, and yet Cora began to whimper a little, though not loud enough to be heard. She knew she could get along all right in the outer world so long as Jerry could be with her, or not very far away. This thought—the need for Jerry—caused Cora to pick up the *Banner* and reread some of those silly stories that exaggerated her husband's greatness.

The door opened to admit the day nurse, Laetitia (Lefty) Sparks. Miss Sparks was tall, angular, graceful and strong, with a decided nose and uncompromisingly red hair. If she'd been a man, she'd have been strikingly handsome, and Cora always thought of Lefty as the sister in a household of big, rollicking, good-looking brothers.

"Hullo, there, chum," Lefty said to Cora. "Ready to be up and at it?"

She'd spied evidence of tears on Cora's face. "None of that. Leave the weeping to us."

"I'm fine, Lefty. In fact, I was just thinking of something that ..."

"Yes?" Miss Sparks held the negligee and Cora slipped into it. "Tell me about it when you've had your bath."

The bath was private and then, negligee-clad, Cora went into a smaller adjoining room where, as a very privileged patient, she was allowed to keep her wardrobe. Springtime dresses and suits hung on portable racks; there was a shelf for hats and another for shoes, and a walnut dresser for her lingerie. For the first engagement of the day, Cora put on a white dress that would have been suitable for a garden party. While she sat at the dresser to do her hair, she resumed the conversation.

"Lefty, I was thinking of a way I might get out of here. Or, I think so."

"Oh?"

"Please don't think I want to leave you," said Cora seriously. "Everybody here means well, and I've been made very comfortable. But it quietly dawned on me that my husband is being driven out of politics."

"Well, for pity's sake don't mention such a thing to the President. He might ..."

Cora turned abruptly and looked into Miss Sparks' face. "You mean he might think it's wishful thinking on my part?"

"It would hurt him, Cora, and we mustn't do that. Come along."

They went into Seven-East, through a locked door and down six floors by elevator to an assembly room where other patients had gathered. Those from the Sevens all wore their own clothes, but they were now joined by patients from the Eights, who wore utility seersucker dresses supplied by the hospital. A cheery little man in tight pants and a roll-neck sweater clapped his hands.

"Your attention, ladies. This is your day for Body Lightness class. Our pianist will now play a march, and I want you to just walk in rhythm with your hands lightly above your heads . . . thus . . . so."

The piano struck up "Oh, Susanna," and the patients started their march. After a reassuring smile or two at Cora, Miss Sparks excused herself, for the room was well guarded with attendants, and hurried down to the ground floor where the physicians kept office. She knocked and entered a door marked: Dr. Alice Hatcher, saying:

"May I, Dr. Hatcher?"

"Certainly." Dr. Hatcher was grey, thin and so nervous that the rumor seemed credible that she'd once been a psycho case herself, and had entered this branch of medicine out of a personal experience. "Something about Mrs. Chase?"

"Yes. She's just confided the feeling that her husband is being hounded out of politics. Driven, was her word."

Dr. Hatcher lifted the phone: "Desk, please ask Drs. Hastie and Grindl to come here if they're free. Say that it concerns Mrs. Chase. Sit down, Miss Sparks. Take that chair."

The two women waited in silence till the office door brought Clem Hastie, a thickset, youngish man with heavy spectacles, and then Edward Grindl, a lantern-jawed, dark-skinned Viennese. When the new arrivals were seated on the couch, Dr. Hatcher asked Miss Sparks to give in the fullest detail all that Mrs. Chase had said that morning. Lefty complied, and Grindl said in his thick accent:

"Iz quite clear. Zee projection of a persecution complex from zee lady to her huzband."

"Yes, I agree," said Dr. Hastie. "The patient is beginning to display delusions. It's perfectly evident that President Chase is an immensely popular politician. He could be carried to reelection on the shoulders of his admirers. If the patient sees him being driven out, that's because of introspective separation from the world of realities. I think we have done wrong to keep her in Seven-East. She should be immediately moved to Eight-West for closer observation and more intense treatment."

Alice Hatcher shakily lit a cigarette. "I might concur in the diagnosis, but not with the proposed procedure. Mrs. Chase is quite comfortable and manageable in Seven-East. To move her to a close-scrutiny corridor might trigger a recession."

"Zee illness is in zee patient, not put there by zee treatment."

Miss Sparks was writhing with indignation.

"May I speak?"

"Certainly, nurse."

"Please pardon me if I speak out of turn. The only reason I reported this incident was to help Mrs. Chase. I thought, of course, that you doctors would try to find out why she made the remark. Perhaps she made it, as you say, out of a projection. Perhaps she made it from a glimmer of hope. Perhaps her remarks represent something more."

"Such as?"

"There's just the off-chance that Mrs. Chase was reaching for reality. Has anybody thought of that?"

"Miss Sparks," said Alice Hatcher, "rest assured we will continue this conference, and leave nothing unexplored. Meanwhile, please rejoin your patient."

When Miss Sparks returned to the assembly room, the patients were tossing gay-colored balloons off their fingertips and dancing to the strains of "When the Saints Come Marching In." When Body Lightness class ended, Lefty accompanied Cora back to Seven-East and waited while the patient re-dressed for the street in a pretty Easter dress of pastel blue and a flowered straw hat.

"How lovely you look, dear. I wish the President could see you just as you stand there. It would cheer his heart."

"Yes, Jerry needs cheering as much as I do. Lefty, I promise not to mention what I said this morning. I would rather die than have him believe that I would want to see him driven out."

"Come on, dear," said Lefty. They descended to the street, and took a cab to Hutzler's Department Store. The treatment called for Cora to feel as free of confinement as the precautions allowed. Nothing gives a woman more sense of normality than to go shopping for things she doesn't need. Cora bought a silk blouse and some sachet powders. She tried on half a dozen other garments which were just enough of a temptation to be delightful. The items were charged and carried off to the Green Door Tea Room where the two women ordered luncheon.

"Lefty, I feel so gay. I truly do."

"Cora, I'm trying to think of a way to help you. Tell me—why did you say this morning that your husband might be defeated?"

Cora's delicate face flushed.

"I said nothing of the sort."

"But you did. You said it twice."

"I most certainly did not."

"Now, dear—" Lefty whispered.

"Be quiet. I won't stay here. I won't have my luncheon. For god's sake, take me back to my room."

The raised voice had attracted the attention of the other women shoppers, and the hurried exit that followed caused a number of stares. By the time the patient and the nurse were safely in a taxi, Cora had found a stony composure. She sat back in her corner, her pale lips pressed tight, her eyes half closed.

"Forgive me," said Miss Sparks softly. "I blame myself so bitterly that nothing you could say or feel could make it worse for me. I will never again intrude, Mrs. Chase. I promise."

When they alighted at a side door of the hospital, Cora lost control and plunged into a sobbing fit. Their entrance to Seven-East was so emotional that the other inmates took up the cries, some laughing, some wailing, some even shrieking. Dr. Hatcher came running and did what the emergency seemed to warrant. She ordered Miss Sparks to get out of sight in Cora's room, and she ordered Cora taken forthwith to Eight-West for restraint and sedation. In the room where the day had commenced so promisingly, the miserable Lefty sat on the bed and roundly cursed herself in the language of her brothers.

"You god-damned, meddling, blundering bitch!"

She took up the morning newspaper from the wastebasket and spread it on the bed. Carefully, she read everything that Cora could have read this morning.

"But why the devil didn't I think of it before?"

Lefty jumped up and began pacing the room. She was still at it, beating a fist into her palm and muttering unladylike words when Alice Hatcher returned.

"Miss Sparks, I must say—"

"Be quiet. I've got it. Yes, I've got it. Listen, here—" She shoved the indignant doctor into a chair and stood over her. "I know that I balloxed things up, and I'll go jump off the wharf if you like. But first, let me tell you something that nobody around here knows. Crazy Cora isn't as crazy as you headshrinkers think."

Dr. Hatcher started up. "Your language—" She was forcibly thrust back into the chair.

"I don't claim to understand politics. Neither does Cora. But she does understand her husband. This identifying him with Greek heroes, Moses, George Washington—even Christ! How would a real, he-man, common-sensical fellow react to all that drivel?"

"This has nothing to do with the patient."

"The hell it hasn't," said Lefty. "When Cora said the President might be driven out, she didn't mean by defeat. She meant that he might be driven to quit rather than put up with all the foolishness that's being written and said about him."

"Well?"

"It sounds to me as if Cora is closer to reality than all the pundits who are writing politics. It sounds as if she's looking outward at her husband, rather than inward at herself. These are good signs in a psychiatric patient, aren't they, doctor?"

"You're forgetting your position here," said Dr. Hatcher, at last succeeding in gaining her feet.

"I admit it," said Lefty. "But that poor lady is no more a D.P. than you are. Cora is frightened of certain things. She's a nervous wreck, but she's far from being a schizoid. You've got no right to haul her off to a lock-up ward. It'll only make her worse."

"We shall see," said Dr. Hatcher. You may go now, Miss Sparks."

Word that the President's wife had been seen in public, in a distraught condition, could not be kept from the gossip columns. Two days after Cora was rumored to have flung a fit in a big hotel dining room, Flynn called reporters into his office but so many showed up that the meeting was moved into the press lounge. Jim got up on a chair with some notes in his hand, and said:

"There's been a lot of speculation . . ."

The place was so quiet that the whistle of a cardinal in the trees outside could be heard in the strained room.

". . . on what that Round Table in the Fish Room is all about that . . ."

Breaths were audibly exhaled in disappointment. Jim wasn't going to talk about Mrs. Chase, his listeners knew. He was going to bury that story under something else that would be so newsy they'd have to write it.

". . . I'm going to give you some names. So get out your pencils."

There was a shuffling of bodies in the crowded room as the news hawks dug into their pockets for the instruments of their trade. Flynn commenced anew.

"The President meets with these so-called Twelve Apostles, who are nothing more than informal advisors. They convene two Fridays of each month. Their discussions are off-record and non-political, so don't ask me to go into that, but here's who they are, with some reasons why they were chosen."

Flynn waited till the notebooks stopped rustling and said:

"The first six are well known public officials: Senator McJay, GOP floorleader. The President respects him highly. Senator Arthur Nestorson. The President sets store by the wisdom of Mr. Nestorson's years. Speaker John Krebs. Mr. Chase believes this young man underwent a deep change of heart as a result of the impeachment episode.

"Vice President George S. Rigor. No need to explain him.

"Ambassador Hazleton, recalled from Argentina to be Deputy Secretary of State. The President likes the way that Hazleton has come to look at international affairs.

"The Honorable Erasmus Hannibal. No man stands higher in the President's regard."

Again Flynn paused to let the note-takers catch up. He continued:

"There are four from the academic world who need no introduction. They are: John Collins, Dean of the Faculty, Princeton University; Daniel Katzberg, President of the University of California; the Rev. J. Silliman Sullivan, President of Notre Dame; Davenport Allenby, Superintendent of the Air Force Academy."

Flynn waited a moment before saying: "Two more men, less familiar to you, make up the twelve knights of the Round Table, as the press insists upon calling it. They are: Harold Bardson, historian, novelist, lawyer, and ponyfarm proprietor. You can look him up in *Who's Who.*

"Finally, a surprise—Miles Standish Smith, head of the Nathan Hale Society."

At the pronouncement of the final name, there was a gasp of astonishment and unbelief which was repeated, in tones of horror and disapproval. By next morning, Washington's leading daily, the *Standard,* exclaimed:

> What next? From inside accounts we learn that these twelve men will be sent as knights errant on missions for His Majesty. Where will the Nathanite be sent—to stir up the kooks?

But Flynn's masterful ploy had checkmated the rumors that had been building up about Cora Chase.

Chapter Thirty-One

Girl and woman, matron and political manager, Nellie Finnigan never expected the course of ambition to run smooth. She didn't mind tossing on the well-known tide of public affairs, enduring its ebbs and whirlpools, for she believed in catching the flood just at the time it would bear her on to the fulfillment of ambitions—the first of them being to get Governor Andy into the presidency, with Senator Barney and Mayor Chester to follow.

Thus, in the sunny suite on the second floor of the New York gubernatorial mansion at Albany, she sat alone these mid-March days, but never lonely—she was too self-possessed for that. She toted up the many twists and turns of fortune since that fateful Thanksgiving Day.

Sam Lepol's crash: As we all agreed he'd have been a tough customer to shave.

Jerry Chase's accession: He looked still tougher at the beginning. Jerry's got a way about him. Nobody's made war popular since Teddy Roosevelt. Eisenhower talked about cutting the cost of government, but he was a bigger spender than Truman, even counting the Korean War. Johnson could be pinch-penny in turning out electric bulbs, but he was a two-fisted splurger on the public programs. Nobody except Chase set out to darn the holes in the Federal purse.

From the way he rose above the impeachment movement, Jerry looks unbeatable—and yet, there seems to be a sort of I-want-to-go-home instinct in him. It was in George Washington—who turned down a crown because he hadn't fought the Revolutionary War to set up another monarchy. And it was in Thomas Jefferson—who really established the two-term tradition.

Cora Chase: If I didn't know that Jerry believes life belongs to the living and not to the half-dead, to the strong and not to the feeble, I'd think—. But, no, I doubt it. Jerry wouldn't retire and let Judge Hannibal take his place on the Republican ticket because—well, because a Southerner has too many instincts going against the elevation of a Negro to the White House. The time isn't ready—not for a good many years more. There's nobody in sight for the GOP nomination except Chase himself, so I'll assume he's going to run though he hasn't announced as yet.

Chase's Fish Room Round Table: Andrew Jackson had a kitchen cabinet, and Hoover had a medicine ball cabinet, and Franklin Roosevelt had all those semi-official trustees like Harry Hopkins and Tommy the Cork. It's not unusual for a President to bring in a special group for private confabs. Truman had his cronies, and Kennedy had his Irish Mafia. But I keep thinking of Chase's homing instinct. There's a don't-give-a-damn about much that Jerry does, and it's both progressive and cumulative. He bombed the SAM sites in Cuba, then he gas-bombed the demonstrators. He practiced straight Goldwaterism, but now he's gone beyond that to Nathanism—bringing Miles Standish Smith into the inner sanctum. By jiminy, that's too much. He'll get hoist by his own petard.

On the evening of these meditations, Ma Finnigan descended at dinnertime to join the governor and Angie Finnigan, her daughter-in-law, a young woman who made herself seen but not heard. After dinner, over coffee in the living room, Ma picked up the *Albany Knickerbocker News* to see what Cal Borton was writing. She cried out.

"Glory be, Andy, did you see this? Borton's got a scoop. He

says Chief Justice Thurgood Rustin will resign and stand for Vice President on your ticket."

"Yes, Ma. Borton's been very close to brother Barney down there in Washington, and Barney leaked him the news. I phoned Barney to ask him why he broke the Finnigan-Rustin ticket so far in advance. He said it was because Borton is leaving town for a trip and needed a yarn."

"Your brother should have cleared it with me!" the old lady snapped.

"Now, Ma—you keep telling us to do things on our own once in a while. It seems that Cal is out to do us a favor, so Barney owed him one in return. Cal's off to camp on the trail of the Nathanite. Cal's promised to get some stories that'll blow Jerry Chase right out of the water."

That very night, though the Finnigans didn't know it, Calvin Borton, with typewriter and valise, stood muffled to the ears across the Avenue from the White House. He was waiting for the emergence of the twelve men who had met in the Fish Room. Borton had never before seen Miles Smith, whom he had so foully maligned, but there was no trouble sorting Smith out from the dozen men who left by the front door under the lights of the portico. Borton was quite familiar with all the others, so by elimination, the short, compact, brisk individual in a tight-buttoned black overcoat, wearing a smart bowler hat, had to be Smith. This individual did not linger to talk with the others, but moved purposefully through the west gate, nodded to the gateman and began flagging taxis that shot past. Borton snapped up a cab on his side of the street, ordered the driver to do a U-turn, and leaned from the window with his handkerchief shielding his face.

"Difficult to get a cab, mister. Can I give you a lift? Where are you going?"

"National Airport."

"Get in," said Borton. "So am I."

Borton was taking a chance, but not a wild one. He'd got Naomi, who couldn't live without him and was back on the job, to work up a dossier on Smith. The man had the reputation of being taciturn and absentminded. There were anecdotes about his being introduced two or three times to the same person during an evening, and of forgetting whether he was in Wilmington, Delaware, or Wilmington, North Carolina.

"You must be taking the Eastern Airlines shuttle," ventured Borton in the dark of the cab. "You haven't any luggage."

"Yes. Thank you for your courtesy. Smith's my name."

"So is mine," said Borton, shaking hands. "Lots of us around. Excuse me if I smoke."

He covered his face to light up, then opened the window and leaned out as he smoked, to discourage conversation. He needn't have bothered. Miles Smith took a well-worn leatherbound book from his inside pocket and, holding a small flashlight in his palm, proceeded to read all the way to the airport. He boarded the eight o'clock shuttle for Boston, selected a window seat and resumed his reading. Borton, in depositing his coat in the overhead rack, was able to sneak a look: *The Federalist Papers.* Borton's eye caught a familiar, heavily underscored passage by Hamilton: ". . . it seems to have been reserved to the people of this country, by their conduct and example, to decide the important question, whether societies of men are really capable or not of establishing good government. . . ."

Settling down, Borton chose his own reading matter from his briefcase. The folder prepared by Naomi began with a candid camera shot. Miles Smith had a round head of fine silver hair. The face was one of arresting frankness, with extraordinarily blue eyes, and a solid chin. The lips, with their courageous lines, carried the faint curl of a man who had suffered anguish. Borton turned to the next page, where Naomi had given vital statistics.

"The subject was born in Concord, Mass., November 22, 1921, of old New England stock. He was taken by parents—U.S. Army—to Canal Zone as infant. Entered U.S. Military Academy, September, 1941, but in December of that year, following Pearl Harbor, requested permission to resign from Academy and enlist as an Army private. When the Superintendent pointed out to him that Miles Smith was the fifth of that name and family to be a West Pointer, that Miles would be far more valuable as an officer than as a GI, the young man insisted stubbornly, 'Sir, there isn't time.'

"His resignation granted, Smith did enlist, rose to master sergeant in the African campaign, received battlefield commission of second lieutenant on Normandy beachhead, June, 1944, and less than a year later was Captain Smith of an advance party that linked up with the Russians on the Elbe River. When his buddies welcomed their Russian comrades-in-armes and fraternized in a wild saturnalia, Captain Smith denounced the celebration, got into a brawl with a Soviet major who jeered at American democracy, and, eventually, because of his excellent combat record, was allowed to appeal his court martial directly to the Supreme Commander, General Dwight D. Eisenhower. Captain Smith was given the choice of apologizing to the Russian Army authorities or of losing his temporary commission and being dismissed from the service without prejudice. He replied in writing to General Eisenhower:

" 'I will never apologize for striking an enemy of my country. To me there is little difference in infamy between the crooked cross of Nazism and the twisted symbol of hammer and sickle. Both are anathema to the American ideal of freedom for the soul of man. Instead of greeting the soldiers of Communism, we should drive them back to Russia, as we are now well able to do. But if we treat them as friends, if we disband our conquering forces, if we withdraw from the territory we have liberated from black totalitarianism, then we will someday have to liberate it from red totalitarianism—or bear the shame of having failed in our mission. M. S. Smith, Captain, U.S.A.' "

Naomi's dossier continued: "Separated under a cloud from the U.S. Army, which his family had served for so long, Miles Smith for a while disappeared from public attention. He married a Boston girl, Bertha Cates. His friends said that Bertha was one of the few persons ever to 'understand Miles.' Being without a college degree, he worked on farms and on construction jobs, studying at night. By 1950 he had received a B.S. in political science, and become an instructor at Johns Hopkins University, Baltimore, where he settled down near the campus with his wife and three sons. This was the time of the controversy over Owen Lattimore of the Hopkins faculty, and Smith was very much in the minority of that academic commotion. He wore a large Joe McCarthy button outside the classrooms. He wrote letters-to-the-editor, denouncing Lattimore as an instrument of the Soviet conspiracy. Smith's wife left him. He lost his job. He moved to Washington where he eked out a precarious living by writing pamphlets on the no-win foreign policy under Eisenhower and Kennedy.

"In 1962, Smith joined the Nathan Hale Society as an organizer and staff writer, but was soon promoted to the board of directors. In accepting the presidency of the Nathan Hale Society, July 4, 1974, Smith wrote the following letter to the membership:

" 'Too often it is forgotten that the twenty-one years granted to Captain Nathan Hale (1755-76) were more devoted to living for American ideals than to dying for his country. At Yale College, and later as an inspired writer and speaker, this young scholar-soldier was a firebrand for American liberties. At the darkest hour of the Revolution, Captain Hale volunteered for a dangerous mission behind enemy lines. He was captured by the British with valuable documents on his person and sentenced to be hanged without trial. At the gallows he quoted a noble passage from Joseph Addison's *Cato*—" 'I only regret that I have but one life to give to my country.' " Hale meant, as Addison's Cato meant, that one lifetime is but a meager contribution to make to the ideals of liberty and justice.

" 'Captain Hale's creed is the creed of our Society. We are devoting our lives to America. Today and perhaps for many years ahead, our work will be negative in nature. We shall continue to discover and denounce every soft-on-Communism trace, every sign of equivocation, within American society. We have already found examples of weakness and treachery within every administration from Truman and Eisenhower through Kennedy and Johnson and Lepol—and we have said so. We are apostles of protest—which our enemies call hate. That's how it must be for so long as there is appeasement and collaboration with the Communist world. We will not change until these accepted attitudes change. Speaking as the chosen head of this Society, I declare in the language of another who strove for American liberation: "I am in earnest—I will not equivocate—I will not excuse—I will not retreat a single inch—and I will be heard." ' "

Having read Naomi's summary, with still an hour's flight to go, Borton set up the portable typewriter in his lap and commenced his next day's column:

> En route to Brookline, Mass.—From the White House the other night, straight from a seance with the President, emerged the Grand Kleagle of the Kooks, one Miles Smith, whose mission seems to be to extend the Chase consensus into the backwaters of Nathanism.
>
> Smith, an ex-McCarthyite, must be the strangest presidential courier of all time. He was born an Army brat, so that he comes by his militarism naturally. He grew up in the Panama Canal Zone, which for years was the scene of our most disgraceful adventure in imperialism, ending only when President Johnson virtually gave the Canal away.
>
> As a World War II officer, Smith was guilty of the kind of insubordination which later led to the disgrace of General Douglas MacArthur. Both men defied their country's policy as being soft on Reds. Both demanded action which might have led to World War III. Like Robert Welch before him, Miles Smith took a position in derogation of the beloved Eisenhower on the subject of coexistence with Communism. Like Goldwater before him, Smith has been an extremist who finds no virtue in moderation.
>
> One may well ask what President Jeremiah Chase needs with such supporters as Miles Smith and the Nathanites? The answer must be that Chase hopes to become President of all Americans—in short, a dictator. This is no idle fear, considering the well-known Fascist tendencies of both Chase and the Nathanites. Your columnist intends to follow Smith wherever he goes and to report upon his crafty, secret misdoings. I hope, by exposing him and his followers, to warn the nation against the fate of many republics that have fallen prey to extremists of the far right.

At this point, Borton folded the sheets into a Western Union envelope that was addressed to his syndicate. He summoned the stewardess with an imperious gesture.

"Send this message, night-press rate collect, as soon as we land," he told the girl more haughtily than one American should ever speak to another.

The man whom Borton was following took a cab from Honey

Fitz Airport in Boston and was driven to a modest apartment house in a nearby suburb. He rode the rickety self-service elevator to the top floor, let himself into a small utility apartment where he poured a glass of milk from the refrigerator. He sipped the milk while he donned wool pajamas, for the weather was chilly and not much heat reached him at this level. Taking the black leather family Bible from the bedside table, Miles read for a while from the Epistles of Saint Paul, then he knelt and prayed while Borton skulked outside the door.

Jim Flynn did what he was told to do. He took off his hat and hung it over the leaping hand of the speedometer. The cream-yellow roadster roared along the Washington-Baltimore parkway where the first white blossoms nodded from the apple trees and yellow jonquils rippled above the grass. Ladybird Johnson's beautification program had made the road—and many roads—a joy to travel in the springtime, but not at 100 miles per hour.

"Sir, I wish you wouldn't do it."

"They'll say I drive too fast. They'll probably invent a beer can I'm supposed to be waving. Jim, the road's been cleared. The faster I get over it the better."

"Mr. President, you didn't hire me for a yes-man. Remember? You're being too reckless."

"That's right." The car eased down to a legal 50 mph, but the restless foot squirmed on the accelerator. "My god, Jim, I give myself three hours a day to visit Cora. If I loaf along the way, I'm taking time that I could spend with her. Don't the people understand?"

"You've never explained it to them, sir."

"No, but I don't think a press conference would be in order right now. I'll hold one soon. Meanwhile—what's Obermeister's term for it?"

"Withdrawal-and-return."

"I'm entitled to it," the President grumbled. "You must take care of the press for a while. Please, wait in the car."

They arrived at the Johns Hopkins Hospital. The President hurried between two Baltimore policemen through the grim portals to the Paca Clinic where his wife was under treatment. Flynn had to sit and wait, had to review in his mind, as he did day after day, the pros and cons of the way things were going:

Pro: Obermeister's term, the withdrawal-and-return, was only a relative situation. The President was on the job, and the country knew it. He was visible to reporters all morning as he walked through the White House corridors for meetings in the various rooms. True, Chase gave only his greetings and never stopped to talk. But bills got signed, delegations were met and appointments kept. Up on the Hill, Congress had expedited its routine Tuesday-to-Thursday pace, and adjournment was in sight by the end of June, the earliest going-down date in memory.

Con: Those damned columns of Borton on the trail of Miles Smith were the Administration's worst headache. Cal was no longer an inside reporter like Eula, nor a reflective one like Phil. His output had become a prolonged flashflood of invective. Nothing from Cal's reportage would indicate that he'd done any more than stand on the sidewalk outside the headquarters building in Brookline, Massachusetts, but his descriptions made that rather commonplace office building seem to glow with the brimstone of its internal iniquity.

Cal had written of pale emissaries going and coming from the building, of shifty-eyed persons arriving by day and weeping secretaries departing at nightfall. One column ran:

> The word is that the head Hater is preparing a Manifesto of some length. One source has it that Smith has discovered a Democratic conspiracy for the forced transmigration of southern whites to Alaska, and of Eskimos to the Everglades. Another tells of a plot at the courthouse level to issue marriage licenses only to racially-mixed couples, forcing the Caucasians to catch up to the illegitimacy record of the Negroes.

From Massachusetts, Borton had followed Smith's private plane on a whirlwind tour of what Cal considered the centers of political paranoia: to Dallas and Los Angeles, to Salt Lake City and Selma and the Florida gold coast. Cal wrote of secret meetings which resounded with yells and hoots, as the attendants joined their hymn of hate.

New Orleans, La.—At last I approach the climax of this series—a press conference by the Mogul of Malice himself will soon be held. From this city I can report the substance of Smith's Manifesto, the details of which he has been spreading among the creep-klans of his organization: a spell-out of all the diseased nightmares of morons. Smith has been contacting his regional subalterns to put before them the proposition of sparing Chase and pouring the vials of their loathing upon the Democratic opposition. But there are degrees of insanity. It may be stated with confidence that there is not enough craziness in the Chase family to satisfy the Smithites. They will eventually turn and rend the President, and this is the message that this nutty knight of the Round Table will bring back to Washington where he will meet reporters in Lafayette Park.

Flynn resumed his count:

Pro: Despite the sensationalism of the Borton series, an opposite trend was moving in the President's favor. Chase's suggestion of the "absent treatment" to Braddock had caused that individual's isolation by the groups he'd once manipulated. It had extended to other shadowy leaders. The FBI had hung their pictures in Post Offices with the admonition: "Americans, snub this man." An exodus of Communists-sans-cartes had moved toward the borders for Cuba, Mexico, Warsaw and Prague, and a sweeping cancellation of passports augured against round-trip passage.

Con: Yet the non-appearance in public of President Chase, and the knowledge of his daily visits to Paca Clinic during working hours, militated against all that was going well, and all that had gone so gloriously in the recent past. "What's Chase done for the country lately?" was the mocking query that came through to Jim Flynn.

An hour had passed. A blue-coated figure surged through the hospital entrance, and the tall form, stooped with undisguised misery, plunged for the waiting car as Flynn jumped out to open the door.

"You drive, Jim."

It took no inquiry from Flynn to learn news of the patient. The President himself might as well have been an animated clinical chart. Every drooping muscle of the sagging face was an index on

Cora. The President's body lying against the seat-cushions was the register of a hopeless psychiatric case inside those gloomy walls. No need for the press secretary to hurtle the high-powered vehicle back along the parkway. The dash each day to reach the bedside was contradicted on every return trip by a lumpish huddle that showed no hurry to get anywhere.

> Love goes toward love, as schoolboys from their books.
> But love from love, toward school with heavy looks.

Wheeling into the White House grounds, Flynn pulled to the south lawn steps. He opened the car door for the President who slowly disentangled his long form from its listless huddle, and moved with a spineless slouch up the steps. The Commander in Chief looked the very embodiment of dejection.

Flynn followed with a sunken heart. Good god, how would the country keep? How would the wobbling world be borne if these Atlas-shoulders shirked their burden?

Inside the great hall waited Vice President Rigor. His aplomb was unshaken but two feverspots of excitement burned in his cheekbones,

"Mr. President, we've got an alert, sir. I took the liberty to call the key personnel of your cabinet.

"I count on you, Rigor. Come along, Flynn."

The languid form of the sickbed caller acquired straightness and hustle as he strode down the hall toward the cabinet room. The Secretaries of State and Defense stood above the heaped ash-trays of crumpled cigarettes. The Attorney General's face wore its ashen color of anxiety. Flynn did not ordinarily attend these crisis-conferences at the big cucumber-shaped table in the cabinet room, but the President motioned him to sit down, and then took his place at the head of the board.

"Let's hear it, men."

"There's a strongly worded demand from Markov," said the Secretary of State. "He regrets your depressed condition. But he says that there will be very serious consequences unless the Sixth

Fleet pulls up anchor at Naples and heads for Gibraltar and the Atlantic Ocean. Meanwhile, he demands a summit conference."

"Rigor!" said Chase.

"Yes, sir!" The ramrod-like man stood up and saluted.

"A jet will get you to the Sixth Fleet flagship in four hours. When you reach there, please notify Markov of your arrival, and sign yourself as Deputy Commander in Chief. Give the Admiral my regards, and ask him to steam full speed for the Dardanelles. I want Markov to know that you're personally looking down his throat, and that we haven't any idea of evacuating the Mediterranean."

"Mr. President," gasped State as the Vice President bolted from the room. "I was going to propose that we let the Fleet remain at Naples and invite Markov to a summit conference. It's one thing to bomb the Cuban coast, but it's quite another to flout the Russians in their home waters."

"That's what Markov is thinking, Mr. Secretary. He also thinks I'm too weighed down with personal worries to stand up to him. He needs to be reminded that this isn't a one-man country. Rigor is more trigger-happy than I am, if anything. You might notify the Russian ambassador that we consider the Protector General's demands to be unworthy of any reply. We would never come to any conference under a threat."

"Yes, sir. I thought that's what you'd say, and I've already informed the Soviet ambassador. But don't you think that Marshal Markov might misinterpret the dispatch of the Fleet to the eastern Mediterranean? Wouldn't we be better off just to hold maneuvers off the Italian boot?"

"No, Mr. Secretary, it's not possible for Markov to misunderstand me. If he starts a war, it'll be fought in his own back yard. Now I need the attention of the Secretary of Defense."

"Yes, Mr. President," said that individual.

"I want you to take necessary measures to see that Vice President Rigor's death is avenged, if it occurs. Don't wait for any further instructions from me. We'll use this message to all unit commanders at the missile sites—'You may fire when ready, Gridley.' And, Flynn—"

"Yes, sir."

"You'd better call the White House reporters into your office and tell them exactly what's going on. Everything said in this room is on the record."

The Secretaries of State and Defense departed, but the Attorney General stayed behind.

"Mr. President," he said when they were alone. "My crisis isn't on the same level as a war scare, but I thought I'd better let you know. Chief Justice Rustin phoned me his resignation just an hour ago. I'm sure it means that he intends to run for Vice President on the Democratic ticket with Governor Finnigan."

"The pompous clown!" ejaculated Chase. "The little publicity he got at the impeachment trial went to his head. The Russians and the Democrats have hit me at the same time for the same reason. They figure I'm in a sinking spell over my poor wife's condition. Well, Erasmus, with a Negro on the Democratic ticket, you'll be the natural choice for the GOP. You've been disappointed in the past. This time you should be a shoo-in for the job that Sam Lepol and I both might have given you."

"I thought of that," smiled Hannibal. "That's why I hurried over here. Do you want me on the Republican ticket, Mr. President?"

"Yes, I do," said the President. "Not because you're black, but because there isn't a better man. I would trust you right here in my place. You've amply proved yourself."

"I think I have at that," the Attorney General nodded. "For six hours last November, I was more President than anybody else. And for four weeks, I campaigned in New Hampshire and delivered you a landslide. Statesman under pressure, politician in the clutch, I qualify."

"You do."

"But, sir—" grinned the Negro. "I didn't say I liked the big cheese act I pulled last Thanksgiving. And between the two of us, I'd sooner be in hell than go through another campaign like New Hampshire. If you're offering to take me on your ticket as Vice President in November, no thanks."

Chase got up and stretched. Hannibal had looked out the window and had seen him arrive at the White House, looking dispirited and beaten. Since then there had been a crisis in foreign affairs, and now this lesser matter, and the President was a different man entirely. Hannibal imagined he could see the electricity run where the blood ran in such men as Jerry Chase.

The President said: "By sun-up, we could have a war on, Hannibal. If that happens, I'll need you in the cabinet. But if Markov backs down, as I think he will, how'd you like to be Chief Justice?"

"Very much," exclaimed the Attorney General.

Chapter Thirty-Two

Late at night, after the meeting in New Orleans, Miles Smith had flown himself to Washington. He had come by cab to a small inside room at a low-rate hotel a block off Pennsylvania Avenue. It wasn't that he liked to live meanly. He had been raised among family possessions of old New England. As the offspring of Army commanding officers he knew the meaning of RHIP—Rank Has Its Privileges. But he had put all that aside, believing he could serve best in this other capacity. He took his salary and expense account from the dues of members, some rich and some poor, and he felt it wasn't right to live high on other people's hogs. So, this night he slept between thin walls that separated him from nearby transients, but not from the annoying, sometimes revolting, intrusive sounds of their bedsqueaks, snorings, quarrelings and ablutions.

Miles awoke at the soft April dawn—a gladsome month of flowers and sunshine, yet a sad month too, which brought the agony and death of Christ before it brought the resurrection. Miles brushed his clothes and buffed his shoes. He always dressed nattily, always looked like an officer who was going out in mufti. He took breakfast on instant coffee, which he made from the hot water spiggot. Today he had the morning ordeal of a press conference, which he felt obliged to hold, and he had another engagement that he dreaded almost as much.

He sat down for a while to read alternately from *The Federalist Papers* and the Holy Bible. He was fully aware that there was double distrust of a man who set himself up as a super patriot and who also happened to be intensely religious. A lot of charlatans, he had to admit, wrapped themselves in the flag and went in for flaming crosses. It seemed too bad that these frauds had caused people to believe it uncouth and chauvinistic to look for national destiny in the Will of God. Miles' New England forebears had gone into battle with a rifle in hand and a Bible in the coat pocket, and he'd done the same thing in World War II. He didn't consider it bad theology to believe that God was always in the fight for freedom.

At nine o'clock, after nearly two hours of reading, he kept the first engagement of the day by picking up the phone and dialing a number that was already in his head.

"Dr. Harrison, please. This is Miles Smith." The doctor took the call. "Well, sir, what's the score?"

"Hello, Mr. Smith. Yes, I have the information. I'd rather not give it over the phone. Couldn't you walk around to my place?"

"I could. I'm at the Evers Hotel right near your office, but I don't need any hand-holding. How did my cardiogram read?"

"I'm sorry," said Dr. Harrison. "It didn't read very well. Do you want it with the bark off—?"

"Yes, I do."

"Degenerative angina. In layman's language, it's more heart failure than heart trouble. I'm forced to make this known to the FAA for which I'm a registered physical examiner. You shouldn't be flying a plane."

"You do what you think is best. Thank you for your frankness, Doctor."

Miles hung up. The diagnosis wasn't unexpected, and he felt no shock. But he did feel—or so, with a smile, he imagined—somewhat as Nathan Hale did when General Howe ordered him to be executed. A bad-news cardiogram wasn't as dramatic as a hanging sentence, but it did remind a man pretty forcefully that he had but one life to give for his country. It made Miles wonder if the life he'd lived, and the way he'd chosen, had been worthwhile.

He closed his reading material, and sat there to think. Last night the hotel clerk had snickered over the registration: Miles Standish Smith, affiliation, the Nathan Hale Society. The bellman who'd carried up the bag to his room had looked at him the way a lot of people look at known and dangerous crackpots. Miles was accustomed to it, but it wasn't pleasant.

The trip he'd just finished wasn't much fun either. He didn't need anybody to tell him that some of the Nathanites really were kooks, but you had to fight battles with whatever troops you could enlist. Many a commander had taken the field with broomstick soldiers in the rank and file. The payoff was what you accomplished with the material in hand, and whether the mission you undertook was of any real importance to the country you were trying to serve.

He stopped trying to figure out any answers of his own, and went back to reading. Within an hour, the phone rang.

"It's Jim Flynn, Mr. Smith. I know you've got a tough press conference coming up. If you'd like to drop over, I might be able to give you some pointers."

"I'd be glad to, Mr. Flynn."

Miles crossed the Avenue, conscious of a few curious and hostile stares. They were partly the legacy of his long-standing notoriety, but also the direct result, he judged, of those cruel Borton columns in this newspaper-reading and personality-spotting town. He gave his name to the White House guard at the West Gate, and was grateful for the man's conditioned politeness. All sorts of characters, the celebrities as well as the nonentities, had to pass muster at the White House entrance.

"Yes, sir, Mr. Smith," said the gateman after consulting a list. "Mr. Flynn expects you. Just go in through the press lobby yonder, and he'll pick you up."

Miles walked along the driveway to the wing of the mansion where a number of men loitered with television equipment. He went through the glass door, and there was the rugged-featured Mr. Flynn whom Miles had met on a previous visit. He followed the press secretary down a corridor, into a small, smoke-hung room where a previous meeting had apparently just broken up. The two men were alone.

"Sit down, sir," Flynn said. "We've been thinking about you."

"We?"

"The President has followed your trip by certain dispatches," smiled Flynn. "Of course, you will present your statement at the regular meeting this evening. I understand your press conference will deal with its gist."

"Yes. I believe that was our understanding?"

"Sure. Sure, Mr. Smith. The President isn't seeing reporters these days, but he wants them to get plenty of news and views from other sources. I suppose you heard General Rigor's broadcast from the S.S. *Clarksburg* in the Mediterranean?"

"No. Did something happen? I've been reading books this morning."

Flynn gave a subdued chuckle. "Oh, that's good, Mr. Smith. Excuse me. You ask—did something happen? No, nothing happened—but here we just assume that everybody in the world is standing around waiting for the bang. We had another showdown with the Marshal. He crawled. Come to think of it, there must be millions of people who just weren't noticing, as well as the other millions who were. I remember once I fell on a fumble and scored a big touchdown. Afterwards I stopped off a few miles out of South Bend for a cup of coffee, and asked the waiter if he heard about the game. 'What game?' he asked. It should have taught me."

"I'm lost."

"No, you're not. I'm rambling. Wait here."

Flynn left him, and Miles felt more lost than ever. Mr. Flynn's falling on a fumble and Vice President Rigor's facing down the Russians seemed to equate a football win with an international crisis. Of course, the press secretary hadn't meant it that way, but was only saying that many epic events didn't get the credit they deserved. Still, it made Miles wonder, as he'd wondered back at the hotel, about the life he'd chosen. If he hadn't been so zealous to fight the Nazis, he'd have stayed on and graduated from the Point, and been a high-ranking officer by now. If he hadn't flared up over that scene on the Elbe, he would have come home with military honors and lived a very different existence from the one of ridicule and social exclusion as the head of the Nathanites. What had driven him? Had he been a Quixote at the windmills, a near-sighted imaginer of threats that didn't exist? He'd followed an instinctive love of country and made a private war on Communism, but was it all a delusion? Mr. Flynn's voice jarred him.

"The President—"

"Hello, Mr. Smith," said Chase, giving his hand. "I've got a few minutes between engagements. I just wanted to wish you luck at your press conference. Tell those fellows the truth. By that, I mean, don't dodge. They can't hurt you if you meet every question with perfect candor. Flynn has taught me that."

"Very well, sir."

The President hesitated. "I might as well be candid myself. No sooner did Dr. Harrison inform the FAA that you should be grounded—and give the reason why—than some busybody told a reporter. The reporter told Jim who told me. I'm very sorry to hear what I heard. Please take good care of yourself."

The desk phone rang. The President lifted it. "Yes? Well, he's a damned fool but I suppose I'll have to talk with him. I'll take the call when I get back to my office." He hung up. "That's a very important Negro leader who'll chew me out for naming Erasmus Hannibal as the Chief Justice. I'll never convince him that it wasn't a white-supremacy plot to keep Hannibal out of the vice presidency. Sometimes it seems that everything you do gets twisted out of shape. Would you believe it—the chairman of the Republican National Committee came in to warn me that I'm seeing too much of my ill wife, and right behind him came a volunteer marriage counselor who said I'm selling out the holy duty of matrimony for a cushy political job. There are times when a man can't seem to win for losing."

The phone rang again. This time Flynn took it.

"Hot line from Moscow, sir."

"I'll take it in my office, Jim. Give me another minute here."

Miles watched the President walk slowly to the window. The full, handsome, deeply melancholy face was silhouetted against the outer light that accentuated the gray in his hair and the hollowness of the round eye sockets. Miles moved a few inches to give himself a fuller view. The President noticed neither the move nor the observation. The gray-blue eyes seemed hazed with far-off thoughts—and Miles was reading from a familiar page. That estrangement! That questioning of whether the game was worth the effort! Why, then, it happened to others too. To great and wise men, to men of action and flawless decision, as well as to mere strivers like himself. There was a commonality between all men of good purpose, no matter how different their methods of striving. The President turned back to his visitor.

"Mr. Smith, I do admire you," said Chase. "I've given only a few years to my country, but you've given a mature lifetime. It gets pretty lonesome at times—and we ask, 'What for? What for?' But, then, the satisfaction is waiting deep down inside—right?"

"Why—yes. It is, of course."

"Good luck." The President nodded abruptly, and went out, back to whatever came next in keeping the world right-side up. Miles took his leave of Jim Flynn. Feeling very different than when he'd come, he left the White House and its grounds.

He crossed the Avenue into Lafayette Park. Gray-winged, beady-eyed pigeons came scavenging around, but he had nothing to give them. They left him for a group of strollers who had nuts and popcorn to scatter. Miles sat there, blinking at the sun, which stood over a corner of the Treasury Building. People drifted past now, a few pausing to stare. He thought he recognized from pictures a spry old lady with three filial younger men in tow. If it wasn't Ma Finnigan, it might have been. She stopped to look possessively at the White House, while scattering crumbs to the fluttering birds.

Some of that mobile television gadgetry he'd seen outside the press wing of the White House was being carried on shoulders and placed to surround his bench. Miles hadn't expected more than a few derisive pencil pushers to meet him here, and he summoned the President's admonition to tell the truth. Now, by a distant bonging from a church tower, he was warned it was eleven o'clock, his hour of ordeal. A honey-haired girl edged in with a mike, and men held notebooks toward him like geiger counters.

Q: For identification, Mr. Smith, are you the head of the Nathan Hale Society?

A: Yes.

Q: As such, how were you ever invited to consult with the President in his Fish Room gathering, known as the Round Table?

A: I anticipated that query. May I read a letter which is signed by James Xavier Flynn and reads: "March 13 (day after the impeachment failure). Dear Sir: The President asks you to join a small discussion group to meet at five p.m. on alternate Fridays hereafter for extra-legislational endeavors and for other general purposes. Please reply."

Q: You have attended such meetings?

A: Just one. The next one is this evening. I shall present a paper.

Q: Before we get to that, how's with this Round Table?

A: There's nothing sinister. The President asked the several educators of his choice to consider the extension of honor systems that exist in the military academies and in many southern schools. He asked the political personalities to give him further ideas about the realignment of the political parties. He asked the ecclesiastical members about the feasibility of using patriotic hymns at all services. All these, you see, are matters that can't be accomplished by federal law or federal programs.

Q: What did the President ask *you* to do, Mr. Smith?

A: I have a short, prepared statement which I'll read at this point: "The President has felt for some time that the various patriotic societies in the United States should be brought closer to the center of public activities. He intends to appoint a special White House aide to keep in touch with patriotic endeavors of all sorts. He plans to issue invitations to all groups in this field to attend a White House discussion of the problems and activities. He asked me to make a field trip for the purpose of talking with leaders and chapters of my Society." That is the end of my statement.

Q: Do you mean to say that Chase considers the Nathanites to be patriots?

A: You're Mr. Borton, of course. Yes, sir, the President includes us with the DARs, the SARs, the American Legion, the Society of the Cincinnati, the Order of the Purple Heart and many others. But he's also well aware that the Nathanites, as they're called, are a special case. Feeling that his invitation perhaps might not be graciously received, he asked me to carry it in person.

Q: A personal message to the Nathanites? Greetings from your President? To those hate-mongers and psychopaths?

A: Mr. Borton, I have another prepared statement if you don't mind. "The President feels that the so-called right-wing extremists are about the only minority that isn't covered by some bill on civil rights. He feels that right wingers have been unconscionably smeared and mistreated for their opinions' sake. Specifically, he feels the Democratic Convention was practicing mob psychology in 1964 when it condemned the John Birch Society in the same resolution as the Klan and the Communists. The President doesn't agree with the Nathanites, but he feels it's a vicious practice and a great waste to read them out of American society."

Q: But I heard them screaming like maniacs! I stood outside the secret meetings and listened to—Bedlam!

Q: Shut up, Calvin, and give somebody else a chance. Mr. Smith, how was the President's message received?

A: Well, Mr. Borton did hear some protest. Most Nathanites are restrained, dignified persons, the best citizens of any community. But we do have our ragged fringe of conspiracy-addicts. They could not instantly kick the ingrained habit of mistrust. They had been against Truman, Eisenhower, Kennedy, Johnson and Lepol. They weren't ready to believe that a true anti-Communist had finally come to the White House. There was a great deal of agonizing when I presented my manifesto.

Q: Your what?

A: The Nathan Hale Society Manifesto of '76 accepts President Chase's invitation and congratulates him. Specifically, we applaud Mr. Chase's firing Secretary Phillipson, his audacious establishing of a free government in East Cuba, his defiance of Red Russia and Red China, his expatriation of Braddock and other Communists. It came hard for my followers to say anything laudatory about a President. They protested. But, in the end, they agreed that Mr. Chase has gone a long way toward eradicating Communist influence in this country. They unanimously adopted the manifesto.

Q: Mr. Smith, what's the significance of all this? Have you and the President caused the Nathan Hale Society to go respectable?

A: The Society has always been respectable. And if I've had anything to do with making anti-Communism more effective, then I haven't lived in vain.

Press: THANK YOU, Mr. Smith.

When the park-bench conference ended, Obermeister took a quick look at his wristwatch and began picking his way through tourists in a southeasterly direction. His destination now was the intersection of 14th and F Streets, where the National Press Building used to stand. That venerable edifice had given way to the Claiborne Pell Rocket Roller Terminal, named for the Rhode Island Senator whose legislation had established jet-propelled tube service between Washington, New York and Boston. Commuter trains still came to Union Station, which was partly converted into a railroad museum, but travelers now found it equally convenient to move up and down the eastern seaboard by the underground or by air.

"Brave man," thought Obermeister of Miles Standish Smith. "How many of us would show that life-long courage of unpopular convictions? He really lowered the boom on Cal Borton. . . . Oh, hello, Eula."

The Mechanical Maiden came jingling to his side, and fell in step. They had not met since the hideous extravaganza at Laker's Acres.

"Can you ever forgive me, Phil? It was a dirty trick I pulled."

"Yes, it was," he said uneasily. He wasn't unforgiving, but his fancy for Eula had definitely passed. He increased his pace till she fairly trotted to keep up as they passed in front of Gallatin's statue at the Treasury Department.

"I'm—for Boston," Eula panted. "An interview with Governor Brooke."

"I'm for New York. An interview with Governor Finnigan."

"Then we'll be on the same tram."

Pell Terminal, nothing but an aluminum kiosk that housed an elevator, enclosed them. Down they shot to the passenger level, and buckled their seatbelts side by side in the cylindrical capsule. The churning of the nuclear reactors that fired the jets was heard, and then the subtram sprang from a dead stop to its swift run-up, and hit its 300 mph cruising speed in a matter of seconds: forty-five minutes to Broadway!

"Phil, you're not still angry?"

"No. I hoped—I mean I thought you were."

"You hoped," the girl ejaculated. "Then, it's going to be easy for us both. When I recovered from the shock, I suddenly realized —it was all for the best. Phil, we're just not the marrying kind. It's our work we're mated to."

"You mean it?"

"Yes. You're free."

They unsnapped their seatbelts and gave themselves over to an embrace that brought whistles from the other passengers. Then, with the eagerness of enchanted free enterprisers, they began to talk shop.

"Eula, I'm not an intuition-writer like Cal. It's led him to his debacle. But I'm worried sick about the way things are turning out with President Chase."

"Lord, Phil, how can you fault his record? Let's admit that he hasn't won a war recently, but have you checked some of the home-front meters?"

"No, but—"

"I have. You won't see the Postmaster General on the cocktail circuit these days. Chase called him to the carpet and said the mail had to go through—or else. The National Labor Relations Board hasn't called a bum decision against business during this calendar year—Chase says to call 'em straight or he'll go on the air and present the facts. Do you know that industrial absenteeism is down by 15 percent, and that productivity is up by 8 percent, and that relief agencies are taking clients off the dole and putting them into jobs and that—?"

"I don't hear the President getting any credit for it," Phil grumbled. "Damn it, Eula, this is an election year. He sends Rigor to the Med. when he might have gone himself. He hands over the Administration legislative program to Senator McJay, and when it comes to signing a bill—where is all that hullabaloo with the ceremonial pens that Lyndon Johnson used to pull? I tell you, Jerry Chase is fading out at just the political hour when he ought to be front and center. That's what bothers me."

"Have you got any answers?"

"The symptoms—yes; the diagnosis—no. But if we could ever land the President in front of a press conference, I know what I'd ask."

"What's that?"

"Mr. President, are you going to run for re-election?"

"Phil—how absurd! Whoever heard of an eligible President stepping down? Or of any man voluntarily relinquishing such power? Of course he's going to run."

"I hope so. But the stakes are so enormous that the uncertainty is ominous. Imagine the catastrophic irony if the Chase presidency should become nothing but a bridge between the administrations of Sam Lepol and Andy Finnigan?"

"It can't happen. The Finnigans could never defeat Jerry Chase."

"No, but they can beat any other GOP possibility. Erasmus Hannibal might have won. But he's chosen to be Chief Justice. General Rigor—but he's given his word not to run. Who's left? Lyle McJay? He's a man like so many of the good ones of the past. He can do everything in politics except win a national election. McJay's as solid as Robert Taft, as brilliant as Henry Clay, as learned as Daniel Webster and as good a technician in his field as Fremont the Pathfinder. But every one of these failed to make the presidency—they were beaten in convention or at the polls by inferior rivals. Let's face it—nobody except Jerry Chase can whip plausible frauds like Lepol and the Finnigans."

"Such is politics. So long as it's a good contest this autumn, I'll get my stories. The only time I was emotionally involved over outcomes was while I was dippy about you, darling, but now—," the girl broke off. "Zooks, we're almost in New York, and I haven't told you the worst. I threw it in the Potomac."

"Threw—what?"

"The evidence," gasped Eula. "I had films to prove beyond a doubt that Phillipson is a Commie."

Phil groaned. The libel suit was coming up tomorrow in the local court. Eula had found something to help him—and had thrown it away.

"It's all right, Eula. I had it coming."

He kissed her good-by and hurried to the exit. The Pellmell Rocket Roller, like the famous Pony Express, barely paused at the way stations.

The elevator that lifted Obermeister to the midtown Manhattan terminal at 42nd and Broadway did not raise his spirits. He decided to work off his glooms by going on foot to the brownstone building in the East 50's where Governor Finnigan kept a city dwelling. Obermeister had seen the Finnigan brothers together, and in company with their mother, but when he entered a cheerful little parlor with its white marble mantle and full length windows opening upon a closed garden, he was meeting the governor for the first time. The cropped head, the florid cheeks, the ivory smile were what he expected, but soon there was a feeling in Obermeister that he had never left the jet-driven tram—that this man was a well constructed, powerfully propelled, artificial conveyor in full motion over greased tracks.

"I'm aware of your high standing in the journalistic market, Mr. Obermeister. I'm aware that a good word in your column would reach conservative readers with whom I have few contacts."

The words seemed to be spoken by rote, and they were uttered with an empty smile. The two men sat in straight-backed chairs, a low table between them, a setting that added stiffness to the scene. "Are you a candidate for President, Governor?"

"I am available to the Democratic Convention. If nominated, I expect to win on the basis of my public record, which is well-known. I would describe myself as a liberal conservative, or a conservative liberal. I would work for prosperity at home, and peace abroad."

"Everybody works for those things, sir. I'm not sure I understand what's meant by the free interchange of liberal and conservative, as adjective and noun. The words seem to cancel out."

"You see, Mr. Ober, it's very simple."

"The name is Obermeister, Governor Finnigan."

"Certainly. You interrupted me. Where was I?" The interruption had flustered the man. "Yes. My conservatism is liberal in that I believe in the fullest freedom under laws and not men. My liberalism is conservative in that I believe in fiscal responsibility."

The unbroken, nearly unbelievable stream of banalities had now begun to fluster the reporter. There was an awkward pause.

"Governor, would your administration in Washington try to undo much that Mr. Chase has done? If so, would you specify?"

"I am a builder, Mr. Obermeister. Not a tearer-downer. There is some of Jerry Chase's work that I would keep, and some that I would change. I would favor lower taxes, with a greater degree of federal assistance to the economy."

"That might mean deficit spending."

"Not with the balanced program that I have in mind."

"How would you achieve the balance, Governor? The country is remarkably prosperous, and Mr. Chase has a pay-as-you-go budget."

"It's a matter of improving methods of management without abandoning any social gains."

Obermeister had forgotten he had a notebook in his pocket. The man hadn't said anything worth taking down, but the reporter unsheathed pad and pencil, a motion that seemed to unsettle the governor again.

"I don't wish to be directly quoted. Whatever you write must be a paraphrase."

"Let's try foreign policy. I understand that Mr. Phillipson would be your Secretary of State?"

"I've read that in the papers," said the Governor, "but I've made no such announcement."

"Then you wouldn't pick Mr. Phillipson?"

"I didn't say that either, Mr. Obermeister. I might. I mightn't."

"How do you feel about East Cuba?"

"I rejoice in every advance of freedom."

"Would you like to see the whole of Cuba liberated?"

"I would repeat the previous answer, but that's not for attribution."

Obermeister pocketed the notebook. He might as well have stayed in Washington for all the information he was getting here. But he looked again at the motionless figure in the chair and felt again the incongruous sense of motion. Even stationary, the man seemed to be in transit by some unidentifiable energy. It was as if Andrew Finnigan were on a time plane that bore him onward just because it was later now than it used to be. He had a momentum about him that made his presidential ambitions less preposterous than the ridiculous conversation indicated. The man, as someone had said about Dewey, had been running for the presidency ever since puberty, but in Andy Finnigan's case there was an outside force at work.

That force entered the room just as Obermeister was rising to leave. Nellie Finnigan sailed in, and she was the remote source of energy that Obermeister had felt. Behind her, muffling the introductions, trundled a double-decker tea tray on noisy wooden wheels, pushed by the butler.

"Luncheon is served," declared Mrs. Finnigan with no invitational preamble. "Young man, you've met the next President. You can put it in your notebook that Governor Andy has the same Democratic organization that elected Roosevelt, Truman, Kennedy and Johnson. Sam Lepol won against a split party, but that's been mended. Cold chicken and slaw. Pass your plate. Jerry Chase is a dead rooster in the sand of the cockpit. He's as old fashioned as a windmill in competition with a dynamo. Sugar and cream?"

"Yes, Mrs. Finnigan."

"Mark my words. Make yourself a name for long-distance prediction. There are three Democrats to every Republican in the country. Jerry's been riding on a hurricane, but we'll have calm weather from now on. By November the people will be glad the storm has blown itself out. Any questions?"

"What's a conservative liberal, or vice versa, Mrs. Finnigan?"

"Andy is. The too, too solid flesh that doesn't need a dictionary definition."

"How can a government tax less and give away more?"

"The people will believe it. Andy inspires faith."

"Which is better, peace or victory?"

"Andy's going to talk plenty of victory. Iwo Jima and Normandy beachhead, San Juan Hill and Yorktown. Don't deceive yourself, young man. The people don't want to go on holding their breaths to hear where the next bomb gets dropped. The rocket's red glare of long, long ago will suffice."

"Won't it be difficult to run against glamour?"

"Young man, Ben Franklin once said you can look at a landscape and not be able to tell whether the sun is rising or setting. Our story will be that Jerry Chase is on the way down, and we'll make it stick. Besides, if he's going to run, why hasn't he announced?"

"There's plenty of time."

"At first I couldn't believe he would step aside. But I believe it now. He behaves like a man who wants to go home. That kind of man doesn't win elections. His biggest satisfaction was the impeachment clearance, and look what it brought him—a lost wife."

Obermeister found himself involuntarily nodding, so cleverly had the old woman evoked a point of agreement: that the President might well have his heart somewhere else than in the election.

During lunch the governor took little part in the conversation, but Nellie Finnigan talked fluently of where the votes would come from. The farm bloc was shrinking, and trade unions were no longer so politically militant, and yet, added to the Negroes, to the millions who had been pinched by Chase's economies, to what was left of the city machines, Governor Andy would start off with a congeries of minorities that toted up well. He would carry his own state of New York, and Senator Barney's Pennsylvania, and Mayor Chester's Florida. Then there was California, where the vindictive Juno longed for revenge upon Chase, and part of the governor's campaign would feature twelve coffins—boys who had died in the undeclared war of the Caribbean. Chase had raised a hot civil liberties issue by driving Communist leaders out of sight and out of mind. And it was an open question whether it would help him to make a home in the GOP for the Nathanites. Phillipson? His wife had filed a divorce action for desertion, and he was probably out of the picture for a while.

"So you see, Mr. Obermeister, we'll make it a horse race if Chase goes to the post, and we'll make it a walkover against any other Republican. Must you leave?"

"Yes, I planned to treat myself to a matinee before returning to Washington. Good-by, Mrs. Finnigan. Thank you, Governor."

He walked back to Broadway, more sunk in spirit than before. Was it all over so soon—this brilliant noontide of the Chase ascendancy? Must the country be ruled by fabricated leaders of inferior mind and cheap cunning? Must America sink again into mediocrity and pusillanimity, her highest office a brass ring to be grabbed for a free ride into the history books? One man, and he alone, had caught and invoked the spirit of an earlier '76, and now he gave every appearance of quitting a winning fight, of putting a personal sorrow above the call of duty. As if to italicize Phil's increasingly bitter thoughts, the electric streamers across the Times Building in the Square were blinking:

> MRS. CHASE TRANSFERRED TO MENTAL HOSPITAL OF INVOLUNTARY CONFINEMENT. PRESIDENT CANCELS ALL ENGAGEMENTS.

Obermeister found his street, found his theater, and received his reserved ticket through the wicket. He was soon in darkness among the debutantes, housewives and male loafers who had nothing better to do than attend matinees. There on the stage was Chi Chi in the role of Rozzie, slut-into-princess, her luminous magic creating worlds within worlds of the human spirit. Obermeister had seen the play in its Washington tryout more than a year ago, but today it was a new experience. He needed only the first act to tell him something that he hadn't expected to get with the price of the ticket, Chi Chi glowed as her marvelous self—and more. She must have gone on stage with the knowledge that her mother's case had worsened, and there came through in her acting such emotion as to set his eyes awash.

At intermission, ashamed of his swollen face, Phil plunged next door into a pink saloon. He swallowed whiskey, tilting off the barstool against a boy and girl who were amorously entwined.

"Can't you find another newsbeat?" the boy accosted him. "Here, Flossie, this is one of the old man's cheerleaders, and I guess he needs 'em."

"You're Granville."

"Don't tell the family I'm off campus in a daydream of fair women. I always bring my dates to see the celebrated Chi Chi. She puts them in the mood, so to speak, Mr. Obermeister."

"Let me buy us another quick round," said Obermeister. From what he'd heard, this wayward boy was a sieve at keeping family secrets. "I'm awfully sorry there's more bad news from the hospital, Granville."

"Harder on Dad than on Mom. He tells Chi Chi and me to go on living our own lives. By which he means he'll take it all on himself to bring Mom around. Dad'll do it too. Come January, he'll never leave her side till she's well again."

"The President's going to retire?"

"Why, sir, all the tea in China wouldn't buy him from her care. Don't print it, please."

"No, I'll wait till the President makes his own announcement. If you go backstage, give Sis a hug from somebody who's never hugged her. She unmanned me in there today, and I hardly trust myself to see any more. Good-by."

But he returned for the final act, and then in a daze descended by the Times Square kiosk. He was whipped down the coastal tube to Washington where he arrived at dusk. As he walked past the White House, the sun had dropped behind the west gate and the mansion stood greying in its shadows.

"Chase's not going to run," brooded Obermeister. "What a depressing thought it is. This must be how it feels at the twilight of the gods. When they depart, the demigods arrive. Another word would be more accurate: the demagogues."

Chapter Thirty-Three 

Judge Henry Knox Pulaski, of the Court of General Sessions, slipped quickly into the highbacked chair at the bench. He took a sip of water, put the glasses across his bony, homely face and read the slip of paper prepared by his clerk. There were two cases scheduled this morning. Smith *v.* Borton and Phillipson *v.* Obermeister. Judge Pulaski didn't like sitting in libel suits, for the law was fuzzy and feelings were high. If he hadn't made a decision in an equity case that offended Juno Lepol some years ago, he'd probably have gone from the Senate to the U.S. Court of Appeals by this time. At the Appellate level he'd be deciding cases on principle rather than watching so many of them fought out as a contest between the skills of lawyers.

It worried Pulaski, a conscientious man, that courtroom justice wasn't as impartial as the justice symbolized by the lady holding the scales. He looked over the top of his spectacles into the small room that was packed with spectators and reporters.

"Please," he beckoned to the attorneys. They came to the Bench: Bardson for plaintiff Smith, and Burnbagge for defendant Borton.

"How do you want this handled, gentlemen: judge or jury?"

Harold Bardson said: "Your honor, our action is in the nature of a satisfaction suit. My client intends to waive damages, but he'll need an apology. We opt for non-jury."

Robeson Burnbagge: "Your honor, we are in accord on that."

"Very well," said Judge Pulaski. "Go back to your tables. I'll hear Mr. Bardson for the plaintiff."

Bardson put his hand on the shoulder of Miles Smith who sat beside him.

"May it please the court, it is common knowledge that on Thanksgiving last, a National Guard plane rammed the presidential carrier with tragic results. I submit in evidence a newspaper column by the defendant, Borton, in which he charged without any qualification that the plaintiff, Smith, was an aerial assassin. We will show that the plaintiff could not have been such, because he was elsewhere."

Burnbagge broke in. "All facts are stipulated, your honor. My client, Mr. Borton, admits to a factual mistake in the heat of a crisis. We'll submit to judgment without further argument, considering that damages will be waived."

Judge Pulaski tugged at an ear: "I see an injury to the commonweal in this case. The criminal libel surpassed the civil complaint. If a groundless accusation goes unpurged or unpunished, what man's name is safe in our land? Stand up, Mr. Borton."

Calvin Borton, pale and shaken from yesterday's debacle in Lafayette park, arose.

"Mr. Borton, I'll be brief. Apologize to Mr. Smith, or I will enter judgment against you in the amount of two million, five thousand dollars, and costs."

Burnbagge, the fixer, had come to his client's side.

"Your honor, my client is an unusual man. Though he regrets what has happened, he is as God made him. Mr. Borton is entirely incapable of giving an apology to anybody high or low. It amounts to a fixation in him. I would say that his obdurateness is the closest thing Cal Borton has to a religious tenet, for his arrogance approaches the fanatical. I feel that your order for an apology would comprise the cruel and unusual punishment which the Constitution forbids. But if the court pleases, I will offer an apology in my client's name."

"Well," said Judge Pulaski, "that's not very good, but I will accept it rather than throw the book at him. This man has already been punished outside the courtroom for his malice and folly. I will set aside the damages, but I now order him to tell the court whether or not he feels he has injured the defendant."

"I refuse to answer," said Borton, stubbornly.

"Then," said the Judge, "you are sentenced to one day and one hour in the city jail for contempt of court. I think that you have that much coming to you. Call the next case. Please come to the bench."

Burnbagge, for the plaintiff, and Obermeister, for himself, stood before Pulaski who arched his eyes again over the spectacles.

"Another matter in libel, it seems. Shall we convene a jury this time?"

"No," said Burnbagge. "The wisdom of Solomon sits here today. Are you satisfied with Judge Pulaski, Mr. Obermeister?"

The columnist nodded. He wouldn't know how to address a jury, and he thought Pulaski had treated the previous case with exceptional insight. A moment later Obermeister listened to Burnbagge introduce in evidence the column which had named Phillipson as a Communist leader. That offended dignitary sat not ten feet away, his veiny hands folded on the table, his eyes cast gently down. Burnbagge recited the former Secretary's distinguished record and asked the full amount in damages. Then Phil was on his feet, feeling thoroughly lost.

"Judge, sir, I am not financially able to retain counsel of the rank that this case would warrant. Moreover, I have no protection other than the facts. For reasons sufficient to my own judgment as a journalist, I came to believe that the former Secretary of State was adhering to the domestic and foreign enemies of this country. Those enemies are the Communist forces which have, again and again, exhibited a determination to overthrow this nation by force and violence. I cannot produce a Communist party membership card on Seth Phillipson. I assert that no such legalistic, difficult and non-existent evidence should be necessary. We are at a time in history when to be a Communist means in the language of everyday life to be just such a man as Phillipson has been. I base my defense upon the sentence at the heart of my column—'when a writer sees Red, he should holler Red.' That is what I did. Not to have done so would have been a sin of omission by the standards of my profession."

"Mr. Burnbagge, any witnesses?"
"No, your honor. Mr. Phillipson feels it unnecessary to take the stand. The libel is manifest. Nobody can prove he's a Communist."
"Mr. Obermeister, any witnesses?"
Before Phil could speak, there was a stir in the back of the room where a bailiff opened the door for two visitors. The disturbance was more noticeable and prolonged because Eula Breck was trying to guide a wheelchair through the portal. In the wheelchair sat Pauline Phillipson with two outsized dispatch cases in her lap.
"Mr. Obermeister," said Pulaski sternly. "Are these your witnesses?"
Catching a signal from Eula, Phil replied: "Your honor, I'm as surprised as you are. Yes, my witnesses. I call Miss Breck."
Eula smilingly took the stand and the oath, and Phil asked her:
"Do you have evidence that the Honorable Seth Phillipson is a Communist?"
"I do. On March 8, which was the Sunday before the New Hampshire primary, I had reason to visit Maison de la Paix, the Phillipson mansion at Surrey-by-the-Hudson. There, sitting on the sickbed of the plantiff's afflicted and deserted wife, I was allowed to examine and photograph the private papers of Seth Phillipson. These documents revealed beyond peradventure, his membership, his contributions, his arrangements and his cooperation with numerous organizations and personalities of the Communist cause."
"Objection," yelled Burnbagge.
"I will sustain it," said Pulaski. "Miss Breck, you will refrain from characterizing unnamed groups and persons as Communists. You say you made photographic copies of certain papers. You may submit them in evidence, and I will decide whether or not they indicate Communist membership."
"Judge, I threw the films away."
"What did you do that for?"
"I had personal reasons at the time, but they won't impair my testimony now."
"Do you remember what was on the films?"
"Vaguely, yes. But I don't have to rely on memory. Yesterday,

I finished an interview with Governor Brooke, hired a car and drove to Maison de la Paix. All I wanted to do was borrow the original papers and bring them here. But Mrs. Phillipson decided to bring them herself. She's got a long story to tell about how a wealthy, famous, respected, peace-loving American statesman can be a Commie for all that."

"I'm sure it will be enlightening," said Judge Pulaski drily. "Do you wish to call another witness, Mr. Obermeister?"

Before Phil could answer, Phillipson had thrust aside his counsel and cried out in a piping voice: "Your honor, I choose to withdraw my complaint. I move dismissal of the case."

Judge Pulaski surveyed the strange tableau over his glasses. The tall statesman stood trembling in every joint, and the invalid of the wheelchair sat with what Pulaski took to be a fevered gleam of long-suppressed indignation in her sickly eyes.

"Let me have your attention, Mr. Phillipson," said Pulaski sternly. "You brought a complaint into this court. In substance, you charge it to be a lie for anybody to call you a Communist. Now, it appears that we have quite a stack of material bearing on the point. We have a witness who seems intimately qualified for expert testimony."

"I claim the right to withdraw my own suit," said Phillipson.

"Not so fast," said the Judge. "The previous plaintiff, Mr. Smith, had a right to waive damages, but I chose to visit a token punishment upon the defendant, Mr. Borton. I felt that he had grossly injured a citizen by fallacious, malicious publication of a lie. If Mr. Obermeister has lied in print about you, then I may want to chastise him as I did Mr. Borton. The judicial system should protect the citizens who come before it, but also the citizens who don't. We can't have libel running rampant through the land."

"I most vehemently protest," said Phillipson. "The exhibition of my private papers would do me incalculable injury, as would the testimony of an estranged wife."

"Mr. Phillipson, I will decide what testimony and witnesses are admissible. However, I will allow you the same opportunity that I offered Mr. Borton. Do you wish to apologize to Mr. Obermeister for bringing him here?"

"No, sir. If I did that, I would be conceding too much."

"That's as it may be, Mr. Secretary. This columnist has asserted that a reporter who sees Red should holler Red. There may be a fine point of law involved here. This suit may become a landmark case."

"None of this concerns me," said Phillipson, tremulously. "Give me leave to go."

"Not yet," said Pulaski. "I have a question. Are you a Communist, Mr. Secretary?"

"I plead the 5th Amendment."

"I'm sorry, sir, but the 5th Amendment is not available to you. You are not on trial. But if you won't cooperate, I shall call the next witness."

Phillipson reeled in his tracks, and the judge relented a little.

"Let me put a different question, Mr. Phillipson. Everything considered, did Mr. Obermeister have a right to holler Red?"

Phillipson collapsed beside his counsel. They whispered in hoarse, agonized tones. Burnbagge, the fixer, came to his feet.

"May it please the court. Rather than have the testimony spread on the record, Mr. Phillipson authorized me to say that Mr. Obermeister was not without justification."

Judge Pulaski replied:

"That's not any more forthright than Mr. Borton's apology was, but I'll allow it to stand. Let it go forth from this time and place that a new hour of freedom has dawned. Next time a conscientious newspaperman finds a Communist, let him speak out loud and clear without fear of reprisal. This court stands adjourned."

Chapter Thirty-Four 

There is a time for all things, and for Eula it was time to get herself in the mood for laying down the guidelines of her book to be called *People's Choice* '76. In Federalia, New Year's Day falls upon July first, which is the beginning of the fiscal year. By a close cooperation among Senator Nestorson, Speaker Krebs and President Chase, Congress had buttoned up its business by June 15. There was the fortnight when the legislators had departed, the press had a breather and only the miserable clerks who punched at computers in the Treasury Department and the Budget Bureau were heavily occupied.

Eula seized upon this relative hiatus to shut herself up in Laker's Acres with a catalogue of all the pictures, interviews, clips and scripts she had thus far collected as raw material for her opus. There would be much else to do, what with the two conventions and the national election, but her material would become unmanageable unless she made a beginning now. The similar book she'd done four years ago, recounting the making of a President in '72, could not be a model, for there never had been anything to match the stunning surprises, the stirring conflicts and the invigorating but often contradictory spirit that had swept the land under Jeremiah Chase.

Sitting cross-legged in her living room amid her collection,

Eula wondered if she were really up to the enormous task. She doubted her knack for profound political analysis. Was it true, first of all, that the President exceeded human stature and deserved the mystique that made him seem a prophet or a reborn hero of the past? Did his still unannounced decision about running for election hang upon the condition of his wife? Was there anything to Phil's theory about withdrawal-and-return?

Then there was the question of whether the American people really were ready for the New Allegiance and the Spartan regime which Chase had brought, or preferred to live under a less demanding paternalism as represented by leaders like Sam Lepol and the Finnigans. Eula had gone exploring for the Zeitgeist, but that was when she had stars in her eyes over Phil—and maybe she'd seen more than was there in the people's remarks and behavior. Now that she'd rationalized herself out of love, and had more or less accepted spinsterhood as a way of life, she hoped for clearer vision.

One day, by chance, she took off her bookshelf Joseph Conrad's *The Nigger of the Narcissus* and read in the penetrating introduction: "My task which I am trying to achieve is . . . to make you hear, to make you feel—it is, before all, to make you see. That—and no more, and it is everything. If I succeed, you shall find there according to your deserts . . . all you demand and, perhaps, also that glimpse of truth for which you have forgotten to ask."

"Glimpse of truth—". But Conrad hadn't sought it from on high. He expected to attain and bestow it through the lowly senses of sight and hearing. Well, the equivalent of that in journalism was to show the great public figures of the era, to let them walk and talk through the pages, so that the truth would emerge, unasked.

After that, work went well for the industrious girl. By the end of the first week she had laid out everything in hand from the coverage of Lepol's last speech in Boston where she'd first become enamored of Phil, down through her salty invasion of Cuba. During the second week, she arranged what she knew of the impeachment drama, and what she had learned from some additional papers supplied by Pauline about Phillipson's visit to Yalta, down to the courtroom scene that had made a celebrity of Judge Pulaski.

A full fortnight of sedentary activity was about all Eula could stand at a stretch. She was glad to accept Phil's invitation for a dinner at the Capitol Hill Club. She found him burbling with excitement over Defense Department clearance for him to cover the civil war in Cuba.

"What war?" ejaculated Eula.

"Where've you been hiding?" he laughed. "Ever since the establishment of East Cuba, refugees from the Communist zone have been executing that famous maneuver called Getting the Hell Out of There. Refugees have done the same from East Berlin and everywhere else where the Reds have taken over. Barbaquito decided to build a Cuban Wall. The Free Cubans keep knocking it down. There's a vest pocket war on. I'm going in."

Eula felt a stab of envy. Professional jealousy could find no nest in her bosom during the months she was in love with Phil, but now the fancy-free maiden felt annoyed at the thought of this rival's getting ahead of her. She could still put in her application to cover the Cuban revolution, but that would be following Obermeister. Not her style! She wanted to get ahead of him, to be the first in an exclusive field.

Though Eula chatted gaily through the rest of the meal, the evening was spoiled for her. It was all she could do to conceal her pique. She hardly took in what Phil was saying about the foreign relations aspects of the contest for the Pearl of the Antilles. Phil, it seemed, had been briefed at the Pentagon on the possibility that the crestfallen Marshal Markov might try to supply tactical nuclear weapons to Red Cuba. U.S. policy absolutely forbade the introduction of such arms into the Western Hemisphere, and a note to that effect had gone to the Kremlin. Obermeister went on:

"But it's never been known what weapons the Russian technicians left behind after the Kennedy-Khrushchev confrontation in 1962. There was no on-the-spot inspection as Kennedy at first demanded. The Cuban caves may be full of nuclear-armed rifles, cannon and land mines. Imagine! I could find myself covering the first ground war in history to be fought with nuclearonics."

"How stupendous," she murmured.

"I asked Jim Flynn—he said under no circumstances would the President escalate by giving the same sort of weapons to Free Cuba. Six months ago, I'd have bet on Lieutenant Commander Chase to lead the first sortie in a punitive strike—but not now. The President isn't the man he was. He delegates these actions—what's the matter, Eula?"

"I've a headache."

"Too much of the midnight oil. Solitary research isn't good for us shoe-leather reporters, darling. Did you hear that Chi Chi Chase is soon opening in a new play at the National Theatre? I'll get opening night tickets for us, and we'll go if you like—if I'm back from the perilous front. All right?"

She proclaimed her headache to be much worse. It would never occur to the naive Phil, she thought, that the only thing more infuriating than his getting ahead of her on news coverage was his mention of another girl. Chi Chi—! Bitchy—!

Eula begged to call it a night, and her subdued escort walked her across the Capitol campus to the Webster Building, as the second Senate Office Building had lately been named. There in the marble doorway they kissed good-night, and Eula took the elevator to the basement where a new subway for the convenience of senators ran to Forrestal Airport. She would walk from the terminal to Laker's Acres, and soon have a good cry about it all.

But coming off the subway car that ran between Webster and the Capitol was a large, heavy-footed man with an armful of leather-bound books. Eula instantly recognized Senator Lyle McJay, the Republican floorleader, whose thick, sparkling eyeglasses and preoccupied ways reminded many oldtimers of Senator Robert Taft, the peerless Mr. Republican who, his Republican rivals claimed, had the wrong kind of personality for running for President—although everybody agreed by now that Taft would have made a great Chief Executive. McJay's chin was literally on top of the stack of books he was carrying, and when Eula said

"Good evening, sir," he tried to look at her and to return the greeting, in the process of which pleasantry he fumbled his burden.

"Sorry, Senator," cried the girl, as she dropped to her knees and began recovering the books. "I made you spill 'em, and I'm going to help you carry them wherever you're going."

"That's mighty kind, little lady," McJay answered with his courteous gravity. "I'm on my way to my office to catch up on work for my Commerce Committee job. Arthur Nestorson has made me ranking Republican member of the Maritime subcommittee. I'll be frank with you, Miss—"

"Breck." It was part of McJay's supposed disqualification for national candidacy that he didn't flatter reporters by first-naming them. "They call me the Mechanical Maiden, and I'm beginning to think it's a backhanded slap at my lack of sex appeal."

"Then we have something in common," chuckled McJay as they took the elevator with their shared burden. "The press thinks I'm stuffed with sawdust because I don't have glamour—whatever that is. As you can see, these are books on admiralty law. I'll be frank with you, Miss Breck, I don't know anything more about admiralty law than a sow knows about sidepockets. However, I don't expect to remain in that ignorant condition. My offshore assignment for the Maritime subcommittee requires that I bone up."

They reached his suite of rooms on the third floor of Webster, and Eula deposited his pile of lawbooks on the desk in the deserted office.

"Offshore assignment, sir?"

"A short trip on a Coast Guard cutter. My subcommittee isn't happy about the way the Russian fishing fleet has been harvesting the catch in the Florida Straits. We don't know if there's a remedy under law, but I shall try to find one. Would you like to come along?"

Thus the chance encounter, often a bonanza in journalism, led to Eula's flight two mornings later to Miami and to her presence aboard the 82-foot Coast Guard cutter, U.S.S. *Old Point Comfort*. They were lazing along in the warm weather off the shores of Cuba, which looked peaceful enough at this distance. Eula couldn't suppress the spiteful hope that Phil had landed in one of those hurry-up-and-wait operations where all he could write about would be the wisecracks of bored soldiers.

She was pretty bored herself, for that matter. The benign, bespectacled Senator McJay was sitting in the stern in yachtsman attire of a white, visored cap and brass-button blazer, still boning up on admiralty law. Crewmen in light blue dungarees manned the 50-caliber machine guns fore and aft, which seemed ridiculously light armament for a war zone. The top rank aboard the cutter was nothing but a chubby-faced lieutenant named Tom Lealand, and a grizzled chief petty officer named O'Brien. A few miles to the eastward lay the somnolent-appearing *Pushkin*, mothership of the Soviet fishing fleet. Two or three distant specks were the diesel-driven Soviet trawlers that periodically brought in the catch to the *Pushkin*.

Tom Lealand sauntered up from below decks to where Eula lounged on a deckchair, slacks-clad and equipment-hung in the unlikely event of some action.

She yawned: "Do you fellows ever hear a shot fired in anger?"

"Not since we swept the coastline of North Vietnam," he smiled. "If you want excitement, you should have come out with somebody more warlike than Old Books and Cobwebs there. He says he's got a piece of paper from the President of the Senate which authorizes him to inspect the fishgrounds—so that's what we're doing."

"Anything going on ashore?"

"Couldn't say, Miss. We've got a signal in the message room that O'Brien is decoding. It says something about Russian submarines on the prowl, but that's old hat. We never see any. O'Brien will have a routine report."

At this point, that black Irishman emerged from a hatch, listlessly saluted Lealand and handed him a yellow sheet.

"Excuse me," said Lealand to the girl. She watched him without much interest as he carried the message to the reclining Senator. McJay scanned it, readjusted his spectacles and seemed to reread with closer attention. He used the message slip as a bookmarker at the page he'd been studying, closed the book and spoke with his usual gravity to Lealand. On the Senate floor, she recalled, you couldn't tell by McJay's manner whether he was discussing science or sealingwax. In the Senate, as now, the gravity was part of his immense but unexciting solidity as statesman and human being. But when Lieutenant Lealand returned his chubby cheeks were pale as milk.

"Chief," he croaked to O'Brien. "It's sidearms and carbines for all hands. The Senator would like a ham and pickle sandwich. I'm going below to change course if my teeth will stop chattering."

Eula hustled over to where the Minority Leader had casually reopened the ponderous law book in his lap.

"May I ask, sir—what goes on?"

He looked up with his avuncular smile, tapping a page with his forefinger. "By the great horn spoon, Miss Breck, I think I'm getting the drift of these maritime mysteries. Very little relationship to the jurisprudence of corporate organization and patent rights where I like to think I have some proficiency. We haven't advanced very far, really, from the days of piracy and privateers. I won't say that *everything* goes on the high seas, but that's hardly an exaggeration."

The ship veered on its gunwales and headed at full speed ahead toward the *Pushkin*. Fourteen enlisted men, headed by O'Brien, appeared on deck. All were wearing holsters and carrying short rifles.

"Had—hadn't we better wait for Navy excort, Senator?" gasped Eula. "I take it you're going to hail the *Pushkin*."

"We're going to board and search, little lady," McJay replied as if he were announcing his intention of a quorum call. "The message told us that the *Pushkin* last night took on cargo from a Russian submarine vessel under cover of darkness. I don't think it was a net full of fish. Tonight, if my guess is right, those little trawlers will stand by for gun-running from the mothership to shore. Nuclear weapons, as sure as I'm a foot high."

McJay patted the adjoining chair as an invitation for her to sit down, and went on with his reading. Eula complied in a daze. Didn't he know that the Russian vessel, guilty or not of taking on contraband, wasn't going to play sitting duck? This stupid noncombatant didn't know his way to the latrine. The Minority Leader traced a finger down the page.

"Nations have a traditional right to apprehend smugglers. We're permitted to seize the goods as evidence and take the contraband ship into port as a prize. At least, that's the way I read it. The instructions I carry make me an officer of the Senate. What could be clearer authority than that?"

"Yes, Senator. But what if the Russian skipper refuses to let Lealand and O'Brien come aboard?"

"My dear, we have the law on our side, don't we? I don't know a better way to serve both foreign policy and the American fishing economy than to seize the *Pushkin* and put her up for bids in Miami. You know, my defective eyesight kept me out of several wars, but I understand the simple act of apprehending a criminal. If I called in the Navy, it would alter the whole case of a civil arrest—and there might be shooting."

White foam rose like a fountain at play as the U.S.S. *Old Point Comfort* closed the distance to the *Pushkin*. Two Coast Guardsmen had uncovered the 81mm. mortar on the foredeck. Lealand came running.

"Now, sir?"

"A mere formality, Lieutenant. Two shots across her bows," said the Senator as if he were ordering two lumps for his coffee.

The two shots zoomed, and McJay said, "Now, get on the bullhorn and inform the master of the *Pushkin* that I'm coming aboard in the name of the Maritime subcommittee of the Commerce Committee of the United States Senate."

Eula's microphone picked up this opulently worded statement, which was soon being echoed through the automated megaphone. The answer from the *Pushkin* was a rattle of machine guns which pocked the still, green waters but did not reach the onrushing cutter.

"Steady as she goes, Lieutenant," said McJay. "Give me a hand, Miss Breck. This is a mighty deep and comfortable seat to come out of." He rose with her light-fingered assistance, more jocular than necessary on his part. " 'Stand by with grappling hooks and throw a gangplank to her deck. . . .' By the way, Miss Breck,

I'm quoting orders by John Paul Jones, so please give him credit in your story."

By now the ships had closed to machine-gun range, and Soviet bullets were thudding as they hit the hull and shrieking as they ricocheted off the deck and superstructure. To enlisted men fell squirming to the boards.

"You may open fire, Lieutenant," said McJay. "See that those poor boys have every care."

His large frame in its high-visibility attire became a looming target as he walked firmly to the side of the *Old Point Comfort*. The seamen began heaving grappling irons at the *Pushkin* and when two of the hooks caught hold, the Coast Guard cutter was hauled alongside the Russian craft, and the firing stopped. Senator McJay, followed by the awestruck Eula, stalked across the unsteady plank. There the Minority Leader came face to face with the burly, bow-legged Soviet skipper who spoke in halting but dignified English.

"I protest this imperialistic outrage. I order you to withdraw in the name of the Union of Soviet Socialist Republics."

"I must insist upon searching your vessel in the name of the Senate of the United States."

"I demand that you disembark, sir."

"No, sir. This is recognized procedure under the laws that rule on the high seas."

To the horror of Eula, the Soviet skipper put down his head and charged the Senator. McJay's glasses flew off at the first impact, but he resolutely stood his ground. The two sizeable men seized one another by arms and torso. They wrestled like longshoremen in a dockfight, while the crews of both ships looked on, awaiting orders.

None came. The rival representatives of two world powers struggled, heaved, fell, rose, grappled again. The Soviet skipper drew back a hamlike fist and cracked it against the Senator's forehead. The American statesman lifted a bearlike arm and brought it down like a pole against his adversary's temple. The skipper fell in a heap. The statesman jumped on him and trussed his arms to his back in a hard-handed grip.

"Miss Breck, my spectacles, if you please. Place them on my face, if you don't mind. There! Very well, Lieutenant—let's have your boarding party, and tell me what's below."

American seamen tumbled aboard the craft, and Lealand descended into the fishy-odored interior from which he returned in a few minutes.

"No doubt about it, Senator. I was checked out at ordnance school in every kind of ammo. There's enough fission and fusion shells, grenades and landmines to blow the Free Cuba forces back to Gitmo. What next, sir?"

"Next," puffed McJay, "take this man off my hands. Accord him every courtesy of the honorably vanquished. I want a prize crew to bring this captured ship into port. . . . I see, we're about to become encumbered with help, now that we don't need any."

Overhead roared a flight of Navy fighters from the U.S.S. *Pedernales*. They were being followed at a distance by the waddling helicopters of a Marine detachment.

McJay rose from the deck and dusted off his hands.

"Well, Miss Breck, I must get back to my books. There is so much to learn in life, and so little time to learn it."

Chapter Thirty-Five

No American actress except the incomparable Helen Hayes had successfully tackled the demanding role of the Queen in Laurence Housman's chronicle play, *Victoria Regina*. When the New York critics learned that Miss Chase was to star in a revival of that masterpiece, which calls upon its star to run the gamut of presentation from a young princess to a nonagenarian great-grandmother, the outcry was one of shrill derision.

"Our Chi Chi can be cute as a button when she plays the relatively shallow roles of the modern stage," declared the *New York Times*. "But we shudder to think how an unready ingenue will mangle a role of such breadth, depth and historical requirements."

"Clearly," said the *Tribune*, "there is an unworthy attempt on the producer's part to cash in on the presidential name. Miss Chase lacks experience and regality. The inappropriateness is compounded when one hears that Juno Lepol was asked to read lines as Victoria, and was rejected in favor of the younger woman. Mrs. Lepol has long been a stranger to the boards, but she is regality itself. The suspicion will not down that gross favoritism was the decisive factor of selection."

On these sour notes, the *Victoria Regina* company holed up at Washington's National Theater for rehearsals in the hot middle of

July. A September opening was planned with a move into New York if the bad publicity could be overcome by passable performance. But another bird of ill-omen soon winged its way into the press. There were dispatches from Broadway that Juno had assembled her own company for a revival of Shakespeare's *Merchant of Venice*. This troupe holed up in Ford's Theater in Baltimore, on a similar schedule, and in patent rivalry of the President's daughter's attempt to scale the heights.

"Of the two ladies," asserted the *Baltimore Sun*, "the presidential widow has chosen more wisely than the presidential child. For the part of Portia in the *Merchant* is incontestibly the most fetching female role in dramatic literature. It is almost actress-proof, so there is no real possibility that Mrs. Lepol may fail—only a question of how stunning her success will be. On the other hand, the part of Victoria can be stodgy and pretentious in anything but the keeping of a mistress of the stage. Miss Chase's is a very pretty neck to be stuck out so far."

The *Washington Standard*, an inveterate foe of the Chase family and too politically oriented to have any aesthetic values, did as might be expected—lowered the argument into the partisan arena.

"While the party conventions won't pick their candidates till next month, we are betting that somebody named Chase comes a cropper and finishes second in a two-horse race before November. Victorian standards won't allow a certain young actress to get by on her legs and figure, which have been quite conspicuous in her former roles. This time she will be swathed in long skirts and petticoats and bustles. We shall have no regret if the Democratic party, to which Mrs. Lepol and her son now belong, benefits widely from Juno's triumph in the role of Portia."

All this was hard to bear at Waverly Farm where Chi Chi had come to spend the summer. She was back in her girlhood home amid an uneasy situation at best. The President took no more morning rides on Yorktown. Following those nights which he spent at home, he was up early to return to his White House desk, so as to justify time off in the afternoons for visiting Cora. That poor soul had been taken in April from the Paca Clinic, where they don't keep hopeless cases, to a far gloomier Baltimore hospital, the Stonybrook Institute, where they do.

"Not that Dad regards it as hopeless," said Chi Chi to the young man who was becoming a regular caller. "Such words aren't in his lexicon. But it wrings my heart to see him so sad. Sometimes I wish he'd throw in the chips. 'High, low, jack and the goddam game,' as Stephen Vincent Benét wrote it for a desperate young Southerner who'd come to the end of it all. I wish Dad would wash it up."

"You don't mean it, Chi Chi."

"I do," she snapped as they strolled in Cora's garden. "My Dad's a giant in chains. Marriage vows! Patriotic duty! Moral conscience! Clang, clang, clang. If he ever busted loose, he'd be Lothario, Genghis Khan and Lucifer in one package. I just want him to have fun with his life, instead of giving it to others."

"He's saved the country."

"Oh, pooh the country. Sometimes I feel like giving it back to the Hanoverians. If the press reflects the taste of the people, there ought to be crocodiles coming out of the slime to gobble up little children so they'll never reach voting age. My blood boils."

"Just because you're getting some bad press notices?"

"The fiends. The fickle, fickle fiends. They liked me as Rozzie. Now they can't wait for me to flop as Vicky. Phil—I was at the airport when Dad came home from Latin America last winter. He was given everything a Caesar had in that triumph. Have people forgotten?"

"Out of sight, out of mind. Chi Chi. People came out to cheer Vice President Rigor after his presence on the Sixth Fleet scared Markov into a backdown. The people raised a big hurrah for Senator McJay when he cut off the nuclear supplies to Red Cuba. If they've forgotten the President, it's because he plans it that way. I think he's teaching others how to carry on."

"They should build him a monument."

"His monument lies around him, Chi Chi. Look what he's done for America—if only she doesn't backslide."

"Serve her right. Oh, Phil—I'm in the doldrums."

He knew when a girl, even a President's daughter, needed to be kissed, but some Presidents' daughters have kid brothers with the well-known propensity for inopportune appearances. Along the moonlit garden path sprinted Granville with news he thought the journalist would like to have.

"Hey, Phil—it's Cuba Libre! Barbaquito has quit. Took it on the lam for Peking."

"Peking's not a bad idea for you, too, Granville," said his sister. "Must you go, Phil?"

"Yes, I'd better get into town. I got royally scooped on that Coast Guard yarn by not being at the right place. What else, Granville?"

"President will meet the press tomorrow. Jim Flynn's announced it."

Flynn had done so only fifteen minutes before, and already the lines were hot from incoming queries. There had been nothing like so many out-of-town requests for accreditation to attend a press conference since the spring of 1956. It was then that President Eisenhower let it be known he would announce whether or not he intended to stand for re-election, following his heart attack. Hundreds of publishers, then as now, desired to come in person from their cities or to send their star reporters for the historic event. All were welcome, but the East Room would never hold them. Flynn took his problem into the President's Oval Office.

"How about the State Department auditorium, sir?"

"No," said Chase, "that's sacred to the memory of Jack Kennedy."

"The Daughters of the Revolution are meeting at Constitution Hall, but we could preempt it."

"I wouldn't do that to the DAR's, Jim. What about Memorial Stadium for the visiting firemen?"

"The Senator baseball team is out of town, but the little leaguers are playing there in the morning. How about al fresco on the White House grounds, sir?"

"No, the lawn is sacred to the memory of Lyndon Johnson and his dogs."

"That leaves the National Theater, Mr. President. There are 1683 seats, and room for 30 standees under the Fire Department regulations. Actors never get up till noon, so we could hold an a.m. conference without interfering with rehearsals."

"Clear it with Chi Chi, Flynn."

It worked out that way. Next morning at 11:30 the theater was packed to capacity, with extra seats on the stage. The President entered down the right-center aisle, followed by Flynn, who went first to the lectern, front and center on the crowded stage. The press secretary announced the meeting open to questions.

Twenty reporters were on their feet, vying for the honor of asking the big question of the meeting. The President moved to the lectern, waited till the photographers had their shots. To many attendants who were getting a full view of him for the first time in months, Chase looked more gaunt and somber than they'd expected. But a smile warmed his features as he selected the first questioner by the traditional system of seniority. He nodded to the veteran representative of United Press International.

Q: Mr. President, are you a candidate for election?

A: No, Smitty, I am not.

Q: Sir, it has been surmised that your decision would rest on family reasons. Is that true?

A: No, Mr. Obermeister, that is not true. As you know, I have always felt that the names and faces of my family do not belong in politics. I have never used my wife, daughter or son for publicity, and I'd never use them for an excuse.

Q: Will you take the subject a little further, sir?

A: Yes. A personal philosophy is involved here. The strong, and not the weak, shall inherit the earth. I would not step down from the presidency for the purpose of comforting my invalid wife. I think that would be wrong for me—wrong for her. On the other hand, I have vowed to cleave to her in sickness and in health. I would do that, in or out of the presidency. Her illness is not a measurable factor in my decision, and I'd be grateful if the discussion now went to other factors.

Q: What factors, sir?

A: First, the preservation of democracy. It is not good for the country to get the false idea that it depends upon one man. I have been the instrument of momentous changes for improvement in foreign and domestic affairs. But an instrument only. It should go without saying that the genius of the nation, and that alone, has made the changes possible.

Q: But millions of Americans regard you as the best man to lead them, Mr. President.

A: If you mean the so-called Chase cult, it's the best reason I can think of for retiring.

Q: No, sir, I mean millions of everyday Americans think you are irreplaceable.

A: Under those circumstances, I may be the worst man they can pick. Nobody is irreplaceable.

Q: At the very least, Mr. President, won't you concede that you are the only Republican who is likely to win? Aren't you letting down your party in this decision?

A: No. I would think we are a very sick nation if we can't produce several men in both parties who are capable of winning a free election. There are dozens of men who are quite competent to run the nation. We'd be a poor example of a democratic republic if it were otherwise.

Q: The general opinion is that Governor Finnigan will be the Democratic nominee. But there is little time for the GOP to build up a ticket. Do you have any suggestions, Mr. President?

A: No. The nominating process belongs to the Republican National Convention. But I will be glad to discuss any names you care to bring up.

Q: Is it true, sir, that Senator Lyle McJay would make a good President except that, like Taft and Clay, he can't win?

A: If there's an American mentality which excludes good men from the presidency, we ought to change it. I can't think of a better year than the glorious '76 to put an end to such gross waste of manpower. I hope all Americans will study Miss Eula Breck's sound films of Lyle McJay boarding an enemy ship like John Paul Jones and pinning the Russian skipper to the deck. Did Senator McJay look like a man who can't win? And can't take care of his country's interests? Next.

Q: What about Judge Henry Knox Pulaski, Mr. President?

A: I have read the transcript of the libel trials at which he presided. Hank Pulaski sounded like a Daniel come to judgment to me.

Q: As you know, sir, Speaker John Krebs has decided to switch to the Republican party. Would he make presidential timber?

A: Not until he's 35 years old as the Constitution prescribes. I hope Johnny Krebs will be elected as a Republican and that the House of Representatives will go Republican this year. If so, I foresee Krebs' being chosen Speaker and I hope he holds the post longer than Sam Rayburn, whom he greatly excels.

Q: Mr. President, should Braddock, Phillipson and other Communists be allowed to return to this country?

A: Never.

Q: Mr. President, in your retirement, will you be on call if the country should need you?

A: Always.

Q: Mr. President, aside from unofficial hurts and disappointments, did you enjoy being President?

A: Miss Breck, I enjoyed it so much that the country should be glad to turn me out to pasture. A dictator lurks in every man, subdue it as he may.

Q: Sir, what's the first thing you intend to do as a private citizen?

A: Have me a tall drink of bourbon.

Press: THANK YOU, Mr. President.

Chase left by the same aisle that he had entered. His audience performed a rising ovation, almost unheard of as a journalistic tribute. His face had gained some animation from this stirring demonstration, but fell back into its mask of grimness as he entered the waiting limousine. By prearrangement, the car, with its V-shaped motorcycle escort, swept through town to the access to the Washington-Baltimore Parkway. There, between halted lanes of traffic, the President and Flynn quickly transferred into the cream-colored roadster with Chase at the wheel.

This car headed for Baltimore.

Overhead, a helicopter was never more than fifty feet away, and behind him came a closed car with three agents in front and one in the rear seat, this last man's feet resting on a tarpaulin, which covered a clunking cache of firearms. The President no longer smashed speed records. That early frenzy of anger and despair had subsided into repressed versions of the same feelings.

"Flynn, I'm a lame duck from now on. There won't be the same retinue of autograph hounds and demonstrators. People won't stand gawking at the White House fence to see me come and go. The picknickers and gatecrashers will ease off at Waverly Farm. Soon it will be Andy Finnigan and the GOP nominee whose words are hung on. I would be sorry—if I weren't so relieved."

"You were good in there today," said Flynn. "I wondered about your answer to Eula Breck."

"Flynn, I'll level with you. I'd like to stay in the race and win my own term, and maybe two. It isn't the people I distrust. It's myself—it's any man with too much power. The Greeks had a system—the one called ostracism. By dropping enough markers in a box, they could banish anybody for a year's duration. Not as a disgrace. As a precaution. If we had such a system, I'd trust Chase."

"That's the first time I've ever heard you mention yourself in the third person."

"When Julius started calling himself Caesar, that was curtains for the republic, Jim. Someday, when this is all over, you tell young Obermeister it was his withdrawal-and-return quotation from Toynbee that decided me against running for election. I did withdraw for a while back there, and I did return a better American. I never served the country better than when I did not choose to run."

Within ninety minutes they drove under the dark stone arch that was the entrance to Stoneybrook—in older days, simply called the insane asylum. The President left Flynn at the wheel and went through a door into an office where a large, billowy man, Dr. Willis Herbertson, the resident physician, awaited this call in a rumpled white coat. The President impatiently waved aside an invitation to be seated.

"I'll take it standing up, Herbertson."

"Very well. I have called the consultation that you demanded.

No fewer than six of the top psychiatrists of the nation have now examined your wife. I have their names."

"To hell with their names. Let's have their prognosis."

"It is a negative prognosis, Mr. President."

"My wife will never recover?"

"That was the unanimous opinion."

"Good God Almighty!" the President exclaimed without blasphemy.

Herbertson had played left tackle at Princeton on some good Bill Roper teams. He'd been fast enough to be sent downfield under punts, and he still moved lithely despite his bulk, as he now circled the room, trapped in a situation he hated.

"I'm twenty years older than you, Mr. Chase. I'm entitled to give you my advice."

"Every man's entitled to his opinion, as Sam Johnson said, and the next man's got a right to knock him down for it."

"Just the same, here's mine. You're still a young man, Chase, and the world lies at your feet. Leave your wife in our hands. Make arrangements for her permanent commitment. Stop coming to see her. Go your own way."

"Why, damn you."

"You can't help her. You can only help yourself. She's better off in complete confinement."

"Nobody's better off in a padded cell."

"We don't pad our sanctuaries. There are no locks on the inner doors. You know that."

"I've got to take her away with me."

"It is not permitted. You would have to go into court to obtain a release, and I would testify against it."

"Herbertson, I'm going to pull my rank. The President of the United States says you're to bring Mrs. Cora Chase to my car—and I'm not going to be very patient. I have four armed men outside. Now—get going."

The President stormed from the building. In the courtyard he picked up the hand telephone of his automobile and reached the White House.

"This is the President. I want somebody to call the Surgeon

General. I want the Surgeon General to have two experienced female psychiatric nurses at Waverly Farm within the hour."

He threw the telephone into Flynn's lap.

"God forgive me, Jim."

"It's all right, sir."

"Have three of the men go into Herbertson's office. I want him to know I'm not fooling."

Herbertson demanded a signing of numerous papers. The President went inside and signed them. But it was another hour before a white-haired huddled figure in a dark cloak came from the building between two attendants and was placed in the cream-colored car. There between her husband and his press secretary, Cora Chase was slowly driven to Waverly Farm where the nurses waited. By supper time the President came downstairs to find his daughter back from rehearsal, and to find that she'd brought Phil Obermeister for the evening meal.

"Would you like me to leave, sir. I can't help knowing what's happened."

"No, stay. But you're off duty. No reporting, Mr. Obermeister. This is my private home."

"That's understood."

"By god, Obermeister, this is one heat I'm going to win."

Phil nodded. He knew the President wasn't talking about any election.

Chapter Thirty-Six

The national conventions of 1976 (wrote Eula in the rough draft for her book, *People's Choice '76*) broke sharply with the past. The Democratic Convention met August 2 at Miami Beach, where Mayor Chester Finnigan was the official host. The Gallup, Roper, Harris, and Quayle polls had in July found such certainty that Governor Finnigan and former Chief Justice Rustin would be nominated, that no more polls were taken on that subject. Mrs. Juno Lepol, a recent convert to the Democratic party, left her rehearsals in Baltimore to make a keynote address of intense drama, including motion pictures of her late husband. Senator Barney Finnigan of Pennsylvania, chairman of the Resolutions Committee, submitted a platform titled The Greater Society, and it was adopted.

But then the feathers hit the fan. When Mayor Finnigan, a delegate from Florida, went to the rostrum to nominate Governor Finnigan, there was a scene reminiscent of Governor Rockefeller's trying to address the GOP Convention of 1964. A group carrying banners that read Democrats Against Nepotism (DAN) infiltrated the galleries and the floor of the convention hall. Hoots and catcalls interrupted the Mayor's man-who speech and drowned out much of what he said. Finally Mrs. Finnigan, like Mrs. Roosevelt at the Democratic Convention of 1960, rose in her box and quelled the disturbance with a few well chosen, motherly words. But a move to make the Governor's nomination unanimous ran into trouble.

Senator Andrews, the permanent chairman, asked for a motion that the nominations be closed. He was howled down.

"I recognize the delegate from—er, the great District of Columbia. Does he wish to make a nomination?"

"Yes," yelled the delegate. "I nominate Mrs. Nellie Finnigan. If it's going to be a family affair, let's have the one who wears the pants."

"The delegate is out of order. Are there further nominations? If not—"

"Mr. Chairman!"

"Very well. The delegate from—er, the great Commonwealth of Puerto Rico."

"I wish to nominate the Honorable Seth Phillipson. Joe McCarthy once called us the party of treason. So let's put a traitor on the ticket."

"The delegate will be removed by the sergeant-at-arms. We will not allow this great convention to become a farce."

But there followed the farcical nomination of Miles Standish Smith, much in the order of the Republican Convention of 1956, where delegates got fed up with going through the motions of naming the fixed slate of Eisenhower-Nixon. Whenever the chairman moved to close nominations, another outrageous name was proposed. For most of that week, the national television audience rocked with laughter at the impromptu comedy. Partly it was caused by long-pent-up feelings that national conventions were a rigged show anyhow, and partly by publication of the Census Bureau report which showed that 57.9 percent of Americans regarded themselves as conservatives, regardless of party.

At last, however, the hidden Democratic machinery seized control. Unruly delegates were expelled, and the faithful professionals rubber-stamped the ticket of Finnigan-Rustin.

In contradistinction, the Republican Convention, opening August 14 at the quiet resort town of Newport, Rhode Island, was lightly attended and lasted only one day. Following advice once given by General Eisenhower, the Republicans broke the carnival pattern and stuck strictly to business. There were no alternate delegates, no chorus line of pretty girls, very few hangers-on and a minimum of whoop-la.

The Republican keynote address occupied nine minutes. It was a reading of the Gettysburg Address by a young descendant of Lincoln. The platform comprised one sentence. It read: "We approve practically everything done by President Jeremiah Chase, and we intend to continue his policies." Nomination speeches were spirited but succinct. Senator Lyle McJay was chosen on the third ballot. Judge Henry Knox Pulaski was chosen as his running mate on a fourth ballot, nosing out three state governors. The GOP Convention opened and closed by reciting the Lord's Prayer and singing one verse of the Star Spangled Banner.

In the polls that were taken between mid-August and Labor Day, traditional opening date of the campaign, ninety percent of the respondents said they had heard of Andy Finnigan and Thurgood Rustin, but only twenty-three percent had ever heard of Lyle McJay and only six percent had ever heard of Hank Pulaski. The odds-makers in Reno, Nevada, established the Democrats as 3 to 1 favorites.

Here Eula's rough draft was put aside until she could cover the election itself.

Another bad omen for the Republicans occurred in early September with the opening of *Victoria Regina,* starring Chi Chi Chase. With the passage in the late 1960's of a Home Rule Act for the District of Columbia, the city of Washington acquired a City Hall regime. There hadn't been anything like it for corruption and confusion since Chicago during the Prohibition era and New York City under Mayor Wagner's waning rule. The only difference in Washington was that the collapse came with a bang. In the dog days of August, gangs of hoodlums so terrorized the police that ordinary citizens barricaded themselves in their homes at night, and only ventured out under the direst necessity. Something went wrong all at once with the city's water works, the power plants, the garbage collections and traffic control. On the last day of

August there was a newspaper strike, followed almost immediately by a transportation strike that immobilized buses and taxicabs.

Under these conditions, a play opening was severely handicapped. Those who attended agreed that Miss Chase had carried the difficult part very well, but the audience was sparse and the reviews were non-existent. In contrast, Juno Lepol opened the next night in Baltimore with a gala performance. Her rendition of Portia's famous lines, "The quality of mercy is not strained," brought such an ovation that she stopped the show and did an encore. There was a suspicion that the Finnigans had papered the house with loyal Democrats, but this did not alter the hard fact that Chi Chi had been temporarily eclipsed by Juno. In Reno the odds increased to 4 to 1 for the Democrats, and the Washington company was forced to close down until further notice.

Echoing a parodied quotation from *Time* magazine of years past, Obermeister opened his October estimate of the campaign with the sentence:

> Backward turn precedents until reels the mind. How it will all end, knows God.

Obermeister's article continued:

> We have a President in office who has run out of crises to conquer—but he is not weeping for more. Now that he has his wife at home, the President walks with her each morning through the dells and woodlands of his beloved Shenandoah Valley. The unofficial word is that Mrs. Cora Chase is making a complete recovery. This became possible when she knew that her husband would not much longer be submitted to the merciless glare of presidential publicity.
>
> After breakfast, Mr. Chase goes to the White House for a day's work, and his presence there gives such confidence to the nation and the world that historians must look back to the days of Calvin Coolidge to find apt comparisons for tranquility and confidence. Yet Chase is no Coolidge, for he is intensely active in keeping other people active by his example. Never have postmen been more prompt and accurate on their appointed rounds. Never has there been less absenteeism at the factories, and never has industrial and agricultural productivity

moved so sharply upward. Perhaps the more accurate comparison is not with Coolidge but with Jefferson, who believed that the people least governed are the best governed. Mr. Chase is inspirational without being intrusive.

If we turn to the progress of the campaign we find precedents still harder to identify. The ludicrous Miami Beach Convention seems to have been a disguised blessing for the Democratic party in that it provided so much exposure. Governor Finnigan draws the massive crowds that might be expected from massive organization. He has a stable of gifted writers who make his speeches boom with bow-wow. His running-mate, the former Chief Justice, should put practically all the Negro vote in the Democratic basket, and he is a dignified person who will not drive away votes of the white population. The Democratic platform of the Greater Society is merely a hyperbolized extension of platforms that won for Democrats from Roosevelt through Johnson, and any commentator would be unwise to underrate it.

And what do we see on the Republican side? The totally unglamorous Senator McJay is campaigning from his front porch which happens to be—of all places—Marion, Ohio, the hometown of President Harding. Every day, morning and afternoon, delegates arrive from around the country, and Mr. McJay addresses them from his vine-covered stoop, often with his thumbs casually fastened in the armholes of his vest. He very sapiently discusses such basic subjects as taxes and tariffs, the gross national product and national defense. All that he says is sound, but has no more sex appeal than a ledger. McKinley and Harding won by front porch campaigns, but can it be done in the late twentieth century?

Judge Pulaski, the GOP vice presidential candidate, is ranging the country in the accepted modern style. He is colorful and attractive, but the Democratic taunts of "Who's Pulaski?" may catch up. On the other hand, James Polk was similarly taunted—"Who's Polk?"—but won handily in 1848 and became one of our better presidents. Without Polk, who was a nervy man like Jerry Chase, we might never have brought Texas, California, Arizona and New Mexico into the Union. But who remembers?

What then are the prospects here in early October? Where it will all end, as was said at the opening of this column, knows God.

Naomi Nathan, tender-hearted prisoner of love, watched with dismay the disintegration of a character once admired and forever adored. The defeats to his proud spirit—culminating in the tongue-lashing by Judge Pulaski—had reduced Calvin Borton to despondency and impotency of expression which, she knew, only some compensating event would alleviate.

Now, in their mornings in their work room, Borton laced his black coffee with brandy as he attempted to regain his powers of finding and of illuminating the subjects for his column. But the liquor which he tossed down his gullet, and the bitterness with which he fed his soul, were the opposite of inspiriting. Time after time as the afternoon deadline approached, he would clutch at his tormented head, muttering thickly:

"You must write it for me, Naomi. Just this one more time."

She did what she could from his outlines. She could produce a pale imitation of his style, and could sometimes sprinkle it with the recondite references and difficult words which were regarded as his hallmark. But the fan letters, which used to come in stacks, had fallen off to a few crackpot repeaters. The mail was likely to bring irksome notes from some editors who complained that the copy had turned monotonous and unusable.

Naomi could believe it. All that Borton wrote, wherever it began, veered to a denunciation of Chase and to a prediction that the New Allegiance would crash in the overwhelming defeat of its ticket. Naomi had no way of knowing if that would happen, and she felt that Borton couldn't know it either. The candidates were making their final bids to the electorate, and other reporters were filing reports fresh from the fields of action, but Borton had not stirred from his lair. How could he know? Of what worth were his opinions?

Obermeister, however, hopping from one political camp to the next, meeting and sizing up the candidates for Senate and House, was finding ideas that didn't lurk between four walls. He wrote:

> Alas, there is no pulling power in coattails, no matter how magnetic they seem to be. Chase can no more drag McJay to victory than Eisenhower in 1960 could drag Nixon. Chase does not make Ike's mistake of a half-hearted try. He feels that the people need no side-line coaching. They will choose for President between a stodgy but sagacious man on his front porch, and a showy but synthetic figure in the driver's seat of the Welfare Wagon. In an atmosphere of crisis and excitement, such as the Chase Administration thrived on so well, the country would undoubtedly vote to retain the men on whom Chase's mantle has fallen. But today the socialistic call of the something-for-nothing fleshpots is heard in the land. It favors the Finnigans.
>
> Oddly, the strongest influence still exerted by the absent hero is

beamed on the Congressional races. All of the House Democrats who connived at the impeachment, except for John Krebs and others who have repented, are in danger. Among Democratic Senators, the surest one to repeat is the ancient Arthur Nestorson of Arizona who prevented the Senate from dismissing the most popular President within easy memory. Mr. Nestorson had added to his hold on his constituents' hearts by one of the strangest political courtships since Alben Barkley became enamored of a fetching widow-lady. Nestorson's antiquated but masculine fancy has lighted upon a grass widow in a wheelchair—none other than Mrs. Pauline Phillipson who recently divorced the former and expatriated Secretary of State. It is a romance that seems to fit these golden autumnal days.

Calvin Borton in his self-imposed immurement within the Georgetown mansion could not match such on-the-spot, perceptive reporting. To Naomi's distress, he took to using it as source material. One day, ill-shaven, ill-clad, ill-tempered, Borton stood dictating over Naomi as she laboriously typed:

Like the degraded and deranged emperors of the failing Roman slavocracy, Chase has tried to force a succession of his line by adoption. The Hardingesque McJay is indeed a bulbous foster-son to the sulking squire of Waverly, but Chase will no more drag McJay to the White House than Woodrow Wilson was able to crown William McAdoo, his son-in-law.

The fraudulent and bellicose game of Russian roulette, which was played under the cheating name of the New Allegiance, was nothing but a nightmare from which the people will awaken on November 6 when they climb upon the Welfare Wagon of the Greater Society with the able and conscientious Andy Finnigan in the driver's seat.

As an example of senile mentality which prevented Chase from being removed at the time he should have been, there is the Rasputin-like lechery of that very senior Senator from Arizona for the invalid beldame of Surrey-by-the-Hudson. Hasten the day when the people turn back to the green pastures from which they were temporarily led astray.

Naomi prepared the script, but it was blotched by her tears as she saw how lamely and dishonestly Borton wrote. Yet all she could hope for was that Cal might stumble into some resurrection. If the Finnigans should win, at least Borton would have been their prophet, and that kind of success might give him another start. Her hope and her nightly prayers gave birth to an unreasoning, improbable faith that Borton's experience and intuition might yet be strong enough to pierce the veil of uncertainty that hung over the election. Obermeister, who worshipped Chase and was beauing Chase's daughter, could not bring himself to predict the outcome that he desired. Eula Breck, objective as her instruments, was not forecasting the election's outcome. But Cal Borton, contemptuous of the striving Republicans and laudatory of the hard-driving Democrats, was making this last desperate gamble, and Naomi let herself believe that he would guess correctly.

Then came a happening which cheered her against all her gentle instincts. Borton himself brought it to her knowledge, rushing into the work room one morning and shouting tidings of death.

"He's dead! I caught a flash over the radio at breakfast. Some fool reporter found him stiff and stark in that coldwater flat of his. Miles Standish Smith! Dead and gone. At last. At last."

"Sir, you really shouldn't—"

"Hurray for the grim reaper, Naomi. I rejoice and I don't hide it. That little lunatic was the beginning of everything that's gone wrong with me. Well, it's true. You know it's true."

"Yes, Mr. Borton. I suppose you can say that. If his passing is helpful to you, then I must say I'm relieved to hear that he's gone, but I know I shouldn't be glad for the death of any man."

Borton went for his coffee, but waved aside the brandy.

"Don't be ridiculous, woman. As long as he lived, he was a mockery to me. Unjustly, irrationally, but a mockery just the same. Listen—! I'm never going to back down from the position I took. Say what you will, the whole cult of radical-right fascist bigotry is what put Jerry Chase into the vice presidency where he could reach the White House by death—the only way he ever could have reached it. Smith was the personification of evil—a Nathanite. Hah! That's my column for today. Smith lies a-moldering in the cold, cold ground, but Nathanism goes marching on."

"Oh, Calvin—don't."

She put her head down on her desk and sobbed. Partly it was relief, for at least this end of another man's life had lifted the spirits of the man she loved. If now Borton could find some liberation in the loss of an adversary's life, she would rejoice with him.

She lifted her head and palmed away the tears, to find Borton staring at her in bewilderment.

"What's the matter with you anyhow? Why are you blubbering? And looking almost happy at the same time? D'you know, Naomi —that's the first time you ever called me by my first name."

"I'm sorry. It slipped out."

"No—." He drew his chair close to hers and raised her chin with his hand. They had lived thirty years together here. Their closeness had never been marked by so much as an endearing word. Yet many a man and wife had enjoyed much less unity and shared emotion. Together, they had scaled his heights of fame and fortune.

Together, they had felt the dizzy exultation of those peaks, and felt inside themselves the terrible fear of falling. Never quite believing it could happen, they had lately shared the sickening knowledge of that first misstep, and the bruising, battering, fracturing, mortifying plunge from the peaks to the gullies of present misfortune and demoralization.

Together, they had ceased to be young, had turned grey at the temples and slower in the limbs and in the mind, an admission that had never been made. Together, now, they were reaching after comfort which only such long propinquity can bring to one person who is proud and another who is shy, to one who cannot confess his faults and to another who accepts the faults, the man and all.

"No—," repeated Borton, his hand trembling at her face. "Don't take it back. The way you said it was—my god, I need so much to hear you say it again."

"Calvin, dear," the woman said, and hid her streaming face against his shoulder. "Anything that's good for you is what I want. If the death of one man, or many men, would help you pull yourself together, I would say they're well gone from the earth. Only don't—for god's sake, Calvin, don't pursue the poor fellow into the grave with your hatred. If it's a change you need, that won't do it. He's dead—then let him go."

"I—don't know what you mean."

"Please—," she put her face to his, her lips to his, and at last they had kissed. He drew her to her feet, holding her tight and kissing her gently, again and again, as if this discovery of her love for him was so precious that words would not suffice.

"Thank you," she said when he released her and turned away his face because he was embarrassed to have shown how he felt. "And, now, Calvin, we will have time to talk this over later, for we don't have time to let you drag on the way you've been going. Go and dress. Have your man pack a bag for a week on the road. I'll get your airline reservations."

"What?" he laughed hollowly to hide the emotions he still could not bring himself to show. "Who's boss around here? And where would I be going?"

"Finnigan is speaking in California this week. You can spend two days with him. Then fly back to Marion and hang around that front porch till you know what's going on. If there's a day or two left in the week, catch up with Rustin and Pulaski. By the time you're home for the weekend, I'll have some engagements lined up in Washington."

"But—I might find something—"

"You goose!" She took him in her arms and kissed him as soundly as if she'd been doing it for years. "You're afraid you might find something to make you change your hopes about the election. Never fear! Your prejudices are too firmly set for that. But at least you can get some facts by doing some leg work and you can give your readers something worth ten cents. Go on. Get dressed."

She had him out of the house and into a taxi within the half hour. Only then, alone and aghast at her temerity, Naomi looked about this familiar place. The desks, the typewriters, the reference books, the attractive fireplace, the burbling percolator—all his, and more than a little sacred to her sight and touch. His person was godlike, even in disgrace and defeat, and this first breakthrough into his reserve was like entering a temple where hitherto she had remained outside with downcast eyes.

But he had held her! They had kissed! She looked at the door that led into his private home. No, that was not for her. She could never be his wife, for the separation of the social caste system remained. But since this morning, she had risen in status. If not a wife in the marital sense she would be an office wife, a stay and comfort, a partner in his work, no longer just his drudge and punching bag.

She dared—she dared to walk to the teakwood chair and sit there. Now she could think—as him, for him, but with an objectivity that he could never reach. In a few minutes he would be airborne for California, and there was a column due for delivery this afternoon. Perhaps he would write one on the plane, but she could beat him to it. She had to beat him to it—to save him from himself. Naomi reached for the phone to call around town and collect some items, but the instrument rang in her face.

"Long distance for Mr. Borton."

"He's out of town, but I'm his—his partner."

A familiar voice came on: "Hello, I'm Eula Breck, calling from Boston. Have you heard?"

"Miles Smith is dead? Yes."

"No. More," said Eula. "I made it to the deathbed ahead of the inspectors. I never saw such repose and tranquility on a face, in life or otherwise. The little man died so happy. There was a Bible by the bed. In one of the Epistles of Saint Paul there was an unsealed letter addressed to Calvin Borton. I'm a snitcher, so I lifted it."

"To Mr. Borton? Are you sure?"

"I'm holding it in my hand," said Eula. "I'm going to use it, but I thought it only fair to notify you. Like to hear it?"

"Go ahead," said Naomi, reaching for pencil and paper, as Eula read:

"Dear Calvin Borton: This is written a week after the Lafayette press conference, and I do not intend it to reach you while I live. You may have heard that President Chase has restored my Army commission, and has offered to bring me into his White House staff as special assistant on Patriotic Affairs, a post that hereafter should become a fixture in every Chief Magistrate's household. While my health has precluded acceptance, I consider myself so honored that to live much longer might be an anti-climax—and my doctor tells me not to worry on that score.

"While I shall leave nothing of material value, I do have something to bestow and I hope that you will accept it in the spirit in which it is offered. You and I have been adversaries, and you have tried to injure me by false witness. I would like to think that in stating my full forgiveness, I can render our antagonism null and void unilaterally. If you feel that I have been the cause of some injury to you—whether or not it was deserved—I hope that you will feel this is a good time to forgive me. Let us part, not friends, but foes who have evened the score. Miles Smith"

Naomi had it down in shorthand. "That's a very private letter," she said to Eula.

Eula answered: "I have no scruples. It makes a bit of news. I'll be using it on my weekend broadcast. Then I'll forward the letter. That's all. Good-by."

Naomi wheeled up her partner's typewriter. She slugged a title into the corner of the page: "An Exchange of Letters." She paused to think for a moment or two and then wrote quite quickly:

"Dear Miles: Though you have left this troubled world, I feel my message will somehow reach you.

"Thank you for your forgiveness. It is a gift of the heart which I return in kind.

"It is true that I have hated you and all that you have stood for in the life of America: not for just the evil which I believe you have perpetrated by the conspiratorial theories of your idiotic Society, but even for such good as you may have done by taking our country's side against its enemies both within and without.

"But, Miles, our country is now engaged in a great civil struggle to see if this land, or any land, can meet the age-old conflict between left and right, and abide by the result. Therefore, we who are combatants must think not only of any particular election day, but of the days and years beyond it when, hopefully, the nation will continue in its course through history.

"I know now, because of your letter to me, that it is incumbent upon those of us in this fight to remember that we are not contesting with enemies, but with friends in disagreement. We must not leave wounds which never heal, nor strike at the nation's life when we wish merely to attack a political opponent.

"I pledge myself from this time forward to foreswear the rancors and the cruelties which I have too often employed. Thank you for your shining example. Calvin."

When she had finished, Naomi stapled the two letters together. They would comprise Borton's column for tomorrow. It was a column, she hoped, that would be the turn-over leaf in his endangered career.

Chapter Thirty-Seven

At six o'clock on November 6, Election Day, President Chase waited in evening clothes in the charming Lincoln Sitting Room of the White House with his wife. In his lap reposed a stack of the latest press clippings, the commentary and the forecast of the experts. This morning he and Cora had voted at a country store near Waverly Farm. Now they sat in this quiet room with a quiet city around them. He smiled as he listened to the soothing click of Cora's knitting needles. Soon they would be going downstairs for a rather large dinner party, and then they would listen to the incoming returns that would tell Jeremiah Fielding Chase how he would fare in the history books.

Yes, the city was quiet—he'd had something to do with that. In mid-September the crestfallen Mayor of Washington, followed by the suppliant city councilmen, had called at the Oval Office. They'd asked for combat troops to quell the riots, but the President had shaken his head.

"Mr. Mayor, this isn't a federal city any longer. It was a failure of government when Eisenhower, Kennedy and Johnson had to send American soldiers into the southern cities. Washington is a municipality now. You have your Home Rule. It's up to you to make it work, or else admit that it was a wrong idea. I thought myself that the District had none of the characteristics of an

American city. There's no heavy industry, no tax base, no solid corps of citizenry. But you're the ones who insisted on having it your way."

"My god, sir, we can't keep order. We can't keep the lights on or collect the garbage. Take us over! Bring on the paratroopers and Marines!"

"It would take an act of Congress to repeal Home Rule and Congress has left town. You men, quit bellyaching and get back to your jobs. Did you think it was easy to run a big city?"

"Yes, sir. But we're up against it now."

"I've been up against it a hundred times in this post, Mr. Mayor. Tell you what. There's a good man sitting around with nothing to do these days. How about it if I lend you General Rigor on an informal basis? Maybe an old soldier can show you how things get done."

They'd gone their way rejoicing. In a few days, the Vice President, practically with one hand, had straightened out the town. Chase grinned. Another crisis, but a minor one by standards of his term. He picked up a clipping.

"Here's a column by our daughter's heavy beau, darling. Obermeister thinks our ticket might get licked just because I've run out of crises. He doesn't exactly wish we had a war on, but he thinks it would help."

"Jerry, are we going to win today?"

"Honey, the only predictable election is a crooked one. No man can say what's in the hearts of the American people. But I reckon we'll see an outcome very much like that of Chi Chi's play. It was touch-and-go at the beginning but it turned out to be a wow. The American electorate will accept Lyle McJay and the New Allegiance. I think it will reject the corny Finnigans. But I'm biased in that direction. Here's Calvin Borton who's biased the other way—and Cal thinks McJay will score."

"Mr. Borton? Really?"

"The temporarily new Borton," said Chase. "Trapped into righteousness by that exchange of letters, Cal hasn't called me a Fascist for two weeks. He honestly wants us to lose, but thinks we won't. Obermeister wants us to win, and fears we'll lose. How does anybody read such a muddle of the tea leaves."

Cora kept to her knitting. So little she knew about politics—or cared. Except where it touched her husband, which was to say, where it touched her heart. She rose from the chair, still knitting, kissed his brow and returned to her seat. That's how it was between them: the companionability of lives entwined. In that relationship there was something far above gratitude for what he'd done. Gratitude sometimes implies a sense of servile thanks, and that wouldn't begin to tell what they were to one another. Twice he'd been her rescuer from total disorientation from this fearsome world.

The last time, after the doctors had given up, he'd brought her home to a therapy beyond professional prescription. Each morning they'd walked the fields and woods together, and where she'd exclaimed with joy to find a wildflower in the grass, or an especially lovely bloom on a bush, the President of the United States (who really didn't care for things in nature unless they were spectacular like mountains and sunsets) would kneel with her while she was rapt with wonder at the fragile beauty. Each evening he was home again, away from the founts of pomp and majesty, to sit and read and hear her needles click, while they talked lightly or not at all. Not gratitude but love was what she felt, and what they exchanged, and love like theirs was a panacea. She could stay at the White House now. She could attend sizeable dinners. The jangled nerves were calm, now that she was in his understanding care.

"Jerry, could there be a write-in? If there is, and you're drafted, I shan't mind."

"Thank you, honey, but that's the one thing which won't happen. The people take their national election too seriously to spoil it. Besides, they envision something for me that's the opposite of being a political draftee. They want to see me make my exit. There will be some who will think of me as a pirate walking the plank. Others are looking for me to go down the Potomac and throw away Excalibur, whereupon a silk-clad arm will arise, brandish the sword three times and disappear. No, they want an exit—a grand one, preferably, but a one-way trip."

"I don't believe it, Jerry."

"Yes, it's true. Many resent my refusal to run. I've rejected the greatest office within the people's gift. Many, like the poetic-minded Obermeister, think I'm withdrawing, only to return when I'm needed. It's the age-old myth of the hero's second coming. But, Cora, it never happens. Later, when the people come to understand why I couldn't let them elect me, they'll know why I can't come back, except in some subordinate role."

"They'll know? Why?"

"Because, believe me, dear, this country hasn't run out of crises, and it never will. And because, if I'm proved right, the country will know that it has plenty of men with the ability to handle the very worst problems that come up. The trick is to elect good men, to support them when they have to do what's temporarily unpopular and risky in order to do what's right. McJay and Pulaski are such men. I think the Finnigans are not. If I've done right by stepping out, our ticket will win. If I've done wrong, or if the people fail to understand, then my name in history is mud—we'll see."

A servant entered to announce that the guests were assembled below. Chase gave his arm to his wife. They descended to the Red Room, hung in opulent satin, and heard the subdued murmur of welcome. It broke into a shout and then into a babble of male and female acclaim as Chase threw out his long arms in an encompassing gesture of welcome and Mrs. Chase opened hers like Ceres.

For these guests were neither political nor diplomatic, nor journalistic nor professional. You might have told from the soft accents and the broad A's that they were all Virginians. You might have thought from the lusty hugging and joyous kissing that they were all close kin and enduring friends—and this was true. The Red Room did not begin to hold them, although it was the center of the melee. They also surged in and out of the adjoining little parlors, called the Green Room and Blue Room, giving their greetings and claiming their embraces. Here were the President's cousins and their collaterals, his old cronies of the county courthouse days, his neighbors of Waverly Farm, and an assortment of female consorts and relatives.

Cocktails arrived on heavy silver trays. The President, taking his tomato juice, walked about, slapping backs, hugging shoulders and bussing cheeks. Cora stood and let them come, the dear ones, for the salute that each deserved. From the great entrance a Marine Band bugler trumpeted and Chase raised his glass:

"Welcome, folks. There are those here whom I have loved from the long, long ago, old friends with whom I went to school, and later struggled with in courts and on the hustings. One-time girls are here for whom my heart used to throb when my hair was longer and theirs was brighter than it is now. When we have drunk our cocktails we'll go to the State Dining Room on this floor for continued merriment. I am reminded of the good old hymn which refers to 'The shout of them that triumph, the song of them that feast.' At least we shall feast, and maybe we shall triumph. After this early dinner, the television account of the election will be shown in the East Room for all who care to stay. You will understand if I later retire to my study upstairs. Meanwhile, we will be serenaded as we dine, and I think it appropriate that the band now lead us in the tune of 'Carry Me Back to Old Virginy.' "

There never was a merrier festival than the one these Virginians enjoyed. Seldom did the White House walls hear more about fox-hunting and trout fishing, old courtships and the wheeling-and-dealing of the courthouses. It was 8:30 before the President mounted to his study, where Jim Flynn already waited, before the television score-keeping.

"Flynn, you look attentive. In 1964, the contest was decided on the computers by suppertime. In 1960 and 1948, it hung on until the early hours. How's it look?"

"It could be a horse race, Mr. President."

"Got a summary?"

"Yes, sir. New England is back in the Republican column, except for Massachusetts."

"New York?"

"Going for Governor Finnigan by a scratch."

"Pennsylvania?"

"Going for Senator Finnigan by a hair. Florida's going for Mayor Finnigan. The fighting Irish!"

"What else, Jim?"

"Can't be sure. If Juno and Young Ike deliver California to the Finnigans, I'd say our side has had it."

"The House and Senate?"

"Republicans will take the House. Democrats will hold the Senate. I wonder if Candidate McJay's front porch campaign caught hold. Wait! Here's Michigan, Ohio, Illinois and Indiana on the presidential balloting."

A handsome face and confident voice emerged from the screen. "Next is NBC's great reporting team of Hinkly-Dinkly. Stand by."

Hinkly-Dinkly showed with the chopping sound of electronic counters as background music.

"There's a landslide in the midwest—McJay and Pulaski are running far ahead. Details in a moment. A flash from California—it goes to the Republican ticket. Scattered returns from the Rocky Mountain States—McJay over Finnigan by a safe six percent. Yes, and the Deep South—from the Carolinas to Louisiana, it's McJay and Pulaski by a country mile."

"Sir, I think we've won it without the Finnigan home states. Massachusetts is still Kennedyland and Texas is on the fence. But all the rest are ours."

"Flynn, I'm going to watch all night. There's not a district or a county that isn't important. But when we're sure of the presidential results, and if they're favorable, I want this telegram to go to Lyle and Hank."

Flynn took a pad: "Yes, sir."

"There was a famous telegram that Stonewall Jackson sent to Robert E. Lee after the battle of New Market. I want just the substance of it."

"Right, sir."

"Providence," dictated President Chase, "has blessed our arms with victory today."

Chapter Thirty-Eight

How does the Muse cut the thread of the finished tale? A spirit, fresh and vibrant, deep and moving, had swept the American nation in '76. The unglamorous man had won—a Daniel come to judgment had scored as his running mate. The victory surpassed all predictions. When the challenges were made, and the recounts were taken, not even New York and Pennsylvania supported the Finnigans. Florida hung in the Democratic column, but not by much. Texas remembered LBJ and Massachusetts clung to the Kennedy nostalgia, but McJay-Pulaski carried 47 states to 3 for Finnigan-Rustin, and the electoral score was 485 to 53.

Was it a testimonial to Jeremiah Chase? He had not stirred out of Washington to campaign for his party. He avoided any tell-tale of the coattail. He knew that the Republican nominees must win on their own, or not at all. The election was a ringing mandate for ideas rather than for personalities. It rang the Liberty Bell. As they had done 200 years ago, Americans endorsed a foreign policy based on fearlessness and freedom, and a domestic policy oriented toward conservatism. There was nothing else at stake, but these two were all-important.

Yet to an alarming extent the American press failed at an immediate interpretation.

The *New York Times* editorialized:

"Mr. Chase had brought peace with the sword, and had turned handouts and waste into frugality and self-reliance. The people embraced peace and consented to the rest. That explains the victory of Senator McJay and Judge Pulaski."

"It just happened to be a Republican year," wrote Calvin Borton. "The G.O.P. victory is exactly the thing that occurred when Coolidge succeeded Harding and Hoover succeeded Coolidge. The nation will be just as sorry this time as it was in the late 1920's."

"The people's spine was still tingling with pride at having such a leader as President Chase," wrote Phil Obermeister. "They could not turn down his party's chosen successors."

"We foresee an Era of Tranquility abroad and Good Feeling at home," the *Tribune* pontificated. "President-elect McJay gets a free ride through a period of normalcy. No more crises in our time."

These, in general, were the sentiments that prevailed on Inauguration Day when the new national officers took their oaths in brisk, clear weather under a brilliant noontide sun. Five hours later the parades were over, the victors had gone to dress for the evening festivities, and Jerry and Cora Chase were at their Waverly Farm hearthside where the ex-President with evident relish lifted a very dark highball. He toasted his wife:

"To you, dear—and farewell to politics."

"Well, Jerry, you'll have to dust off the law books."

He luxuriated in his bourbon and his pipe: "Cora, they say the roughest road an ex-politician ever treads is back to making an honest living, but I expect to enjoy it. About the only question the press never asked me is: 'Why did you almost exclusively serve the rich clients, Mr. President?' I might have answered, as Willie Sutton, the bank robber answered: 'That's where the big money is.' Or I might have said with equal frankness: 'I like to play for high stakes.' I believe with Calvin Coolidge that the business of America is business."

"That would have been much too frank, dear," said Cora. "It's just as well you didn't drink while in office."

Granville galloped into the living room with a dizzy blonde with whom he was going out celebrating on the town. He kissed his mother, wrung his father's hand, and was gone. Chi Chi, rosy and chilly-cheeked from a nipping day in the open, arrived with Phil Obermeister and flew upstairs to dress for the main Inaugural Ball at the Mayflower Hotel. The ex-President gave the columnist a drink.

"You were faint-hearted about our chances to win, Phil."

"No, sir. I was scared stiff that your men might lose. The voice of the people may be the voice of God, but—as Jefferson said—I tremble for my country when I think that God is just. I was afraid we deserved further punishment for our mistakes of the past. The Finnigans would have been a retribution too dreadful to contemplate."

With the young people gone, Jerry and Cora dined together, tended by their butler and maids. Later, he read and she knitted, and they went early to bed.

At midnight strokes upon the frosty city, it became another day—the first full day of a new Administration.

On that day Ma Finnigan and her brood collected in a hotel room with Juno and Young Ike to scheme further domestic mischief.

On that day Calvin Borton became his old self again and wrote a column that predicted a century of calamity, caused by the events of '76.

On that day Communist revolutionaries in Haiti brought along their Molotov cocktails and plotted to overthrow the dictatorial government.

On that day the slant-eyed scientists of Red China gathered to flight-test a missile that would shoot down the American MOL, Mark IV, as Francis Gary Powers' U-2 had been shot down over Russia on May Day in 1960.

On that day Marshal Markov prowled his map room at the Kremlin, and poked his stubby fingers at geographical points where the American will-to-fight might be probed.

On that day President McJay was wakened by an aide who reported that crises were breaking out all over.

On that day, their arms entwined and their lips fragrant with wine and warm from kissing, Phil and Chi Chi alighted from a car in the milky dawn at Waverly Farm.

"Look there," said Chi Chi.

They stood and watched the stalwart figures of man and horse rushing through the mists in the meadows below. The rider who sat his saddle like George Washington and the steed named Yorktown charged uphill at a tall, stiff fence, surmounted it in a tremendous leap and disappeared into the mists.

"Will he come again to lead us?" murmured Phil. "I used to hope so, but Jerry Chase has finally taught me to think. Different eras, different heroes. The old ones live only in legend."

Chi Chi hugged her escort's arm. The love that she bore for the older man became one with her love for the younger one. She was thinking of them both, and of what they both stood for when she said:

"God bless America."